Is There Anything You Want?

BY THE SAME AUTHOR

FICTION

Dame's Delight
Georgy Girl
The Bogeyman
The Travels of Maudie Tipstaff
The Park
Miss Owen-Owen is At Home
Fenella Phizackerley
Mr Bone's Retreat
The Seduction of Mrs Pendlebury
Mother Can You Hear Me?
The Bride of Lowther Fell
Marital Rites
Private Papers
Have the Men Had Enough?
Lady's Maid
The Battle for Christabel
Mothers' Boys
Shadow Baby
The Memory Box
Diary of an Ordinary Woman

NON-FICTION

The Rash Adventurer:
The Rise and Fall of Charles Edward Stuart
William Makepeace Thackeray:
Memoirs of a Victorian Gentleman
Significant Sisters:
The Grassroots of Active Feminism 1838–1939
Elizabeth Barrett Browning
Daphne du Maurier
Hidden Lives
Rich Desserts & Captain's Thin:
A Family & Their Times 1831–1931
Precious Lives
Good Wives?
Mary, Fanny, Jennie and Me, 1845–2001

POETRY

Selected Poems of Elizabeth Barrett Browning (Editor)

Is There Anything You Want?

Margaret Forster

Chatto & Windus
LONDON

Published by Chatto & Windus 2005

2 4 6 8 10 9 7 5 3 1

First published in Great Britain in 2005 by
Chatto & Windus
Random House, 20 Vauxhall Bridge Road,
London SW1V 2SA

Random House Australia (Pty) Limited
20 Alfred Street, Milsons Point, Sydney,
New South Wales 2061, Australia

Random House New Zealand Limited
18 Poland Road, Glenfield,
Auckland 10, New Zealand

Random House (Pty) Limited
Endulini, 5A Jubilee Road, Parktown 2193, South Africa

The Random House Group Limited Reg. No 954009
www.randomhouse.co.uk

A CIP catalogue record for this book
is available from the British Library

ISBN 0 7011 7745 4

Papers used by Random House are natural,
recyclable products made from wood grown in sustainable forests;
the manufacturing processes conform to the environmental
regulations of the country of origin

Typeset in Palatino by Palimpsest Book Production Limited,
Polmont, Stirlingshire

Printed and bound in Great Britain by
Clays Ltd, St Ives plc

To the memory of

GILLIAN PRYCE –

for her cheerfulness,
her spark,
her optimism

And did you get what you wanted from this life, even so?
I did.
And what did you want?
To call myself beloved, to feel myself
beloved on the earth.

'Late Fragment', Raymond Carver

PART I

1

The Clinic

MRS HIBBERT was a Friend. In her own mind, it gave her a status she otherwise lacked: she was a Friend of St Mary's Hospital, someone known to give her time to help others. She was the most senior of all those who belonged to this association of Friends and was regarded with respect and, in some cases, awe. She rarely spoke to the other Friends, except to say a polite good afternoon, and her arrival in the little room off the hospital's main entrance hall, where Friends met and deposited their coats, stopped any conversation instantly. This did not worry Mrs Hibbert in the slightest. She was perfectly comfortable with the sudden silence, taking it as a tribute to her seniority. There was work to be done, serious work, and it ought to be approached solemnly. She took off her jacket and busied herself fixing her armband to her sleeve. The armband was red with 'Friend of St Mary's' stamped in black letters upon it. It fastened with a Velcro strip, making it easy to fit on to any arm except for the very fattest. Mrs Hibbert's arm was stout and strong but the armband encompassed it easily. Ready to take up her position, she nodded at the other Friends and walked out into the entrance hall to begin her particular duties. As ever, she felt alert and eager, ready to support all those who were coming in fear and trembling for their appointments and unsure how to make their way. She would sort them out. She would give them confidence. She would soothe their troubled spirits.

Taking up her position in the centre of the busy entrance hall, to the left of the reception desk and immediately in front of the doors, Mrs Hibbert hummed. She hummed to the tune of her favourite hymn 'Who would true valour see', knowing that such was the constant commotion no one could possibly hear her. While she hummed, she scanned the faces of everyone entering, trying to assess to whom she would need to offer help. Some were easy to spot. Those who went on hovering near the desk, even though they had been given directions, were approached by her before they had any more time to worry. 'Can I help you?' she would say, and their gratitude was touching. Sometimes, she took very nervous patients all the way to wherever they were supposed to go, chatting to encourage them to relax. Their appreciation was gratifying. She would hear moving stories of suffering and try to reassure the narrators. 'Never give up hope,' she would say. But sometimes, nerves made patients utterly silent. Who knew what was going on in their heads? Who knew how great was their need?

Mrs Hibbert was in her element.

*

Edwina talked to herself in her head. Avoid that woman, that Friend, she said, that creature out to catch people. Edwina sidestepped her, as she always did. She would follow the yellow line, oh yes, follow the thin yellow line, that was all she needed to do, that was what she'd been told to do at reception, the first time, just follow the yellow line. It wasn't yellow, not what she would call yellow, it was cream, a sickly cream. The red beside it wasn't red either, it was maroon. Were they colour-blind? Only the green was green, fresh and bright beside the others. She wished she had to follow the green, but where did it lead to? No, hers was the yellow line: follow it, pretend to be Dorothy, pretend the Tin Man and the Scarecrow and the Cowardly Lion are beside you. Dance along, think of the magic. Oh, it's what is wanted. Magic!

End of the yellow line. Full stop. No, not a full stop, a right turning, an arrow. Bye-bye red and green lines, wherever you are going. The clinic. Mr Wallis's clinic. Quite small, the area. A square. Metal chairs, arranged in rows. Grey metal chairs, three rows of ten. All joined together, riveted to the floor. Who would want to steal them? Who would want to throw them? Such hard seats, uncomfortable, no cushions. Where should she sit? Oh, at the end of a row, certainly. Nearest to the door, yes. At the end of a row, then she won't be stuck between two others. Good thinking. Near the door, then she could escape easily. If she had to, if she dared, if she was silly. Silly to think of escape. This is not a prison. Isn't it? No. Nobody is here yet. Well of course they're not. She is early, very early; not even the clinic's own receptionist is here yet. Much too early. No one else is foolish enough to come forty minutes before the clinic begins. But it isn't foolish. It is smart. It shows she is experienced, an old hand. They can't fool her. Come for 2 p.m., the time on her card, the time of her appointment? Three other women will have been given the same time. She knows they will. She can't be fooled. First card handed in, first patient seen. Simple. She will be first.

So. Here she is. Early. Sitting alone in this dreary place. Heuga felt squares on the floor, moved around many times, stains on them all. Doesn't seem hygienic. Why not lino? Why not wood? Such a dusty rubber plant in the corner. Needs cleaning, needs some cotton wool, soaked in milk, wiped over each leaf. Tin wastepaper basket, lined with a black bin-liner. A black plastic table, coffee-table size, piles of magazines. Old, torn magazines, much thumbed. At least look through them. Mostly women's magazines, the covers promising makeovers of rooms and faces, offering free packets of shampoo attached inside, but taken out long ago, naturally. One copy of a wildlife magazine at the bottom, mysteriously pristine. She takes it to her seat. Lovely photographs. Lovely birds. Lovely colours. She can't read the words, though. They blur. She blinks repeatedly, to clear the blur. She blinks in time to a beating in her head. She tells herself to *stop it*. Be calm. Calm.

Footsteps. Brisk, confident footsteps. It's the receptionist. Good afternoon, she says, snapping on the lights in her corner. It isn't a corner really, more of an alcove. Has she said good afternoon in reply? No, just grunted, but the receptionist doesn't notice. She is busy. She bustles. The small space is filled with her bustling. Switching switches on, connecting unseen things, emptying her bag, listening to messages on the answerphone, making notes. Arranging herself, getting ready. She's organised now. Get up and present the card. Accepted. Return to seat, no words spoken except thank you, by both of them. More footsteps. Other early arrivals, though not really so early, it's two minutes to two. Do not look up. Fatal. No eye contact, ever. Still, two people are within her line of vision even as she studiously avoids looking up at them. Two sets of legs, both wearing trousers, but one set obviously female, one male. The man here as a support. Crowded clinics because of women's support systems. Hardly anyone comes on her own. Husbands, partners, brought to endure with them, willing or not. Sometimes mothers, sisters, friends, all taking up places on the thirty chairs. Feeble. She should not be scornful, why shouldn't women have support, if it helps, but momentarily she is proud of herself. She is terrified, sick with apprehension, but she manages alone. Why put Harry through this misery, why drag Emma or Laura through it? No. She will manage. And not just to spare them. Harry would make her even more nervous. He can't sit still. Up, down, up, down, fussing, complaining. It would drive her mad. Harry doesn't do waiting, for anything. Emma might cry, she's sensitive, and Laura might get angry. Easier to be on her own. Easier not even to have told them she's here. Harry forgets the date. She doesn't conceal appointments from him but she doesn't draw attention to them either. He ought to remember, but he doesn't. She won't even tell him she's been today, unless she has to. Unless she is obliged to because . . . No. Please, no.

These other early arrivals have chosen to sit in the middle of the left-hand row of seats. The legs are seated. The man is wearing trainers, the woman moccasin-type shoes. Rather jolly ones, red, with little tassels. She can just glimpse their hands hanging down in the narrow space between the seats. They are holding hands, slightly furtively. They are talking. The man is saying something very quietly. Something personal, she's sure. Comforting, maybe. She can't quite hear. There is a sound of sniffing. Is the woman crying? Possibly. The hands separate and a tissue is pushed into the woman's hand. Well, there's often crying going on, if it is crying, in this place. Never laughter. She's never heard laughter among those waiting, though sometimes there are inexplicable bursts of it from staff rushing through. It's always a shocking sound, such hilarity. But now there's another familiar noise. Rumblings, squeakings. She knows what it means. A bed. In a minute, through the open door, a bed passes, wheeled along by a porter with a nurse in attendance, holding a drip steady. There's a woman lying in the bed, eyes open and staring upwards. She's quite young. Hair scraped back, bones of the face startlingly prominent, a yellow tinge to the skin. Her hands, above the bedcovers, are plucking at the white, open-weave blanket. She is travelling from one ward to another, or perhaps from or to an operating theatre. Travelling like a Pharaoh to another world, but where are her worldly goods? The bed has sides to it, which are pulled up, and as it passes the clinic door the woman suddenly switches her stare, gazes through the bars into the clinic. Help me, her eyes plead. But that's fanciful. Probably she is doped up. Mercifully, she probably has no idea where she is or what is happening.

Edwina feels nauseous. She swallows repeatedly, but can't prevent the rush of saliva into her mouth, filling it. Hastily, she takes a handkerchief from her bag and surreptitiously spits into it. Then she delves into her bag again and finds some tissues and blows her nose. This helps. A glass of water would help more, but she does not want to draw attention to herself by going in search of one. Her discomfort is her own fault. She broke her own rules. She looked up, she saw that woman in the bed. Never look at anyone, it is the only way. She has learned again a lesson she thought she had learned before. She goes back to looking at people only from the waist down, and now there are plenty of them coming into the clinic. A sequence of trousers and skirts, of boots and shoes. The seats are filling up. Each time someone sits down, all the seats shake. They might be firmly attached to the floor and welded together, but the combined weight of ten people in each row seems to affect their stability. It is going to happen any minute. Yes. A woman sits down next to her. A large woman, a fat woman. Her thighs spill over the sides of her seat, her bottom is cruelly caught. Move away from being touched by her. Move! But it's impossible, there is no room to move. The contact can't be avoided, the pressure of this fat woman's thigh, so warm, pressing so tightly. Perhaps crossing legs will help. It does, fractionally. The fat woman is sighing. She is murmuring, Oh dear, Oh dear. There is no doubt about it, she is going to want to talk. Here it comes, the starter question, what time is your appointment? She answers. She has to. But she will not let this go any further. Politeness is one thing, friendliness another. She does not have to be chummy, absolutely not. So, after she has replied that her appointment was for two o'clock, she ostentatiously closes her eyes and leans back in her seat to signify that she does not want to talk. But the fat woman does not read these signs correctly. 'Are you all right, dear?' she asks. This has to be dealt with. She says she is. But there is no stopping her neighbour who resorts now to a monologue. She is enraged because it is already twenty minutes past two and nobody has been seen, and the clinic is nearly full. She thinks this is a scandal. She says nobody could run a business like this. She wants agreement that the NHS is collapsing.

She isn't going to get it. Stay silent. Good, the fat woman has turned to the patient on her other side who, by the sound of it, is happy to chatter. Edwina keeps her eyes closed still, but ponders whether she does indeed think it a scandal, all this waiting. Not really. She assumes there are reasons for it. Doctors wouldn't deliberately keep patients waiting. It would be bad for their health. Anyway, she hasn't the energy to get worked up about it. It is better to be cow-like and simply accept how things are, though Laura wouldn't agree. She herself can only cope by staying remote from everything, it's as basic as that. She opens her eyes cautiously. She thinks about changing seats. Her face feels so hot, her forehead greasy with sweat. She wants to get away from the fat woman's presence. But there is only one seat left and it has women on either side who are clearly in a bad way. One is wearing a bandage round her neck and is having trouble holding her head up. It lolls pathetically. The other radiates tension. She sits ramrod-straight, handbag on knees pushed tightly together, cream-coloured raincoat buttoned up to the neck. She is wearing dark glasses. What a good idea, one to be copied, Edwina thinks. There is a lot of activity now, constant comings and goings, people carrying boxes, people with clip-boards. Hardly any of them wear uniforms. It is impossible to tell who on earth they are. Not even all the doctors wear white coats. In fact, she can't recall seeing a white coat for years. White coats have come to be thought of as intimidating, or so she'd read. She didn't find them intimidating. She found them re-assuring, she liked doctors to wear them. The receptionist's tele-phone rings all the time. The receptionist takes her time answering. Resentment is beginning to build up. It is not only the fat woman who is agitated. A man has gone up to the desk. He is saying his wife's appointment – he gestures, it is the woman with the neck bandage – was for two-fifteen and now it is two-thirty-three and no sign of anything happening. He is saying, in a bad-tempered, hectoring manner, that he is not prepared to put up with this sort of treatment, his wife deserves better, yes, she does.

And at that moment a nurse comes in. A nurse in a dark blue uniform. A Sister. At least nurses still wear uniforms, their rank clearly denoted. All eyes follow her. There is a general shuffling of feet, an outbreak of coughing, a general minor agitation. The nurse says she's sorry about the late start but it has been unavoid-able. She doesn't say why. Nobody asks her why. Then she reads out the first five names. Hers is the very first, as it should be since her card was the first handed in.

'Mrs Edwina Green?' she calls.

*

Edwina knows the procedure. She knows the routine. She moves towards the weighing scales without being told, and slips her shoes off. Nine stone 3 pounds. The nurse says her weight out loud before writing it down. She gives it in kilos, but Edwina has already looked at the dial and translated it into the meas-urement she understands. Nine stone 3 pounds is good. It is excellent. She feels a flutter of relief, a lifting of the weight in her head. She knew she was 9 stone 3 pounds, she'd weighed herself that morning, but it is good to have it confirmed and written down. No weight loss in a year. In fact, 1 pound weight gain. Very, very good. Cubicle three, the nurse says, pop your clothes off except for your pants and put a gown on. Cubicle three is good news too. For some reason, it is more spacious than the others, she always feels less claustrophobic in there, not so much like a horse trapped in a horse-box. She goes into cubicle three and snibs the door. There are two parts to the cubicle. This first section reminds her of the changing cubicles at the swimming baths when she was a child, with its shelf-like seat at the back and the wooden pegs above to hang clothes on. She takes her clothes off and hangs them up. She's dressed today with this stripping in mind. Nothing that takes time to undo. A sweater which pulls over her head, a pair of trousers with an easy zip and no buttons, slip-on shoes. The floor feels cold to her bare feet, but she welcomes the chill. The floor doesn't look too clean, though. She will probably pick up a verruca. She puts on the blue cotton gown provided. At least that is clean. As usual, the Velcro fastenings have come adrift. Two ripped off, one not sticking, only one working. She clutches the gown round her and opens the other door which leads into the examination cubicle.

There is a bed against the wall, with a sheet of thick, coarse paper spread along the length of it. She climbs on to the bed, and stares at the curtain drawn across the end. The curtain used to be blue with tiny white dots on it. She used to try to count the dots. Impossible task, though once she got to 350. She thinks it was 350. Perhaps she cheated. Perhaps she wasn't seeing the dots distinctly at all, such was her fear. But now the curtain is pink. They changed it two years ago. A very pale pink with grey squiggles running vertically down its length. It is rather soothing to follow each squiggle up and down. Better than dots. It's thinner material. Not quite transparent, but she can see shadows through it. Nurses, doctors. Consulting notes, fetching things. The ceiling was painted when the curtain was changed. Not white. It's a cream colour. Magnolia, maybe. A deeper shade than the walls. She knows the walls are not proper walls. Just hardboard. There is talking going on next door but she can't quite distinguish the words. Some woman rabbiting on to a nurse. She herself doesn't talk to the nurses, beyond saying thank you and that yes, she is quite comfortable. And she is. Very comfortable. She could fall asleep if it were not for her pounding heart. Her face feels flushed. She wonders if it is. How strange she must look, with a bright red face above a pearly white body. Harry once said that, he said her skin was beautiful, pearly white. Pearls aren't actually white. She'd said that to him.

The curtain is pulled back so suddenly that she jumps. 'Hello, Mrs Green, how are you? I'm Dr Fraser.' He isn't the consultant, nor the registrar. She knows that is a good thing. They only look at the serious cases. Once, she was serious. She always saw the consultant. Then they down-graded her and for several years she saw the registrar. And now she doesn't quite know who looks her over. The lowest of the low, probably, except they are all qualified, there are no students in this clinic. This doctor is the hearty sort. Looks like a rugby player. Ruddy face, thick buttery yellow hair. She takes an instant dislike to him. She loathes heartiness. She doesn't want her doctors to be jolly. She prefers them quiet and serious, like Mr Wallis himself. This one is smiling in an inane sort of way. He will want to be chummy. He does. Stuff about the weather, stuff about the lunch he'd just had. She doesn't respond, just smiles, vaguely. He asks a couple of standard questions, about how she is feeling, and then he says let's have a look at you, then. She lets the robe fall open. Here come his hands, big hands, here come his fingers, thick fingers. She braces herself. They all examine differently. Mr Wallis has such a light, delicate touch. He never prods, just seems to let his fingers glide over her body, smoothing it down, soothing it. His touch is so gentle it almost tickles. She guesses this one will prod and push. He does. Quite hard, especially round her neck, digging his fingers in. He keeps saying good, good, fine, fine, but she is ignoring him, distancing herself. He asks her to sit up. She sits. His face is very near. He'd used aftershave liberally, a gingery scent coming off him. She closes her eyes, not wanting to meet his.

He is finished with her neck and armpits. He tells her to lie down again while he feels her tummy. She hasn't much of a tummy. She is slim and, lying down, her stomach is almost concave between her hip-bones. She thinks of the big fat woman who'd sat beside her. Her tummy would be vast, how could anything be felt in such a mass of flesh? A doctor would need big hands, thick fingers to examine it, he would need to prod and push. Right, he says, everything seems fine. Seems? Why does he have to be so equivocal, sowing doubt in her mind? Well, she knows why. They can never be certain. They have to cover themselves. He is picking up her notes again. He says he wants her to have a blood test. He says she should have had it before he saw her, but that everything is topsy-turvy today, nobody has been sent for their blood tests, but it doesn't matter, he is sure it will be fine, he'll only contact her if there is any cause for alarm, all right? No. It is not all right, but she is afraid to say so. Letters could go astray, phone calls fail to be made. She needs to know the result of all tests, whatever they are for. But he is still talking, talking and looking at his watch. He is saying something else important. He is saying that next time, next year, she is due for an X-ray, and then if everything is fine, as he expects it will be, she will be discharged. *Discharged*? She is shocked. The shock sounds in her voice. He looks puzzled, says yes, discharged. She would be reckoned to be clear of cancer after ten years without any further trouble. Doesn't that please her, doesn't it please her to think she wouldn't need to come to this clinic again, or does she love it so much that she can't keep away? He says the last bit teasingly, but she won't be teased, she ignores his flippant remark. She sits on the edge of the bed clutching her robe and asks, her voice tremulous, how, if, in a year's time, she is discharged, she isn't seen at this clinic after that, how will she know? He frowns, looks again at his watch, and says know what? That nothing is wrong, she says, that it hasn't started again, because I'm not cured, am I? I'm in remission. He looks embarrassed. He doesn't know what to say. Finally, not meeting her stare, he explains that ten years is a long time. Her tumour had been tiny and of a low malignancy with no spread. She was one of their success stories. 'But that doesn't mean I'm cured,' she repeats, timidly, 'does it?' He hesitates. She'd got him there. What will he say? What has he been taught to say? He hadn't been prepared for her question. 'You're as good as cured,' he says, sounding irritated. Where this disease is concerned long-term remission counts as a cure. 'It doesn't,' she says, quietly, shaking her head. He's had enough. 'Look,' he says, 'maybe you should talk to your GP.' 'Why would I do that,' she says, almost in tears, 'he knows nothing, he didn't even find the lump, he wasn't even going to refer me, I had to insist. I need to be checked out here, at this clinic.' He says he is sorry but that they can't go on checking patients who are perfectly healthy and symptom-free after ten years, there isn't time, there aren't the resources, and there is no need. He says he has to go, he has other patients.

*

She didn't thank him. He left. She sat quite still. She heard him pull the curtain aside in the next cubicle. She heard talking, low and indistinct. A nurse came in, surprised to find her still there, and asked if she was all right. She didn't reply but slowly she got up from the bed. The nurse screwed up the paper on the bed, the noise violent, and spread a clean sheet. Another nurse came in, carrying a slip of paper, telling her to trot along with it to haematology. She asked if Edwina knew where that was but didn't wait for an answer, said follow the yellow line back to the entrance hall, then follow the red line. Edwina took the paper, retreated to the changing part of the cubicle, dressed herself. She didn't feel hot any more, didn't put her jacket on top of her sweater. She unsnibbed the door. The clinic was so full that some people, men, were standing. There must have been some kind of commotion. Nurses were clustered round a woman sitting huddled on the floor. Edwina walked past them, found the yellow line, followed it, though she had no need to, she knew the way. That Friend was still standing, lording it in the entrance hall. She went behind her, picked up the red line starting at the reception desk. She'd no need of that line's guidance either, but she followed it, looking down dully at it as it turned corners and shot down corridors. She arrived at haematology. She knew the system. Little numbered tickets came out of a machine, like they do at the deli counter in a supermarket. Take one, sit, keep an eye on the screen flashing up the numbers. She was thirty-seven. They were at twenty, but she knew things moved with speed here. They did. In no time, she was on her feet, moving to the door where a nurse took the slip of paper. It was a long, narrow room. It always reminded her for some reason of a shoe shop. The only shoes in sight were on people's feet, but the atmosphere was like a busy shoe shop, slightly frantic, chaotic. Something to do with how the seats were arranged, all along one wall, with arm-rests to the right of each one. They were all men, the technicians who took the blood. She thought they were some sort of technicians, not nurses, though they wore white coats. Did she mean laboratory assistants, she wasn't sure. No one ever told you anything. They were too busy to talk. It was all sit down, bare your arm, small prick. So busy. Blood pouring out of everyone into phials. Don't be silly, not pouring, tiny amounts, dribbling. The man in the middle of the row was free. He beckoned to her. Come into my parlour, said the spider to the fly. She went to him. Sat. He tightened the rubber thing round her upper arm. Asked her to clench her fist. The vein came up nicely. He was skilled. The needle went in easily. She watched the blood, her blood, squirt into the test tube. It looked rich. It looked good blood. And then the man said something. He patted her arm, the arm he'd taken blood from, and said, very quietly, almost whispering, now you take care, dear.

Did she smile? Did she acknowledge his little bit of kindness? Did she say that yes, she would take care? She had no idea. She could hardly see for tears, hardly gather up her strength to leave the room. Her progress from the room was unsteady. She couldn't see the red line to follow. Twice she lost the way to the entrance hall, twice turned corners into corridors unfamiliar to her. Miles of floor stretching in front of her, sign after sign directing her everywhere but to the exit. She had to stop and collect herself, breathe deeply. Then she felt a hand on her arm. 'Are you all right, dear, can I help you, where are you going?' She tried to say she was fine, but the words wouldn't come. She coughed to cover her confusion. The coughing helped, it cleared her head. She saw it was that woman, that Friend, the one who waited for prey in the entrance hall. She pulled herself away from the helpful arm and said she was perfectly well, thank you, just a coughing fit, and strode off briskly. She could see the exit sign now. She passed swiftly through the big entrance hall and as soon as she was outside, found a bench and sat down.

She felt better. Tired, but no longer in a panic. Taxis drew up, people got out. An ambulance shrieked past. People milled about, the comings and goings were tremendous. They came from so far away to this hospital, the biggest in the area. She had 30 miles to travel home and couldn't yet face making her way to the bus station. But the terror had finally faded. She'd been in its grip all day. She ought to feel elated, joyous even, the clinic visit over for another year and all well. More than all well. She had the prospect before her of having done with clinic visits for ever. In a year's time, she might never have to follow the yellow line again. It should thrill her, but it didn't. Elation, joy, was not what she felt. It was the fault of that kind man who took her blood. Telling her to take care. Exactly. That was what depressed her, all the care she needed to take, all the time. Taking care meant battling with her fear, grappling with pessimism, blanking out images of cells in her body grouping and splitting and gathering into tumours. They might be anywhere. They might be in her bones already, cosily sleeping, waiting. Waiting for a year, till she was discharged from the clinic and then waking up and getting to work. Nobody would know. It didn't matter how much care she took, she wouldn't know until the pain began. It wouldn't be like last time, the tiny crumb of a hard lump giving the game away. Her own care then had saved her. Mr Wallis had congratulated her on her vigilance. But next time it wouldn't be like that. The secondaries would steal through her bones or creep into her liver or drain into her brain, and no amount of vigilance would prevent them. That was how she reckoned it would be.

The burden of her dread was so heavy. She couldn't sit here all day. She wished she had her car, but she hadn't trusted herself to drive. She got up and trudged along to get the bus home, feeling dragged down by melancholy. It weighed as heavily as a bag of stones. She told herself that tomorrow she would feel relieved. She would, it was true. The glorious relief of the clinic being over would start as pin-pricks of happiness, a physical thing. She'd feel them in her skin, the skin of her face first. It would relax, the tautness would slacken. Then they would trickle through her whole body, these minuscule jolts of energy, and she'd feel suddenly vibrant. Harry would say she was looking particularly well. He liked saying that. She would hold herself back from any bitter remark about wondering why that was, had he not remembered she'd just been through the ordeal of the clinic. No, she wouldn't say that, or anything like that. He'd only want to know how she'd got on, and when she told him he'd beam and say what brilliant news. Brilliant!

She couldn't cope with his euphoria. Best to keep quiet. Always best.

*

Chrissie dreaded the walk across the clinic floor, though she hoped her dread was not apparent. She tried to look cheerful, smiling, making her walk brisk and bouncy, and forcing herself to look to right and left, nodding a greeting to anyone who looked her way. She knew she didn't look as a doctor was supposed to look, but she couldn't help it if her appearance didn't conform to the stereotype. Mr Wallis looked as people wanted a doctor to look – tall, imposing, serious – and, in different ways, so did Ben Cohen and Andrew Fraser. They didn't have Mr Wallis's dignified bearing, and they were not immaculately dressed as he was, but each in his own fashion inspired confidence. She did not. It wasn't just that she looked schoolgirlish, or that her hair was always coming loose from the combs holding it up and making her look untidy, or even that her clothes (grey skirts, black or grey tops) made her look dowdy, but that her whole demeanour was somehow apologetic. It made her despair. She'd catch sight of herself in mirrors sometimes and think who is that funny little woman scurrying by like a squirrel. So she tried to counteract the impression she knew she made by always smiling; she tried to radiate friendliness.

God knows, these patients needed friendliness. The atmosphere in this waiting-area was always dreadful. She smiled and nodded, but there were never any smiles or nods in return. Faces were frozen, expressions fixed, and who could blame them. Today, especially, there was an air of settled misery. It had filtered through by now that Mr Wallis was on holiday, and Dr Cohen ill, which left only her and Andrew. Somehow, they were going to have to cope. What was worse was that officially she was in charge, because she'd been in Mr Wallis's team a year longer than Andrew. It didn't make any difference, really, they would both share the load, but she felt apprehensive. She'd never done a clinic without Mr Wallis in the background, always there to be turned to. She should be pushing for promotion herself by now, but she didn't want it. Andrew would make registrar status before her, and she didn't care. He'd probably become a consultant within five more years, at some other hospital if not this one, and she never would. Her mother used to say lack of real ambition was her fatal flaw, but she didn't see it as a flaw. She felt dedicated to her work but not to reaching the top of her profession. Making decisions was always hard for her and if she became a registrar, never mind a consultant, she'd be turned to all the time for advice. She didn't want that.

It was a relief to leave the patients behind and arrive in the other part of the clinic. It was like a maze, this part, the other side of the cubicles. The dividing walls were hardboard, the general impression one of a shanty town, everything waiting to be swept away by a bulldozer. Two little rooms had been created at one end of the corridor, one for Wallis, one for Cohen, and another makeshift area, without even a door on it, acted as a staff-room. It was a very old hospital waiting to be knocked down and rebuilt. Plans were in progress, building rumoured to be starting next year, but meanwhile this shoddy arrangement had to be put up with. There was no proper space for anything. The corridor that ran between the curtains of the cubicles and the outside wall of the building was especially narrow and awkward, with the flimsy shelf that ran along under the windows further reducing what space there was, and making passing backwards and forwards like an endless excuse-me dance. The lighting was ridiculous, so poor that to read notes you had to hold them up high to catch the best illumination. The whole place was a shambles, and yet their work there was a matter of life and death.

Andrew was waiting for her, slouched in the sad, old leather armchair he found so comfortable and which she herself avoided ever sitting in. 'You've heard Ben's ill?' he said. She nodded. 'We'll be here all night,' he said. 'You'd think they'd have arranged an extra pair of hands.' It was a silly thing to say, so she didn't reply. Sister Butler came in with the lists. She extracted folders from the trolley she was pushing and dumped them on the table, almost knocking over Andrew's coffee. 'Hey, steady on,' he protested. The pile was huge. Andrew stood up, divided it into two, and asked which did she want, the right-hand pile or the left one. She said it didn't matter, so he took the left lot. Sister Butler, in such a bad temper she could barely speak at all, said that the division couldn't be done like that, and they should know that the folders had to be arranged according to the times of the appointments, or there would be a riot. She started shuffling through the folders, checking them against the list in her hand. Chrissie and Andrew watched. When Sister Butler had finished, the table had ten small piles on it. 'Right,' she said, 'you'd better get started.' She swept out, and Andrew raised his eyes to the ceiling and shook his head. 'Who'd believe that woman,' he said.

There were four patients booked in for two o'clock. Andrew took Mrs Green and Mrs Stanley, cubicles three and four, and she took Mrs Yates and Miss Nicholson. Andrew went into cubicle three with barely a look in Mrs Green's folder, but she stood outside cubicle two reading Mrs Yates's notes for a long time. She always read notes carefully before going to examine a patient, needing to concentrate without their presence, whereas Andrew chatted and read at the same time, in front of them. It was important to her that all the details should have been memorised before she was ready, and even then she needed a minute or two to gather her energies to banish the anxiety she still often felt. Mr Wallis told her repeatedly that she worried too much. Let the patients do the worrying, he said, it's your job to be reassuring and you can't reassure if you're allowing yourself to worry on their behalf. All true, she knew that, but what she didn't know was how to detach herself from the patients, to stop herself absorbing and empathising with their worries, for which, in this clinic, there were nearly always valid reasons.

She closed the folder, straightened her shoulders, pulled the curtain back gently – Andrew yanked curtains, it set her teeth on edge – and smiled. 'Good afternoon, Mrs Yates,' she said. 'I'm Dr Harrison. How are you?' Some day she imagined a patient would shout back, How do you think I am, lying here waiting to be told the state of my cancer, eh? But Mrs Yates loved the inquiry. 'Awful,' she said, loudly, closing her eyes and screwing her face up. 'Awful, I feel terrible, I don't know what you've done to me. I feel worse than I ever did before you lot got your hands on me. I do, really.' Chrissie made a sympathetic noise. She'd read the notes. She knew about Mrs Yates. She'd understood the neat little initials peppering reports about her case. It was important not to get bogged down in all her complaints but, instead, to concentrate on examining her. 'Let me have a look at you, then,' she said, and she helped Mrs Yates sit up (groaning) and remove her wrap which barely covered her enormous breasts.

A body was a body, but this one was memorable. It wasn't just the size of Mrs Yates's breasts which made them extraordinary but the shape of them – they stretched wide across her chest, as full at the sides as underneath so that there was this temptation to adjust them, to push them back towards the centre. And then there were the veins in them, which stood out more like the veins in a leg. Mr Wallis, during Mrs Yates's lumpectomy, had given them all a little lecture on the unique appearance of her mammary glands while he was operating. She thought he'd rather enjoyed digging through the blubber to find and extract the tumour, which was in one of the milk ducts. Good news for Mrs Yates. Three years on and no recurrence. Carefully, Chrissie felt round the scar. It was still very visible on the dull, pale flesh, but it had mended beautifully. There was a patch of reddened skin left from the radiotherapy but no irritation present. About a quarter of the breast had been removed, all the tissue around the tumour, which Mrs Yates had complained ruined her appearance and upset her husband. Chrissie palpated the reduced breast gently, then moved on to the other. She could feel lump after lump, the whole breast was a mass of lumps, but the notes had told her these were common in this patient's case and that they were benign cysts. She went on feeling them, searching for any with a bullet-like centre, like a ball-bearing, but found none. All the time she did this she scrutinised the nipples. Mrs Yates's nipples were dark brown, with black hairs sprouting from the areola. Chrissie had a sudden image of a cowpat, crusted on the top, and said hastily that everything seemed fine and would Mrs Yates raise her arms slightly, but was told this was impossible, her shoulders were too sore, she could hardly move her arms at all. Chrissie said just the slightest movement would do, and this was grudgingly managed.

She wished she were wearing gloves. Mrs Yates's armpits were hot, sweaty caverns, thick with strong hairs. Her fingers slipped about and she felt as though they were being sucked in and trapped, never to be released. Mrs Yates, apart from not removing underarm hair, didn't use deodorant, and she was perspiring freely. Surreptitiously, Chrissie wiped her fingers on her own sleeve before putting her hands on Mrs Yates's neck. All the lymph glands seemed normal. Only the ovaries to check, in so far as they could be checked, but probably she'd be unable to feel much in this case. She tried, all the same, thinking as she pressed Mrs Yates's stomach that though the image was unoriginal it reminded her of kneading dough. The colour of the skin, never mind the texture, was like the bread dough they used to play with in cookery lessons at school, punching and pulling it and fooling around until it was grey in colour and revolting to touch. She was aware suddenly that Mrs Yates, who had been talking throughout the entire examination, though Chrissie had taken little in, had stopped. She was staring at Chrissie with a strange expression on her face. 'Is Mr Wallis away?' she asked. Chrissie said yes, he was on holiday. 'Who's in charge, then?' Mrs Yates said. 'Well,' said Chrissie, hesitating, 'I suppose I am.' Mrs Yates snorted. 'You are? How old are you?'

Chrissie knew she didn't have to answer that. She didn't have to answer any personal questions. All she needed to do now was tell Mrs Yates that all seemed well, see you in a year, must get on to the next patient, and whisk out, Andrew-style. But she answered. She said she was 30. 'Married?' asked Mrs Yates. Chrissie smiled and shook her head. (The smile had never left her face, just faded slightly now and again.) Mrs Yates, if she had been harbouring any contemptuous thoughts, seemed to relent. She sighed. She said she felt sick, and couldn't she be given something for this nausea, which was constant, and that her back ached, and she was tired and would like a tonic. Chrissie said she should visit her GP, that that would be the best thing, and backed out of the cubicle. She felt exhausted. She leaned against the shelf along the back wall, holding the next patient's notes and closed her eyes for a minute. She heard Andrew coming out of cubicle four – he'd finished two patients in the time it had taken her to do one – and coming along the passage. He patted her on the shoulder as he passed. 'In a trance, Chrissie?' he said. She didn't reply. Yes, she was in a trance. Had to be. Andrew was whistling as he went in to the next patient. Nothing got him down. If he was tired, it was always just physical, the result of being on his feet all day, or some other simple cause. He was never tired to his soul, thought Chrissie. I am tired to my very soul. Tired of bodies, tired of their workings, tired of their malfunctions. Sometimes, in spite of all her training – and oh, how brilliant she had been at exams! – she didn't understand the body at all. Mr Wallis, to whom she had confessed this in an outburst she'd then been horribly embarrassed by, had said that this was nothing to be ashamed of. He said it was a good thing to feel humble (though humble was not precisely what Chrissie had indeed felt). 'Don't get too clever,' he said, 'it doesn't do in our work. We're not God, though the patients would like us to be, they'd like miracles.'

Chrissie sighed, and got on with Miss Nicholson's notes. She was young. Only 35, unmarried, childless. Chrissie read her notes twice, though she could not afford the time. Wallis had seen Sarah Nicholson last month and sent her for a mammogram and a blood test. The results of both were in the folder. Wallis had written that the lump Miss . . . no, Ms – she wanted to be Ms – Nicholson had found was in his opinion a benign cyst, but that the patient was extremely anxious, so he was ordering the tests. The tests were clear. Relieved, Chrissie drew back the curtain, thinking this one would be over quickly and cheerfully. She was taken aback to see not only a young woman on the bed, but a man standing beside her, holding her hand. It was against the rules. These rules were not actually written down but they were always obeyed: only the patient in the examining cubicle, unless special permission had been requested and granted. No one had asked her if Ms Nicholson could have a man – friend? relative? – with her. How had Sister Butler allowed this? Hesitantly, Chrissie stood at the foot of the bed, hand still on the curtain. She should say something. There wasn't room for anyone but doctor and patient. She would need to get round the side occupied by the man, she would have to ask him to move. It was going to be awkward.

But all she said was 'Hello, I'm Dr Harrison.' Ms Nicholson didn't reply. Tears ran down her face and she gave a hiccuping sob. The man squeezed her hand. Chrissie could see his knuckles whitening as he tightened his grip, and thought how this must be hurting the woman if the pressure was so great. She would have to address him. 'And you are?' she said. 'Her friend,' he said. 'I'm Sarah's partner, her friend.' His voice was deep and hoarse, a smoker's voice. 'She can't talk,' he said. 'She's too scared, she won't be able to answer any questions, you'll have to ask me. I've seen the nurse and she said it would be OK.' Well, Chrissie thought, did she indeed, and flushed with irritation. She'd been going to start by saying she had good news, the tests were clear, but instead she said she'd like to examine Ms Nicholson, so would she slip her robe off. The woman went on weeping and the man who, Chrissie suddenly realized, had neither given his name nor been asked for it, helped her remove her robe. 'Just try and relax,' Chrissie said, but now Ms Nicholson was shaking as well as sobbing. 'There's no need to be frightened,' Chrissie said, 'the tests were clear, I'm just having a last look and then you can go.' 'It's no good telling her that,' the man said, 'she's got herself into such a state.' Chrissie didn't reply. Instead, she indicated with a nod that he should move, but he misunderstood the gesture and thought she was trying to send him out. 'I'm not leaving her,' he said loudly. 'I wasn't asking you to,' Chrissie said. 'I only want you to move to the end of the bed.' Reluctantly, he let go of Ms Nicholson's hand, saying, 'I'm still here, darling.' It was ridiculous. Of course he was still very obviously there. Then he blew her a kiss.

She felt him scrutinising her all the time she was carrying out her examination. Every time she uttered a reassuring 'good' or 'fine', he echoed her, repeating the words with great emphasis, and adding, 'There you are, darling, everything's fine.' The tears did not entirely dry up but they were less plentiful. Chrissie was palpating Ms Nicholson's breasts and looking at the nipples. They were quite unlike Mrs Yates's. They were tiny, pale pink, very pretty, like the furled buds of wild roses, the sort entangled in hedgerows in June. There was nothing wrong with them, no sign of any discharge or crustiness. She felt the cyst Wallis had noted, but then, higher up the breast she thought she felt something else. She let her fingers circle the whole breast again before returning to it. It was small, much smaller than the cyst. She asked Ms Nicholson where she was in her menstrual cycle. The man replied that her period was due in a couple of days. If Wallis had been in the clinic she would have gone to get him, but he wasn't and the decision was hers. 'Look,' she said, speaking directly to her patient and ignoring her male mouthpiece, 'it's probably nothing again, but I'd like you to come back . . .' But before she could explain why, Ms Nicholson started to scream and the man rushed back to her side and flung his arms round her, pushing Chrissie out of the way so that she banged into the thin partition with the next cubicle. She was furious. 'There's no need for this,' she said, but the couple were locked in each other's arms. Chrissie took a deep breath. She wasn't going to order another mammogram or a blood test. The way to resolve this was with a needle biopsy. It was maybe an extreme measure, but the patient was neurotic and hysterical, and the new lump did seem suspicious, much more so than the cyst. She must become brisk and sound confident and efficient. 'If you'll get dressed,' she said, 'the nurse will give you an appointment for a needle biopsy. It's a simple process and . . .' But at the word 'needle' Ms Nicholson said she was going to be sick, and Chrissie grabbed a dish and offered it to her. She wasn't sick. Chrissie carried on with her explanation and the man asked if the biopsy couldn't be done now. 'She can't stand the waiting,' he said. But it couldn't be, not today. Chrissie said so, and the two of them shuffled back into the changing part of the cubicle, the man holding Ms Nicholson as though she had just had a major operation.

Chrissie stood in the passageway, leaning on the shelf, her head in her hands. She'd mismanaged the whole business. Everyone would've heard the commotion, and there would be questions to answer from Sister Butler and Andrew, but what appalled her wasn't the shame she felt but the antagonism towards Ms Nicholson and her partner. It was bad, it was unprofessional. What was happening to her, that she couldn't deal with such situations? But the next patient was waiting. She needed to study her notes and carry on. She must *not* be agitated. Most patients were not like Ms Nicholson. They were stoics, the majority of them, they put up with things, they were humble and deferred to her knowledge and training, and most of them never queried what was said to them. She had marvelled often at the acceptance with which her words, whatever they were, were greeted. Fear made patients timid, usually. Mrs Morgan was very timid. Chrissie remembered her. She'd seen her six months ago. Nice woman, mid-fifties, doing well. No need to fear Mrs Morgan. She smoothed her hair down, dabbed her face with a tissue, wiped her hands on another, and went into cubicle one again, smiling.

*

Smiling, always smiling. Didn't fool anyone. Rita wondered if Chrissie Harrison ever looked in a mirror and saw how strained her smile appeared, how much the smiling mouth was contradicted by the worried eyes. She was nice, well liked, but she was pitied too. Something pathetic about her. She was always so anxious, always checking and rechecking things. Rita got tired of it. She felt she wasn't trusted to do her own job properly.

She'd known there would be chaos this afternoon. Inevitable. Full clinic, no Mr Wallis, no Dr Cohen. The moment she'd arrived and unlocked the door to her little area she'd anticipated trouble. A woman was already there. It annoyed Rita. There was being early and there was being absurdly early. The woman knew the routine. She let Rita get settled before walking up to the reception desk – well, it wasn't a desk, it was a counter – and handing in her card, then she returned quietly to her seat. Rita got organised.

She sat facing the clinic on a chair that had wheels so that she could swivel backwards and forwards as she needed to. Her computer was to her right, the telephone to the left. She always let it ring seven times before answering. It was her system. Even when she wasn't doing anything she never answered it instantly – it only encouraged people to imagine she had nothing better to do than answer their calls. Sometimes, patients would stare at the ringing telephone and Rita could sense them willing her to answer it at once, but she rarely obliged. If a patient came to hand in her card, or to ask something, Rita always put the patient first. A receptionist in such a clinic had to have standards, and Rita had them. Small things mattered, she knew that. Some of the doctors didn't, they didn't realise how being offhand could hurt. Chrissie Harrison knew, but even she had her faults. Weak, she was weak, could let certain patients dominate her. Rita never let that happen. Sometimes patients, or more often their companions, would stride up to the counter and complain loudly about how long they had waited. They could be abusive, but Rita remained polite and calm at all times. She explained, she apologised, she reassured. That's all it took to defuse most situations, a bit of kindness, a bit of understanding. Allowances for bad temper had constantly to be made, and she made them. Compassion, she liked to think, was her middle name.

It was put to the test on days like this one. By 2.30 p.m., half an hour after the first person was supposed to have been seen, every seat in the clinic had been taken, and two people (men, so not patients) were standing. Rita surveyed the scene before her with an experienced eye and calculated where trouble would come from. The truly terrified patient had a way of sitting which she had learned to recognise. It wasn't the one in the buttoned-up raincoat, the woman whose back was rigidly straight, and knees pressed together, who might faint or have hysterics, but the overly casual one, trying to look as though she hadn't a care in the world, the one sprawled in her seat whose fingers endlessly plucked at each other. In a minute she would get up – she promptly did – putting her bag on the seat, and walk to the notice board where she would read the posters about Art Therapy and the Befriending Service and the details of the Cancer Bacup freephone. She'd read them twice already and, Rita was prepared to bet, hadn't taken a word in. She might be the one who in another half-hour, if she wasn't called, would come and burst into tears in front of Rita. Or it might be the man accompanying the woman with the neck bandage who would come. He would be angry. He would harangue her in a fierce whisper about how scandalous it was to keep patients in his wife's condition waiting. Others would follow him but not be so much angry as worried. There were buses to be caught, work to be returned to, children to be collected. People came from so far away to this hospital, it wasn't easy for the majority to come and go. Rita bore that in mind. She came a considerable distance herself.

Today, though, she hadn't had to bother with two buses. She'd got off the first to catch the second, which went from the same stop, and Mrs Hibbert had offered her a lift. Rita hadn't thought the car was stopping for her, and had looked around to see who was going to be lucky. But Mrs Hibbert (whose name she didn't at the time know, though she knew her by sight) lowered her window and said, 'I know you're going to work at St Mary's, would you like a lift?' She'd been delighted to accept. They'd had a nice chat on the way in. Mrs Hibbert introduced herself and said how long she'd been a Friend, and Rita responded with similar information about herself. She said she admired what the Friends did, and Mrs Hibbert said it was nothing, she just wanted to help. Rita confided that her husband was always trying to persuade her to be a receptionist somewhere that paid better, in a hotel or a health club, but she loved the hospital and wouldn't think of it. Mrs Hibbert was glad to hear this. She said it restored her faith in human nature. Rita felt a little uncomfortable, wondering if maybe she had boasted about her own virtue. They moved on to discussing the state of the hospital, agreeing that the fabric of it was in a deplorable state, and that the building of the new one couldn't happen soon enough. They were in perfect accord about Rita's clinic, how shabby it was, how inadequate in every way to deal with its particular patients. Mrs Hibbert said that if she won the lottery she would spend some of the money on the clinic, and for the last few miles they vied with each other in suggesting improvements: sofas, new carpet, soft lighting, pretty pictures, fresh flowers, a fish tank maybe, glossy magazines – oh, they had such fun.

She was an odd woman, though. Posh. People were a little wary of her, Rita knew. There was something forbidding about her, even though she was elderly. You could tell she wanted to be comforting but she was too forceful, too strong, to exude sympathy, however hard she tried. Sometimes, she brought patients all the way to Rita's clinic and they would have a shell-shocked look about them, as though they had been completely taken over and could no longer function by themselves. There was nothing gentle and motherly about her, though that was what patients craved – tenderness, motherliness. The more Rita thought about it, the more it seemed to her strange that a woman like Mrs Hibbert wanted to be a Friend. She was more of an organiser than a helper, surely. Rita instinctively felt she had mistaken her calling and would have been better off behind the scenes directing the efforts of others. Except, of course, she was too old now. Rita wondered what Mrs Hibbert had been like when young. Like Paula, probably. Paula had been Rita's assistant for a brief period. Very brief. She was smart and capable but her personality wasn't suited to the job. She was bossy and abrasive and answered back. Asked by some distraught patient how much longer she'd have to wait, Paula would snap back, 'How should I know?' She only lasted two weeks. Rita never snapped at anyone, no matter how irritated she felt. Her smile, she suspected, might become a trifle glacial under pressure, but she always remembered her manners. She liked to react to rudeness with extreme courtesy. It was, she'd discovered, extremely effective. It made her feel good, too, superior in a way, though of course she was not superior. These people were under stress, she was not.

Sister Butler swept in. Good. Things would get started, and just in time. When she'd sent the first four women into the cubicles, she came rushing in to Rita's reception area. 'Bloody nightmare,' she hissed, scrabbling around looking for something. Rita didn't turn round, but made a tutting noise. She could hear Sister Butler – Anne, she was called – pulling open the filing cabinet. She must know that whatever she was looking for wouldn't be there. Only long-forgotten, useless stuff was in that old cabinet now that everything was computerised. Sister Butler – nobody actually called her by her Christian name – probably just wanted an excuse to get out of the clinic for a minute. She was supposed to be a good nurse but Rita could see no evidence of any particular skills. She would like to have been a nurse herself, and fancied she would have made a better one than Sister Butler. But she wasn't clever enough, simple as that. Only passed one GCSE and that was in Religious Knowledge. Maths, English, any sort of science were all beyond her, and a girl had to have them these days to get into nursing. Rita was sure Florence Nightingale hadn't had to pass any exams, but then nobody did in those days. At 16, it had enraged and humiliated her to think that because of her lack of academic qualifications she could never become a nurse when she had so many of the qualities that a nurse needed. She was kind and capable, she wasn't squeamish, she knew how to make sick people comfortable, she was compassionate, she was efficient and organised and trustworthy. Nobody was interested in all that. Her mother had suggested that she took some sort of course which would qualify her to work in a nursing home, but that wasn't proper nursing, she wasn't interested in being less than a proper nurse. She didn't just want to bathe and feed people, she wanted to be in an operating theatre handing the surgeon instruments, or in the intensive care ward, administering life-saving drugs. Nothing else would do.

Dr Fraser came across the clinic and leaned on her counter. 'How are we today, Rita?' he said. The nurses liked him, but Rita didn't. He patronised her. And he was flirtatious, his eyes openly appraising her, lingering too long on her chest. He spent his whole working life examining breasts and yet he still ogled them, or at least ogled hers. Her mother always said that if she didn't want men to look she shouldn't wear close-fitting tops, but she didn't see why she should hide herself in baggy jumpers just because some men couldn't stop leering. 'Fine, thank you,' she said, turning away to fiddle with some papers, and adding, 'Can I help you? Is there anything you want?' in a deliberately off-hand tone. He laughed his big, booming laugh, a shocking sound in that place, and said that she certainly could help him, she could get him out of this madhouse and whisk him off to that tropical island she came from, which one was it again, remind him. Rita was livid. He knew she had been born right here, and so had her parents, and that it was her grandparents, both sets, who had come from Jamaica. When the telephone rang, she snatched the receiver off the hook at the first ring, not caring that she was breaking her own rule. He went on leaning there while she spoke to the caller and when she'd finished he said did she have a mint or a cough sweet, that was what he wanted, he had a horribly dry throat, and he opened his mouth and pointed, as though she might not understand him. He had lots of black fillings. She pushed a tube of Polos towards him, and turned away again.

Once, when he first started work at the clinic, he had asked her out for a drink in the pub round the corner. She said she didn't drink. True. She didn't, never had done. (He, she later discovered, drank a lot.) He said she could have a soft drink, couldn't she, and she'd said she didn't like pubs and preferred going straight home to her husband. That told him. He hadn't asked her again, but he kept up the patter at every opportunity, always coming over to chat, or try to chat, however busy the clinic. Mr Wallis and Dr Cohen and Chrissie Harrison never did. They only came over when they needed her to do something for them, and then they were brisk and polite and in a hurry to get back to their job. All of them were preferable to Dr Andrew Fraser, yet the odd thing was that she got the distinct impression that most patients preferred him. He was thought of as friendly, he made jokes and was jolly. But Rita knew that if she were ever forced to attend this clinic she'd rather have any of the others.

Only four women left now.

*

People looked poor. Rachel knew they couldn't all be poor, but somehow they looked it. They were all cowed, that was what created this impression of deprivation. The fear, the apprehension, mysteriously seeped into clothes, turning perfectly presentable garments into charity shop purchases, shabby and worn. Or else it was the effect of the lighting. No windows in this horrible room, no natural light. The clinic was in a basement where the darkness was kept at bay by harsh strip-lighting which hurt the eyes and distorted every colour. A pretty pink became a sickly violet, a leaf green a bilious lime. Rachel wore only black and white on clinic days. It made her look like a sad little crow perhaps, but she felt safe only in neutral shades. Black trousers, black cotton shirt, black slip-on shoes, white jacket, white ribbon, tying back her thick black hair. Her ear-rings were opals. The only touch of colour she allowed was red, red lipstick, red nail varnish.

She'd arrived, as she always did, determined to be busy. She had a novel with her, and a writing pad and pen, and in her briefcase a stack of papers to check. But she knew none of them would be much good. Her attention would wander, the printed word blur. The interruptions and distractions were endless – calls to come and be weighed and measured, the phone ringing, a regular procession of people passing in front of her, disturbing concentration. She'd tried, that first time, to detach herself, to rise above what was happening, but it hadn't worked. It was no good straining to avoid involvement. Instead, she was alert to everything going on, it was the only way. She didn't initiate conversation, nobody really wanted to talk (except for one big, fat woman), but she observed everyone in the clinic, and even those passing through, closely. She felt she might be in the transit lounge of an airport for all the connection between her and these people. A clinic full of women (only four men) and yet there was such a silence among them. The noise was all extraneous, it didn't come from them. If anyone did speak, it was in whispers, apologetically. And the more she thought of the comparison, the more she thought it was appropriate: she, and all these women, *were* in transit, between health and sickness, hope and despair. Yet in spite of this feeling of identification with the others, she felt the odd one out. She couldn't see anyone really like herself. It wasn't just a matter of age – there were at least two other women about her age, though the majority were older – it was that none of the others looked professional, they didn't look as if they were fitting in this clinic with a day's work. She felt too well dressed, though she was not in fact in her working clothes. She didn't belong here: it didn't suit her to be herded here with the others. Why, she asked herself, had she not gone private? She could afford it, or at least she could have afforded a private consultation. But she had always thought the NHS perfectly satisfactory. Till this, this *thing*, three years ago now, she had never been ill, never been in a hospital. For thirty-five years she had been glowingly healthy. And now it seemed too late to change. She was sucked into the life of the clinic.

The doctors liked her. She had the impression they found her a relief. She wasn't emotional, she didn't fuss, she wasn't aggressive. She knew her questions were intelligent and gave the doctors the opportunity to demonstrate their expertise – they enjoyed that. She made it clear, too, that she appreciated that they couldn't perform miracles, that there were limits to what they could achieve. She acknowledged that they were tired and overworked and couldn't spend all the time they liked with each patient, and she took pains to let them know this – oh, she was a model patient! As a consequence, or so she judged, she received if not better treatment then certainly more attention. Doctors would perch on the end of the examination bed she was lying on and chat, and often had to be hurried on to the next patient by the nurse. In just a few minutes she always managed to create some sort of relationship with them and she could see in their eyes their recognition of her as an individual, like themselves.

But afterwards, on the way home, she would realise she'd overdone the calm, reasonable, rational image. She'd been too bloody convincing. So full of sympathy for *their* problems and giving not a hint of her own. Where was the sense in that? There she was, working hard at the charm, making everything easy for them, and all the time containing her fear and misery. They had her down as bright, confident, well informed and in control. Who could blame them? She never had tears in her eyes, her hands did not tremble as she shed her robe, her voice did not shake when she replied to questions. She was a fraud, but none of them ever guessed, except perhaps the woman doctor, Dr Harrison. She didn't like being examined by Dr Harrison. The woman's permanent smile, vague and vapid, irritated her. Rachel knew perfectly well that for a woman to be working in this clinic was a sign of how good she must be, probably better than the men (though she wasn't quite sure how she'd come to that conclusion). At any rate, there was no justification for doubting Dr Harrison's abilities as compared to any other doctor's. It was just that she didn't convince. She gave the appearance of being scatty – her shirts always had buttons missing, her skirts were creased, and her hair needed brushing and properly fastening back. Rachel was particularly critical of the doctor's hair. It was not unlike her own, thick and dark, but whereas her own was well groomed and neatly caught back from her face and secured with a ribbon, Dr Harrison's cried out for attention – it looked as if it had been shoved into a bundle on top of her head and had been escaping from a few clips and an elastic band ever since. It was a mess of wisps and strands falling into her eyes, making her look distracted.

She was smart though, not just clever at her job. Rachel had only had her once, but had known right away that she was different from the other doctors and not just in gender. She had this steady gaze, appraising and searching, whereas with the others eye contact was always minimal. When Dr Harrison had asked her, as they all did, how she was, it had seemed a genuine inquiry to which she was awaiting the answer with concern and not a routine question hurriedly got out of the way. That was pleasing, but it was also unsettling. Rachel had almost forgotten to be the model patient, she'd teetered on the edge of confessing that she was scared and confused and wasn't sure if the treatment had worked or not. Instead she'd smiled and made a joke, but the joke hadn't gone down as well as it should have done. Dr Harrison hadn't laughed. Her smile had stayed the same, but she'd made it clear that Rachel's flippancy didn't fool her. Considering that what she really wanted (even if it ran contrary to what she seemed to want) was for some doctor to realise the state she was in, it was absurd that Dr Harrison's rejection of her banter should depress her. She'd fallen silent instead of chattering away, showing off, giving her usual performance, and her own unaccustomed silence during the examination had the strange effect of making her feel humiliated. She'd felt abject, spineless, lying there being prodded, and a rage had built up inside her for which she blamed Dr Harrison. She contained it, and everything that day had been pronounced fine, but she'd left the clinic distraught. Somehow, Dr Harrison, in refusing to let her act as she usually did, had made everything harder to bear.

She hoped she wouldn't get her today. She couldn't tell how many women were before her; the system was impenetrable, seeming to bear no relation to who had arrived first or the time of an appointment. She'd tried, on other occasions, asking the receptionist why some patient, whom she'd seen arrive long after her, had been seen almost immediately, and the question had been met with a polite disclaimer and a promise to look into it. Not for one minute did Rachel believe the promise would be kept. The receptionist was a relaxed young woman, strikingly good-looking, who queened it behind her counter, an attitude well calculated to discourage complaint. Rachel had often witnessed how Rita – she'd heard her being called Rita, though the name did not fit and was a disappointment – dealt with anger, and she admired it. She didn't feel she wanted to cross Rita who, at this moment, was listening to a man raging about how long his wife had been kept waiting and she was defusing his rage with a combination of patience and tact – she listened, she nodded, she made notes, she clucked her tongue. Then there was a sudden commotion, which had Rita out from behind her counter at a run. A woman, who had just got up from her seat, collapsed. She did it so neatly, so silently, that Rachel had no idea why Rita had been galvanised into action, but then watched helplessly as a nurse appeared and the woman was attended to. The patient was young and pretty. Rachel had watched her arrive almost an hour ago, hesitant and nervous, and she'd noticed how fidgety she'd been, twisting a scarf over and over in her hands until it looked like a rope and then untwisting it and flattening it out and folding it carefully into squares. Now she lay on the floor, her eyes shut, her skin grey. A doctor arrived, and Rachel turned away – it was appalling to be staring – but she heard the words 'panic attack', and when she next allowed herself to look, the patient was on her feet and being helped into one of the rooms next to the cubicles. No one had been with her. She'd spoken to no one and no one had spoken to her.

Rachel swallowed hard. She felt shaky and dismayed. A woman in such a panic, but nobody had noticed until now, nobody had been kind and reassuring. She went to the water fountain and filled one of the ridiculously small cardboard beakers with water and drank it greedily. Her mouth was dry, as though she, too, was about to panic. Maybe she would just leave, just walk out of this clinic. Her heart beat rapidly as she considered the idea. She couldn't stand the tension any longer. She would go. Nobody would care. Rita might notice, but she wouldn't stop her. One less patient to deal with. Her business, if she was silly enough to leave before being seen, more fool her. But Rachel was not a fool. She went back to her seat, ashamed of the impulse to which she had almost succumbed. And at that moment her name was called. Cubicle two. It was as though her decision not to be silly but to stay was being rewarded and she went into the cubicle eagerly. Clothes removed, robe on, she positioned herself on the bed. The curtain twitched. Dr Harrison came in. 'Hello,' she said, 'I'm Dr Harrison.' 'I know,' Rachel said, 'you've seen me before, two years ago.' 'So I have,' said Dr Harrison. 'I remember.' Rachel knew it would be in the notes and was not impressed. 'Good to see you looking so well,' said Dr Harrison. 'And are you well?' 'Yes,' said Rachel, 'but then I was perfectly well before I was told I wasn't well at all, so I don't suppose feeling well means much.' She knew she sounded bitter, but she couldn't help it. 'Oh, I wouldn't say that, I wouldn't say feeling well was of no significance, not at all, it's a very positive sign.' 'How can it be?' Rachel said, quite sharply, 'when all the time I was feeling well I had a malignant tumour.'

Dr Harrison ignored this. 'Let's have a look at you,' she said. Rachel took off the robe and waited. Dr Harrison had smooth, gentle hands. Her nails were bitten but otherwise her hands were pretty, long-fingered and slender. 'Good,' she kept saying, 'good, excellent.' Leaning over Rachel, her untidy hair came loose even more disastrously from its moorings, but she ignored it except to blow the strands falling into her eyes, little puffs of breath lifting them. At least she washed it. Rachel could smell some sort of lemon shampoo, and her skin had the same faint scent. But the hands had stopped. Rachel's wandering thoughts stopped with them. The hands were on her left breast, the one not treated. 'What's wrong?' she asked. Dr Harrison went back to the right breast without replying, and then returned to palpate the left one again. 'There's a thickness,' Dr Harrison said, thoughtfully, and she turned her head slightly away from Rachel's body as though she was listening. 'Probably nothing.' Then she stopped and went to the notes and leafed through them. 'Yes,' she said, 'it's been observed before. Dr Cohen once noted it down, but it had gone at the next check-up.' Rachel's heart slowed down a little, but her face felt burning hot. 'He didn't tell me,' she said, 'nothing was ever said about any thickening.' Dr Harrison put the notes down. 'I like my patients to be fully informed,' she said. 'Why?' Rachel asked, gathering her robe around her, glad to feel its thin blue cotton cover her and gaining confidence as it did. 'Why tell me if it's not important, if it's been noticed before and found to be nothing? Why tell me? It just worries me, it will haunt me until next time.' 'Best to be fully informed,' Dr Harrison repeated. 'Don't you think?'

There was no time to argue. She was given an appointment slip and then Dr Harrison left the cubicle. All the words Rachel wanted to use popped into their correct order only when she found herself walking back along the yellow line to the entrance hall. She demanded, in her own head, in a loud and clear voice, to be told exactly what the significance of this thickening amounted to, and she wanted an explanation of how it could come and go. Dr Harrison boasted – it had sounded like a boast – that she liked her patients to be fully informed, but full information was exactly what was lacking. So proud of myself I am, thought Rachel, that I'm intelligent and unemotional and can ask the right questions, and I've been stupid and nervous and haven't asked what I should have asked. She couldn't do anything about this thickening. She didn't need to know about it. It was cruel to have told her. Dr Cohen hadn't told her. He hadn't said it was there, and he hadn't said it had gone. He had saved her from unnecessary worry and now that bloody woman had plunged her into it. She'd sounded so virtuous, with her 'I like my patients to be fully informed', but it was spiteful. Rachel thought she should register an official complaint. She should write to the consultant, to Mr Wallis, and tell him what Dr Harrison had said and how cruel she had found it. But she had just enough sense to realise that he might defend Dr Harrison's attitude and criticise Dr Cohen's policy of *not* informing her of the thickening.

She hadn't the energy for complaining anyway. By the time she got to the entrance hall she was drained of all anger and only wanted to get to her car quickly and return to work. But she found herself suddenly at a full stop. She stood in the hall only a few steps from the doors, unable to move towards them. Her body was shaking, visibly trembling. She clutched her bag to her chest and closed her eyes and ordered herself to be calm and sensible. Stop it! You are perfectly all right! Proceed to those doors! The fresh air will restore you! Go! Now! This is not a panic attack! Go! Slowly, she began to inch her way forward, relieved to find she was obeying her own instructions, but then she felt a hand on her arm and a voice saying, 'Are you all right, dear? Would you like to sit down for a minute? Would you like a glass of water?' It was that woman, one of the Friends, the elderly one who always plonked herself in the middle of the hall. It had amused Rachel many times to see her pounce, and now here she was, caught herself. 'I'm fine, thank you,' she managed to say, and as she said it, she did begin to feel in control once more and was able to smile and to attempt to disengage the Friend's hand from her arm. But she failed. The Friend's grip only tightened as they both approached the doors. 'Deep breaths!' she was told, as they went through them. She took deep breaths, irritated because she hadn't needed to be told to do so, and finally her arm was released. 'Better now?' the Friend said. Rachel saw that she had a name tag on the white blouse she was wearing. 'Thank you, Mrs Hibbert,' she said. 'You've been very kind, though really I was fine.' 'Good,' Mrs Hibbert said, but she smiled in a knowing way, as though humouring Rachel, and she looked so pleased with herself. Walking to her car, Rachel pondered on the nature of women like Mrs Hibbert – imagine, lurking in that entrance hall trying to spot people who needed your help and then being thrilled when it could be offered and accepted, delighted to be the good Samaritan. But then Rachel felt ashamed of wanting to mock her, the stranger who had seen her difficulty – she might very well have been thankful for that supportive hand and that kindly inquiry as to her well-being. They should have a Mrs Hibbert on duty in the clinic itself.

Maybe at the next appointment she would suggest it.

*

Only four women left now, each of them an hour and a half over their appointment time. They all looked calm enough, except perhaps for the one with red hair who, Chrissie noticed, had a scarf round her neck though the clinic was hot. She must be sweating profusely. She looked up as Chrissie returned to the cubicles and there was an air of bewilderment about her. Chrissie saw, as she edged past her into the corridor, that the red-head had collected some of the leaflets available and had been studying them. Patients found them scary. They were supposed to be reassuring, but she'd seen women read them, then drop them as though they were hot.

She knew she would get the red-head, and she did, though if she hadn't had to leave the clinic for those few minutes, Andrew would have taken her. She'd had to rush out to be sick. It wasn't real nausea, only a nervous reaction to the patient who'd been so angry about being told of the thickening in her breast. She'd just felt she was going to vomit, and had grabbed some notes and dashed out as though on some emergency. There was a lavatory near the door of the clinic and she'd rushed into it and stuck her finger down her throat and brought up a lot of bile, that was all. Once this was over, she felt better. Hastily, she'd washed her hands and splashed her face with water as cold as she could make the tap produce, and she was back behind the cubicles before anyone had missed her. Rita had seen her dash out, though. She would have to think of some explanation to give Rita later, but now she had the red-head to concentrate on and then one other and it would be over for today. She'd have survived the clinic and could go home, and hide.

It was a first appointment. The red-head, a Miss Collins, Carol Collins, had been referred by her GP. Chrissie read his letter. Miss Collins, who was a mere 26, had been to see him on four occasions suspecting that she had a lump in her left breast. The GP had found no evidence of this on the previous three examinations, but now he had felt what he was pretty sure was a cyst, and in view of Miss Collins's very obvious fears he'd thought it advisable that she should be reassured by being seen in the clinic. It all seemed straightforward. Mr Wallis never minded obliging GPs even though such unnecessary referrals made the clinic's load heavier. He said a spot of reassurance cheered everyone up. Chrissie went in to see Miss Collins, who gave her a tremulous smile and answered the routine questions in a whisper but at least did not cry. It was definitely a cyst. Chrissie was relieved, but the young woman didn't seem to be. She asked if the cyst could 'turn bad', and whether it would go away or would have to be removed, and because she was tired and it was the end, almost, of clinic, Chrissie was a little abrupt in spite of her smile. She said Miss Collins shouldn't worry, but if she liked she could return in three months' time and if the cyst hadn't gone they could discuss its removal.

Meanwhile, Andrew had seen all three of the other women in record time. He was slumped in the little staff-room eating biscuits when she went in. Mr Wallis loved biscuits, he practically existed on them, and his secretary Norma always saw that there was a new box available on clinic days. It was kind of her, Chrissie thought, to have put a box out even though Wallis was not there. Andrew was taking full advantage. He had already eaten half the top layer. His mouth full, he held the box out to her. She didn't really like biscuits, but she took a chocolate cookie and nibbled at it. Andrew poured some tea for her. She didn't much like tea either, preferring coffee, but it was comforting to be drinking it and munching a biscuit. The sweetness was cloying but when she'd finished one biscuit she took another. She needed comfort so badly. 'You look pale,' Andrew said. 'Are you OK?' It was only a casual inquiry but it made her want to cry. She choked on the second biscuit. 'You're not crying, Chrissie?' said Andrew, laughing. 'Hey, you're not crying, are you?' She said that of course she wasn't, that she had some crumbs stuck in her throat and coughing them up had brought tears to her eyes, that was all. But Andrew had stopped laughing. He was looking at her curiously. 'You need a few days off,' he said, 'it's getting to you. No good letting all this get to you.'

No good at all. Silly, silly, silly. It was absurd, but she could not get Ms Nicholson out of her head. *She* wanted to be lying in a cubicle with a man sitting by her bed calling her darling and blowing her kisses.

*

End of clinic, for another week. Rita liked the end of clinic. She and Sister Butler and the two other nurses on duty had a cup of tea and a piece of cake. Rita brought the cake, always one she'd baked herself. Gingerbread, this week, with real pieces of ginger generously mixed into it. It was delicious. Cake, Rita reckoned, was wholesome whereas those biscuits Mr Wallis lived on were not, but curiously he did not care for cake, any sort of cake. 'What an awful clinic,' Sister Butler said. 'Everything went wrong from the beginning. That Chrissie Harrison is going to pieces.' They discussed the scene when the young woman had screamed, and then they discussed the woman who had collapsed, and then it was time to put the lights out and leave. Rita left last. She always did. There was a little tidying up to do and, though it was not her job, she liked to do it. She didn't mind collecting up the magazines and stacking them neatly, or gathering the stray leaflets and empty cardboard cups together and putting them in a plastic sack to be disposed of. It didn't take long. The clinic was soon returned to its soulless state. A drab room, not a hint within its claustrophobic walls of the tension which had hung in its air all afternoon. Everyone was always so glad to vacate it. Rita put out the lights and closed the door. All those women, all gone home now, released, if only temporarily.

*

Mrs Hibbert took off her armband and put her jacket on. She'd done some good today. That was all she wanted to do. As she came out of the Friends' room, she saw Chrissie leaving, head down, hands thrust into the pockets of a rather scruffy navy blue coat which wasn't long enough to cover her skirt. She thought about calling out her name, but decided not to. Chrissie would be tired, exhausted. She wouldn't want to be detained. Walking to her car, and keeping an eye out for anyone to whom she could give a lift, Mrs Hibbert reflected that it was more than six months since she and Chrissie had spoken, and then it had only been to exchange a few hurried words. She hardly knew the girl, though they were related by marriage, or had been. Francis, Mrs Hibbert's late husband, had been so proud of his niece even if he hardly saw her. A clever girl, Cambridge degree, now working in oncology. Wonderful. Mrs Hibbert had agreed with him. Chrissie had done well. She envied the girl her education and training. But there was something lacking in her, as there was in so many of the doctors. Chrissie might smile all the time, that rather silly smile of hers, but she failed to reach out to patients in the way Mrs Hibbert felt she herself could and did. Cleverness wasn't enough, that was the point. As she got into her car and settled herself, Mrs Hibbert sighed. She was tired. It took a lot out of her, her afternoon at St Mary's, being a Friend. She thought of all the women she had helped, the ones she had guided to the oncology clinic. Poor things. What were they going home to? What had their attendance at the clinic done to them?

2

174517

HOW QUIET everything seemed the next day, how quiet her head, all the worry no longer bouncing about, leaping and jumping from one side to another as it had done waiting in the clinic. Edwina felt dreamy, pleasantly sleepy, all her movements languid and gentle. She didn't have to do anything. All day, she could do what she wanted to do, whatever she wanted. It was a warm, sunny day. She thought she should be outside, walking along the river, or in the park, but she felt too lazy. She could garden, but there wasn't much to be done. So she settled herself on the sofa in the conservatory and reached for her book. She couldn't read in the week leading up to the visit to the clinic. Strange, when she most needed it, reading was impossible; she could never concentrate, the words drifted and floated away without meaning.

Edwina bought a lot of books. Harry didn't mind, he encouraged her. For years now she'd bought what she wanted to read and hadn't been near a library. She'd spent all her working years in libraries and they were no longer the places she'd loved. Public lending libraries were no longer quiet. They weren't church-like. A good thing, she supposed, that they were now what was called 'user-friendly' and full of modern technology, but they had lost their appeal for her. She bought what she wanted and loved possessing the books. Mostly, she chose biographies. This was expensive, but then each biography lasted her a long time. She read slowly and carefully, stopping regularly to think about what she was reading, learning so much as she went on. She was particularly drawn to biographies of women whom she felt had had difficult lives, sometimes because of the men they had married. She'd enjoyed Mary Soames's biography of her mother Clementine Churchill, and another about Jane Carlyle and her husband. She liked to contrast her own married life with theirs. It made her feel fortunate.

Harry wasn't famous and he wasn't difficult. He was a cheerful, kind man who liked his job, had plenty of leisure interests, and was devoted to his family. Edwina had nothing to put up with, and yet she was drawn to women whose husbands required great sacrifices of them. It was odd, but she explained it to herself as a feeling that she had something to offer which was not required of her. She felt that she could have been a rock for Harry, or alternatively an inspiration, but that he had no need of either. She was *important* to him, of course she was, but that was not the point. All that had been required of her in her marriage was that she should be a good housekeeper and mother, a pleasant companion and a willing lover, content to share Harry's own evident contentment. There had been no challenges, nothing to test her. Harry had never leaned on her heavily, never turned to her in a crisis, never been unable to go on without her support. And, though she fully realised it was perverse, there was something in her that would have relished having to rise to the occasion if it had occurred.

But it hadn't occurred. She wondered sometimes if what she secretly yearned for was to be the wife of a famous man – but surely not, she was too shy, too diffident, for such a role. She would have hated to be in the limelight, having her clothes scrutinised and mocked. No, it wasn't fame she wanted for Harry. It was some other sort of importance, to do perhaps with his work, which others would not necessarily know about. It excited her to imagine being the wife of a scientist engaged in medical research, for example, on the edge of discovering a cure for cancer, say. She could see herself taking Harry's coat in the hall when he came home from spending hours and hours in the laboratory, weary with the weight of the work he was doing, exhausted with the strain. She could see herself soothing him, settling him down to a nourishing meal, patiently listening to his account of what he was doing and the stage he was at (though she did, in this fantasy, have doubts about her ability to understand). He would say he didn't think he could go on and she would encourage him. Behind every successful man, the saying went, there was a woman, or something like that. She wanted to be that woman, she wanted to be a part of some great scheme, claiming no glory for herself but privately knowing she shared in it. It was, she supposed, a shameful longing but since she never gave voice to it, she avoided shame.

She wondered sometimes if she could even have settled for less than the fame. Maybe this irritating longing of hers would have been satisfied if Harry had become a mayor, or the chairman of some charity organisation, but then she would have had to appear in public, at his side, and it wasn't that sort of prominence she craved. It was ridiculous in any case to imagine Harry in any such position. He was the most modest and the least public-spirited of men, lacking in ambition and utterly uncompetitive. She'd known that before ever she married him. It had been part of his charm – he had charm – that he was not pushy or aggressive. She'd heard his mother complain about it ('You've no ambition, Harry') as though it were a grievous fault. As far as Harry was concerned, helping his father to run his business suited him fine. He liked the product (greetings cards, mainly) and enjoyed selling it, and when his father retired, he was perfectly comfortable becoming head of the firm, following exactly the paths well marked out for him. He didn't talk about work. What was there to talk about, when it was so familiar? He never seemed to have any problems he wanted to discuss with her.

Edwina's book was still lying unopened on her lap as she stared at a robin perched on the stone urn in front of the conservatory doors. When the bird took off, she would start reading and sweep away these foolish meanderings of thought. Daydreaming, people called it. She'd always daydreamed. Harry was always snapping his fingers in front of her eyes and saying, hey, daydreamer. He used to be curious as to exactly what she was daydreaming about, but she was never able to tell him. She'd say something vague, like holidays, or Christmas, and that satisfied him. He quite liked her dreaminess. He'd told her once how sweet she looked wearing what he called her 'faraway' expression, her face so still, her eyes heavy-lidded. Like the Sleeping Beauty, he said, though she wasn't asleep. He never got impatient with her, the way her parents had done, constantly urging her to snap out of it, to pull herself together, for heaven's sake. It had made her feel guilty, Harry's tolerance of her daydreaming, because she knew he thought her head was full of fairy-tale imaginings. And it was not. It was more often full of dark thoughts and frustrations. Her sweet expression was a lie, it betrayed nothing.

The robin had gone. She opened her book. She didn't use bookmarks, or turn down the corners of pages. She always knew where she had got up to, always remembered the page number. This was an unusual book for her to have bought. It wasn't about a woman. It was about a man, about Primo Levi. He didn't fit in to what she thought of as her special interest and, in fact, she had never heard of him, though after she'd bought the book and seen who he was, she couldn't believe she had been so ignorant. What had attracted her was the size of the volume. It was vast, it would keep her going a long time. She'd read the jacket copy and when she saw that Primo Levi had been a survivor of Auschwitz, she'd bought the book immediately. Ever since she'd read Anne Frank's diary when she was at school she'd been drawn to Holocaust literature in a way that she worried wasn't healthy. It appalled and frightened her to read about Auschwitz and Belsen, and Ravensbrück and Treblinka – she knew all the names – but at the same time the horror of what had happened, of what had been endured, was something she could not keep away from. It was the fascination of knowing it had really happened, that nobody had made it up, it was not simply a terrible story, worse than any nightmare thriller. But what worried her was the fear that reading about the camps, and what had been done in them, was somehow disgusting, until, one day, she came across the phrase 'bearing witness'. She read in a newspaper article that bearing witness to the sufferings of those who died in the Holocaust was right and proper and the only way of honouring their memories. It was wrong to suppress the truth, wrong to argue that it should not be talked about because it was over, that it had happened a long time ago, and no good was done by dwelling on such atrocities. Edwina was relieved. Afterwards, when she sat reading and wincing and even weeping over a survivor's story, she said to herself that she too was bearing witness, and that she was not being masochistic by torturing herself with the images.

She was two-thirds of the way through the biography, the Auschwitz experience over (except she knew it never would be for Primo Levi). Surprisingly, the book was proving easy to read – she'd been afraid it might be too academic for her. The author's style was clear and direct, the sentences simple and short. She was reading about Primo Levi's wife, Lucia, and as she read on she began to feel there was something missing here. Lucia was surely more important than she was presented as being. This man had come back from Auschwitz and had had to rebuild his shattered life. He married Lucia (whom he had not known before) and she enabled him to do so. His real love, or the woman suspected of being his real love, had perished in the camp but Lucia was the one he married and with whom he had two children. Without her, would he have managed as well as he did? Edwina stopped reading, and frowned. She stared into the garden and wished there was more about Lucia. In spite of the photographs in the book, she couldn't see or hear the woman in her mind. Lucia was vague. She was (to Edwina) the all-important wife, but she was shadowy. Not enough consideration was being given to what it had been like for her to marry a man with 174517 branded on his arm.

Harry was Jewish. His paternal grandparents had originally come from Poland to Germany, and then to England, changing their name from Greneski to Green when they arrived. Their son, Harry's father, had married a Jewish girl, Rebecca Rubenstein, so Harry was indisputably Jewish, though he never went to the synagogue and observed none of the Jewish laws on holy days after he left home to get married. Edwina was blamed for this lapse by her mother-in-law, but it was not her fault. She would have been quite happy for Harry to practise the faith and observe the customs of his parents and grandparents, though she had not sought to please them by converting and marrying into that faith. They had married, she and Harry, in a register office, and his parents, though upset and, in his mother's case, resentful, had attended. When Laura was born, Edwina had been glad she was a girl, which avoided any dispute over circumcision. Harry had been strangely emphatic: if he had a son, the child would not be circumcised, however much his parents pleaded. Why not? Edwina had asked and been told it was barbaric. It fascinated her that the mild-mannered, conventional Harry, always anxious to please, had in this one respect proved such an unlikely rebel. She'd wondered if this rejection of Jewishness was a kind of fear, but he said it wasn't. 'Look,' he'd said, 'you were brought up a Methodist and rejected Methodism and all religious belief. I'm no different. I don't believe in any of it, it's all a nonsense.' She'd said to him once, 'Do you ever think about what would have happened to your family if you'd lived in Germany when Hitler came to power?' He'd said no, but then later admitted that he had thought about it but had stopped himself, because such speculation was morbid and sick. Edwina never mentioned the subject to him again. She thought about it often, though she hadn't confessed that to the impressionable Emma (who, unlike her dark-haired sister, was blonde, taking after her mother, and didn't look at all Jewish). She'd fantasised the knock on the door in the night, and the SS arriving and dragging Harry away. She'd shuddered as she imagined him crammed into an overcrowded cattle truck (she'd seen the films so her imagination hadn't had to work very hard). And then she'd tried to imagine him surviving and coming back to his family (who, miraculously, would in her fantasy have been on the last transport to England). At this point, her imagination had always failed. What would she have done, as his wife, greeting such a man after what had happened to him? It was a test she was overwhelmingly glad not to have had to face; but reading about Primo Levi, and thinking about Lucia, she saw it in a different way. The test would have been Harry's more than hers. It would have been up to him to dictate how his recent hellish past should be dealt with. And knowing Harry she knew what he would have decreed: forget it.

Primo Levi didn't want to forget it, he had had no intention of ever doing so even had it been possible. To forget would have been to betray those who had died, a victory for their murderers. But it occurred to Edwina as she took up the book again that Lucia might have wished he could, if not forget, at least not keep hammering home the memories over and over. The biographer related how Primo Levi always wore short-sleeved shirts, even in winter, and that the number 174517 tattooed on his skin stood out. It was intended to stand out. No one could avoid seeing it. Lucia certainly couldn't. She had to look at it all the time. She couldn't escape it, or its significance. During the most intimate moments of her relationship with her husband it was there. She saw it, she touched it, she felt it. The pity of it caught in Edwina's throat. She wondered if Lucia ever suggested that her husband should wear a sweater, it was cold, he would be warmer, might it not be a good idea . . . She wondered if Lucia hoped the ink would fade over the years, that given time and hundreds of baths and showers and dozens of bars of soap the colour would fade, the number at last become so faint, it would not call attention to itself and its meaning.

She admired Lucia Levi, much more than this biographer seemed to. She would like to have been her, providing her brave husband with the love and tenderness of which he had such need. But at this stage of the book Lucia seemed to be receding. She was off stage, coping with the children and her mother and her mother-in-law. Edwina read that people said the Levis seemed happy a lot of the time, but how could anyone know? She thought of how her own unhappiness was hidden, even from Harry. She was sure that people thought she and Harry were happy and on the surface they were. She had a sudden mad impulse to put the book down and go and write to Lucia Levi, to ask her if she had indeed been happy with her husband or whether throughout her marriage she'd been struggling to fight the great sadness engulfing it. The moment passed. She smiled slightly to herself at her own absurdity. She was, as Harry would put it, getting carried away, so immersed in the lives of others, and one of them dead, that her own life hardly existed. She herself was a background person, someone upon whom attention would never focus. If it did, on the rare occasions she was noticed, it scared her – when that woman at the hospital, for example, that bossy Friend, caught hold of her she couldn't wait to escape and merge back into the crowd. *She didn't want to be noticed.*

It suddenly struck her what an advantage that might have given her, if, like Primo Levi, she'd been taken to Auschwitz. It was good not to attract attention. She had no skills that might have saved her, as his knowledge of chemistry saved him, and no beauty that might have preserved her life as a sexual slave, but maybe she had other qualities which she had never recognised. Primo Levi, she read, said that years after he left Auschwitz he could still tell within the first five minutes of meeting someone new whether they would have survived in the camp. He'd said this without needing to know what talents people had – it was all based on a reading of character. Character was everything, character and personality, which had nothing to do with either physical strength or cleverness. Did she have it? Was there within her an innate toughness in spite of her reserve and shyness? Would it have been a life-saver, looked at through Auschwitz eyes, that she was usually quiet and rarely spoke up for herself and avoided confrontation unless provoked? Would all these traits she despised in herself actually have proved to be assets?

She read for another hour and then put the book aside. Harry would be home soon. When she'd brought the book home, he'd groaned and said couldn't she have picked something more cheerful. It's bad for you, he'd said, reading this kind of depressing stuff. But he was wrong. On the contrary, she knew it was proving good for her. Primo Levi's survival consoled her. It was making her more respectful of her own survival. What she had had to survive was as nothing compared to Primo Levi's prolonged ordeal, it was offensive to speak of her own ordeal in the same breath, but nevertheless she saw that by not collapsing or breaking down, but instead carrying on as normal, she had shown some small measure of courage. Bravery didn't have to come in dramatic form, it could emerge in tiny doses and be built on. She should give herself some credit. All those nights she'd lain awake sweating with terror, convinced that in spite of all the reassurances her disease was terminal, but she hadn't woken Harry, she hadn't turned to the girls. She'd got up in the mornings and made breakfast and sent Harry off to work and the girls off to school, all with a smile. Didn't that count for something? She hoped so.

When Harry came in, she was rolling out pastry, but the Primo Levi biography was on the table in the conservatory where he settled himself for a drink. She finished making the chicken pie, put it in the oven, and joined him. The book separated their two glasses. 'Still reading this?' Harry said. She nodded. 'I might give it a go sometime. On holiday. Except it would fill a suitcase.' She smiled, but said nothing. He would never, of course, even open it. He read crime fiction on holiday, or else sports biographies. She didn't want him reading it in any case. It was too precious to her. He would madden her by fidgeting and yawning and reading so slowly he never seemed to turn a page. But she knew that she in turn irritated him by becoming so absorbed in the books she read that, though she heard his voice, she couldn't pull herself out of them to answer him. The pull of what he was saying was not as strong as the pull of the print. She didn't want to leave the alternative world she was inhabiting even if it was Auschwitz. It made him jealous, though he was not a jealous man. 'Talking of holidays,' Harry was saying, 'how about being adventurous for a change and going to Thailand?' 'Thailand?' she queried, astonished. Harry usually thought it madly adventurous to go to Scotland. 'Well,' he said, 'the young seem to like it. Laura loved it, and Emma's dying to go.'

'We're not young, Harry.'

'We're not old.'

'No, but we don't back-pack, we like a bit of comfort. And Emma wouldn't come with us, she's finished with family holidays, you know that.'

'Finished with wet weeks in Scotland,' said Harry, 'but I bet she'd be keen to have her fare paid to Thailand whoever she was going with.'

'I doubt it. She's got a Saturday job anyway. You said she had to earn her own pocket money, remember?'

'She could still take two weeks off.'

'I don't know. I don't know if I want to go to Thailand. I mean, why? Why Thailand? Why not Greece or Italy? We've hardly been anywhere, why go so far?'

'Because we can.'

'Oh, Harry . . .'

'And we should. We're stick-in-the-muds.'

'What's got into you?'

'I feel restless, sort of restless.'

He got up suddenly and asked if she wanted some more wine. She said no. She watched him go through to the kitchen and refill his glass. He wasn't a big drinker, two generous glasses of wine before his meal was unusual. She saw him stand, glass in hand, facing the wall. He stood quite still. She knew what he was looking at: the calendar. Well, she hadn't specifically marked the clinic day on the kitchen calendar, just put a tiny cross by the date, he would see nothing significant there. She didn't need to write down clinic appointments anywhere. The date, even a year ahead, was fixed in her mind. She kept her hospital card in her jewellery box, in a little drawer at the bottom of the two-tier box, a place neither Harry nor the girls would ever have cause to look. Harry came back into the conservatory and sat down. She knew what was coming. 'It was yesterday, wasn't it?' he said. 'What? What was yesterday?' she asked. 'Don't be silly, Edwina, you know what. Don't play these games. Was everything OK? I assume it was good news.' 'Oh, do you?' she said, and got up and went into the kitchen and began banging about.

He sat on, not moving. She was being unfair, of course. It was ridiculous, her anger, her fury that he hadn't remembered till now. Why should she expect him to remember a date a year ahead when she'd taken such care to hide it? Nothing he could do or say was ever right. She didn't even know what she would have wanted him to say or do. From the very beginning it had been like this, distancing herself from him on clinic days, freezing him out, and then raging because he wasn't giving her the nameless something she wanted. She blamed herself for this state of affairs, but she also blamed him. It was his refusal at the beginning to consider the possibility that the treatment might fail and that she might die which had separated them. She'd wanted to contemplate the worst outcome and he'd refused, point-blank refused. There was no need. She was going to be fine. She would not only survive, she would flourish. He even said that he was sure there had been a mistake and there was nothing wrong with her; though he admitted he knew at the same time that this was absurdly wishful thinking. He had said – his only concession to the kind of discussion she wanted – that if she did only have a short time to live (though he had referred to this as 'if things go wrong') he didn't want to waste it talking about her dying. He wanted it to be a happy time.

She didn't hide the scar. She had no need to do so, from Harry's point of view. He wasn't squeamish and it wasn't a very big scar, but on the other hand she became expert at turning away when she was dressing and undressing, turning away at just the right moment. In bed, Harry's fingers sometimes strayed towards the scar and she pushed them away. She didn't want it touched. He obeyed. He didn't want to do anything to upset her and there was all the rest of her body to fondle. Her illness hadn't made any difference to his desire for her, or hers for him, which seemed to her extraordinary enough to make her weep sometimes. She even felt, at the beginning, soon after the tiny tumour was removed, that all her fear was moving out of herself when she was making love – for that short while the pleasure annihilated the sickening worry. But then, later, as the years went safely on, that had ceased to be true. Panic over, the anxiety had burrowed deeper and dulled her senses, the terror had withdrawn from the forefront of her mind to bury itself cunningly in the very centre of her body, biding its time. She could never be sure when it was going to surge through her again and this made her first tense and then numb. It was the strangest feeling, one she couldn't have begun to explain to Harry even if he had wanted to listen. He seemed to notice nothing. It amazed her.

'Dinner's ready,' she called. They hadn't spoken for a full half-hour. Harry had gone on sitting in the conservatory, she'd stayed in the kitchen watching the vegetables simmer, peeping unnecessarily at the pie in the oven. He came through and sat down, looking wretched. She knew she was being cruel, refusing to tell him about the visit to the clinic. 'There was nothing to tell,' she said, 'so it didn't seem worth mentioning it, that's all.' He stared at her, food untouched. 'What?' she said, eating her own food with exaggerated enthusiasm. 'Ages since I made this,' she said. 'It's good, don't you think?' Slowly, he began to eat. After a few mouthfuls, he nodded, but still he didn't speak. The clink of their knives and forks on their plates was awful. When they'd finished, he cleared his throat and said, 'They must have said something.'

'Who?'

'Please, Edwina.'

'Oh, you make such a performance of it. They said I *seemed* fine. They said that if I still *seem* fine next year they won't see me again.'

His face expressed such delight she could hardly bear it. 'But that's terrific!' he said. 'That's brilliant news, how can you say there was nothing to tell, it's wonderful!'

'Is it?'

'Yes, it is, how can you not think so, what more could you want? We should celebrate, it's incredible how well you've done.' He got up and came round the table to her and tried to hug her. She felt like weeping.

'I've survived so far,' she said. 'I'm in continuing remission, Harry, that's all.'

'That's *all*? That's everything.'

'Yes, it is, but it's not what you think, what you keep trying to make it out to be.'

But he was so happy, singing away (tunelessly) a Beatles song, smiling to himself as he cleared the dishes, and she felt envious. Emma came home while he was stacking them in the dishwasher and asked him what he was so cheerful about. She'd only been 8 when all this began, and Laura 10. Harry had told them that Mum had a bad bit in her breast and was going to have it taken out in hospital. Like in an apple? Emma had asked. Yes, Harry had said, like in an apple. That had quite satisfied Emma, but not Laura. She'd tied her father in knots with her demands for explanations and no talk of bad bits in apples had satisfied her. But after Edwina came home and was well, and hadn't needed any more treatment, even Laura had lost interest. Sometimes, Edwina reckoned, her entire family had forgotten what had happened. A good thing, of course. What she wanted, she supposed. Her own mother had been such a trial with her overwhelming concern, but she was the only one who had reacted with horror, and she was dead now. No one left to weep and wail over the words 'tumour' and 'malignant' and 'cancer', and watch her so intently that it had been a relief, always, to leave her presence.

Emma didn't really listen to the explanation Harry was giving for his high good humour (to do with trying to persuade your Mum to come on an adventurous holiday, he said), but then she rarely listened to the answers to her own questions. She had no, or only a slight, interest in her parents' lives. Harry hadn't even finished replying before she'd cut in with complaints about how little she was going to be paid for the gardening job she'd just got. 'She's a funny old woman,' Emma told them (in contrast to how she listened to them, they hung on her every word), 'sort of posh. It's a big garden, really beautiful. She's got a man who comes to do the hard stuff when it needs doing, but she needs me to follow her round and do all the bending. At least it'll be easy.'

'You don't know a thing about gardening,' Harry said, laughing. 'You don't know a daisy from a snowdrop, and you wouldn't recognise a weed if your life depended on it. I can't think why this poor woman's taking you on.'

'I'm young and willing. She can train me.'

'Wish I could,' Harry said, and pointed out to his own garden. 'There you are,' he said, 'I'll train you out there, if you're so willing.'

'*That* isn't a garden, not compared to hers,' Emma sneered, 'and anyway, you wouldn't pay me.'

'No, I certainly would not.'

'Well, then, I need the money. You said I had to earn my own pocket money now.'

'At 18, you should.'

'I'm not 18 till August.'

Edwina had gone into the sitting-room. Their voices drifted off behind her. She'd brought her book through from the conservatory, and now she switched on a lamp and sat down, but she didn't start to read again. Emma probably wouldn't come through from the kitchen. She'd find something to eat and eat it standing up and then rush upstairs and ring Luke. Luke never came near the house, though Edwina had suggested inviting him for a Sunday lunch when his name was so often on Emma's lips. It would be nice, she'd said, to get to know this boy. Emma had groaned, said she wouldn't think of inviting him, for heaven's sake. But Edwina had caught sight of him in town. She hadn't liked what she had seen, but had chided herself for being prejudiced, because Luke looked dirty and unkempt and he smoked. She just hoped Harry, if he came across the boy, would show the same restraint.

'Mum?' Emma said, suddenly appearing in the doorway. 'Could you lend me a fiver? Dad won't, and I really need it to pay Luke back.'

'What do you owe him for?'

'Mum, that's not the point, I just need the money. I really need it, *please*, I'll pay you back when I start this job at the weekend.'

'My bag's in the hall. Bring it here.'

She held the five-pound note out, trying to meet Emma's eye, but failing. The money was almost snatched, with a quick thanks, and Emma had gone leaping up the stairs to ring Luke from the extension on the landing. Laura never borrowed money. Laura looked like her father but she was like Edwina, quiet and reserved and careful – or, as Emma put it sarcastically, 'a paragon of all the virtues'. Yes, if those were virtues.

Edwina started reading again. She was dreading getting to Primo Levi's death. She knew, because she'd been unable to resist looking it up, that he was thought to have committed suicide many years after surviving the camp, and she couldn't bear to contemplate such an end or what it signified – all that struggle, all that endurance, for nothing, a life once so valuable it had been clung on to during the whole ordeal of Auschwitz, and then suddenly, in better times, worth nothing, found unbearable. And yet, preparing herself to read about it, she thought for some reason of how she felt each time she came away from the clinic with everything all right – no joy, no instant happiness that her little ordeal was over, but instead such grief, as though instead of being cleared she had been condemned. She strained to make a connection, however tiny, however absurdly different in scale, with Primo Levi's ultimate response to the safety and ease of his life so long after coming out of the camp, but it made no sense. It was outrageous for her to seek any empathy with such a man. All she had in common with him was a kind of survival ludicrously different from his own.

But what was she doing with her survival? Jogging along in the same old way, not using it at all for her own benefit or anyone else's. She'd isolated herself, tried to protect herself these last ten years by not allowing herself to feel anything. That was why reading had become so important, why it was comforting – within the life in the books, she could *feel*. But keeping herself apart had damaged her too. She was remote from her family, she'd trained herself to be. Harry didn't seem to mind. He just thought she had become a calmer person, and he approved. But she wasn't calm. Inwardly, she seethed with all kinds of unreconciled emotions that only erupted on clinic days and then subsided.

It had to stop. Her control had had its use, but it was time to let the brake off.

'Harry?' she called.

3

Is There Anything You Want?

THERE WAS no one watching, but Mrs Hibbert turned away abruptly from the glass door opening into her porch as though she were trying to hide. She screwed the beastly letter up, then passed it from hand to hand before throwing it into the waste-paper basket in her kitchen. She stood and looked at the offending little ball, lying in the corner of the otherwise empty basket. Ten seconds later, she bent down and took it out and, smoothing the paper as best she could, reread the letter. Her face burned. She was *mortified*. She wished the letter had arrived the day before, on a hospital day when, doing her job as a Friend of St Mary's, she would have soon got things in proportion and laughed it off, whereas today she would have to struggle to do so. She was always tired on Fridays – it took more out of her than she ever let anyone realise, being on her feet for four hours in that hospital. But now she badly needed to be busy, to get over the nasty letter, and so she was glad she had Dot to take shopping.

She took the crumpled paper to the table and told herself to be sensible. It was not a nasty letter at all, merely an official one. It declined her offer to help in the Mental Health Research charity shop, saying that the charity's policy was not to employ people over 70 because it was felt the standing required was too wearing for them. Such nonsense! Those women sat most of the time. She'd seen them. There were two chairs behind the counter where one went to pay and they sat on them. Some of them didn't even stand up to take the money, they were so lazy. And rude. As for not employing people over 70, that was ridiculous – there was hardly anyone working there *under* 70. Lucy Binns was probably only around 50, true, but Adelaide Priest was definitely either 70 already or just about to be, and as for Mrs Jarrett, she was indisputably nearer 80. Why was she being told this lie about age? She peered at the signature again. Barbara Bell. She didn't know any Barbara Bell, or a Barbara, or even a Bell. It said 'co-ordinator' in brackets beside the name, whatever that meant. Probably someone in head office, not anyone local. Her own letter offering her services had been passed on. She wondered how many people would have read it. Would anyone in the shop itself have seen it? Had any of those women there read it and thought, oh heavens, here is that bossy Mrs Hibbert showing off? It made her shudder. She wished passionately that she had not put that bit in about having time now that she was no longer a magistrate. (And if she hadn't said that, it occurred to her, no one would have known her age and she somehow doubted if it would have been asked for.)

Suddenly, screwing the wretched letter up yet again, Mrs Hibbert dropped it this time into the bin where she put potato peelings and used tea-bags and other such waste. She would not now be tempted to take it out again. For a moment, she thought about writing back to Barbara Bell, thanking her for her communication and then, just in a casual fashion, throwing doubt on the age of certain women who already worked in the shop. She wouldn't, of course. She was not small-minded or malicious. She had her pride. Determined to be busy, she pulled out the cutlery drawer and emptied the contents on to the kitchen table with a curiously satisfying clash of metal. The drawer had long needed tidying. As she sorted out the fish knives from the steak knives (neither used since her husband died) she decided she would most likely have been terribly bored working in that pathetic shop. And, she remembered, it had an odd smell, rather unpleasant, fusty. It was alleged that all the clothes they received were either washed or dry-cleaned before being put out for sale, but Mrs Hibbert doubted this. It was one of the things she would have been interested in establishing as true or not. That, and how prices were decided on, because, frankly, it seemed to her that the pricing policy was entirely haphazard. The books, for example: she had found three copies of Monica Dickens's *One Pair of Hands* on the shelves, all priced differently and yet all in paper-back and all in the same condition. She had felt obliged to point this out to Mrs Jarrett, who was on duty that day. She'd shown her the pencilled-in prices: 70*p*, 75*p*, £1.10. And what had been that silly woman's reaction? She'd laughed. She'd said how funny, and that it didn't matter, and that Mrs Hibbert could have any of the three for the lowest price, for 70*p*. As if the price was the important thing and not the discrepancies! And in any case she'd read all of Monica Dickens's books years ago. What Mrs Jarrett had failed to understand was how foolish, dishonest even, it made the shop and therefore the charity itself look. How would someone feel if they'd bought the £1.10 copy and then later on saw the other copies so much cheaper? Cheated, that's what.

She had the cutlery all lined up on the table and now she cleaned the compartments of the box she kept it in. Placing the knives and forks and spoons back in the compartments pleased her. She liked order; confusion and muddle irritated her. She had so longed to sort out the manifest confusion in that charity shop. Some charity shops, she'd observed with approval, had the clothes colour-co-ordinated, but not this one. This one, the one to which she had offered assistance, had everything jumbled up with the only distinction one of separating men's and women's and children's clothes. In fact, the *look* of the shop was what upset her most. A mess. It unsettled her. Her hands always itched to start reorganising it. Take the window for a start (and it *was* the start, after all). A large, plain, open-style shop window, crying out for an attractive display. And what did people looking into it see? A scruffy pile of jig-saw boxes in the centre, some shoes next to them on one side and three hideous vases on the other, one containing dusty ears of corn and the others empty. Otherwise a great void. Yet inside the shop she'd noticed a beautiful, almost complete, set of blue willow-pattern china which could have been displayed with great effect on one of the pristine lace table-cloths draped at the back of the shop over a chair. Nobody had any *idea*, and it grieved her.

She knew she was getting in a state over nothing and that she must control herself. Dot would be waiting. She could not let her down, especially this week when the poor woman would have been worried to death by that daughter of hers. Mrs Hibbert had spotted her going into the clinic but had managed to make sure Sarah didn't see her. She'd been with that ghastly boyfriend of hers. He'd been half carrying her along. It was a dreadful thing to say, but Mrs Hibbert suspected there was not much wrong with Sarah Nicholson. Women who attended Mr Wallis's Thursday clinic did not always have something wrong with them. She knew they'd often just been sent by GPs for reassurance if they were the neurotic type, and Dot's daughter was certainly that. But Dot wouldn't have it. She didn't see how Sarah manipulated her. She was such a foolish girl, always had been, and she caused her mother endless anxiety. She could not help having cancer (if indeed she did have it, which was by no means yet proven) but she undoubtedly could have helped taking up with Mike Allen, a married man with three children, all young. However, best not to mention to Dot her feelings about that man. Maybe Dot guessed she did not approve of him – she was aware that she tightened her lips when he was mentioned and that her expression probably betrayed her – but she would never *say* anything.

Her coat on, she picked her car keys off the hook behind the door. She must have another key made for the garden shed so that this girl who was coming to help could get into it for tools if she was out, not that she intended to be until she'd trained her. It would take some doing – the child clearly had no idea what to do in a garden, but she'd seemed nice-natured and was eager for the job (yes, for the money, Mrs Hibbert knew that) and she'd been the only person to answer the advert in the post office. It had taken Mrs Hibbert a long time to face up to the fact that she had to have more help in the garden – she hated the thought – but though she had Martin Yates for the heavy work she needed someone to help her weed, now that her arthritis increasingly troubled her. She didn't want her beautiful garden to fall into the same state as Dot's. She didn't blame Dot, none of the neglect was Dot's fault, it was all Adam's. Once he'd become crippled himself he should have organised help, but he had been too stubborn (always expecting to get better) and too mean to see to it. How Dot had stayed married to that man Mrs Hibbert could not imagine. He was a bully and a tyrant, whereas her Francis had been a gentleman, and a truly gentle man.

If Dot was not ready and waiting she would be annoyed. Being annoyed with Dot was something she had to struggle with continually – Dot *was* annoying, and the most annoying thing about her was how she let Adam take advantage of her. On the occasions when she was not standing outside on Fridays at the agreed time, it was always because Adam had demanded attention just as she was putting her coat on. Dot would whisper as an excuse that he had needed help to get to the bathroom and this enraged Mrs Hibbert. Adam claimed he couldn't walk without assistance but why in that case did he not use sticks or crutches? Anyone sensible, and wanting to be independent, and eager to spare his wife would do so. Dot was tiny and fragile, under 5 feet tall and weighing a mere 7 stone, whereas he was huge and heavy. Leaning on her shoulder he was in danger of fracturing it with his immense weight. 'Get him crutches,' Mrs Hibbert had told Dot, but Dot said that when she had suggested this to Adam he had been furious and had shouted that resorting to crutches would signify the end and he was not ready for that yet. He had had his bed moved downstairs so that he had only a few steps to get either to the bathroom or the kitchen, but whenever he wanted to move at all he summoned Dot. The rest of the time he lolled in their living-room watching television with the sound very loud even though he had a deaf aid and could hear perfectly well with it when he wanted to. It was an awful life for Dot.

She knew, or rather guessed, that people found her friendship with Dorothy Nicholson a little odd. Partly, it was a matter of class, and matters of class were still alive and well in their part of the world. Mrs Hibbert, in local terms, came from a well-off, once landowning family. She had been educated privately and spoke without a trace of the regional accent. Dot, on the other hand, was a tenant farmer's daughter, a tenant of the Lawsons in the old days. As a girl, Mary Lawson (as Mrs Hibbert then was) had been in the habit of going to the farm to collect eggs and it was Dot who took her to the shed and picked the eggs out for her. She was such a tiny, thin scrap of a girl, and so eager to please, and she'd always seemed to admire Mary, regularly marvelling at how tall she was and how nice her nails were (Dot's were bitten) and how pretty her dresses (Dot was dressed in awful hand-me-downs which drowned her, with her older sisters being so much bigger). They became not exactly friends – the gulf in social status was too great – but pleasant acquaintances. When Mary Lawson returned as Mrs Hibbert after her years down south (though 'south' had been still north, in effect) Dot was about the only person who had bothered to welcome her. At the time Mrs Hibbert came back, Dot had been married to Adam Nicholson for fifteen years and had a 5-year-old daughter. Mrs Hibbert had felt even more protective than she had done years ago when they were both children.

She drove the mile or so to Dot's house reflecting that this shopping trip to the out-of-town supermarket must be the one bright spot in her friend's life. Heaven knew, there was nothing very thrilling about going shopping, or not this sort of mundane shopping, but it meant Dot got away from Adam and had a ride in a car (the Nicholsons no longer had a car) and had someone to talk to. It pleased Mrs Hibbert to think she was providing such a treat, but it did *not* please her when Dot took advantage. Taking advantage meant not being ready and waiting. In Dot's place she would have positioned herself at a window ten minutes before the friend was due, her coat already on, key in her pocket, shopping list in hand, and she would have been out of her front door the moment she saw the car turn the corner. But Dot was never ready. Sometimes, like today, Mrs Hibbert had to peep the horn, and still no sign of her. Well, she was most certainly not going to get out of her car and go up those steps and ring the doorbell. It was bad enough being obliged to turn the engine off. She peeped once more, and looked at the clock. She would wait two more minutes and then she was just going to drive off. But then, as she was checking her watch against the car clock, the front door opened. Dot stood there, smiling and waving and mouthing something. She did not, Mrs Hibbert noted, have her coat on. She disappeared back into the house leaving the door open and then a minute later reappeared pulling her coat on as she closed the door. Half-way down the six rather steep steps, she stopped. Exasperated, Mrs Hibbert lowered her car window and shouted, 'Dot! Do come on! I haven't all day!' But Dot had retreated back up to her door and was taking her coat off again. Furiously, Mrs Hibbert watched as Dot struggled to remove the apron she had just remembered she'd left on and tried to shove it through the narrow slit of the letter-box. Oh, as if it mattered! But apparently it did, because Dot would not give up until the yellow spotted material had finally been disposed of. She trotted to the car, pink-faced and breathing heavily. 'Sorry, Mary,' she whispered, 'it was just that as I was getting ready Adam wanted . . .' 'I don't want to know what Adam wanted,' Mrs Hibbert snapped. 'I have no interest in the matter, or anything to do with him, as you very well know. You are quite aware, Dot, of how absurd I think it is that you let yourself be a slave to that inconsiderate man. Now, get in and settle down.'

Dot settled. She was so small she could hardly see through the windscreen and kept stretching her neck up like a tortoise. Mrs Hibbert cleared her throat, ashamed at having spoken so sharply and only hoped Dot understood that it really was Adam she was annoyed with. She badly wanted to say something sympathetic, or to apologise, but did neither. She would try to show Dot by her actions that she hadn't meant to sound so angry, for after all, actions spoke louder than words (an aphorism of which she was particularly fond). She drove confidently on, feeling not quite so guilty having decided this, negotiating roundabouts with aplomb and gathering speed once the dual carriageway was reached. It was only 3 miles along it to all the big supermarkets, a hideous collection of them, all more or less next to each other. There were plenty of shops in their small town but almost everyone made a weekly trip out here because of course everything was cheaper and the variety of goods much greater. Mrs Hibbert didn't need to save money and she had no desire for a wider choice, but she liked the outing, though she would never have admitted this – she was going for Dot's sake, no other reason. Adam kept her very short of housekeeping money and wanted every wretched penny accounted for. He regarded his wife as disorganised, scatty, impressionable and hopeless at knowing what was value for money. Mrs Hibbert had been bound to admit that there was some truth in this. She had seen Dot forget to buy essential items like soap powder or toilet rolls and come away from the shop with a pound of grapes long past their best ('Reduced!') or expensive frozen chocolate eclairs which would rightly infuriate Adam. She loved cream cakes and was always 'fancying' them.

'Dot,' said Mrs Hibbert, when they were nearly there, 'Dot, buy something for yourself today. Is there anything you want? I'd like you to. My treat, dear. Some cakes, or biscuits. What about those chocolate wafer things you like? Do they come in boxes or tins as well as packets? Choose yourself a box.' 'They do come in tins, Mary,' Dot said. 'But they're expensive, because you're buying the tin too, you see.' Mrs Hibbert controlled her irritation with difficulty – good heavens, as if she needed Dot to explain that to her! It was amusing, really. 'Never mind the cost,' she said, 'you get yourself a tin. You can always use it to store something in, when it's empty, so it won't be a waste.' 'I could give it to Sarah,' said Dot, brightening up, 'she could keep her paintbrushes in it, if she took the lid off.' Again, Mrs Hibbert tightened her lips. If Dot wasn't thinking of how to please Adam, she was thinking of how to please that ungrateful daughter of hers, a girl who never thought of treating her mother. She had never known Sarah give Dot anything but trouble. No doubt it was all to do with her upbringing and Dot had indeed brought Sarah up very, very foolishly. She had over-indulged her from the beginning, petted and cosseted her, been at her beck and call. Mrs Hibbert had found it painful to witness and had never been able to resist contrasting Dot's lamentable style of mothering with how she herself would have approached the role. When she saw Dot so neglected by her only child, who must know how much in need of support her mother was, she could not help fantasising about how *her* daughter if she'd had one would have responded to her needs, whatever they might have been.

She parked as near as possible to the trolley bay. Dot wouldn't have a pound coin ready for the trolley, of course, but she had one for each of them, as she always did. Sometimes, Dot forgot to return the coin and had to be reminded (laughingly, nicely). 'Now, Dot,' Mrs Hibbert said, 'have you got your list?' She knew it was Adam who made the list and that he would play hell if Dot forgot any of the items on it. Dot flourished it, beaming. 'And your purse?' Dot pulled it out of her bag and said, 'All present and correct.' They both laughed. It felt most companionable, almost jolly, going into the supermarket together. Once inside, Mrs Hibbert reminded Dot that she herself would be back in the car, her shopping done, in forty minutes precisely. She didn't mind waiting a little longer for Dot, but no more than another ten minutes at the absolute most, was that clear? It was. They parted. Mrs Hibbert had no need of a list. Having to make lists was a sign of a weak mind and, unlike her body, her mind had shown no sign of weakening. The truth was, and she acknowledged it to herself, she didn't *need* to buy anything. Need didn't come into it. She had six oranges left (she had an orange every day, mindful of vitamin C requirements) and half a wholemeal loaf (she ate two slices each lunchtime) and plenty of cheese (2 ounces a day, with the bread), and her freezer had ample supplies of fish and chicken (she no longer ate red meat). In her fridge she had three carrots, a cauliflower, some green beans and a pound or so of tomatoes as well as a cos lettuce. A string of onions hung in her kitchen and there were potatoes in the shed. She was well provided for, but this was Friday and Dot's shopping day, and she could not let Dot down. Dot, she was sure, had not the slightest idea that this trip was for her sake only.

There was no harm, though, in stocking up on supplies and in keeping up with what was on offer. She wandered slowly down the aisles, leaning slightly on her trolley, comparing prices. She could have managed with a basket, but they were such awkward things and pulled on her arm even with just a few items in them. There was something pleasing about knowing she could buy anything she wanted – anything – and that she didn't need to worry about the cost as so many of the other shoppers, Dot included, were obliged to. Harassed mothers were forever rushing past her trying to stop small children snatching goods off the shelves – to them, shopping was a burden, something to be got over as quickly as possible. She saw them looking at wrist-watches and sighing, and, at the check-out, looking in purses and groaning. She felt sorry for them. If she found herself behind one of these demented beings she always offered to help unload her trolley and the offer was nearly always accepted. She tried not to be judgemental but really, the stuff these women bought! It wasn't so much the packets of crisps and cans of Coke – she knew she must not be snobbish – but the ready-made meals that shocked her. If she had had a family and been on a tight budget, no ready-made meal would ever have found its way into her trolley.

She stopped in front of the fruit. It seemed extraordinary to her that supermarkets these days were willing to let shoppers pick their own fruit and vegetables so that anyone discerning could always be sure of perfect produce – marvellous. She selected four Granny Smith apples with the greatest care, a small melon which she tested for ripeness, and a bunch of watercress. Watercress was very nutritious. She'd read that there was more vitamin C in a sprig of watercress than in . . . she couldn't remember what. She moved on to the next aisle and searched for the right sort of tinned sardines. The right sort had to have been canned in sunflower oil and be boneless. Sardines in spring water, or brine, were better for you but she thought them tasteless and preferred risking her health by selecting those in an acceptable sort of oil. People made themselves ill by fretting about cholesterol, whatever it was. They went on foolish diets when there was no need. Mrs Hibbert herself was proud to claim she had never been on a diet in her life. If she got fat, which in her fifties she had begun to be, she had simply eaten less. Her trolley (of the smaller type) now looked quite respectable after she'd added two boxes of All Bran to the apples and six tins of sardines. She was finished and could no longer delay making her way to the check-out.

Amazingly, Dot was already there with a great heaped trolley plus a wire basket perched on top. She looked even more nervous than she usually did, but Mrs Hibbert thought maybe she appeared so shaky because she'd been rushing in an effort to please her friend. She was touched by this and even felt a little guilty. They got into place at the check-out, Mrs Hibbert graciously indicating that Dot should go first. But Dot hesitated. She took the wire basket and held it out and said, 'I thought I'd keep my treat separate, Mary.' Mrs Hibbert understood at once: Dot didn't want the treat to go on her receipt, even though Mrs Hibbert would give her the money for it afterwards, because then Adam would know about it. She wanted to hide her biscuits and enjoy them secretly. 'Very sensible,' Mrs Hibbert said. 'Put your treat in my trolley, Dot.' Still hesitating, and seeming about to say something but thinking better of it, Dot picked a packet of biscuits and put them in the other trolley. 'No tins?' Mrs Hibbert said. 'No larger boxes? I told you you could have a tin or a box, Dot, don't you remember?' 'Yes,' said Dot, 'but the tins are twice the price of the packets and so I thought if I just got a packet . . .' She paused, and repeating 'just got a packet' she lifted something else out of the basket and held it up. Mrs Hibbert stared. She felt her face flush. 'No!' she said. 'No, Dot, I said I wanted to treat *you*, not your husband. I have no intention of treating him. I'm sorry, but I am not prepared to pay for those. If you want to treat him, that is your affair.'

She couldn't bear to stand behind Dot any longer and suddenly moved to the next till. She was through it in minutes, before Dot had even unloaded her trolley, and marched out to the car. Once her shopping had been deposited in it and the trolley returned, she sat herself down and switched on her tape of Beethoven's Ninth. Not very soothing, but it was the first that came to hand. The music thundered through the car and made her feel worse, not better. She knew she had over-reacted and made herself appear mean, but she was upset out of all proportion that Dot had actually thought she might buy Adam Nicholson salted peanuts. She should have been amused. She should have laughed. Dot had pointed out, obliquely, that the packet of biscuits together with the packet of peanuts (a very large packet) came to the same price as a tin of the same biscuits would have done. The only loser was herself, deprived of more biscuits for the sake of treating Adam. And yet it was not as simple as that. Dot knew she hated Adam. Had there not been at least an element of mischief in her flaunting of those peanuts? Had it not been a deliberate test of her friend's kindness? Mrs Hibbert sat and pondered and could come to no conclusion. She felt that her desire to be kind and helpful was always being tested. It was tested every week at the hospital whenever a patient was curt and ungrateful. It had to be endured then, she had to rise above rudeness, constantly reminding herself that virtually everyone who stepped through those hospital doors was suffering stress of one kind or another. But in the rest of her daily life she didn't see why she should submit to such small tests without registering her resentment that they were being imposed. Dot had known what she was doing.

Still, Adam Nicholson's peanuts were not worth getting in a state about. The silly little incident was over, and when Dot came she would be perfectly friendly, as though it had never happened. The sight of Dot when she did lurch towards the car reinforced Mrs Hibbert's determination not to be cross with her. The poor woman could hardly wheel the trolley straight and when she started to unload the bags into the boot of the car one of them burst and there was the sound of glass breaking. Mrs Hibbert got out to help, but not in time to stop a large box of Persil slipping from Dot's grasp and falling into a puddle. 'Oh dear!' Dot kept wailing, 'the light bulbs. I've broken the light bulbs!' and Mrs Hibbert found herself consoling her and then searching the boot until she'd established only one light bulb had smashed. It was all so exhausting. By the time both of them were back in the car, she felt worn out. 'Sorry,' Dot kept saying. 'Sorry, Mary, sorry to have been . . .' It was so pathetic. Mrs Hibbert closed her eyes for a moment to compose herself. 'Don't worry, Dot,' she said, breaking into the still ongoing litany of apology, 'let's just go home.' She lowered the volume of the music and started the car. Neither of them spoke. When they arrived at Dot's house, Mrs Hibbert did not get out. She remained in the car while Dot ferried her six carrier bags and the soggy big box of soap powder up the steps, lining them up in front of the door. 'You go now, Mary,' she panted, as she took the last bag from the boot and closed it. 'Don't wait, you don't need to see me in.' Mrs Hibbert didn't reply. She *always* saw Dot in. The woman was such a scatterbrain it would have been unthinkable to leave her without checking she had her key, because if she'd forgotten or lost it that lazy brute of a husband of hers could not be depended on to open the door. She watched Dot fumble for her key in pocket after pocket and then start to search her bag. She was tempted to peep her car horn vigorously in an attempt to alert Adam to his wife's arrival home and her need of assistance, but she didn't. Finally, Dot located her key and, stepping over the bags, opened her door. She stood and waved as Mrs Hibbert drove off at last.

Ten minutes later, taking her own shopping out of her car, Mrs Hibbert discovered a packet of bacon and a pound of sausages lying in the corner of the boot. She was always telling Dot to tie the plastic carrier bags securely together – she'd shown her how easy it was to take the two handles and knot them firmly – so that this kind of thing would not happen, but Dot always forgot. Bad-tempered now, Mrs Hibbert started the car again. It wasn't far to Dot's, but she was nevertheless annoyed to have to drive there again instead of being able to put her feet up and have a cup of tea. She realised, as she neared Dot's house, that she ought to have telephoned before she left so that Dot would be waiting and could come down the steps and collect the missing items. Now, she would have to toil up them herself, unless she could make Dot hear her by sounding her horn. She resolved to try this. She gave three short blasts when she'd parked dead in front of the steps, but nobody appeared. Sighing, she got out of the car and clambered up the steps. She put her finger on the doorbell and kept it there. It was a very loud bell and she could clearly hear it blasting through the empty hall but still Dot did not appear. Furious, she plonked the bacon and sausages down and carefully began to negotiate the steps. She was just on the last one when she heard the door open behind her and a shout. It sounded like 'Hey! You!' She paused, stepped safely on to the pavement and turned. Adam Nicholson stood in the doorway, his clothes dishevelled, his face a livid scarlet. 'Hey! You! Mary

Hibbert! I want a word with you!' She froze, shocked by the violence of his manner. 'I beg your pardon?' she managed to say, annoyed that instead of sounding icy and dignified, her voice shook. 'You! I want a word with you, upsetting my wife. Who do you think you are, eh, with your treats? Patronising bitch! My wife doesn't need treats, she doesn't want anything from do-gooders like you!' And then, as Mrs Hibbert felt for the door of her car, he threw something down the steps and went back inside, slamming the door.

The packet of chocolate wafers split as it hit the third step and half the biscuits scattered down the remainder. Mrs Hibbert was breathless, she felt she was going to faint, and clung on to the steering wheel until she had regained her composure enough to drive. A dog pattered past. She watched it sniff a biscuit which had bounced right down on to the pavement and then gobble it up. Excited, the dog mounted the steps and finished off all but the paper wrapping. So that was that. Mrs Hibbert at last felt recovered enough to start the car and drive very slowly home. She hadn't the strength to back it into her garage, which she usually did, and left it for the moment in the driveway. Her legs felt weak as she let herself into her house and she had to sit down for several minutes before she could raise the energy to make herself some restorative tea. She sat quite still, thinking, her hands clasped in front of her. It was at times like this that being on one's own was so very hard – no one to be comforting, no one to take one's side, no one upon whom one could unload all the distress. It had to be contained and gradually processed, and that was horribly wearing and difficult to do.

He was a monster, that man. His behaviour had been outrageous. There was no excuse whatsoever for it. But it wasn't Adam Nicholson's disgraceful shouting which worried her most, it was the thought of what Dot might have said to provoke it that upset her. *Had* Dot said she was patronising? Had Dot complained to Adam about her? Had Dot accused her of being a do-gooder? No. She didn't believe it. Dot couldn't have done, wouldn't have done. It was unbelievable. Dot and she had always been friends. She had always helped, and often indulged Dot, and Dot had always been grateful. Adam had somehow twisted whatever Dot had said. He'd probably found the biscuits and it had come out that Dot had been treated to them. But if he thought he could ruin her friendship with his wife he was greatly mistaken. Once she got Dot on her own it would all come out, how he'd, no doubt, bullied her and resented her being given a treat. Dot would tell her the truth. Probably Dot would have heard him hurling his vulgar abuse – she could hardly have avoided hearing – and was even now sick with shame and embarrassment. Mrs Hibbert nodded her head as she came to this conclusion, and then made her tea.

It helped, sipping the hot liquid, but she felt drained and sad and a little tearful. She wondered if it would be wiser not to call for Dot next week – now that would make Adam suffer! Dot would have to rely on the corner shop which was much more expensive than the supermarket and didn't sell fresh meat or fish. Adam Nicholson would soon regret his outburst. He and Dot had no one else to rely on. Their own daughter wouldn't be of any use, she never had been, and since Adam had turned her out of the house she had to sneak back into it to see her mother without his knowing (not that she made the effort very often). But if she didn't turn up to take Dot shopping as usual, would Dot ring her? It was tempting to find out. She rather liked the idea of Dot having to ring her – it put the ball into her court and was perhaps the most satisfactory way of dealing with this unpleasantness. Years ago, when she'd first said to Dot that if there was anything she wanted at the supermarket she'd be happy to take her when she went herself, Dot had been thrilled at the invitation but had nevertheless said she'd have to ask Adam if it was all right for her to go. Hearing this, Mrs Hibbert had reflected that Dot needed a lot more than help with shopping. She needed help to stand up to her husband. She had absolutely no life of her own. How she'd survived the constant crushing of her spirit was impossible to fathom.

And yet Mrs Hibbert was bound to admit to herself that Dot must have an inner strength not to have broken down or fled from her husband. It was such a mystery, how she'd managed to put up with his tyranny. Yet there she was, fragile maybe, nervous and anxious perhaps, but also always cheerful and smiling and putting up with things.

There was some secret there, something to be envied after all, and Mrs Hibbert wished she knew what it was. Dot didn't want anything that really mattered from anyone. Whatever it was, she had it.

4

We're Always Here, Dear

COMING OUT of the supermarket, Rachel saw her, that woman, the Friend of St Mary's, the one who'd taken her arm that day. She was getting into her car, parked right next to Rachel's own car. Rachel lingered, feeling strangely reluctant to risk being recognised, though she knew the chances of Mrs Hibbert – she'd remembered the name – knowing her were slight. Still, she waited. A tiny woman meanwhile staggered with an overloaded trolley up to Mrs Hibbert's car and tried to open the boot. Mrs Hibbert got out. Some sort of confusion ensued and voices were raised, but she couldn't catch any words. Finally, the boot was closed and the two women got into the car and drove off.

Following them, minutes later, Rachel thought how her own behaviour had been typical. She was always avoiding people, for no reason whatsoever. Coming to live here at all had been a sort of avoidance. Avoiding her family, avoiding old school friends, avoiding the entire area in which she had spent her childhood, and why? No good reason. She didn't hate her family, or her friends, and the place where she'd been born and brought up was pleasant. But she'd left. She'd left everyone and everything she'd known in London to move north, in direct contrast to most of her contemporaries. She'd wanted to live in a town where she'd soon know every street and building, just as her grandparents had done. She'd wanted to get out of the confusion of London – so many streets, so many houses, so much choice of every kind on offer and never a hope of sampling it all. They'd thought her mad, of course. 'Not exactly a good career move,' her father had said, but then he hadn't any idea what sort of career she'd wanted.

She was taking the long route now, in a wide arc round the town. More avoidance. This way, she avoided passing close to St Mary's, though it was impossible entirely to blot out the sight of its main building which still could be glimpsed through the trees. A foolish decision, to come this way. It meant a 2-mile detour and the tedium of having to queue at three sets of traffic lights before she reached home. But if she'd taken the direct route, her eyes would have caught the sad sprawl of dilapidated buildings spread out round the base of the hill and it would, as ever, have depressed her. Familiarity had not bred indifference. Always, the buildings themselves got to her. She hated to think of the patients lying behind those closed windows, and it seemed to her that a horrible, composite hospital smell wafted its way through the doors and into her car. She liked to keep away from St Mary's.

She should go home to London this weekend, but she wasn't going to, she hadn't actually promised. She'd gone home after that first visit to the clinic, when they'd told her the news and then what they were going to do. She'd needed to test herself. Could this *thing* be kept secret from them? From all of them? Could she get through a weekend without blurting it out? Was it possible, considering the state she was in? When she knew what was scheduled to happen? Was it fair, to them, to herself? Was it unnatural to want to conceal something so important? Probably. Once she'd admitted this to herself, she'd felt better. She'd never behaved as a daughter with loving parents would be expected to behave, so why should she now? She was the odd one out in her family and they all knew it. Her sister, who lived only five minutes away from their parents, was in and out of their house all the time and seemed never really to have left home in spite of being married and having children. And her two brothers, though they lived further away, slotted back into their places in the family with no difficulty at all whenever they returned. It was just Rachel. She couldn't function properly there any more. She was 38 and had her own life, but being at home made it vanish and that scared her. Three nights were the most she could endure being there, but this had been accepted for a long time now. Her father no longer wondered aloud why she bothered to come home at all and her mother no longer made excuses for her – they were resigned to her peculiarities, maybe even more than that. It had crossed Rachel's mind that her parents were not actually sorry to see her go, though nothing was ever said or directly intimated. Her mother would sometimes ask 'You are happy, darling, aren't you?' and she would reassure her that she was.

That weekend after the first visit to the clinic, three years ago, she'd tried hard to be especially cheerful and friendly, but soon realised this was a mistake. It caused comment. 'You're a little ray of sunshine this time,' her father said. 'Had some good news?' The irony of this was hard to take but she'd called it forth herself. And it had decided her: she would tell them nothing. What was the point? Their concern would not help her. They suspected nothing, why should they, and living so far away she would not be under their scrutiny. She'd come back to her own home perfectly clear as to how she would manage things and manage them she had. She'd kept up her regular phone calls without difficulty, helped by the fact that though regular they'd followed no absolute set pattern. Sometimes, especially during the radiotherapy sessions, it had been surreal chatting about every triviality she could think of when something so important was going on, but she'd kept going. She'd given herself full marks, and still did. But, walking out of the hospital after each appointment at the clinic, it was strange the way she always thought of her parents' home. Her mother, she'd decided, was a bit like that Friend who'd helped her, Mrs Hibbert, though physically there was no resemblance. She loved to help people, or think she was helping them, and had the same unwittingly smug pride about doing so, liking to detail precisely how helpful she had indeed been. She had the habit of ending some account of how she'd helped someone with the words, 'I think they were grateful, I think what I did was appreciated.' It made Rachel shudder.

They'd asked, in the hospital, before the operation, if she had someone at home who could look after her while she was convalescing, and having the radiotherapy. She'd said yes, her partner, though she no longer had a partner. They'd been satisfied with that. They knew nothing of her personal life in spite of all the notes they'd taken. It had worried her slightly that in fact she might need help when she came home and she'd rung round a few nursing agencies to check out what kind of help might be available. The replies had been quite encouraging – if need be, she could engage a nurse, and she could easily afford it. And she had a girl who came to clean her house who, she was sure, would be willing to shop for her. But in the event, she hadn't needed help, except for the journey home, because the hospital wouldn't let her leave on her own. Her friend Annette had collected her and there had been no harm in her knowing the truth. They were not intimate friends but they'd known each other for the twelve years they'd been neighbours and had grown to depend on each other in a loose kind of way which left neither of them feeling beholden. 'I don't want any fuss, I'm fine,' Rachel had said, and Annette had nodded and after seeing her into her house (where, unasked, she had left provisions and put the heating on) had left her in peace, telling her to ring, or even just thump on their party wall, if she needed anything. 'I'm always there, if there's anything you want,' Annette had said, which was very sweet of her but echoed rather too accurately Rachel's mother's oft-repeated words at the end of every phone call, 'We're always here, dear' – as though that wasn't obvious.

She'd wept, that first night out of St Mary's. She hadn't wept out of pain – she wasn't in much pain – or out of fear, but out of pity for her body. She hadn't done anything wilfully stupid like look in a mirror at the scar, but she hadn't needed to, she could feel it and knew what it must look like. She'd wept, and then she was done. It had been quite luxurious to be able to weep alone, away from sympathetic eyes, but it had to stop or she would be turned into a pathetic shadow of her former strong, resolute, independent self. She didn't weep during all those weeks of radiotherapy, but sometimes she'd come close to it, always at the same point, just as she was descending the stairs into the basement where the radiotherapy department was housed, in the bleakest, most run-down area of the hospital. She always had to stop, half-way down, and get a grip, clutching tightly at the hand-rail and breathing deeply till her heartbeat had calmed down. Then she had always managed to continue, arriving cool and calm-looking, even smiling a greeting at whomever was going to operate the machinery that day.

Exactly why keeping her feelings strictly to herself made her feel better she wasn't sure. It avoided explanations, for one thing, and explanations as to her state of health were upsetting. They would, if truthful, alter her identity in the minds of others. She wouldn't be Rachel Hurst, solicitor, but Rachel Hurst who, poor thing, had cancer. It wasn't shame she felt – or she hoped it wasn't – or even embarrassment, but a determination not to allow herself to be treated differently. She was *not* different, she was the same person. George would have understood exactly, but George had gone before all this began. Three years of loving and being loved had ended: the scar it left hurt far more than her physical scar. He wasn't going to come back, she'd accepted that. She would have liked to be able to try to tell him how she felt about the cancer. He'd have grasped how she wanted not to have a body any more, only a mind.

Partly to shut thoughts of George out of her mind, she decided to go for a walk – she had the day off – as soon as she'd put the shopping away. She set off, not knowing in which direction she would go, but drawn as she always was to the river and the twisting path along it leading to the old stone bridge. Most of the town was to the west of the bridge, and the river path continued on that side, passing under one of the arches of the bridge, but she decided to cross it and explore the east side, which she rarely did. It was steep on this side, a long flight of old, worn stone steps leading up the hill to a ruined fort, and she was shocked to find herself out of breath and clutching the iron hand-rail before she was half-way up. She had to rest, leaning on the railing and pretending she was admiring the view, though there was no one around to be concerned with what she was doing. Slowly, she continued up the steps until she reached the top, where across the grass in front of the ruin she could see a bench, facing the sun.

It was pleasant, sitting there. The bench was comfortable. Not a wooden one but made of metal and curved at the back so that her body felt moulded to its shape. She closed her eyes, enjoying the sun, and thinking that she would walk on to the road and get a bus back to the town centre when she had had enough of sitting there. Then she felt the weight of someone lowering themselves onto the bench beside her, but she didn't open her eyes. There was a sigh, loud and deliberate, and then a burp, followed by 'Pardon!' Still, she remained with her eyes closed, but aware suddenly of a smell, of beer, she thought. A tramp. She would have to move. She started to get up, but a restraining hand appeared on her arm. 'Give me the time of day, love,' a voice said, and Rachel saw it was not a tramp, or not exactly a tramp, but a woman, holding a bottle of lager. She was wearing a battered-looking sheepskin coat, in spite of the warmth of the day, and had heavy-duty green wellingtons on her feet and a headscarf tied tightly under her chin. Uneasily, Rachel allowed herself to be detained, though once the woman's hand was removed she aimed to escape quickly. The hand stayed there. The woman took a swig from the bottle. 'Nice day,' she said. 'Nice to have a bit of sun, isn't it?' Rachel nodded. 'I might not have many more of them,' the woman went on, and then 'my days are numbered, see, my card's marked, that's the truth.' Rachel tried to detach the hand pulling at the sleeve of her jacket, saying, very politely, that she was afraid she would have to go, but she couldn't without its turning into a tug-of-war.

'Listen,' the woman said, whispering, 'listen, I've something to tell you, something personal. I've got cancer. There. Did you hear me, did you hear what I just told you?'

'Yes,' Rachel said, startled and horrified, and this time she did manage to stand up, yanking sharply at her jacket.

'Don't run off,' the woman said, 'it isn't infectious. You can spare me the time of day, can't you? You can give me five minutes when I've told you something like that. You've got a heart, haven't you?'

'I'm catching a bus,' Rachel mumbled.

'Then sit down, you've a long wait, there isn't another for half an hour, I know the buses round here. What are you frightened of? Why can't you sit?'

'I'm not frightened,' Rachel said, but she did sit down again. The woman, she'd seen, was not old or senile, and in spite of the bottle and the smell, her eyes were sharp enough to show she was not really drunk.

'I am,' the woman said. 'I'm frightened. Wouldn't you be? Told you've got cancer? Told there's nothing can be done about it, and you're going to die?'

'Yes,' said Rachel, hating having to respond at all.

'Well then, there you are. That's what it's about, that's why I'm making an exhibition of myself.' Rachel noticed that the words were not slurred so much as spoken very slowly, each one carefully enunciated. The woman gave a little cough, and then groaned. 'Have you got a good doctor, dear?' she asked.

'I think so,' Rachel said.

'I haven't. My doctor's crap. Eight weeks, and still no X-rays.'

Rachel knew this didn't make sense, but she kept quiet. She had given the woman a couple of minutes, and that was enough. 'I'll have to go,' she said. 'If there isn't a bus, I'll have to walk.'

'Meeting someone, are you?'

'Yes.'

'Where?'

'In town.'

'A man, is it?'

'Yes,' Rachel lied.

'Good luck to you, then. Go on then, run away. I'd run away if I could. I would, I'd run away, run, run, run, rabbit, run.' She drained the bottle and handed it to Rachel. 'Here, put it in the waste bin over there. I like to be tidy. I might have cancer, well excuse me I *do* have cancer, but you won't catch me chucking bottles about. Off you go then.'

Rachel took the proffered bottle, standing in front of the woman now, facing her and able to see her clearly for the first time. Her face was bloated, her skin poor, but it had obviously been pretty once. It seemed cruel to leave her on the bench, without even the comfort of her lager, and looking as if she was going to fall asleep any minute. Indeed, as soon as she was relieved of the bottle, she put her hands in her pockets, and her head fell forward and she started to snore. Rachel stood and stared at her, wondering what to do. She looked around desperately, but there was no one else about. The woman, she reasoned, couldn't actually come to any harm – she would just sleep off the lager in the sun and then wake up and make her own way to wherever she lived. There was no need to feel she had any responsibility for her, no obligation to look after her. Her sleeping was perfectly healthy.

Slowly, Rachel walked, not to the road to wait for a bus, but towards the steps. She kept looking round at the slumped figure on the bench until the steps took her out of view, and even then she didn't feel comfortable. Distracted, she went back over the bridge and then took the river path once more, thinking that she'd never seen anyone in the clinic in the state that woman was in. No woman had ever arrived there drunk, or if they had been drinking it was never evident. Afterwards, maybe, some rushed to the bottle, but she doubted it – there was something about the clinic experience that made the thought of alcohol sickening. Her stomach wouldn't have tolerated it. What would the woman have said if Rachel had told her that she too had cancer? But she knew that never, under any circumstances, would she have done what that woman had just done, chosen to tell a stranger. The idea appalled her. It was no one's business but her own.

She went home by a different route, turning left at the end of the river path to make her way through the old warehouses, now being converted into expensive flats. Some workmen high up on scaffolding looked down and whistled at her and shouted, 'Hello, gorgeous!' She shouldn't have laughed but couldn't help it – they sounded not so much offensive as cheerful, harmless, just having a bit of fun. She was still smiling when she came out unavoidably at the bottom of the hill crowned by the main building of the hospital. A woman who was coming down the path leading from it almost bumped into her. She was half running, and not looking where she was going, and when she grazed Rachel's shoulder as she rushed past, she said, 'Sorry.' Her eyes were full of tears. Rachel walked on, no longer smiling but thinking now not about the stranger on the bench but this other stranger, escaping from the hospital and on the edge of weeping. She thought how odd it was that crying was almost encouraged when one was given bad news. It was definitely all right to cry when you were told you had cancer. She remembered how the doctor's voice had lowered and softened dramatically – it was laughable, that special 'caring', creepy tone. It had made her scornful, and probably the contempt she had felt had shown in her face.

Walking through the park, she tried to shake off this memory and all the other musings to do with cancer – it was so maddening to find her head full of the subject when she'd set out determined to enjoy a long walk without a thought of it. She was sick of it, this constant, repetitive going over of old ground. She didn't want to do it, she wanted to fill her mind with other concerns. Work, for example.

On Monday, she was going to represent a client before an employment tribunal. It was a case of unfair dismissal and she was looking forward to fighting it. Her client was a funny little woman, not impressive in appearance and with an unfortunate stutter which sometimes made what she said unintelligible. But the story she had to tell had roused Rachel to fury on her behalf and she had worked long hours meticulously amassing evidence of malicious treatment by the client's employer. She was going to show him for what he was: a bully, a cheat, a man who had done his best to humiliate and distress her client in order to make her resign, and then, when he had failed, had concocted the most absurd charge of negligence against her, giving him grounds for dismissal. Rachel could hardly wait to stand up and face him.

But before that, there was a weekend ahead, and the Sunday would see her begin to do something she had wanted to do for a long time. She was going to learn to fly, to fly a glider. She was going to learn to get as near to the flight of a bird as possible, to soar over fields and rivers in perfect peace and quiet, leaving all the cares of earth behind.

5

A Garden is a Lovesome Thing . . .

STANDING IN her garden, waiting for the girl to arrive, Mrs Hibbert watched a small plane fly away to the east, towards the aerodrome, and then she looked at the lilac trees. She had three lilac trees, two of the purple variety and one white. She had planted them herself when she first bought her house and they had thrived over the years so that now they were indeed proper trees and not bushes. She loved them, both for their scent and their beautifully shaped blossoms. She filled jugs with the lilac she picked and distributed throughout her rooms so that the whole house smelled of them – intoxicating!

Her grandfather had wanted her to be named 'Lilac', a ridiculous idea, laughed to extinction by her mother. Nobody was called Lilac. Rose (her sister's name), Daisy, Iris, Violet, Lily – plenty of flowers gave their names to girls, but not lilac. It was her Grandfather's fault, though, that she had been christened not Mary (the name she told people was hers) but Marigold. Her parents had found Marigold acceptable, and they had wanted to please the old (and wealthy) man. Besides, they had quickly seen that Marigold could be shortened to Mari and, when grandfather Lawson died, turned into Mary, which was precisely what happened. She hated her real Christian name, though liked the flower and always had marigolds in her borders. All massed together they made a gloriously cheerful sight. Francis had been amused when, on their wedding day, she had been obliged to divulge it. He had often thereafter referred to her as his sunny little marigold, usually when she was being cross. It had made her laugh, and brought her out of her temper.

Nobody called her Marigold now, and only Dot addressed her as Mary. To everyone else, she was Mrs Hibbert, and proud of it. She couldn't understand the modern fashion for married women keeping their maiden names and being known as Miss or, absurdly, Ms. Her status as a married woman had pleased her and once she had been widowed the prefix 'Mrs' had comforted her. It meant nobody could mistake her for a spinster. She remembered how her grandfather used to refer to his own wife as Mrs Lawson when in company, never as Clara, even if those present were family. As well as a liking for formality, it was from her grandfather she had inherited a love of gardens and gardening.

His garden had been a work of art (that was how it had been referred to locally, in the most reverential way). It was not part of his house, which had only a thin strip of land round it, but was separated from it by a field. The garden he had created was enclosed by a wall, built with mellow, old yellow bricks. Along the outside he'd planted pear trees so that in the spring the wall was almost obliterated by white blossom. It was quite a walk to the garden, across the road (a quiet, little-used road, barely wide enough for a large car) then along a track down the side of the field and over a stream at the bottom. Her grandfather enjoyed the walk, liked seeing the cows grazing. He owned the field, and all the fields surrounding his garden, and let them out to farmers to graze cattle or sheep. Because of the trees and the high, solid wall, these animals were no threat to his garden, entered through strong oak doors. It was always exciting for Mari to watch her grandfather lift up the metal bar which held the double doors together and step over the threshold to be met, in the summer, by the sight of scores of rose bushes, all of them in shades of red. He would walk her round the roses, telling her their names, and it was like a kind of poetry, reciting them after him.

The roses grew wild and straggly when he died. Mari's father had wanted to sell the garden itself and the fields, but her mother, Irene, had protested that this would be an act of vandalism, so her father had agreed to keep the garden (though he went ahead and sold the fields except the one giving access to the garden) with one proviso: Irene should be responsible for its upkeep. This alarmed Irene who knew nothing at the time about gardening, but she agreed. She kept on Mr Thompson, who had been Grandfather Lawson's chief gardener, and hired a young boy, Adam Nicholson, the local butcher's son, to help him. She got Mr Thompson (though he thought it a form of heresy, and muttered on about its being a scandal) to dig up most of the roses and began to plant shrubs instead. She liked lavatera and lavender and other flowering shrubs. She also had Mr Thompson make a little pond at the far end of the garden and round this she grew purple iris and blue-flowering hostas. Her whole idea was to create a natural, graceful bower and do away with the formality of the rigid rows of roses. Blues and pinks were her favourite colours and she was delighted when bluebells naturalised (Mr Thompson had vowed they would not) and forget-me-nots flourished. It took several years, but by the time Mary was ten, her mother had the kind of garden she wanted.

Mary used to go with her mother down to the garden every day in the spring and summer. She would come home from school – this was before she went to boarding-school – and change her clothes, and hand-in-hand the two of them would set off, her mother carrying a basket to fill with flowers for the house. Mary was always glad when she could see that neither Mr Thompson nor Adam was in the garden. She wasn't afraid of Mr Thompson, it was just that she felt awkward when he spoke to her because she couldn't understand his accent, but she was afraid of Adam Nicholson. He was a big boy, bigger than she, though they were roughly the same age, and he had a habit of stopping whatever he was doing to stare at her in the most disconcerting way. He stared first at her feet (which were large, she knew, but not monstrously so) and then slowly moved his stare up her body, taking a very long time to get to her face. When he did, he always dropped his stare and turned away. It made her blush. She thought him impudent, and complained to her mother. Her mother had a word with Mr Thompson, and the next time she met Adam in the garden, sent there early one evening to deliver a message to Mr Thompson, he blocked her path. She'd told him to get out of her way, but he'd stood his ground, and stared. It was she who stepped off the path and ran home, telling her mother she couldn't find Mr Thompson. She said nothing about Adam, feeling, as she did, confused about her feelings, and sensing she'd somehow lost a peculiar contest of wills.

Irene taught Mary how to prune and graft, how to nurture seeds, how to treat the various diseases to which plants were prone. When people asked Mary what she wanted to be when she grew up she said: 'A gardener.' This amused them, but she was not taken seriously. Gardening, for a girl, was a pleasant enough hobby in the 1930s and 1940s – it went with being a home-maker – but it was not a career. A career, in any case, was not something the Lawson parents envisaged for their daughters. A daughter's role was to stay at home and look after her parents in due course. One of them might get married. Till that happened, they could both occupy themselves with church activities and good works in the neighbourhood. It was their brothers who would have the careers, one in law, one in business.

The Second World War changed things for the Lawson girls. The fortunes of the family suffered a reversal of a kind Mary never quite understood – suddenly, her parents were no longer well-off and Grandfather Lawson's money had been used up. She did once ask what exactly had happened to cause the frightening talk of tightening belts and doing without, but nobody ever enlightened her. She had hoped to go into the sixth form but was abruptly taken out of school when she was 16, in 1946, and was told she must get a job to help out. 'What job?' she had asked her father, and he had been cross. 'Any job,' he'd said, 'anything that will bring in a little money.' To say this was a shock was not precisely true – 'shock' implied something unpleasant, and Mary had not thought of it like that. She'd been excited at the prospect of being allowed to *earn money*. Until, that is, she tried to do so and found how hard it was going to be. Once more she had ventured to suggest she could find employment as a gardener, but her father had been furious, saying they had not come to that yet, that he felt disgraced enough by having to tell her and Rose to get jobs without having to witness his daughter being a manual labourer.

There had been enough money, just, for her and her sister to do a shorthand and typing course. Afterwards, Rose got a job immediately in an insurance firm but only worked for six months before marrying the younger partner, much to her parents' satisfaction: that was Rose off their hands, one less mouth to feed, or so they thought (in fact, Rose was widowed within two years and returned home). Mary, though she had been much better than Rose at both shorthand and typing, took a while to secure employment. She knew why. Rose was pretty. Simple as that. Mary took her certificates, attesting to her competence, along to interviews, but they did not seem to impress. Eventually, after several humiliating weeks when she was turned down for position after position in their small town, she was offered a job in a solicitor's office. Her boss was an elderly, bad-tempered, very demanding man but she suited him. She didn't get upset when he shouted at her, or flustered when he asked her to do three things at once. Everyone else in the building was frightened of him (including the other two partners) but Mary was not. It was reckoned she could cope with him. In time, Mary became a valued employee and was treated with respect and caution in spite of her youth. She might have stayed there for ever if her parents had not died, one after the other in the space of a year, and she came into some money when the house and garden were sold.

It hurt having to watch the garden be sold, but her brothers insisted. She was determined to put her plan into action. Her plan was to train as a gardener. She was by then 23, past the normal age for college entry, but she didn't care. Her two years at Ramsbeck were among the happiest in her life. Once she'd qualified, the problem was that yet again she found it hard to get a job, not, however, because of not being pretty but simply because she was a woman. Men were preferred for all the posts she went for. She had to go back to being a legal clerk in yet another solicitor's office, this time further south in Manchester. For a while, she'd toyed with the idea of studying law and becoming a solicitor herself, but she felt too old to embark on yet another period of study. Becoming a legal assistant, a step up from clerk, was as far as she progressed in the practice. Slowly, her life had settled into two distinct compartments: work, where she was not unhappy, enjoying her job even if it wasn't one she had wanted, and pleasure, her garden, to which she devoted all her spare time. Her friends were all male (with one exception), made through gardening, and they were good friends, who appreciated her knowledge and skills. She belonged to a gardening club, and went on visits to gardens and to lectures about them, and had thought her life centred round gardens until she met Francis.

Every time she walked round her garden at this time of year and admired the lilac, Mrs Hibbert saw in her mind's eye Francis standing under the white lilac tree in the square opposite the office. She'd looked out of the window in front of her desk, where she was pounding away, typing out the dreary details of someone's will, and she saw a young man motionless under the tree. He had golden hair, curly and quite long, and his face was tilted up, an expression of rapture upon it. She could tell he was breathing in the scent of the lilac and she found herself breathing in too, though in the office all there was to breathe was the stale smell of too many people in too small a room with the windows closed. Later, she'd taken her sandwiches into the square to eat, but the man had gone. Every day till the lilac blossom was over, he was there, standing in the same position. One day, she managed to be there at the same time. She would never have spoken to him if it had not been for the wind that day blowing the lilac blossom into her eyes. She'd given a little cry and taken a handkerchief to flick the blossom away. 'Let me,' he'd said, and carefully removed the bits in the corner of her left eye.

Mrs Hibbert looked up now at the white lilac, and smiled. No one knew how romantic the moment had been. Fate had brought them together, courtesy of a lilac tree. She walked on, looking at her wrist-watch now and again, hoping this Emma girl would be on time. First of all she would give her a tour of the garden, pointing out particularly precious plants, and then she would take her into the greenhouse. There hadn't been a greenhouse when, after Francis died, she'd moved back here and bought this house. The garden had been in good shape, though, and the couple she had bought the property from had had plans for a greenhouse, though not in the position she'd selected. The Emma girl *was* late. Mrs Hibbert hated unpunctuality. She had seen this day coming, the day when she would have to start being at least partially dependent on other people. Neglect showed so quickly in a garden – even a two-week holiday at the wrong time of year could be pretty disastrous. A house could survive very well without constant care, it could remain undusted for ages and then be put to rights in a matter of hours, but a garden couldn't. She already had Martin Yates to cut the hedges and the grass but he didn't want to weed, alas. He was a good worker though and they had become friends; she valued his support when she had to do tricky things like invest in a new lawn-mower. She took him with her and recognised at once that he knew about lawn-mowers and could give her good advice. He wasn't a mechanic, but he had worked in a car factory at one time and seemed to have some mechanical aptitude. At any rate, he was good at mending things and Mrs Hibbert had begun to depend on him as a general handyman too. He was quiet and dependable, and the only mystery about him was how he came to be married to Ida Yates.

At last, she was here. Mrs Hibbert saw the girl dismount from her bicycle and fling it down carelessly on the path. She was entirely inappropriately dressed for gardening, wearing some sort of floaty skirt and those absurd flip-flops on her feet. Mrs Hibbert warned herself not to start off this relationship by being critical. She practised speaking gently and softly in her head as she walked towards Emma but heard her own voice sounding harsh as she said, 'I hope you've brought proper shoes and some overalls, young lady,' which was not what she had meant to say at all. Surprisingly, Emma had. She brandished a bag, and out of it she took a pair of denim dungarees and some training shoes. She promptly put them on, pulling the dungarees over her skirt which seemed to disappear quite easily inside them. She was a pretty girl, blonde and slim with a sweet, open face and a cheerful countenance. Nothing Mrs Hibbert said seemed to offend her – she took correction very well and was quick to say sorry. She would do (that was Mrs Hibbert's verdict after the first session). Her ignorance of all things pertaining to gardening was not, after all, going to be an insuperable handicap, because she was intelligent and picked up instructions quickly. But, Lord, how she talked, chatter chatter all the time. Later on, while she was being shown how to graft cuttings one afternoon she chattered non-stop about her mother (an apparently very depressed woman who did nothing but read) and her sister (a musical genius) and her boyfriend. It was the chatter about the boyfriend which irritated Mrs Hibbert most. She moved away whenever Emma got going on how wonderful the boy was, but the hint was not taken – a full 20 yards down the garden from Emma and she could still hear her droning on. It was inevitable that, though she had no desire to, Mrs Hibbert found herself soon knowing more about Emma's problems, especially with regard to the boyfriend, than she wanted to. The girl beseeched her for her advice and that was one thing Mrs Hibbert could never resist.

He was called Luke. He had the impertinence to telephone during the third afternoon Emma was gardening and ask to speak to her. 'It's Luke,' he said, though his diction was so frightful that this came out as, 'It's Sluke.' He said he needed to speak to Emma as a matter of the gravest urgency and he was so convincing that Mrs Hibbert found herself almost running to the greenhouse where Emma was transferring seedlings from trays to pots. It turned out that the 'gravest urgency' was that 'Sluke needed to change the time of their proposed evening meeting. Mrs Hibbert was outraged and told Emma he would cry wolf once too often, but the girl didn't seem to get the reference. After this, whenever 'Sluke rang, he was told that Emma was unavailable but that a message could safely be left for her. The messages were always the same: 'Tell her to ring a.s.a.p.' Mrs Hibbert did pass them on but said that Emma would have to wait to use the phone, because she was expecting an important call. (Well, she could play that game too.)

After the fourth Saturday, Mrs Hibbert realised that Emma would never be on time. She seemed incapable of punctuality and, what was worse, couldn't understand its importance. When Mrs Hibbert tapped her wrist-watch and said, 'Emma, it is twenty past two,' Emma just smiled, and if the time was repeated she looked puzzled. 'So?' she said, once, not cheekily, simply seeming to be confused. '*So*, Emma, you are supposed to be here at 2 p.m. We agreed your hours would be two to four every Saturday until you've finished your examinations.' 'Well,' said Emma, cheerfully, 'I'll stay twenty minutes later, all right?' It was not all right. Mrs Hibbert liked to listen to a certain radio programme on Saturdays at 4 p.m. but she didn't want to tell Emma that. It didn't sound important enough to be making a fuss about. So she just had to put up with Emma's tardy ways and, as time went on, her occasional non-appearances. Now those *were* infuriating and definitely not to be tolerated. 'You might at least have had the courtesy to tell me about this dental appointment,' she complained. Emma was contrite, and said she had meant to. There was nothing Mrs Hibbert could then do, except sack Emma, and she didn't want to do that. She liked the girl, and she was coming along nicely and proving useful.

But she was concerned by how deeply Emma was in thrall to 'Sluke. He came to collect Emma once and Mrs Hibbert's dislike of him increased. He had long fair hair tied in a ponytail (with what looked like a bit of pink wool) and wore torn jeans (though Mrs Hibbert knew enough to recognise that the tears were deliberate and therefore fashionable, she supposed) and a T-shirt with 'If You Want Me, Have Me' on the front. Mrs Hibbert happened to be in the greenhouse when he made his appearance, but she heard Emma shout and heard her drop her trowel, and when she looked out of the greenhouse it was to see the girl flying down the garden path towards this creature, her arms outstretched. They stood swaying together, bodies locked together, faces squashed together. Mrs Hibbert turned her back on them and focused her attention on her tomato plants. She looked at her wrist-watch: ten to four. Emma had been fifteen minutes late, so was not due to finish until four-fifteen. She waited. As she expected, Emma duly appeared at the door of the greenhouse, looking flushed and very happy. 'Mrs H. . . .' she began (Mrs Hibbert was quite amused to be called Mrs H. and had allowed it) but then, seeing her employer's expression, she stopped. 'It's just,' she began again, 'that Luke thought – I mean, he's here, and . . .' 'I have eyes, Emma,' Mrs Hibbert said. She could hear the boy kicking stones along the path as he patrolled impatiently up and down, not even having the good manners to come and introduce himself. 'I'm afraid,' she went on, 'that I need you to finish planting those geraniums. Rain is forecast for tomorrow and I wish them to be bedded in.'

Emma didn't say a word. There was no argument. She raced back to where she had been putting the geraniums into the soil, and picking up her trowel began planting them. 'Sluke stood and watched her. She was finished in record time, and ran to get the watering-can and water the plants in. 'Sluke, of course, could have been standing ready with the can filled, but he hadn't moved. Before Emma could come to the greenhouse again Mrs Hibbert called out that she could go now, after she'd cleaned her trowel and put it back in the shed and disposed of the empty trays the geraniums had been in. She watched as, all this done, Emma once more embraced 'Sluke and then they went off together, having difficulty walking straight because they were so closely entwined. 'Sluke's hand, she noticed, cupped Emma's right buttock. She could see what was likely to happen. It didn't take a genius. Emma, to use an old-fashioned phrase, was going to get into trouble. Mrs Hibbert only hoped that that bookworm mother of hers had talked to her about birth control, or that she didn't need to because Emma was already on the pill. But even if she was, other versions of trouble loomed. The foolish girl would do anything 'Sluke asked. If he asked her to live with him, she would, and Mrs Hibbert knew where and how he lived. Emma had described, excitedly, his squat. Mrs Hibbert had thought squatting belonged to the 1970s and only happened in big cities, but apparently not. 'Sluke and two of his chums had taken over a hut in a children's playground. Mrs Hibbert hadn't been able to understand how this could be possible, but Emma, full of admiration, had explained that ages ago 'Sluke had noticed a playground where the asphalt surface was all cracked and broken up, and the swings chained together, and that the park-keeper's hut had been boarded up and had a notice on it saying that the playground was closed until further notice owing to the damaged asphalt. He had kept an eye on it for a few weeks and when still no work had begun, he'd climbed over the railings and investigated the hut. He found that it had a sink, and a lavatory (though the water had been turned off) and a small Belling cooker. So he'd taken it over. He left the boards over the windows, so it was pretty gloomy inside, but he spent the nights there often and had a paraffin lamp which, Emma said, made the little room really romantic. Mrs Hibbert had stopped her at that point. She didn't want to know about the so-called romance since she felt that if she'd been told she would have been honour-bound to inform Emma's parents.

She worried about the girl. Emma was impressionable in a way Mrs Hibbert knew herself never to have been, and easily deflected from her studies. Mrs Hibbert had asked Emma about her GCSE results and which A-levels she had just taken, and knew she was a clever girl who had a conditional place to study medicine at Newcastle. This pleased Mrs Hibbert enormously, and she was moved to tell Emma about Christine, her niece by marriage, and how well she had done, and what important work she was involved in at St Mary's. But Emma hadn't really listened. She'd said, to Mrs Hibbert's alarm, that Luke wanted her to go travelling with him and she was attracted to the idea. She didn't, she confessed (a confession which made Mrs Hibbert feel ill), want to lose him. He was 'special', he was 'different'. With that, Mrs Hibbert could agree: 'Sluke was different, different from the clever, hard-working, and up to now ambitious Emma. He was ignorant, lazy and had no ambition except to ensnare Emma and get out of her anything he could. This included the money she earned from her gardening – Mrs Hibbert's cash. She had seen Emma hand it over when 'Sluke came for her, and when she'd tackled the girl about this she'd been told that Luke bought food for both of them and it was only fair.

By this time, as Mrs Hibbert knew, Emma had moved into the playground hut with 'Sluke. She'd phoned Mrs Hibbert the day she did this, saying she couldn't come because she and Luke were making the hut more 'homely'. Luke was going to make a table out of some packing cases and they'd got hold of an inflatable mattress they were going to mend (it had a puncture) and blow up, and she, Emma, was going to paint the walls. The following week when she did turn up she was wildly enthusiastic about what she referred to as 'our little pad' in which she and Luke were blissfully comfortable. Mrs Hibbert, aghast, had wondered aloud what Emma's parents thought. They'd gone away, on holiday, a long holiday, completely unlike them, according to Emma. She and her sister Laura were on their own, but at the moment Laura was away on holiday too and knew nothing about Emma's squat. She assured Mrs Hibbert that she was looking after the house, visiting it each day to feed the cat and to check that everything was fine. She went there for baths too, but – and Mrs Hibbert found this rather telling – didn't let Luke go there, because she knew her parents would not like it. He had, in fact, suggested that they could use the Greens' family house while her parents were away, but Emma had vetoed this. She preferred the hut, she said.

That evening, when Emma had gone off to the hut, Mrs Hibbert tried to analyse why she felt so dreadfully anxious. There was no need for her to feel responsible for the girl, none at all. She hardly knew her and whatever happened no blame could ever be laid at her door. But that was a cheat. Mrs Hibbert hated cheats, people who absolved themselves from what they perfectly well knew was their *moral* responsibility. The point was, Emma had put her in possession of the facts by telling her about the squatting, and so she could not truthfully claim to have no involvement in the girl's life. Emma was vulnerable. 'Sluke dominated her easily and completely. This was dangerous, and something should be done about it, but what? That was what kept Mrs Hibbert awake at night. She went over and over what Emma had told her about 'Sluke: he had dropped out of the sixth form, he worked in a bar 'sometimes', his parents were divorced, he lived with his mother when he wasn't in the hut, he didn't get on with her, he was going to go travelling when he'd got some cash together. Emma was worth ten of him, but it was no good telling her that. Mrs Hibbert just wished that Mr and Mrs Green would hurry home, or that at least the sister would.

Meanwhile, living in the squat Emma started to look worn. If 'Sluke was using her gardening wages to buy food (which Mrs Hibbert doubted – she was convinced he was buying something else entirely) then he was buying the wrong sort. Emma's healthy complexion vanished. She became very pale, no colour in her cheeks at all, and spotty. Her hair grew lank, and she lost weight. She still smiled cheerfully, but the smile was strained and looked false. Mrs Hibbert began making her nourishing fruit juice drinks and offering her a bowl of home-made soup with some wholemeal bread at the end of her gardening. Everything she offered was gratefully accepted and gobbled up in seconds. One day, just as Emma was about to leave, it started to rain heavily. It had rained at the end of many of Emma's afternoons in the garden and Mrs Hibbert had not offered to drive her home, but suddenly she decided to do so, realising that she needed to see this hut to be able properly to assess Emma's situation (that was how she justified her offer, but really she knew it was just that she wanted to satisfy her curiosity). Emma was not as keen to be driven home as might have been expected, though the rain was torrential and she would have got very wet cycling. She hesitated, and said she didn't want to put Mrs Hibbert to any bother, and suggested maybe she could just wait in the kitchen till the rain eased off, but Mrs Hibbert said no, that would not be convenient. So the bike was put in the tool shed, to be collected later in the week, and the two of them got into the car. Emma told Mrs Hibbert where the playground was – right on the other side of town, on its very outskirts – and she drove there in fifteen minutes. She pulled up at its gates, which were of course padlocked together. Emma got out, thanked her, and went on standing there, getting soaked. Mrs Hibbert had no intention of moving. She sat watching as the girl finally turned away from the car and trudged along the railings until she reached a gap where they were bent out of shape. She squeezed through, and skirted the swings to reach the hut. Mrs Hibbert saw that it was a very small hut and that as Emma had described it was boarded up. Emma looked round, gave a limp wave to Mrs Hibbert, took a key from her pocket – so 'Sluke had either found or fashioned a key to the lock – and went inside.

It was too pathetic. Something had to be done. Mrs Hibbert raged all the way home, thinking of that poor girl alone in that horrible dark hut, waiting for that feckless boy to join her. Scandalous. She felt she should have marched across to that hut (except she couldn't have got through the railings, she reminded herself) and hammered on the door, and when Emma had opened it, grabbed her by the hand and pulled her out. She should have brought her home and insisted that she see sense and return to the family home. She would have been called an interfering old busybody perhaps, but sometimes one had to interfere. She couldn't settle to anything that evening. Her hand kept going to lift the telephone but she couldn't think whom to phone. And then, about nine o'clock, she found herself dialling (she had kept her old-fashioned telephone, not wanting one of those push-button abominations) the Greens' family house, just on the off-chance that Emma's sister had returned. When Mrs Green answered, Mrs Hibbert was so surprised she was momentarily speechless. 'Oh!' she managed to say, sounding stupid. 'Yes?' Mrs Green said, impatiently. 'Who is this, please?' Mrs Hibbert told her who she was, gathering her normal confidence as she went on. She expressed her concern for Emma, said she knew the Greens had been on a long holiday and probably were unaware that Emma was squatting in a derelict playground hut, but that she had taken her there today and had been appalled at the circumstances in which their daughter was choosing to live. She didn't mention 'Sluke. Mrs Green's reaction was very strange. There was a long pause, and then she said, 'Emma is nearly 18 now. She isn't a child. She knows what she wants.' There was no thank you for calling, thank you for caring, thank you for informing us, how kind and thoughtful of you. Just

'Emma is nearly 18 now. She isn't a child. She knows what she wants.'

Finally, the woman did add that she understood Mrs Hibbert's concern but urged her not to worry. Emma was stronger than she looked and would be able to survive such minor hardships as living in a playground hut. 'It will probably do her good,' Mrs Green said. And then she asked, 'What did you say your name was?' and when Mrs Hibbert repeated it there was another silence. 'Thank you,' said Mrs Green and hung up. As soon as she'd replaced the receiver, Mrs Hibbert regretted what she had done. What would Emma think, what would she say? She would surely feel betrayed. But then, as she got ready for bed, Mrs Hibbert consoled herself with the thought that, as Mrs Green was so very odd, she might never mention the phone call at all. This, it seemed, was true. The next time Emma came (twice a week, now her exams were over), nothing was mentioned about a phone call to her mother. She just said her parents were home again and that she'd told them she'd moved in with Luke. Mrs Hibbert didn't ask what they had said, but Emma volunteered the information anyway. 'Dad's furious,' she said, 'but Mum says it's my own affair.' 'How extraordinary,' Mrs Hibbert couldn't help commenting. 'What?' said Emma. 'Well, that your *mother* should be so untroubled.'

She gave a great deal of thought to Mrs Green's attitude after that. Did her lack of concern, or apparent lack of concern, mean that she didn't care about her daughter? Or was it, on the contrary, a sign that she trusted her and respected her wishes? Mrs Hibbert couldn't decide. The father's reaction, on the other hand, was entirely appropriate and easy to understand. She wondered if he would seek out 'Sluke and try to talk to him. Emma did let drop that she wasn't going home at the moment because her father's anger had not abated. This meant, as Mrs Hibbert quickly noted, that she was not having a bath or shower. She looked grubbier each time she came to garden and finally, when she'd arrived bedraggled anyway, with her hair positively greasy, and had dug out and transplanted some small potentillas, Mrs Hibbert had offered her the chance to have a bath. Emma stayed in the bathroom an irritatingly long time and emerged with her skin glowing and her hair smelling sweetly of lemon shampoo. This was a little disconcerting. The shampoo had been in the bathroom cabinet, which meant the girl must have opened it. Permission had not been given to do this. Still, Mrs Hibbert let the trivial intrusion go. What she could not let go was how Emma left the bathroom: wet towel in a heap on the floor, hairs in the plughole – quite disgusting for someone else to have to remove. She spoke sharply to the girl, but privately blamed that mother of hers for not bringing her up properly.

Having a bath before her tea soon became Emma's habit, but though this improved her appearance it did not improve it enough. Her clothes sometimes looked filthy, especially her jeans. Emma said she hadn't been able to wash them because of the weather. 'The weather?' said Mrs Hibbert. 'Good heavens, what an excuse. There are two launderettes in town, Emma, and I believe they have drying machines.' Emma's eyes filled with tears and she said she couldn't afford to use a launderette, and she didn't want to take her dirty clothes to her parents' home to put them in the washing machine there because her father would be sure to find out and he'd say it was proof that she couldn't manage on her own. 'Well, you can't,' snapped Mrs Hibbert. Emma then wept. Between hiccuping sobs, she said that she and Luke had run out of money. They hadn't enough to feed Charlie's dog. It was the first Mrs Hibbert had heard of Charlie or his dog. She was scandalised to hear that Luke had agreed to look after his friend's dog, because he, Charlie, was going to work on an oil rig for three months. Charlie had left money but Luke had lost it. Naturally, Mrs Hibbert wanted 'lost' defined. It turned out that the money had to be used to pay Luke's fine, which was for a driving offence – it was all so ridiculous. She began to lecture Emma on the necessity of 'Sluke getting a job and of Emma herself returning home, but the sobs only grew louder. By then the girl had her head down on the kitchen table, where she'd been having her tea (and Mrs Hibbert had certainly observed scones being slipped into the bag at her feet). Her arms were over her head and what she was saying was muffled, but her words could still be made out: 'I love him! I can't leave him! You don't understand! I *love* him!'

It was all rather upsetting, and Mrs Hibbert felt quite shaky when Emma had trailed off. What upset her most was that the girl would imagine that she knew nothing about what it was like to be hopelessly in love. She would be bound to think, from everything she knew about her employer (not much, so far as feelings went) that she would be scornful of being in love. Mrs Hibbert had badly wanted to tell Emma that this was not true, but it was too embarrassing. She simply could not have embarked on the story of how much in love she had been, not just with Francis, long before he had even noticed her, but with someone before that. The emotion – love, not lust, definitely not lust – welling up inside her at the mere sight of Francis had made her light-headed and giddy and for the first time in her life she had lost weight. It had all been torture. She had known she wasn't pretty, that she was too serious, she wasn't young, and that there was nothing about her to attract him. If Francis had asked her to live in a derelict playground hut with him, she would not have hesitated.

She could tell none of this to Emma. Her role was to be the voice of common sense, to repeat over and over again that Emma must extricate herself from this situation before she made herself any more miserable. Then something unexpected happened. Emma was left some money. She arrived one afternoon, breathless and with cheeks flushed, waving a letter in her hand. She'd been left the enormous sum of £10,000 by a great-aunt whom she had never met. Her sister Laura had been left the same. She was almost hysterical with joy, smiling as she had not done for weeks, but Mrs Hibbert glared at her and was immediately at her most formidably stern. 'Emma!' she said. 'Emma, I hope you are not going to be foolish. I hope your father has spoken to you, I hope he has told you to bank that money in a deposit account while you take advice on how to invest it.' Emma laughed. She said he had. 'And Emma,' went on Mrs Hibbert, 'I trust you will not tell Luke.' Emma looked shocked, but before she could speak Mrs Hibbert added that it would be most unwise because Luke was a spendthrift and would encourage her to waste it. 'But I can't keep secrets from Luke,' Emma said, eyes wide with innocence. 'We share everything.' 'As far as I am aware,' said Mrs Hibbert, 'he has nothing to share. You earn the money and you do the only sharing.' Emma was silent, and stopped smiling, but she looked mutinous. 'I want to tell Luke,' she said. 'It will relieve him. It will mean we can rent a flat and maybe buy a second-hand car, and . . .' 'A car!' shouted Mrs Hibbert. 'Are you quite mad, Emma? The money will run out in no time if you buy a car, second-hand cars eat money. This is your insurance, it's your rainy-day money, you must *not* squander it, you must listen to your father. And what does your mother say? You haven't mentioned her.' 'She says I should give it to charity,' Emma said, 'to a Jewish charity. Or else to Cancer Research.'

This did stop Mrs Hibbert's ranting. She was completely taken aback. Emma couldn't help being pleased. She watched Mrs Hibbert struggle to decide what she thought about this, and then she said, 'I'm not going to, of course. I don't see why I should. Aunt Marlene could have left it to charity if she'd wanted to, but she didn't. She left it to me and Laura, and I'm sure she wanted us to enjoy it. Dad says she had a terrible childhood, she was in some awful camp, and then afterwards she was ill. She never had any fun. I'm sure she would have wanted Laura and me to have fun.' Mrs Hibbert groaned. 'You having fun is one thing, Emma, but Luke having it at your expense is another. Be sensible. At least bank half.' Emma nodded. She said that was what she would do. But she refused to promise not to tell Luke the whole truth. She said she trusted him, even if no one else did, and she wanted no secrets from him. Mrs Hibbert had to be content with that. For a while, all went well. Emma turned up nicely dressed in a new bright red shirt and black cotton shorts and her hair was always washed, with no need of Mrs Hibbert's shampoo. She and Luke had moved into a rented flat which had a proper bathroom and a washing machine. 'Bliss!' said Emma. The only problem now was Charlie's dog (known simply as 'Dog'). Pets were not allowed in the flat, but Luke had been unable to find anyone to take the dog until Charlie returned from the oil rig, and so they were trying to keep it hidden, which was difficult. Emma admired Luke for keeping his word to

Charlie and was hurt when Mrs Hibbert said that there was nothing to admire in someone flouting rules. 'Luke is loyal,' she said. 'He's like that, he's that sort of person.' Privately, Mrs Hibbert thought, he was quite a different sort of person, but she managed to say no more.

But then, a couple of weeks later, on a Wednesday, 'Sluke turned up to collect Emma in a car. He sounded the horn, and both Emma and Mrs Hibbert jumped, it was so very loud. 'That'll be Luke,' Emma said, putting her trowel down and preparing to leave the greenhouse. She was blushing. Mrs Hibbert followed her. 'Sluke hadn't parked in the drive, he'd just pulled up in the road, half on the pavement. She saw Emma lean into the car and say something and then hurry back up the path. 'A car, Emma?' Mrs Hibbert said, before the girl could say anything. 'It's only second-hand,' Emma murmured, 'it was cheap.' 'I can recognise a cheap, clapped-out old car when I see one, thank you very much, Emma. It will, I assure you, turn out not to have been cheap, whatever foolish sum you paid for it. It will end up costing you a fortune.' Emma tried to smile. 'Can I go?' she said. 'If you make up the two hours next time,' Mrs Hibbert said. She watched the car roar off and went slowly back up the path to tidy the greenhouse. All the little methodical tasks she carried out soothed her, but by the time she was in her kitchen drinking tea she was feeling depressed. She said it to herself – 'I am feeling depressed' – and then decided she was being silly. She had nothing to be depressed about. Besides, the next day was a hospital day and she couldn't carry out her duties as a Friend of St Mary's in a depressed state of mind.

She set off for St Mary's worrying about Emma, but after her day at the hospital, thoughts of the girl were wiped out of her mind, because she came home far more concerned about Chrissie, Francis's niece. She never listened to gossip, or indulged in it, but nevertheless she had ears and her ears could not but help hear what was being said in the Friends room and on the reception desk. It seemed a young woman, one of Mr Wallis's patients, had committed suicide straight after a visit to his clinic, and Chrissie had been the doctor in charge that day. There was to be an inquest and Dr Harrison would have to appear, or so it was said. All this, it emerged, had been in the local newspaper ages ago, but Mrs Hibbert thought it a rag and never read it. Hearing all this information distressed her – any mention of suicide made her heart pound alarmingly – but she forced herself to look through a stack of old papers and magazines in the Friends room. She couldn't find any newspaper for the date mentioned. She was certain that Chrissie could not possibly be in any way to blame – she had total faith in her – but she also knew that whatever the truth of what had happened, Chrissie's reputation would be smeared. Wanting to show support, she went downstairs to the clinic but was told that Dr Harrison was not on duty, so before she left the hospital she wrote a note and gave it to Rita to pass on.

Poor Chrissie. How worrying all this would be for her. She wished she knew her better but, once Francis had died, the links with his family, never strong, had faded. She'd only known Chrissie as a child, and otherwise as a vague acquaintance to whom she occasionally said hello in the hospital. She was deep in thought about Chrissie – turning over and over in her mind what would be the right thing to do, should she telephone? – when Emma next came, and Mrs Hibbert did not at first notice the change in the girl. It was only when she had to tell her twice that she was spreading fertiliser in the wrong place that she realised Emma was red-eyed and distraught-looking. Mrs Hibbert wondered if perhaps her A-level results had just come and they were poor, but no, the results were not due for another week. 'Then it's that car,' Mrs Hibbert said. It was not the car. Emma would not say what was causing her obvious misery. She drooped round the garden listlessly, doing nothing properly, and Mrs Hibbert decided to let her be. She had deduced that it must be 'Sluke trouble of some sort. Was 'Sluke going off Emma? Could that be it? She jolly well hoped so. Heaven knew, she'd tried to make the girl see how utterly useless that boy was. He hadn't ever been able to look her in the eye, because he probably knew she had him worked out. It could only be good news if, no matter for what reason, he and Emma were splitting up.

But she tried to be kind. Later, when she was so furious with what had happened, it pained her to think of how kind she'd been, leaving the gardening and going into her kitchen to make Emma a batch of the cheese scones she so adored. She'd paid her extra money too, by not asking for change from the £20 note. Emma had thanked her, but without much enthusiasm. 'Sluke hadn't picked her up. Off she'd gone, promising to come early next time, to sweep up while Martin cut the big hedges so that he could do them all in one session. Mrs Hibbert had watched her go and found herself humming, not quite knowing why. It was wrong to take pleasure in someone else's unhappiness, but with her intuition that out of Emma's present distress would come liberation from 'Sluke, she couldn't help it. She felt she had had an influence, after all.

And then Emma hadn't turned up. Martin had, but not Emma, and consequently only three-quarters of the hedge-cutting was done, because Martin had to clear up himself and didn't have time to complete the whole job. Mrs Hibbert was irritated. The following week, she was even more irritated by the girl's non-appearance. There was no phone call to explain. Mrs Hibbert didn't want to phone Emma's parents, but she had no alternative, never having had a number for the flat Emma had rented with 'Sluke. Mrs Green answered, which was unfortunate – she had hoped to get the father, whom she liked the sound of. Mrs Green was abrupt. 'All we know is that she's gone travelling with her boyfriend, we don't know where. She's left a note, promising to ring us regularly, but she hasn't rung yet.' Mrs Hibbert felt stupefied. 'But she said nothing to me, not a word, and she promised to come early next time. She has let me down badly.' Mrs Green didn't even attempt to apologise on her daughter's behalf. Instead, she said, her tone weary, 'She's young, it's natural she wants to travel. Who knows what will happen, it's best to take one's opportunities while one can.' This was far too lenient and philosophical for Mrs Hibbert. 'I'm afraid I can't agree,' she said, stiffly, 'especially knowing her boyfriend as I do, and in view of the vast sum of money Emma told me she had inherited. I think this absconding will prove disastrous. And if I were Emma's mother I would not be taking this news so calmly.' There was a pause, long enough for Mrs Hibbert to regret being so outspoken, but just as she began to say she was sorry if she'd been rude, Mrs Green said, 'I think we've met, at the hospital, at St Mary's. You're one of the Friends, aren't you?' Surprised, Mrs Hibbert said that yes, she was, and then Mrs Green, sounding shaky but determined, said, 'Well, you should know, there are worse things than going off travelling and having fun with your boyfriend, much worse things, things to get really worried about. I'm sorry, but you of all people ought to have a sense of proportion. But thank you for calling.'

Whatever had the woman meant? Feeling that she had somehow been outflanked, Mrs Hibbert wondered if Emma's mother, who sounded a cold woman, quite unlike her daughter, had been right and that she had indeed lost sight of what was important and what was not. Her head ached unbearably and went on aching in spite of her taking two aspirins. She kept going over that last afternoon with Emma, trying to find clues as to why the girl had said nothing about leaving and going off with 'Sluke. What hurt, she well knew, was that Emma had not chosen to confide in her. She'd thought that, in spite of the age discrepancy, they had become friends. She'd even thought of herself at one point as being a substitute mother (or did she mean surrogate, she wasn't sure) since in so many ways Emma's own mother appeared to have little interest in, or influence over her. But Emma had not asked her for advice (though, since she would have known what it would be, perhaps that was not surprising). Mrs Hibbert vividly recalled how miserable Emma had seemed on that last visit, how red-rimmed her pretty eyes, a sure sign that she'd been crying. Did this mean she hadn't really wanted to go travelling with 'Sluke? Or did it mean her conscience was bothering her?

She had nurtured her relationship with Emma only to have it exposed as a sham. It was the lesson of her life, but one she kept having to relearn. She lay in bed, head still throbbing, pondering over Mrs Green's words. Surely she had got it wrong, surely the logic of what she had said was faulty. Why, because there were much worse things to worry about – with the reference to St Mary's, she must mean illness – should one stop worrying about lesser things? It simply provided an excuse for not acting. She was right to worry about Emma, and to feel something should be done. Maybe Emma had counted on her doing it and she had failed her, a thought so alarming she promptly tried to take evasive mental action by forcing herself to think about the next committee meeting of the Friends of St Mary's. There was going to be trouble, arguments about how a legacy left to them should be spent. And the new vicar of St James's, not yet arrived, was to be there. She fell asleep, wondering if her own opinion would prevail and she would carry the committee with her.

PART II

6

Mysterious Ways

IT HAD been a long, wearying drive and all the time he had been worried that his old car would conk out. But now he was almost there, at the top of the pass, the town no more than ten miles away. He stopped the car and got out. Below him, the valley, clearly visible, was every bit as beautiful as the bishop had said. A river ran through it with hardly a twist or a curve, and on a day such as this it shone silver, a flat, narrow band of silver shooting towards the sea. On the far side were dense woods, of fir trees, he thought, a plantation of some sort. The sun touched the tops of the trees but the massed bulk of the forest remained dark, almost black. On the near side there were fields stretching down to the river, with tawny-coloured cattle grazing. As yet the town was not visible. It was hidden, he supposed, by the hill to the east. He could see a few scattered buildings, that was all, a few whitewashed cottages, a stone farmhouse, some barns. He smoked a cigarette and went on studying the landscape. He watched the wind stroke a puddle on the road, ruffling its surface over and over again. Everything so still. The stillness, the beauty, ought to calm and reassure him. The bishop had said it would. He had said this peaceful place would mend his sickness – 'It is a sickness, it is curable' – and soon he would no longer want to spend his days lying in a darkened room, weeping.

He crushed the cigarette in the puddle, firmly stamping it down with the heel of his shoe. He didn't feel in the least calm. He felt more agitated than ever. He dreaded reaching the town, finding the church and the vicarage, dreaded meeting his parishioners, the people, dreaded the strangeness of it all. It took courage not to turn the car round and flee back to where he had come from. But I will manage, he told himself, and got back in the car.

*

They had some difficulty opening the vicarage door. It had been shut and locked for so long that the keyhole seemed to have got bunged up, but eventually Ida managed to force the key in and turn it. The door creaked dramatically as she pushed it open. 'Pongs,' said Ida. Dot didn't say anything. It seemed obvious to her that a building shut up for very nearly three months would smell fusty. Nothing a few open windows wouldn't deal with. She followed Ida in, wishing she was with anyone else. She hated it when the church cleaning rota threw her together with Ida Yates, though it wasn't the rota that was responsible for her being with Ida today. This was a special job. They were to give the vicarage a thorough cleaning, make it spick and span for the new vicar. Since it was an extra job, every lady on the regular church cleaning rota had been asked if she wanted to volunteer. They had all volunteered and so their names had been put on bits of paper in the collection pouch, and then Joe had been called in from tending the churchyard to pull out two names. He'd made a performance of it, teasing them, jiggling the pouch around on the end of its stick.

Dot's name was the first to be picked out. She beamed. There was a stiffening of backs all round her. Mrs Harris said, 'Are you sure you want to do it, Dot? Are you sure you're up to it? I mean, with Adam . . .' Dot had said she was quite up to a bit of extra cleaning, thank you, but she did not add what was really in her mind, which was that this would give her the perfect excuse to get out of the house – anything to do with the church Adam allowed. She felt delighted to have been chosen. But then the second name to come out of the pouch was Ida Yates's. Mrs Harris hadn't bothered asking *her* if she was up to it. Ida moaned and groaned her way through her stints of cleaning the church, and constantly emphasised her poor state of health, but everyone knew she would never pass up the chance to have a good snoop round the vicarage. So Dot was stuck with Ida.

'Too big for one man,' Ida was saying, as she peered around the draughty hall. It was a large, square area, with a patterned, tiled floor giving way to a dark brown carpet near the foot of the stairs and continuing up them. The general impression was of dinginess and shabbiness. All the doors opening off this dreary hall were painted dark brown and the glass bowl round the overhead light was a murky beige. Dot coughed. 'Dust,' said Ida. Dot nodded. She could actually see the layers of dust and didn't need Ida to draw a finger along the window ledge beside the front door to prove it. 'Too big,' Ida repeated. 'Don't know why they've chosen a bachelor.' 'They all used to be bachelors,' Dot murmured. 'What?' said Ida. 'They all used to be bachelors,' repeated Dot. 'All the vicars, once upon a time.' 'That's not the point,' Ida said, 'it's now I was talking about. This is a family house. One man will rattle around in it, ridiculous. You take upstairs, Dot. I'll take downstairs.'

Dot didn't argue. She didn't argue with anyone, didn't see what was gained by argument. Sometimes it seemed to her that she was surrounded by strong-minded people and that she was the only one who kept her own counsel and avoided disputes. It meant, of course, that she could be taken advantage of, but that, in her opinion, was a small price to pay for avoiding unpleasantness. She was relieved that the unpleasantness with Mary was now over (she'd rung up and apologised for Adam, explaining he had misunderstood her, though that wasn't strictly true). She toiled up the stairs, encumbered with her basket of cleaning materials, knowing full well that Ida would start by having a rest. She would have found her way to the kitchen and be putting her feet up whereas Dot would be hard at it, which she soon was. She wished she had a hoover, but there didn't appear to be one in the house and she had to make do with a stiff hand-brush and pan. But she soon saw that there was no engrained dirt – it was all just dust and responded well to a dusting and careful sweeping. Three bedrooms upstairs and a bathroom. Nothing had been said about making the beds up, but she thought she ought to make up the double bed in the main bedroom. First she opened both windows there (which was almost as much of a struggle as opening the front door had been). A breeze blew through the room and she could smell the scent of the honeysuckle growing up the wall outside. She leaned out of the window for a moment, enjoying the sight of the garden below, a leafy, flowerless garden, overgrown and wild now, but pretty all the same. She liked it. Mary Hibbert's garden was reckoned to be a showpiece, but Dot preferred this neglected garden.

She cleaned all the surfaces thoroughly, thinking what a fine piece of furniture the mahogany dressing-table was, and wishing she had some polish worthy of it, her own polish, instead of the spray stuff in her basket. And then she went in search of sheets and pillow-cases for the bed. She found them in an airing-cupboard in the bathroom, but the last thing they were, was aired. They felt damp and smelled musty. She draped them over the bedroom window-sill while she cleaned the bathroom. Big, solid bath on claw feet, awkward for someone as small as herself to reach into. The walls were painted a shiny blue and the ceiling a darker blue. A gloomy room, functional and unattractive. She hurried out of it and cleaned the other two bedrooms. The children of the previous vicar had slept here and she could see the evidence in the marks on the walls, never properly cleaned off. She had a go herself, but the scribblings wouldn't budge. The walls needed a coat of paint. The whole house needed a coat of paint. Returning to the main bedroom, she hauled the sheets up and made the bed. She was enjoying herself, though her heart was racing and she was a little breathless.

Dot perched on the bed she'd just made and gave herself a moment to think about the new vicar. All that was known about him was that he was a bachelor and that he'd been ill. No one knew what kind of 'ill' though, and fears had been expressed that the parish was being treated as a convalescent home and that this man would be altogether too delicate to be of much use. His predecessor, the Rev. Paul Barnes, had been anything but delicate – a big, bull-like man with a loud voice and personality to match. Dot, as a general rule, liked everyone but she hadn't been a big fan of the Rev. Barnes, though he'd been popular. His wife hadn't interested herself much in parish affairs, but then she'd had four wild boys to look after, boys she could barely control. The Barneses had been moved to Liverpool (to the delight of the Liverpool F.C.-obsessed sons). Most parishioners had been sorry to see the Rev. Barnes go – he liked a joke, and took the occasional drink, and was an asset at any social function. It was going to be hard for the new vicar to follow him. All he had going for him was his single status. Mary Hibbert, who was not a churchgoer, had said she felt sorry for the poor man, knowing, as she did, how his eligibility would fuel speculation. 'Jane Austen knew all about it,' Mary had said. 'She knew that he will be considered to be in need of a wife even if he is poor.' This comment had rather mystified Dot, though she'd understood its underlying implication. People would want to marry him off. Unless he turned out to be gay, and the parishioners of St James's were not so unworldly as not to have considered this possibility.

Dot could hear Ida downstairs. There was a lot of banging going on. Ida Yates was a noisy and rough worker, always knocking chairs over and dragging tables across floors instead of working round them or asking for help to move them. But she was a lovely singer. Still sitting on the bed, and surveying with satisfaction the room she had cleaned – it was being useful she liked, that was what made her happy – Dot smiled as she listened. Ida was singing hymns in her deep, contralto voice. 'Oh God, our help in ages past' she was on to now. Dot marvelled at the sound, and wondered how it could come out of Ida's lumpen body. She felt guilty, labelling Ida in her mind as ugly, but even Dot had to concede that she was. Nobody who had known Ida as a young woman, as Dot had, would be able to recognise her now if they hadn't seen her for twenty years – there was nothing of the young Ida about her. Dot liked to think that in spite of the lines on her own face and her white hair she herself looked much the same at 70 as she had done at 20, but then that was because her shape was much the same. She'd never put on weight. Ida had put on at least 3 stone. She was vast, and lop-sided. She'd told everyone about her operation, and how much breast tissue had been cut away, and she'd said she wasn't going to disguise how they'd hacked her about. Worse than that, she'd invited other women to look at it. There had been one terrible afternoon, after she started attending Women's Fellowship meetings again, when she had unbuttoned her blouse and unfastened her bra and exposed her scarred breast. Every eye had been riveted, everyone had been shocked, and urged her to get dressed, but Ida had been defiant. 'People should know,' she'd said, 'people should see what's been done to me. Why should I hide it? If it was my arm or leg, you'd all see it.'

They'd appreciated, of course, that she was distressed and hardly, at that time, responsible for her actions, but mixed up with their sympathy was a touch of disapproval. Nothing as strong as contempt or disgust, but nevertheless a feeling that Ida had not behaved as they themselves would have behaved (or liked to think they would have). But Ida was like that. She talked openly about her cancer and, it was quite clear, she expected a certain sort of reaction and response. Dot always tried to be kind, but sometimes it was difficult. Ida was shouting now that she'd put the kettle on and that Dot would hear it whistle in a minute and should come down. When it did, Dot descended and went into the big kitchen. It was a bare, draughty room with old-fashioned appliances – huge stone sink, old cast-iron cooker – and not a touch of colour anywhere except for the picture of roses on a calendar hanging on the back of the door. Dot peered at it. She turned over three leaves of the calendar. 'What are you fiddling with?' Ida asked. Dot said she was just correcting the date. 'Here's your cuppa,' Ida said. Dot took it, saying nothing about the milk in it. Ida knew she didn't take milk. 'Sugar?' Ida asked. Dot shook her head. Ida knew she didn't take sugar either, and for some reason resented the fact. Ida put two heaped spoonfuls into her own tea and stirred it vigorously. 'Enjoy life while you can, I always say,' she commented. Dot supposed the sugar was the enjoyment. They sat at the kitchen table drinking their tea in silence. It was a small, spindly table, and looked peculiar in that enormous kitchen, which called for a large, solid farmhouse table. Dot couldn't imagine how on earth the entire Barnes family had ever managed to sit round it. They must have had to eat in relays. 'You're very quiet,' Ida suddenly said. 'You've not much chat today, Dot.' Dot thought about replying that Ida hadn't much chat either, but of course she didn't. Ida was trying to provoke her and she didn't rise to it, but just smiled. 'Well,' Ida said, 'I wonder what he'll be like, eh? They say he's good-looking, but we'll be the judge of that.' Dot coughed. 'What?' said Ida. 'Nothing,' Dot said. 'I was just thinking, it isn't his looks that matter really, is it?' Ida laughed. 'You're a caution,' she said. 'Looks not matter? Of course they matter. I could tell you a thing or two about how they matter. Believe me, I know. I know what happens when you lose them. Then you realise looks matter.' Dot got up, carried her mug over to the sink and washed it out. 'Best get back upstairs,' she murmured.

She wasn't frightened of Ida but she didn't like being with her. Ida made her nervous in a different way from Mary. Ida always seemed to be about to attack her, or at least to trap her into saying things which Ida could then scorn. With Mary, it was more a matter of impatience, but, behind her impatience with unpunctuality and indecision, Mary was kind and Dot knew it. She pondered on this difference as she washed the window-sills, and wondered how she had come to be bossed about by everyone she knew, even her own daughter. She knew she shouldn't always put up with it. Ironically, it was bossy Mary who was forever telling her this. 'It is one thing to let your husband dominate you, Dot, but really it is the limit to let Sarah do it too.' She'd tried to explain to Mary that Sarah didn't mean to act as she often did but that she wasn't always in control of herself. She was a strange girl, as nervous as Dot herself. She'd been given to awful attacks of panic as a child, she'd shaken and shivered with fright over terrors she couldn't describe. She worried all the time, over quite trivial things, and was regularly overcome by fears hard to understand. A lot of them were to do with health. She only had to feel hot and sweaty to be convinced she had some terrible fever, and as an adolescent a cough to her was a sign of the consumption she read about in the nineteenth-century novels she was studying at school. Dot had more than sympathised, she'd empathised (which, said Adam, was their daughter's undoing). When Sarah was little, she'd been able to calm her simply by holding her tight, but after she'd grown up this kind of soothing embrace had been impossible, partly because Sarah had turned out so tall. For Dot to hold her had meant clasping her somewhere around her waist. She'd started telling her mother please not to touch her, to stop it, and Dot hadn't known what else to do. Adam had said the girl needed to be disciplined. Her over-active imagination should be curbed, he'd said, as though imagination was like a horse. He hadn't understood that, unlike her parents, Sarah was artistic and that having a vivid imagination was part of her creative nature. Adam saw this as a curse whereas Dot marvelled at it. It made her feel humble, but then humility was part of her nature anyway. She could never get over the fact that out of what she felt was such 'poor stuff' (as she put it) as herself and Adam the gifted Sarah had emerged.

Once the window-sills were as clean as they could be – she couldn't do anything about the chipped paint – Dot gathered her cleaning materials together and put them at the top of the stairs. Then she had a last look in the bedrooms, hesitating over whether to leave the windows open in the main bedroom where the new vicar would sleep. Odd to think of him taking over this room, all on his own, beginning a new life. All vicars, she supposed, were used to it, forever being moved on by their bishops.

There was a pleasant, dreamy feeling to all these meandering thoughts, with no one to jar her back to more pressing matters. She shook her head slightly, and bent to pick up a duster she'd dropped from her basket. Fluffy and bright yellow when she'd started and now a grey and grimy rag. Then she began walking along the landing towards the stairs but stopped, transfixed, before she got there. There was a long window on the staircase, above the front door, and through it she could see that a car had stopped and a man had got out and was looking at the house, a man wearing a clerical collar and vest stock under his linen jacket. Below her, Ida was singing again, not a hymn this time. Dot knew the tune but couldn't remember the name and couldn't quite catch the words. The new vicar was walking towards the front door and she urged herself to hurry down the stairs to alert Ida. She scurried along to the kitchen and called, 'Ida!' but Ida had her back to her and was singing – it was 'Oh for the Wings of a Dove' – and at the same time running water into a metal bucket, so she didn't hear her. Dot touched Ida's arm and repeated her name. Ida jumped and turned round and put a hand on her heart. 'Oh!' she gasped. 'Creeping up on me like that!' 'Ida,' whispered Dot, 'it's the new vicar, he's here!' The doorbell pealed just as she spoke, and Ida's expression changed from one of surprise to excitement. 'Well!' she exclaimed, struggling to take her apron off and at the same time fussing with her hair, running her fingers through it to fluff it out. 'Go and open the door, Dot, while I put the kettle on.'

Dot didn't want to go and open the door but, because she was so used to obeying orders, she went to do it. The bell had rung again before she got there and she called 'Coming', though doubted that her little voice could be heard. The stiff catch wouldn't move. She wrestled with it, trying desperately to turn the knob, using both her hands and standing on tiptoe. At last, she managed, and the door swung open so suddenly that she almost fell backwards. There he was, the new vicar, smiling and holding out his hand. 'Stiff old door, I see,' he said. 'I'll have to oil it. But good afternoon. I'm Cecil Maddox. Can I come in?' Dot nodded and stood aside. Meanwhile, Ida had appeared (her hair, Dot noted, newly brushed) and was booming a greeting, her arms outstretched as though to embrace the new arrival. 'Vicar! Welcome! You've caught us on the hop, we're still trying to make this place spick and span, but come in, come in, sit yourself down, have a cup of tea.' The vicar seemed a little taken aback, Dot thought, but followed Ida into the kitchen, apologising for being early and explaining that he'd made such good time it hadn't seemed worth staying the night somewhere near just to arrive on the right day. He didn't sit down while Ida poured the tea. He took the proffered mug (Dot felt pleased that he, too, took tea without milk and sugar) and prowled around, Ida tracking his every move, and chattering away about the vicarage and how big it was, then asking would he like a tour of the rest of it. The vicar said no, he'd bring his luggage in first.

They all went outside to the car, with the vicar protesting that he needed no help, but both Ida and Dot insisting that they could surely carry something in. He gave Ida an umbrella, a big golfing sort, and Dot a camera in a canvas case. He himself hauled out a large suitcase and a holdall and deposited them just inside the front door. He had some boxes of books in the boot, he said, but they could stay there for the time being. Then he stood on the steps and held out his hand and thanked Dot and Ida for their help in such a way that Dot realised he wanted them to go. She said she'd just get her coat and bag and her basket, and the vicar moved aside to let her pass. Ida stayed stock-still until Dot re-emerged, coat on, bag and basket over her arms, and the vicar said, 'Can I get your coat, Mrs . . . Good heavens, I haven't even asked your names.' There was some confusion for a moment while they told him their names, and Ida had to accept that she was being dismissed. Then the vicar retreated into the house and the door was closed. He seemed to close it rather quickly. 'You were in a hurry to leave,' Ida snapped, as they walked down the drive. 'Very rude of you, and it wasn't very friendly.' Dot said she'd picked up the hint that the vicar wanted to be left in peace to settle in. 'Rubbish!' Ida said. 'You're imagining it, hint indeed.' They walked in silence to the gates, Ida now groaning and saying she'd hurt her back carrying that damned heavy bucket and that she would pay the penalty. 'And I was told at the clinic,' she complained, 'not to lift anything heavy, not after what I've been through. I was told to look after myself.' Dot tried to make noises of sympathy but Ida would not be placated. She hardly said goodbye as they parted to go in different directions.

Dot knew that Ida would go straight home and start ringing other parishioners to boast about having met the new vicar. Once Ida had given her description to the other women they would want to check it out, distrusting her judgement as they were bound to. They would ring Dot. Well, what would she tell them? She thought she had better practise. She would say he seemed nice. Would that do? No, it would not. She tried to think what she would actually be asked: was he good-looking? Well, he had a nice face and a nice smile. She would say that. But was he tall, was he fat or thin, did he have blue eyes or brown, what colour was his hair? Dot stopped walking. Ida would have had all the answers. She tried hard to remember: no, he wasn't very tall, he was definitely thin, but she had no idea what colour his eyes were or his hair, except that it was vaguely dark and plentiful. Another certain question would be: was he posh? No. Yes. Was he? She strained to recall his accent: faintly southern, but where? He was pale, she'd noticed that, quite strikingly pale. But then he'd been ill so, of course, he would be pale.

Dot was still standing there, a mere few yards along the road from the vicarage gates, when Mrs Hibbert saw her and pulled up, giving a light toot of her car horn. 'Dot!' she called. 'Can I give you a lift?' Dot looked startled, and then gathered herself together and trotted eagerly to the car. As she drove along with Mrs Hibbert, glad they were friends again, she related what had happened and tried her best to describe the new vicar. Mary wasn't interested in how he looked or in his age or accent, which was a mercy, but more in his previous experience and his education. Dot knew nothing about either, nor had she sounded him out on his views regarding women priests or the marrying of divorcees in church. Mary had strong opinions on these matters. She wasn't on the parish council, but she seemed to know a great deal about what had gone on at the meeting when the Rev. Maddox had been accepted. According to Mary, the bishop had more or less instructed the council to take him, and they hadn't liked this one bit. The other information she had mysteriously collected was that Maddox was an Oxford man and very clever. Dot wondered why, in that case, he had ended up coming to St James's, but she said nothing.

*

Cecil Maddox, prowling round his new home, was wondering much the same thing. Those two women had depressed him. He had known the moment the little one opened the door and stared at him with what looked like awe that he was not the sort of vicar she needed and wanted. He couldn't stand the thought of being depended upon. Trying to cope with the effusiveness of the fat one was worse. He was no good at being jolly and hearty, he couldn't respond to matiness. These were people with expectations he'd never be able to satisfy and he'd tried to explain this to the bishop when this parish had been suggested, but his objections had been brushed aside, and he'd been told that after his illness the simple, good folk of St James's would be balm to his soul. He would be able, he was assured, to repair his damaged nerves once removed from the large inner-city parish where he had come to such grief in spite of his splendid efforts (it was the bishop who referred to them as 'splendid efforts'). But the bishop had missed the point. It was 'simple, good folk' who terrified him. He couldn't deal with either their simplicity or their goodness – both made him feel exposed and inadequate. If he had to work with people – well, of course he had to – he was best working with people like himself, neurotics, tortured minds, uneasy people. He liked to lose himself in big cities, too, and dreaded small towns or country villages. The bishop had said that he would be ready for the greater challenge of a city again when he had spent some soothing years at St James's.

Standing, looking out of the window of his dismal bedroom, Cecil felt the greater challenge had arrived already. He'd felt such dismay from the moment he had seen the valley at the end of which this town lay, long before he had reached the parish. It was impossible to account for the way the sight of those forested hills and that shining river had made him want to weep and run away. The peace of the scene, its beauty, made him want to scream. Who could he expect to understand that? It was insane to want traffic thundering along filthy roads, and blackened buildings, and ugly tower blocks and litter blowing everywhere, and exhausted people rushing around ignoring each other, but he did. He wanted to be lost in that sort of chaos, and yet it had brought him to what the bishop called grief. He opened the window wider and took several deep breaths – he had only met two women, only seen the inside of this house, and yet was basing a whole set of prejudices upon these brief encounters. He knew he should not have bundled the women out so quickly. Not a good start.

He decided to close the bedroom windows before he left the room. The scent of the honeysuckle made him feel sick. He wandered about the rest of the house slowly realising that it faced north and that at the back, where the sun shone so brightly, there were only two small windows. The larger windows looked north or east. Someone had built the house expressly to shut out the sun. It felt cold even now, on a hot day. He could see no radiators, which meant there was no central heating: just as well, because he couldn't afford to use it. He poked about and located two storage heaters and an electric fire of ancient design, and noticed two of the fireplaces had coal in the buckets beside them. One of these fireplaces was in a small room off the hall, which he took to be a study. It had a desk in it, a rather ugly, dark wood thing, squat, and with the wood badly scratched and the handles missing from three of the drawers. There was a leather armchair in the corner with an antimacassar over its back and an embroidered cushion perched against it. He would live here, he decided. He would shut the sitting-room up. The kitchen he would have to use, though its size and chilliness were daunting, but he would never eat there. He would bring his food into this study on a tray. For a moment, he thought of dragging a mattress down here so that he could sleep in this study as well, but dismissed the idea as too ridiculous. Hiding in a little room was not going to help.

He couldn't think what *was* going to. This was a family house and he had no wife or children to humanise it. The silence made him shudder. It felt dangerous, as though it might suffocate him if he didn't do something about it. He hated the sound of his footsteps echoing as he walked around and every time he closed a door he winced at the absurdly loud noise. He hadn't unpacked a thing, or attempted to settle in, but he had to get out. Once he'd opened the front door, which creaked horribly, he felt a bit better. The thing to do was to stay out of the house as much as possible. The key safely in his pocket, he decided it was time to acquaint himself with the church. He'd passed it driving here. The bishop had told him it was a late nineteenth-century building, of no architectural merit but with a fine east window donated by a local merchant of the time. It had no spire or tower, and the limestone was from local mines. He walked to it along the tree-lined road, a mere three-minute walk, and entered by a side gate. The graveyard surrounding the church was in excellent condition, the grass neatly cut and flowers in urns in front of many of the gravestones. He stopped and read some of these, noticing that Nicholson was a local name, from the frequency with which it occurred, and that gilt lettering on black marble appeared to be the preferred form of memorial. The church had a porch, not quite in proportion to the building itself, and the door was open. There were notices inside, pinned on boards to either side, but he didn't stop to read them – he knew what they would say and he didn't want to dwell on the inevitable bring-and-buy sales and fêtes and teas. Inside the church at last, he paused. The east window, as promised, was indeed fine and commanded attention at once. He studied it carefully, imagining the morning sun turning the yellow of the angels' hair into a blaze of glorious light. Slowly, he advanced down the nave along the rush matting, touching the pews as he went. They were made of oak, he thought, and seemed light in the general darkness of the church. Reaching the altar, he knelt and prayed to find the strength to do good work here. This was what he wanted. This was what made him happy: a silent church, a stone floor beneath his knees, light coming towards him over an angel's wings. Here, praying, he was sure of his faith and of himself. Even the smell, musty, slightly acrid, pleased him. He breathed in deeply and bent lower, almost prostrating himself, the palms of his hands flattened on the cold stone. 'O Lord,' he began, saying the words out loud, in a whisper, 'O Lord, help me be worthy of thee . . .'

Even before he had finished his prayer, he heard someone enter the church behind him. They came in as quietly as he had done himself – he heard the light footsteps and then a pause. Bracing himself to encounter whoever it was, he stood up and turned round. A woman was standing stock-still in the middle of the nave, her hand at her throat and a look of utter astonishment on her face. He smiled and began to walk towards her, his arm outstretched to greet her, but in one swift movement she turned and walked quickly away. He couldn't shout to her, not in the church. He hurried after her, but was thinking, as he tried to catch up, that since she obviously hadn't wanted to meet him he ought surely to let her go. She had, in any case, vanished – by the time he came out of the porch all he could see was a flash of her skirt as she went through the gate, a good 50 yards away.

He stood still, wondering if she hadn't realised that he was the new vicar, but she could not have missed his collar even if his jacket and trousers gave nothing away. Somebody who wanted to be alone in the church, then, as he did. Alone on a sunny weekday afternoon. And he had spoiled her intended reverie, her need, perhaps, to pray. Another fine beginning.

He dreaded the thought of returning to the vicarage, so instead he sat on one of the benches placed round the graveyard. It was quiet, but not oppressively so. There was quite a bit of traffic running along the road into the town centre and he could hear a pneumatic drill working somewhere nearby, and lawn-mowers nearer still. He reached into his jacket pocket and brought out a small notebook and a pencil, thinking he should jot down ideas for his first sermon here. It would, he decided, have to take the form of a confession – he would talk about his illness openly, about how his terror of people had grown until he could barely speak to anyone at all, and throw himself on the mercy of the congregation, asking them to help him overcome his inadequacies. It was a risk, of course. He might embarrass these people, or worse still, horrify them. They would want their vicar to be strong and confident, friendly and ready to help them, and not a man in need of help himself. There might be complaints lodged against him with the bishop. He stared at the blank page in his notebook, sighed, and put it back in his pocket. He felt the letter there, the only one that had been waiting for him at the vicarage. It was from St Mary's Hospital, asking if he would fulfil the same duties as the Rev. Barnes had done as a relief hospital chaplain and inviting him to a meeting of the Friends of the hospital. He supposed he ought to accept, though the last thing he ever wanted to have to do again was go into a hospital.

Eventually, after an hour of wandering around, he returned to the vicarage. He'd put it off as long as possible, pretending that he needed to familiarise himself with the locality so that he could set his new home in context. The context was much as he had surmised on his arrival. St James's was on the edge of a small market town stuck at the end of a valley cut off from the coastal plain by what seemed to him formidably huge hills. The town itself had little bustle about it – the general cleanliness and orderliness were to him astonishing. There were no supermarkets or chain stores, just a succession of small shops selling mostly food. He noticed people standing talking to each other in the streets, with nobody hurrying, and greetings were called out across them. He walked down the tree-lined main street and round the square at the end, noting the ugly war memorial at its centre, and then back again to the unnerving emptiness of the roads around the church. There seemed to be no one at all about – a few cats prowling along the hedges, and that was all. The roads were clean, the gardens tidy. He'd made a square round the vicarage and by the time he turned into the right road again he was dismally aware that he'd landed in small-town suburbia. The vicarage now looked totally out of place among the semi-detached houses, gross in size compared to them and its gaunt stone exterior, incongruous next to their whitewashed, rendered-concrete fronts. Trudging up the short, gravelled drive, he wondered if he could find somewhere else to live. Couldn't the vicarage be let out, for a rent that would go into the church coffers and be useful? He only needed a bed-sitting-room. But this was not the sort of place that had such rooms to let, and in any case the vicar would be required to have the status an imposing vicarage conferred.

There was someone sitting on his doorstep. A man, middle-aged, or older, strong-looking, dressed in a tweed jacket and old-fashioned flannels. He got up as Cecil approached, and straightened his jacket, pulling it down firmly and buttoning the middle button, and cleared his throat. 'Sorry to disturb you, vicar,' he said, 'on your first day, and that, but could I have a word?' There was nothing Cecil could do but say yes, of course, but he felt flustered and dropped the front door key twice before inserting it in the lock, and then he had to fiddle with it before the wretched door would open. 'Needs a spot of oil,' his visitor said. Cecil agreed. He stood in the bleak hall, wondering where to take this man, and decided it had to be the sitting-room, after all, a room he'd merely glanced into before shutting the door. He led the way fearfully, dreading the discomfort of not knowing where to sit, or whether to sit at all. There was a gigantic three-piece suite in the room, hideously covered in a drab, dark maroon material, and two chairs facing the sofa with a small, glass-topped table between them. He gestured to one of the chairs. The man sat on the very edge, feet planted apart on the worn, brown carpet. Cecil sat opposite, the table between them like a barrier. 'How can I help you?' he said. 'As you see, I haven't settled in yet.' The man nodded. 'I'm Ida's husband,' he said, and waited. Cecil raised his eyebrows enquiringly. 'The lady who was cleaning when you arrived, the bigger of the two.' 'Oh, of course,' Cecil said, relieved. 'Very kind of her, of them, very kind.' The man smiled. He looked a nice man. Straightforward, decent, friendly. Cecil relaxed a little. Maybe this would not be too difficult. 'It's about Ida I've come,' said the man. 'I thought I'd come straight away, in case.' He paused, as though waiting for encouragement, but Cecil warned himself not to try to give it – it was one of the things he'd learned (if little else), always to wait. 'She might bother you,' the man said. 'She gets pretty desperate, and then she comes running, and you just have to be patient, not that I'm trying to teach you your job. The name's Martin, by the way. Martin Yates, pleased to meet you, I should have said it first, my name, I mean.'

He half rose and held out his hand, and Cecil leaned forward and took it, the edge of the table digging into his knees. 'Cecil Maddox,' he said. Then there was silence. Was he supposed to ask in what way Ida Yates might bother him and why she became pretty desperate? It didn't appeal to him. 'Ida was christened here,' Martin Yates was saying, 'and we were married here, in the church that is, and in times of trouble she's always turned to the vicar. The Rev. Barnes was very good, very understanding.' Cecil nodded. Comparisons with his predecessor would be inevitable. 'Well,' he said, 'thank you for filling me in, Mr Yates. I'll try to do my best, if your wife does need comfort.' He stood up, but Mr Yates didn't. Should he sit down again? But that felt foolish. Slowly, the other man got up too. 'It's cancer,' he said, 'that's Ida's trouble, or was, I never know whether to say it is or it was.' His hand went to his chest. 'Here,' he said, 'she gets frightened sometimes, she panics. I thought you should be told, in case she can't say it, in case she's confused when she comes, hysterical, maybe. Then you'll know what to do.'

Cecil almost laughed at the absurdity of the idea in this man's head – that *he* would know what to do! He was dreadfully afraid that a spasm might have crossed his face and looked like a smirk, and so he said, very hastily, and not making sense, 'Don't worry, don't worry, that's fine.' They shook hands again, and then there was the awkward business of moving towards the door side by side, and edging through it and out into the hall and then at last Mr Yates had gone. Cecil leaned against the closed door and closed his eyes. A vision of Ida Yates hysterical and weeping rose before him and he groaned. What would he do with her? What if she were to come in the middle of the night – but no, surely her husband, the caring Mr Yates, would stop her. What had Paul Barnes done to calm her? Suddenly, he rushed into the study. Paul Barnes might have left some explanatory notes for him. There was a folder he'd noticed, in the top drawer, marked 'Parish Matters', which he hadn't been able to face looking at. Now he took it out and flipped through it: dross. Merely telephone numbers for the church wardens, bills for new hymn books, nothing about any parishioners at all.

His forehead felt sweaty and hot. He wiped it with his sleeve, then went to wash his hands and splash cold water over his face. He was still drying it when the telephone rang and he froze, staring at himself in the mirror above the sink. He would have to answer it, would have to, but his footsteps dragged as he went towards the ledge in the cavernous hall where the instrument stood. 'Hello! Am I talking to the new vicar? I hope I am!' 'Yes,' said Cecil. His voice was a croak. 'Who is this, please?' It was a hearty, booming Paul Barnes, ringing to wish him luck, glad he was at last in residence, pleased to find him at home, hoping he was settling in, and finally telling him he was a lucky chap, couldn't be a nicer, easier parish. Cecil hesitated and then decided that he had to take this chance to ask about Ida Yates, explaining about her husband's visit. 'Oh, Martin's a lovely chap, salt of the earth, that's typical of him, typical, but of course he knows his wife, he knows what she's like, quite unhinged sometimes, but don't worry about it.' Cecil said he couldn't help it, he was worried, he felt very apprehensive at the thought of this woman perhaps arriving in a distressed state. 'Part of the job, surely,' said Paul Barnes. 'Never come across it before? Ida wants reassurance, that's all. Say a prayer with her, give her a cup of tea, and she'll be on her way. She's an unhappy woman these days, can't face up to dealing with breast cancer, though I gather she's fine now. It's hard for Martin, wonderful chap. You'll like him.'

Cecil could find no food in the kitchen, but then he hadn't brought any with him and there was no reason why anyone else should have provisioned for his early arrival. There was tea, though, left by the two women, and he wasn't really hungry so much as thirsty. He sat in his study with a large mug of weak tea and tried to compose himself. He thought of Ida Yates and her possible hysteria, and of the woman who had run away from him in the church, and wondered if his mission here was to act as psychiatrist not vicar. But then the administering of religion, if it could be described like that, was a sort of psychiatry. The only problem was that he still needed psychiatric help himself. He was close to mad sometimes. Could the half-mad help the temporarily unstable? It sounded as though he would have to find out. It had all been in his head, to deliver as his first sermon, the confession of his weakness, but now he realised he couldn't deliver it. What would Ida Yates think? What would her solid husband think? What would the nervous woman who'd run away think? He could not publicly advertise his own frailty. He had to show how comfort and healing could be achieved through faith. Everyone wanted help of some sort and only God, working in his mysterious ways, could give it.

He found a can of oil in a cupboard in the kitchen. It was actually labelled 'for troublesome front door'. Cecil went slowly to the door, opened it, and began applying oil to the hinges.

*

It took Edwina a while to recover – she couldn't think what had made her do such an unlikely thing. Churches were places she shunned, only entering them on the kind of occasions when not to do so would offend others. St James's was not like the Methodist chapel of her youth, it was an interesting and attractive building, but nevertheless it held no charm for her and she had never in fact been inside it. But passing the church that afternoon she had paused near the gate into the churchyard and thought how pretty and well-kept it was. Graveyards were bits of history, and she was interested in history. She'd gone through the gate to look at the gravestones not in any morbid fashion but to see how old they were, and then it had suddenly seemed to her like a dare: could she overcome her aversion and enter the church itself?

There was no reason why not. Maybe, she'd thought, it would calm her. Her head seemed to throb with worry about Emma – where was she, was she safe? – and it was partly for that reason that she'd come out to walk. She couldn't read any more. When she most needed to, she couldn't concentrate on the words, they'd failed her. She pushed the door of the porch open and almost tiptoed inside. It was cold, as it always was in churches, cold and musty, a combination which made her shiver. For a moment, she had turned to go straight back into the sunshine but then she'd thought no, she must enter the church itself. The inner door was slightly ajar. Hesitantly, she slipped inside and stood beside a table laden with hymn books. The intense silence, instead of soothing her, agitated her. All the dreadful things that might be at this moment happening to Emma crowded in on her and she put a hand across her forehead as though to try to subdue them. It had been a mistake to imagine any kind of comfort could be found in St James's. But since she would never enter the church again she thought she should just look at its famous east window and then go, quickly. Crossing the stone flags, she glided towards the centre aisle and then, turning to face the window, she saw a man rise up and come towards her.

The shock was violent. Her heart raced and without pausing to reflect that this must of course be the vicar, she ran from the church and down the path to the gate, crashing it behind her and never looking back. Once home, she was mortified by her behaviour – what must the poor man have thought? She should have collected herself, at least nodded, said good afternoon, before leaving. Or she should have explained her presence, told him she was just admiring the window. She'd run away as though she were frightened, as though she'd thought him an ogre. It was inexplicable, that leap of terror. She didn't need anyone to tell her she was getting everything out of proportion. Emma was young and healthy and even if she seemed dominated by Luke, she must surely have some notion of self-preservation within her. That was what Edwina told herself she had to hang on to: Emma's own resilience and her innate respect for her own life. She would not let Luke lead her into danger, she would *not*.

7

Think about Your Life

THERE HAD been a little clutch of cards and notes, and a flurry of messages on her answer machine, but Chrissie had derived no comfort from them. Her misery about the whole awful business had wrapped itself round her like cling-film, sealing up every nook and cranny of feeling. She was numb with guilt, even though guilt was what she had been publicly absolved of and told not to feel. Again and again she replayed that day in the clinic, the day Mr Wallis wasn't there, the day Ben Cohen was ill, the day she and Andrew had struggled through that heavy load, but the dreadful thing was that she couldn't remember clearly what that poor young woman had looked like. She could vividly recall some of the patients she'd seen that day, though she couldn't remember their names, especially one rather striking, dark-haired younger woman, but she could not bring Carol Collins to mind. The newspaper had described her as red-haired and pretty, and her own notes had told her Ms Collins was twenty-six and single, but none of this information brought her to mind, which in itself was an indictment. Even looking at the photograph after the inquest hadn't helped. Carol Collins was a blank.

A blank. That was how she felt herself to be now, a faceless person, remote, unable to connect with anyone. A person who had been unable to provide reassurance at the right time for a vulnerable and needy young woman. No good excusing herself on the grounds of having been tired and overworked, no good repeating that Carol Collins had a history of mental instability and had tried to kill herself before over another imagined fatal illness. She felt responsible, and was sure the young woman's family still blamed her. 'Take time off,' Mr Wallis had said. He wanted to be rid of her, she was sure. Her drawn features, and her eyes red with lack of sleep, alarmed his patients. And so here she was, with time off, and it didn't help at all. What was she to do with herself? Fret and wonder endlessly why ever she had become a doctor, though the answer was simple: because her mother had wanted it. So many times, as a child, she'd heard her mother say, with conviction, 'Chrissie is going to be a doctor, aren't you, Chrissie?' And she had never once replied, 'Am I?' Instead, she'd been eager to agree, yes, yes, I am going to be a doctor. Her head had filled with romantic notions of saving lives and curing the sick; the white coat and stethoscope had been seductive badges of office. She was good at science, all the sciences, sailed through exams, had no trouble getting into medical school. But there, once the reality of doctoring impressed itself upon her, the doubts had begun. Did she want to be among all this blood and disease? It was sad, it was depressing, it was not as worthwhile and noble as she had envisaged, and worst of all was the fearful weight of the responsibility. But she'd gone too far, she couldn't bring herself to back out. Her mother's proudest day was when she saw her daughter entitled to put the magic word Doctor in front of her name.

But the next step, the one her mother had wanted her to take, she had not taken. She hadn't become a GP. Being a GP was all about personal involvement with people and the idea horrified her. It was better for her to be in a hospital environment and to keep the personal at a distance. She still had to deal with people but she didn't have to get to know patients. In the clinic, a body could be a body in a way it could not be in a GP's surgery, and it was bodies she could deal with, not people. But she'd dealt with Carol Collins as a body, couldn't remember her face, couldn't even recall the red hair. Carol Collins had been just a few notes, until she became a dead young woman.

She wondered how she was ever going to go back to St Mary's, with everyone looking at her and whispering who-knew-what, and feeling sorry for her. But she knew that to think like that was vanity. Memories were short. To her, and to Carol Collins's family, what had happened was overwhelmingly important, but to those others in a busy hospital it was not. Aunt Mary had pointed this out in her note. 'Nobody blames you, dear,' she had written, 'you did nothing wrong, and people here have more pressing things to worry about.' It was kind of her to write, but the letter was in itself an indication that Carol Collins's death *was* being talked about. Chrissie knew she hadn't bothered to stop and speak to her aunt for months, though she'd regularly seen her doing her duty as a Friend. She'd avoided her, always had done. Aunt Mary embarrassed her. Even referring to her as 'aunt' embarrassed her, suggesting as it did a degree of affection and closeness which did not exist. 'Aunt Mary' was the widow of her mother's only brother; she sent Christmas and birthday presents, letters of congratulation after exam successes, a card of commiseration after the death of Chrissie's father. And, of course, she came to the funeral of Chrissie's mother. It was the first time Chrissie could ever remember meeting the woman and it had not been a comfortable encounter. They had said hello in the entrance hall of the hospital over the years, but no more. Until now, and the note, which ended with the words 'If there is anything you want, or anything I can do, please let me know.'

What do I want, Chrissie wondered, that a woman like Aunt Mary could possibly give me? A woman I hardly know, whose connection with me is an accident of marriage, a woman to whom I do not feel in the least drawn, who simply happens to do voluntary work in my hospital and about whom I know nothing else. I do not, Chrissie thought, want to be part of her good works. I don't want to be pitied or fussed over. And yet as the days passed, and she dragged herself around her little house, listlessly, she longed for someone, anyone, to pull her out of her apathy and break through the wall of indifference she seemed to have erected round herself. She didn't want another doctor. She didn't want the kindness of colleagues who had all experienced something similar in their professional lives (and without those colleagues she had precious few friends). Gradually, she began to play with the idea of taking Aunt Mary at her word, and summoning her, saying 'Help me', and then waiting to see what would transpire. She could pretend to be ill. Well, it would not exactly be a pretence – she *was* ill, but not in the way she would pretend to be. Something simple would do, some physical malady, which would mean she needed to be visited and perhaps looked after; and then, once Aunt Mary came, if she came, she could recover rapidly should the whole thing prove a disaster. She remembered her mother saying of Aunt Mary that whatever else, she was a sensible woman, dependable, loyal, and full of common sense.

Sitting down and forcing herself to summon up the required energy to write the short letter, Chrissie suddenly wondered what her mother had meant by that 'whatever else'.

*

It was true, she had said that if there was anything Chrissie wanted, just to let her know. Holding the letter in her hand, Mrs Hibbert remembered writing this, and meaning it. Meaning it, but not expecting a response of this sort. She remembered, too, that other occasion, five years ago (or was it four?) when she had said the same thing in person to the girl, at her mother's funeral. She had looked so forlorn, so utterly pathetic, her thin face so pale, her great brown eyes swamped in tears which somehow never quite spilled over, just remained there, lakes of sorrow. Mrs Hibbert had been shocked at the evidence of such raw grief, she had been unprepared to discover that a 25-year-old woman, and a doctor too, could be so overwhelmed by the death of her mother. It must mean, she had concluded, that Chrissie and Sandra had been very close indeed. She hadn't known this, but then she hardly knew Sandra – four times they'd met, while Francis was alive – and could not claim to know Chrissie in the slightest. She'd been surprised to be invited to the funeral and had only gone out of loyalty to Francis. And when she'd offered to help, Chrissie had touched her briefly on her arm, a little pat of gratitude (or so she'd judged it), and tried to smile.

What she wanted at this moment was a calming cup of tea,

because Chrissie's letter had made her agitated, there was no denying this. The tea made, Mrs Hibbert wished for the hundredth time that she had someone with whom she could discuss what she should do. It was the worst part of being on her own. She'd never got used to it. Friends were no substitute for Francis, to whom she had been able to confess her meanest thoughts, knowing he would understand. Telling friends things she would later regret was fatal to friendship, whereas telling Francis had no repercussions. He'd listened and sorted her out and never made her feel ashamed. She knew that what she would have been saying to him now was that, although *of course* she had meant what she had written to Chrissie, she had never envisaged being put to this kind of test. She would have asked Francis why on earth the girl had asked her, of all people, a virtual stranger, to come and stay with her. He would surely have agreed that it was peculiar and that Chrissie must be desperate to suggest it.

In the silence of her tidy kitchen, Mrs Hibbert could clearly hear in her head that Francis was saying 'Exactly'. He was saying something else too. You must go to her at once, he was telling her, his voice very firm. 'Oh, *really*!' Mrs Hibbert said aloud, and got up, scraping the legs of her chair on the floor in the way she hated others doing, and washing her mug noisily at the sink using an unnecessarily large amount of water. She felt rebellious. Liberties were being taken, surely. She wasn't a nurse, Chrissie must know enough real nurses who would oblige. 'I am not well at the moment,' she had written, 'and feel in need of someone to help, just for a little while, and I wondered, after your kind note, whether there was any chance of your coming to stay?' It was polite enough, but why didn't the girl say what was wrong with her? Mrs Hibbert suddenly wondered if Chrissie's ailment was of the nervous kind, a breakdown, if long delayed, after the inquest of that young woman. It would explain why she hadn't specified what she was suffering from.

She had to make up her mind how to respond. There were several convincing excuses which immediately presented themselves, but she knew she would not use them. It would be despicable. Hadn't she said 'If there is anything you want'? And hadn't she now been told it was her presence that was wanted? The alarm and anxiety she experienced as she faced up to this was mixed with a weird feeling of something like excitement – she had been chosen, sent for, she would be answering what could only be described as an emergency call. Francis would have been proud of her. And in fact she could not help feeling quite proud herself as she wrote to Chrissie, saying how sorry she was to hear that she was not well, and telling her she would come at once, the very next day (that is, the day after her letter arrived – she made that clear). She could have telephoned, but as Chrissie had written, she thought she should reply in kind.

It worried her that she knew nothing about Chrissie's house, never having visited her. Would it be cold? Sandra's house had been horribly cold. The only time she and Francis had stayed there, she'd been so cold she'd had to get up in the middle of the night and put a cardigan on. She decided to pack her warmest clothes even though it was still summer, just in case. It was enjoyable to get her suitcase out again and begin selecting items to put in it – she'd always liked this part of going away, the pleasures of preparing. Years since she'd indulged it. She'd lost the habit of holidays. Once, she'd been quite adventurous, valuing her own independent spirit, never minding that she had no one to accompany her. She'd toured Scotland and then Ireland after Francis died, perfectly comfortable to stay in bed-and-breakfast places. The driving had given her great satisfaction, and she'd been a skilled navigator, expert at reading maps. But then the urge to travel had mysteriously left her. She preferred to stay at home, where she was comfortable. The last holiday she'd taken, seven years ago, had been to Cornwall, and every bed she'd slept in had seemed either too hard or too soft and she'd ended up with a sore back.

But, she reminded herself, she was not going on holiday. She was going to stay with a young woman she hardly knew who was unwell in some unspecified way and needed help. She would very likely be going to spend her time indoors doing a lot of listening and looking after. It would be like her role as a Friend, and yet unlike it. Chrissie was a doctor, a professional woman, who would not want advice or guidance in the same way as patients coming in a state of confusion to the hospital. And she was not like Dot, craving direction, or even Emma, looking for a substitute mother. The more she tried to decide what exactly Chrissie would want of her, the more Mrs Hibbert was overcome with the awkwardness of the situation. At least she wasn't going far – the drive to Chrissie's house was not much longer than her weekly drive to St Mary's. She would be there in under an hour.

Chrissie's house was a new one, on the other side of the river from St Mary's. Mrs Hibbert knew the area because she frequently drove that way on her visits to a garden centre specialising in azaleas. She'd seen these houses being built, a row of them, screened from the road by conifers. They were advertised as town houses, though they were a mile at least out of the town, and looked odd to her, standing where they did, a terrace more suited to a street than the bank of a river. She expected them to be poky inside, though their external appearance was attractive enough. The narrow balconies, she'd noticed, had pretty wrought-iron railings and in summer there were window boxes on them full of petunias and geraniums. The front doors were painted black and had brass knockers and letter-boxes (hell to clean, she'd reflected). All this she'd glimpsed as she'd driven to and from the garden centre. It rather pleased her to think of going inside one of them and she looked forward to comparing Chrissie's accommodation with her own. She'd often thought that she herself should perhaps move to some smaller dwelling, easier to look after, in preparation for her old age, but the prospect of giving up her garden had squashed that idea.

Pulling up outside Chrissie's house, Mrs Hibbert reflected that this was a good place for a single woman to live. There were neighbours either side – Chrissie's house was in the middle of the twelve houses – and though it was a quiet spot the road was near. There was space for her to park without any trouble, which was a relief (parking was not her strong point these days). She got out of the car, locked it after removing her suitcase, and began to walk up the short, paved path to the front door. As she did so, a movement at one of the first-floor windows caught her eye. The windows were covered by white Venetian blinds – several houses had them – and she had seen the slats in the middle widen, as though someone was peering through. Convinced that Chrissie had seen her arrive and would be coming to open the door, Mrs Hibbert did not at first ring the bell, but then, when the door didn't open, and she could hear no movement inside, she pressed it lightly. Silence. She shifted uncomfortably on the step – really, one felt like a travelling salesman, standing like this with a suitcase on a doorstep – and rang the bell again, harder. She was just becoming exasperated, and ready to march back to her car, when she heard sounds of footsteps inside and at last the door began to inch open, but so slowly the effect was creepy. Mrs Hibbert coughed nervously, and said, 'Chrissie? It's me, Aunt Mary, dear.' The door opened a little wider, pulled back by the fingers of a delicate white hand. Mrs Hibbert stepped inside, leaving her suitcase for the moment, and repeated, 'Chrissie?' Behind the door she saw a young woman in a white nightdress whom she knew to be Chrissie, but who bore little resemblance to the person she had last seen some weeks ago in St Mary's. She seemed to be trembling, her hair was unbrushed, and her complexion was putty-coloured. 'Dear me, Chrissie,' Mrs Hibbert said, and Chrissie began to weep.

*

Two days later, Mrs Hibbert was in control. Chrissie had been put to bed with a hot drink, and there she was going to stay until this supposed 'fever' had passed. She hadn't tried to argue with the girl, who had diagnosed herself as having a fever, but frankly she didn't believe it. If this was a fever, it was of the mind, not the body, but Chrissie was the doctor and so it was best to accept her word. But the young woman was happy enough to stay in her bed and be brought tea and toast the first day then soup the next day. She sat up nicely and let her hands and face be washed and obediently lay down again when the tray was taken away after she'd drunk the soup. She said thank you all the time, and tried to smile. It seemed a relief to her to be cossetted and it was a relief to Mrs Hibbert to do the cossetting.

But at night, she worried. The bed she was in was perfectly

comfortable and the room pleasant if smaller than she was used to, but she could not sleep. Chrissie was like a little girl, polite and obedient, pathetic in her eager dependency, and it made Mrs Hibbert uneasy for reasons which had very little to do with Chrissie herself. It was the echoes which bothered her, echoes at first of her own past – her mother looking after her and the bliss of it all, of her brow being soothed and her cheek kissed, and the way her mother tiptoed out of her room and her voice shushing her brothers on the stairs, a voice heavy with concern. Where did it go, that concern? Mrs Hibbert strained to remember. It seemed to have evaporated when she went to boarding-school. That first holiday, back from school for Christmas, she had had flu and her mother seemed annoyed more than anything: it was suddenly a trouble for her to bring hot drinks and feel the invalid's forehead. There was none of that anxious tenderness for her welfare which used to be such a comfort. It was all to do with growing up, she'd supposed, a natural process of separation, and she had tried to be brave about it. Once, her mother had seemed to recognise this new distance between them, she'd said, 'What an affectionate child you used to be, Mari!' as though it was her daughter and not herself who had spoiled their intimacy. Then there was another kind of echo. Inevitably, she was reminded of Francis that last week, when she had mistaken . . . She forced the memory away. This would not do.

She concentrated instead on thinking about Chrissie, wondering if she had ever had a boyfriend. (Actually, she meant a lover, but that was how she put it in her mind, a boyfriend, feeling deeper speculation would be prurient.) Surely she had. She was pretty and pleasant, even if she made nothing of herself and spoiled her looks by her untidiness of dress. She wanted to ask the girl about friends but could not quite find tactful words. Certainly, there were few phone calls about Chrissie's state of health. Mrs Hibbert had been in residence three days, and the phone had rung only once, and that had been Mr Wallis's secretary saying he thought she should take a much longer break once her flu had gone, have a real holiday. Mrs Hibbert hadn't known that Chrissie's ailment was flu, but she went along with this and said she thought the invalid's temperature was down and she was feeling a bit better. This was true, Chrissie did seem better, whatever had been wrong with her, and on the fourth day she got up and dressed and came downstairs. Instantly, things were much more awkward. Dealing with Chrissie when she was a wreck was one thing, dealing with her when she had recovered was another. It was her house, after all. Suddenly, Mrs Hibbert was not in control. She was a guest, and she was not good at being a guest. She didn't like how Chrissie did things but it would have been impolite to complain about her never making tea properly (tea should be made in a teapot, not by merely dunking a tea-bag in a mug of not-even-properly-boiling water) or leaving bread in the toaster at too high a setting so that it burned. The kitchen quickly became an area of confrontation over trifles, and Mrs Hibbert wanted to get away from it.

'Chrissie,' she said, on the morning of the fourth day, after an uncomfortable hour during which they said nothing to each other, 'Chrissie, I think I'll go home now that you're better.' The response had been entirely unexpected and alarming. 'No!' Chrissie had almost shouted. 'No, please, Aunt Mary, not yet.' 'But I'm doing no good,' said Mrs Hibbert. 'I'm just in the way now you're up and about.' 'You're company,' Chrissie said, 'I want company, please, for a little while longer. I can't explain . . . I . . . I know I'm being feeble, but . . . with everything that's happened.' 'Well,' Mrs Hibbert said, 'I'll stay until the weekend, then, but on Thursday I must go to the hospital for the afternoon. I'm on duty, I can't let the Friends down. Will you be all right on your own for a few hours?' Chrissie nodded. 'And I can't go on doing nothing here,' Mrs Hibbert went on. 'I can't sit around like yesterday. You must let me give the place a good clean and do something about the garden. You can help me, sitting around does no one any good, you should know that.'

But Chrissie did sit around while Mrs Hibbert tackled first the housework and then the gardening. She obligingly shifted rooms, so that Mrs Hibbert could wash the floors without hindrance, and she went upstairs while the hoovering was being done, but mostly she sat watching as her house was thoroughly cleaned, a kind of baffled wonder showing in her expression as the (to her) strangest things were done. She had never thought of taking all the cushions off her sofa and using an attachment on the hoover, which she hadn't even known existed, to suck all the dust and crumbs out of the crevices beneath. She could tell that her aunt was shocked at what she was uncovering – the evidence of sheer neglect. When, in the afternoon, the garden was tackled, Chrissie stayed inside and watched through the window. She saw her aunt standing, hands on hips, surveying it and frowning hard. There was a patch of dandelion-filled grass, 12 feet by 12, with a border of soil round it, covered in weeds and nothing else. Her aunt spent two hours digging up the dandelions and digging over the soil, and then hauled out the brand-new Flymo and cut the grass. Afterwards, she spent some time measuring the fences at the back and the sides, announcing when she was finished that the next day she'd be going to the garden centre on her way home from St Mary's.

Why, Chrissie wondered, as another difficult evening was spent together, the atmosphere restless and frustrating, do I want her here? Her presence, so far from being congenial, was oppressive. Her aunt, she saw, was a woman of energy and vigour who had always to be doing something or about to do something. There was nothing peaceful about her, nothing companionable. Her style of conversation was abrasive, endlessly querying perfectly harmless remarks, and trying to make something of them. Silence was preferable, but even her silences smouldered. And yet there was a confidence and power about her which, in her present state, made Chrissie feel protected. They both sat ostensibly reading, but Chrissie's eyes were fixed not on the print of her book but on her aunt, who was immersed in a newspaper. She was, Chrissie noted, systematic in this as in everything, beginning at the top left of the front page and working her way down to the right bottom corner before turning over. She should have been a doctor, Chrissie thought. Patients, my patients, would have loved her assurance even if they would also have been a little intimidated. She would have told Carol Collins not to be so silly, there was nothing wrong with her, and she would have been believed. Chrissie's eyes filled with tears at the thought. Unfortunately, Aunt Mary chose that moment to look over at her.

'Good heavens, Chrissie, what on earth is the matter? Are you feeling ill again?' Chrissie shook her head. 'Well, then, what is upsetting you? What is this about?' Chrissie blew her nose, dabbed at her eyes. 'Nothing,' she said. She felt about 10 years old. Aunt Mary held her gaze, seeming to come to a decision. 'It's guilt, isn't it?' she said. 'You're feeling guilty about that young woman. Oh, I know you haven't said so, but I'm not a fool, Chrissie. I know what all this is about, and I know it's nonsense. You've nothing to feel guilty for. The young woman was unbalanced, she jumped to conclusions because of her mental state. She was ill, and when people are ill, they do things they wouldn't normally contemplate. You ought to know what that feels like, being in a state, you're in one now, *you're* not of sound mind at the moment.' Chrissie lowered her eyes. 'No, it's not that, not just that,' she whispered. 'It's me. I can't do it. I can't do the clinics. I can't stand it. I don't want to do it. I'm useless, it scares me.' She wept, waiting for the order to stop being so silly, but it didn't come. 'I'm sorry,' she said, after a minute or two. 'I'm sorry.' 'No need to be,' Aunt Mary said. 'We've all felt like crying over our uselessness at some time or other. What we have to decide is what to do about it. That's the hard part, what to do once one has realised what the trouble is. Now, what can you do? Think about your life and how to change it. What steps can you take?'

Chrissie stared at her, transfixed. She felt as if she were at school again, called before the headmistress to explain herself and quite unable to do so. She did what she always did in such circumstances, smiled, dropped her head, mumbled. What she mumbled was indistinct. 'What?' Mrs Hibbert said, trying not to sound irritated, though really it *was* very irritating when people did not speak clearly. 'What was that, Chrissie? I didn't quite catch what you said, dear.' Chrissie sighed and repeated, 'I don't know what I can do. Give up being a doctor, I suppose. Do something else. Or become a different kind of doctor, do something that doesn't mean seeing patients, research maybe.' There was silence. She was obliged, eventually, to raise her head. Mrs Hibbert was staring at her as though in serious doubt now as to her sanity. 'Give up?' she repeated, but quite gently, sounding not so much incredulous or scandalised as bewildered. 'But Chrissie, you're needed, you're the sort of doctor women want.' 'No,' said Chrissie, 'I'm not. They want decisive, confident doctors, that's what they want.' Aunt Mary was shaking her head. 'What women want,' she said, 'is kindness and sympathy and understanding, as well as expertise, of course. You have all those qualities in abundance, Chrissie. It is your duty to carry on. Have a long holiday, dear, go away somewhere nice, then come back and you'll be fine.' 'I won't,' said Chrissie. 'I can't bear it, I'm sick of it. I have to get out.'

Mrs Hibbert took a deep breath. The thought of the sheer *waste* made her heart pound and she knew her blood pressure was soaring. Trying to speak in measured tones, she said, 'Chrissie, look at me, please. What do you think you see before you? An elderly woman, of course, but what else? You've no idea, have you, how I would like to have been you. I would like to have been a doctor. I would like to have had a career a great deal more fulfilling than the one I had. I would have liked to be in a position to help people, as you help them. I would have liked to go to university, but I allowed my father to push me into secretarial work. *You* have done all the things I would like to have done and I cannot bear to hear you disparage yourself and your achievement. To hear you say you want to give up shocks me. It is your *duty* to stay. I feel I speak in place of your mother, who . . .'

Chrissie had got up and was walking slowly to the door. 'Chrissie, dear, I'm sorry, I didn't mean . . . Chrissie, please, this is childish, do sit down, do come back . . .' But the girl had gone, there was no reply, and upstairs she heard a door gently close. It was so rude, to disappear like that, and after all the effort that she had made. She would leave. Not tonight, that would be foolish, and she was in no state to drive, but tomorrow, when in any case she was going to do her stint as a Friend. She simply would not come back. She would leave a note, informing Chrissie of this decision if the girl did not have the grace to apologise in the morning.

Going to bed herself half an hour later, having drunk too much tea and with the uncomfortable prospect of having to get up frequently in the night to get rid of it, Mrs Hibbert found her anger fading. In its place came embarrassment. She could not bear to think about what she had said, and not just said but made into a veritable speech. Her words, in so far as she could accurately recall them (and that was all too accurately), hadn't begun to tell Chrissie what she had wanted to say, but then how was it possible verbally to convey her sense of frustration with the way things had turned out? Her whole body ached with longing to be able to use what she had known was in her, that deep sense of having more to offer than was being asked of her. Francis may have been the only one to understand her, but even Francis had not appreciated the gnawing passion of an ambition which had not only never found its mark but never been properly identified, nor had he realised how much she blamed herself. Of course she was to blame, but what had she told Chrissie? That her father had pushed her into secretarial work. But had she tried to resist his direction? Had she tried to do what she wanted to do, become a gardener, later on, when he was dead? Well, she'd tried, but failed, given up easily. And what's more, she had lied to Chrissie: she had never wanted to be a doctor. The sight of blood made her faint.

She wished Chrissie had questioned her, she wished she had wanted to know more, to inquire into the details of what she had been told. She seemed unaware of what it had cost her aunt to make those admissions. Probably, Mrs Hibbert reflected as she lay wide awake in the dark, she thought she was being preached at and could not stand it. Or else despised, being made to feel ashamed, reminded of her duty. A mistake, Mrs Hibbert now saw. It never worked, trying to shame people into things. She should instead have boosted Chrissie's ego, told her of what high regard she was held in by staff and patients alike, impressed upon her the good she did. But did she know anything of how Chrissie was regarded? The odd complimentary remark, made within her hearing and impossible not to register, had come her way. Rita, the receptionist in Mr Wallis's clinic, had been heard to say, 'Dr Harrison will see you soon, you'll like her, she's very gentle and kind' to a distraught woman; and a patient leaving the clinic and losing her way, till Mrs Hibbert rescued her, had remarked that she felt so relieved because that nice young woman doctor had made her feel there was hope. Not much to go on, but she could have made much of it. Too late. Chrissie's self-esteem was wrecked.

Shifting restlessly in the bed, Mrs Hibbert tried to be practical. What was it she had urged Chrissie to do? To think of what steps she could take to solve her problem. Well, there were surely steps other than entirely giving up being a doctor. Chrissie needed to get the doctoring into proportion. It seemed to consume her life, and the anxiety and responsibility that went with it, together with all the attendant misery, overwhelmed her. So far as she could make out, Chrissie had no other life. Few friends, no hobbies, no recreational life. Mrs Hibbert knew how being on your own you risked madness when in the grip of some obsessive idea. Work, work, work. Worry, worry, worry. Chrissie believed herself to be self-sufficient. On the contrary, she was in desperate need of support, and of distraction. The girl was emotionally exhausted, quite drained. She needed something put back, but where was that something to come from?

Sleep came finally, just as she was beginning to feel demented at the lack of answers, but when she woke up, Mrs Hibbert felt as though she hadn't slept at all. Her head ached and her eyes felt heavy. Washing and dressing were an effort. Before she went downstairs, she packed her case, but left it for the moment in the bedroom – it would look far too melodramatic to walk down the stairs, humping her case. There was a pleasant smell of coffee floating up from below, which seemed a hopeful sign (though hope of what she wasn't sure). Francis had ground his own beans and the smell had been delicious. Her mood was affected by this memory and she walked into the kitchen feeling less harassed than when she woke up. The thing to do was be calm, calm and polite, and to make no reference to the evening before. Yet she could not help feeling a little hesitant and nervous at the thought of facing Chrissie again. It annoyed her to feel this flutter of nerves. She was too old for nerves, this was absurd.

Chrissie was not in the kitchen. There was evidence that toast had been made, and a jar of marmalade stood open beside the bread board; and feeling the coffee machine, Mrs Hibbert almost burnt her fingers. The coffee had been very recently made, poured out and taken elsewhere. Elsewhere could only mean the sitting-room, so Mrs Hibbert called out, 'Good morning', to show she was not in a sulk, and began cutting bread to make her own breakfast. She put the kettle on, made tea, and all the time she was listening. It was beginning to make her curious that Chrissie had not responded to her greeting – anxious, and then, as time went on, annoyed. It was not polite to ignore a greeting. She did not feel inclined, in the circumstances, to take her tea and toast through to the sitting-room. Instead, she sat at the kitchen table, a circular affair of white painted wood, and ate and drank. It didn't take long. Then she scrupulously washed and dried her mug and plate, and put them away. She would go now. 'Chrissie,' she began, walking towards the sitting-room door, which was ajar and opened wider to her push, 'Chrissie . . .'

But there was no Chrissie. She stood perplexed, and then began to search the house, calling out Chrissie's name. The house was empty. She had not heard the front or back doors opening and closing, but Chrissie had left. The last place to check was the garage, one in a row about 50 yards from the terrace of houses. Mrs Hibbert hurried over there, breathless, uneasy, but the up-and-over door was closed and locked, and there was no sound. It was all too distressing for words. Back she went into the house, and up the stairs to fetch her suitcase. Chrissie had left no note, made no goodbyes, but she felt it would be petty of her to do the same, so she wrote a brief note, saying she had decided to return home after she'd been to the hospital, and that she hoped Chrissie would telephone her in the evening to reassure her all was well, because she could not help but be worried. She left it prominently displayed, propped up against the fruit bowl on the kitchen table. Then she left the house and drove to St Mary's, feeling aggrieved but at the same time relieved. At that moment she didn't care if she never saw Chrissie again.

*

Chrissie had walked a long way, for an hour, following the river path, before she allowed herself to stop. She'd walked fast, arms swinging, head in the air, glad that with the path so clear she did not need to decide which direction to take. She'd met no one. It was early, rain threatened, no one except dog-walkers went this way at this hour. It was something so new to her, to be out walking with no purpose in the morning, that the novelty of it was almost exciting. It made her want people at St Mary's to see her – look, look, it's Dr Harrison enjoying a walk! She's swinging along! She's happy! Look and be amazed! She smiled a real smile, at her own teasing, and felt the skin on her cheeks stretch and bunch. She wished she had a mirror to admire herself, to check that she looked as transformed as she felt. She wasn't any longer that worried creature she'd become, always fretting, and she was going to prove it. Aunt Mary could not know it, but the effect of her little homily had been the opposite of what she had intended. It hadn't made her ashamed of wanting to give up being a doctor but, on the contrary, convinced her that she should do so, as soon as possible. She'd written to Mr Wallis at three o'clock in the morning. The official letter of resignation to the hospital board could wait until later, but she felt the deed was done. She was free.

The river path ran out and turned inward as it neared the town, cutting through warehouses and coming out on to the main road. Chrissie turned back, content to retrace her steps, no longer in such a hurry. Of course, she had behaved badly to Aunt Mary, leaving like that, abandoning her without a word of explanation, but guilt couldn't spoil her sense of elation. She would apologise, and then she would have to try to justify her behaviour. 'Think about your life,' Aunt Mary had urged, and that was what she had done. She'd thought, and realised that she was spending it agonising, always fearful that she might make the wrong decision. She was spending it unable to separate women from their diseases, haunted by what they were going through, or about to go through, and which she could not protect them from. She was a *hopeless* doctor and yet she had no other existence except as a doctor. 'Think about your life,' Aunt Mary had said, expecting to fill her with pride at her role, but she wasn't proud, she was appalled. She'd tried hard enough, for years and years, and now she was not going to try any longer.

So what would she do? It didn't seem to bother her. As she

sauntered along now, admiring the view of hills in the distance, and passing several people walking dogs, and a lone cyclist, she thought that a decision about what to do could wait. Maybe she could indeed turn to some kind of medical research which involved no direct contact with people, or maybe go into some kind of administration where contact with people would not mean coping with their emotions. She could see herself at a desk in a quiet room, perhaps sifting through material or else writing reports. Or maybe in a laboratory, carefully checking experiments. She was after all a careful person. The important thing, whatever she did, was to remain detached, not to allow herself to be crippled with worry. She wanted a job that started at nine and ended at five and did not go home with her. Aunt Mary would despise this, but then she craved the very intimacy with people's lives which Chrissie knew she had to free herself from. At this very moment, as she was relishing her walk, Mr Wallis and Ben Cohen and Andrew Fraser were all preparing to begin clinic, and in that clinic would be terrified women praying for news that was more likely not to be good, as they desired, but bad, or at the very best equivocal. Why would anyone in their right mind want to be in the position of power of those doctors? Not I, not I, sang Chrissie to herself.

She saw Aunt Mary's note from the front door, even before she got as far as the kitchen. What luck, she thought, what luck not to have to explain eyeball to eyeball. Not that she would have weakened in her resolve, but she was glad not to have to see disappointment and maybe worse in her aunt's eyes. Her aunt would feel let down and upset. Better to do the telling at a distance. She would ring her, later, when she was back from her stint at the hospital. But now Chrissie had the first day of her freedom to savour and though she did not quite know how she was going to do it, the prospect pleased her. Already, the images in her head were not as troublesome, the faces that had pressed in upon her not as clear. They had crowded in on her for so long, dozens of them, patient after patient with eyes fixed on her beseechingly, looking for what she was rarely able to give, and wearing expressions of barely concealed anxiety with real panic not far away. She'd felt she was stemming a great tide of hopelessness and was being swept away by it herself. So often, so very often, she had wanted to push the patient off the bed and climb on to it herself. She'd wanted to be cared for, she'd wanted someone else to be in control. That had been her mistake. Aunt Mary had shown it to her. She only wanted someone else to be in control because she couldn't cope with what she was doing, she was wrong for it. It was the work, not herself, which she wanted someone else to control. She could be in charge of herself perfectly easily if she let the work go. If this meant she was a failure, she could accept that.

There was nothing to do in the house. Aunt Mary had left it immaculate. She'd watched her bustling about and marvelled at the satisfaction the older woman clearly derived from imposing order and from all the cleaning and washing that went with it. It occurred to Chrissie that she could ask her aunt to help her carry out the plans she had outlined for the garden, get her to buy the plants she had mentioned at the garden centre, offering the money to do so, of course. Maybe they would go together, make a day of it, have lunch at a riverside pub, make friends with each other, why not? She would take the initiative. And thinking that she would do this, she thought of other ways in which she could, and should, do the same thing, take the lead for once. She felt pulled back from some catastrophic breakdown – it took her breath away to think how close she'd been to collapse. She stood in her kitchen looking out on to the bare soil borders Aunt Mary had dug over and imagined them full of colour, brimming with flowers. All she had to do was plant them. It made her look forward to the evening and the call she would make to Aunt Mary.

*

Arriving home was not quite the exquisite pleasure that Mrs Hibbert had expected it to be. After the light and sparseness of Chrissie's modern little house, her own seemed dark and cluttered, and much too big. Martin had watered the indoor plants as instructed, but she suddenly didn't care for them any more and in a fit of irritation banished the two palms to the greenhouse.

There hadn't been much post: a reminder that she had a dental appointment, an invitation to the opening of the new wing of the local public library, and the gas bill. Nothing interesting, though why she expected there to be she couldn't think.

She must get a grip. The familiar tiredness after an afternoon at the hospital seemed more enervating than usual, but then it had come at the end of a difficult week, and she had had more demands made of her patience than was normal. It seemed to her that from all sides she had been harassed by patients clamouring for help and no one else had responded to their obvious need except herself. She had actually left early, her head aching and her legs sore. For the first time that she could remember, the hospital had seemed an awful, chaotic place, full of mad people rushing around, and not a place in which to be healed. Everywhere she had turned there was something pitiful to catch her eye and she had been shocked at her own despair. It was only a little after half past six but she decided that the only thing to do was go to bed, straight away. She would have tea and toast – and *that* was not very sensible, she lectured herself, considering she hadn't eaten anything else since she'd had tea and toast for breakfast – and then have a hot bath and go to bed. In the morning, she would feel better.

Martin was coming to do the back hedge again, it would help to talk to him. The telephone rang as she got into her bath. She didn't answer it. Too much was asked of her, everyone wanted something from her and there was no one to listen to what she might want.

8

Soaring

THE ENTRANCE to the airfield was difficult to find – Rachel had missed it the first few times – situated as it was behind a thick hedge running along the track marking the foot of the ridge. She was early, deliberately. The gliding club officially opened on Sundays at nine o'clock but it was only eight-thirty. By nine there would already be a queue for the winch and she wanted to be in the air by then. It was a perfect morning for gliding, with just the right amount of wind, just the right scatter of cumulus promising excellent thermals.

John, her instructor, was already waiting, as keen as she was to be ahead of the crowd. He was a man of few words, which suited her fine. He hadn't once asked her what she did for a living, or where she lived, or if she had a boyfriend. Greeting Rachel with a mere nod, he watched as she went through the routine inspection of the glider: cockpit, wings, tail, fuselage, all gone over carefully, checked for cracks, holes, dents or bruising. He attached a rope to the glider and gave the thumbs up to the driver of the car, to which the other end was tied. Then she took hold of the nose of the K13 and he took a wing tip and together they balanced the glider as it was pulled gently along. This walk to the launch pad always felt exciting and there were flutters of anticipation in her stomach.

She put on the slim back parachute, opened the canopy, and settled herself in the front seat while John climbed into the back. The controls had baffled her at first – they'd seemed so much more formidable than those of a car – but now she was familiar with them and able to operate them on her own (though her confidence came from knowing that John had his own set at the back). She zipped up her jacket and pulled her woollen hat down over her ears. It was always cold in the air, no matter how warm the day seemed. Then she gave the signal for the winch to be wound in, and they were off. But the tricky bit, the releasing of the cable at the point when the winch had done its work and no more height could be gained, was still to come. Her heart always raced and her mouth went dry until she'd done it.

Then came the exhilarating part. They were in the air, cable released, at a little over 1,000 feet, with the whole of the valley before them. The glider flew into the air rising faster than it was sinking down, and she felt the thrilling lift as they soared higher still. It made her gasp, to be so buoyant, but she remembered to correct the angle of the nose so that the glider would not stall. They were coming already to the first turn and she tensed, not yet expert at using the ailerons to bank the wings. Checking that her airspeed was steady, she applied a little rudder to the left, the direction in which she had been instructed to go. It was a beautifully executed turn, making the most of the thermals circling in the air. There was time now to look about, to notice the huddle of sheep on the flank of the hill to the right, and the scarred ground above the river where trees had been felled.

She forgot about John. He'd said that today he was coming for the ride and didn't expect to have to do anything – she should just enjoy herself. She thought about what he'd said during her first lesson: she could only stay in the air by her own efforts. She wasn't depending on an engine but, once airborne, was entirely dependent on making use of what nature had to offer. That was precisely what appealed to her about gliding. The structure and fabric of the glider were between her and the air, but she felt herself attuning to its invisible currents, swaying and lifting and swooping with them. It was like a kind of dance and she gave herself to its rhythms. But she didn't manage the second turn so well, misjudging the angle, and John had to correct it for her. Annoyed, she concentrated harder and made no more mistakes. She longed to fly on and on, but her time was up, the K13 had another booking, and she had to make the final turn and land. Always, there was that sense of disappointment as the glider wobbled to a standstill – she was greedy for more, more. It would be another six months, quick learner though she was, before she could fly off on her own and make a proper journey.

For a while, Rachel stayed on the airfield, busy now, watching gliders take off and land. It was extraordinary the way that on the ground they were so ungainly and yet in the air so graceful. In the distance, they were like giant birds, seagulls, swooping above the tiny puffs of clouds. Some soared to great heights and she gazed up at them in envy, longing to be able to do the same, to dip and wheel and skim in the sky. She already knew, even though she had as yet only made circuits of the airfield, how powerful was the psychological effect – she could swear that, while flying, some mysterious current was sweeping through her veins and she fancied that it was a cleansing current, burning up all that was bad as it coursed through her. Excitement, that was all it was, and that edge of danger within it.

She'd no desire to go home. Sitting in her car she wondered where she could go on this lovely morning. To the sea, maybe, or into the hills, or along the river. The options were generous. Slowly, she began to drive away.

*

Morning service over (only seven present), Cecil Maddox went back to the vicarage and changed his clothes. He chose old flannel trousers, a white open-necked shirt, a blue V-necked thin sweater, and a grey linen jacket. He didn't reckon he would need a jacket but he wanted pockets in which to put his sandwich and his apple, and in any case the warmth of the day might disappear. He made some coffee and poured it into a flask which went into a holder with a strap he could slip over his shoulder. It was only just after midday and he didn't need to be back until an hour or so before evensong, but as he stepped out of the vicarage and into his car he felt guilty. No reason why he shouldn't go walking but he felt that in this parish there would be bound to be those who would feel it was unseemly – a vicar ought to be in his study on the Sabbath, reading his Bible.

He drove rather fast out of the town, noting that everything was shut and that an air of abandonment hung over the place, as though life itself had departed. He'd no idea, once he'd crossed the bridge, which way he would choose to go but he hardly gave the signpost a glance. A car ahead of him took the road to the next town, the bigger one, and another followed the road to the sea, so he chose the empty road, leading he knew not where. After a mile or so, he realised he was heading towards the hills. He shivered slightly, knowing that this meant he would have to climb one of them. It was a sign and he would obey it. Once, while still in his Manchester parish, he had volunteered to help take the boys in the church youth club to this part of the country, to go climbing, even though he'd never climbed a real hill in his life and never wanted to. His services had been declined. There were enough adults going, the youth leader had said, but he had felt that that was not the reason why he had been excluded from the party.

He had neither map nor guidebook. No need for either. All he was looking for was some very clear path, which he would follow to the top and then descend by. Nothing ambitious. About ten miles along the narrow road, he saw a lay-by and in the middle of it a stile, a strong, ladder-type construction going over a wall. It was bound, he felt, to have a path the other side. There was a car parked there already, which put him off a bit, but he couldn't see anyone around and concluded it must belong to a farmer who was perhaps inspecting his field and would soon be gone. Climbing the stile, he was gratified to find the kind of path he had been looking for. It cut across the empty field then turned sharply right and disappeared into the wood only to be visible above it, coming out and climbing straight up the slope of the hill. It would do. He was so pleased that he found himself murmuring out loud, 'God's in His heaven, all's right with the world.' Not true, of course. All was not right, either in his own world or the world at large, but he liked saying it.

The wood was dense. He hadn't realised how dark it would be inside, the sun failing to do more than prick through the tightly packed trees. But the path was still easy to follow even when fallen tree-trunks occasionally blocked the way. The sound of his own feet was loud – twigs snapped, stones were disturbed and, though he had always thought of himself as nimble, he felt like an elephant charging through the undergrowth. Once out of the wood, the path became grassy and he no longer advertised his presence with every step. He couldn't imagine how this path could have become so smooth – it was as though someone had taken a lawn-mower to it – or so even, 2 feet across all the way. There was an unexpected satisfaction in gaining height so rapidly, and a sense of definite achievement in the physical effort involved. He thought that in spite of his sedentary life he must be quite fit because he was hardly out of breath until he reached the last stretch before the summit. Here the path narrowed and became stony, and there was some scrambling to be done but he enjoyed it. And then at last he was on top, where there was a cairn to which he added his own rock, taking pleasure in choosing a stone whiter and rounder than the ones already piled up. It was windy up here, and he was glad he'd kept his jacket on, buttoning it to the neck and turning the collar up.

Settling himself against the cairn, he ate his cheese sandwich and his apple, and drank half the coffee. Far off, the sea was a stretch of silver light below the dark outline of more hills on the other side. He was looking, he supposed, at an estuary. The first settlers must have come up it – from where he didn't know, his ignorance shamed him – and then followed the river until they found the valley with its fertile land and the shelter it promised. The scene below was not, he realised, an empty one. Everywhere he looked, he saw the work of man. There was evidence of human endeavour all around, not just in the cottages and farmhouses and barns, but in the stone walls and the roads and the fences and hedges. Arriving, on that first day, he had not been aware of this. A conviction that this was a desolate land to which he had been condemned had filled him, and the loneliness he'd experienced had overwhelmed him. But up here, where truly he was alone, he did not feel lonely. He felt master of himself – it was being down there that made him feel lonely.

Reluctant to descend, he took his time, pausing often to admire the view. Then, half-way down, before he once more entered the wood, he saw a figure standing by his car. He couldn't be sure – the distance was still too great – but he thought it was a woman, waiting for him. At once, the contentment he had been feeling vanished. The owner of the other car, almost certainly. But why was she waiting for him? What did she want of him? He immediately felt anxious and suspicious, and wondered if he could delay going down, even hide, until this person grew tired of waiting. But she would have seen him, he was sure that he stood out on the path at this point. And he couldn't delay indefinitely, with evensong to think about. He had to get back. All the way down through the wood he was rehearsing what he would do and say. He would climb briskly over the stile, a man in a hurry, and rush at once to his car, avoiding eye contact. Maybe he'd shout, 'Hello! Must dash, lovely day', so as not to cause offence. He wished he had a clerical collar on so that his status would make it easier to add, if necessary, that he had a church service to take and shouldn't have been climbing at all. This person would not know him, they were strangers to each other, which might make things less difficult.

His panic was foolish. Just before he left the sanctuary of the wood he paused to scold himself. It was always the same, he dreaded these kinds of encounter, and there was no need to. He could see the waiting person clearly now. It was indeed a woman, a young woman. She let him climb the stile and then, as he stepped backwards off it, she said, 'Hello. I'm so glad to see you. I thought I'd be stuck here for ever. Not another car has passed since I got back half an hour ago.' She pointed at her own car and he saw the flat tyre. 'Ah,' he said, 'I see. I'm afraid I won't be much good to you. Dreadful admission, but I don't know how to change a tyre, terribly sorry.' She would ask for a lift. He would have to give her a lift to the town, to a garage, which would mean a longish drive and having to talk to her – oh, stop it, he told himself, this attitude is unchristian and absurd. But she didn't want a lift. What she wanted was to borrow a jack, if he had one, claiming to be perfectly capable of changing her own tyre. To his own surprise, he did find a jack in the boot of his car, though he had no recollection of having put it there. He was about to say that she could keep it, and that he must go, but then she would be bound to want to return it and would need his address and might turn up . . . No, he would have to wait. So he stood watching the young woman, her deft performance making him feel more incompetent than ever. She had the job done quickly, and handed back the jack. He felt obliged to say how he admired her ability to change a tyre, more to prove that he was not boorish as well as unskilled at such tasks. And then he found himself actually asking her a question. It was only a simple, obvious inquiry, but he was startled at his own daring.

'Do you live near here?' he asked. She said no, and named the town thirty miles away. 'I'm a solicitor,' she volunteered, and then stopped abruptly, and blushed, as though startled at what she'd told him, ordinary piece of information though it had been. She said she belonged to a gliding club, and that after her lesson she had gone for a walk. As she finished speaking, a glider came into view and they both stood in silence watching it soar higher and then float away in the distance. 'So graceful,' he murmured, and then 'Do you fly alone?' She said she hadn't yet done so, that it would take her another six months before she would be able to, but that she was longing to reach that stage. It was she who said goodbye first, and got into her car with another expression of thanks. No names had been exchanged. Too late, he regretted not introducing himself, but then as he drove home decided he was glad this had been a brief meeting of strangers, one of whom had helped the other. There was something pure about the interchange which appealed to him.

He tore up the sermon he'd prepared as soon as he got to the vicarage. Making some rapid notes first about his climb and his feelings during it and then about the young woman and the changing of the tyre, he went on to weave all the topics together until he felt he had an original and uplifting new sermon to deliver on the subject of chance and how God allowed for it and valued it. His argument took cunning twists and turns – he had to admit that there was some forcing of connections – but the end result was, he judged, powerful. He strode across to the church inspired in a way he had not been for a long time. There were only twelve people in the congregation but this did not depress him. In a clear, strong voice he delivered his sermon and was for once sure that he held everyone's attention and that he had been understood – there was no coughing, no fidgeting, and he had a strange impression that if this had been a theatre and not a church then applause would have followed.

He went to bed almost happy.

*

He slept well that night, the first time for ages that he was not plagued with dreams in which he was forever stretching out his arms and begging to be held. Refreshed, he dressed carefully for his visit to St Mary's Hospital, choosing his one good dark suit, though he disliked wearing it. At the end of his convalescence, he had gone for a holiday to Italy and had been so happy to dress in white or cream trousers and delicately coloured shirts, lilacs and blues – he had felt better, quite liberated (though that feeling had almost been his undoing again). But today he had to look like a vicar and so his dark suit and clerical collar and highly polished black leather shoes were appropriate. He put his notebook and a pen in an inside pocket, and his spectacles in another. They were unattractive spectacles which did not suit the shape of his face, but he had been unable to bear looking in the mirror in the optician's while choosing them – his own image had repelled him and he had made too hasty a decision. Still, the unfortunate spectacles made him look suitably serious and grave, which was a good thing. Everything was an act, after all.

St Mary's was easy to find but the entrance to it was not. He had to go twice round the one-way system before he found it and was irritated with himself for becoming flustered. Once, he'd negotiated the streets of Manchester easily but already his living in a small country town appeared to have eroded his driving skills and made him nervous in traffic. Given more time, he could see he would end up like the majority of his parishioners, scared to drive anywhere busy. Finding the room where the committee meeting was to be held took almost as long as getting into the hospital itself – he seemed to trudge miles, constantly bewildered by signs and having to ask directions in spite of them. St Mary's, he discovered, was a rabbit warren of a building, full of odd connecting passages which sometimes seemed more like tunnels and came out at different levels. He started to perspire, not with any physical effort but with the memories. He'd walked other corridors such a great deal, backwards and forwards for hours, needing to keep moving, until the drugs had calmed him and made him sleepy.

They were all waiting for him, though he was not late. He hated entering a room full of people already seated and staring at him. Most of them half rose, some smiled and nodded, and the man at the head of the table, obviously the chairman, welcomed him. There was only one vacant chair, next to a large, imposing woman who looked vaguely familiar and yet he was sure he had not met her. 'Mrs Hibbert,' she said, sticking out her hand. 'We live quite near each other, I think. So pleased you could join us.' There was a general clearing of throats and then the chairman said how glad they all were that the Rev. Cecil Maddox had accepted the invitation to see how the Friends worked. If, during this meeting, he had any questions he must feel free to interrupt and ask them. Cecil stared straight ahead, avoiding all eyes, and composed himself to listen. The woman next to him, Mrs Hibbert, had a great deal to say, and the more she said the more obvious it was to him that the chairman could not bear her. He was wary of her, though. Every time he tried to cut across her interruptions he did so with suspiciously excessive politeness. Taking quick looks round the table, Cecil could see that everyone found Mrs Hibbert annoying, but nobody appeared to have the nerve to object to the way in which she was dominating the meeting.

'It is quite ridiculous,' she was saying, 'to spend money on refurbishing the chapel. It is hardly used, and it is not in any case our responsibility.'

'But the legacy is to the Friends, Mrs Hibbert,' said the chairman, 'and therefore the spending of the money is our responsibility.'

'We have many other calls on our purse,' Mrs Hibbert said.

'Ah, yes,' agreed the chairman, 'but, with respect, you are forgetting that our benefactor specified that she wished some of her money to be spent on the hospital chapel – '

'Then she should have left it to the hospital, or the church, whichever church looks after the chapel.'

'But she didn't, she left it to us, with this one request – '

'It is only a matter of buying some paint to freshen the walls, and material to run up new curtains,' a woman, timidly ventured.

'That is not the point,' Mrs Hibbert said. 'The point is, it would be a waste of good money. Patients who go to the chapel, and precious few even know where it is, don't care what the walls or curtains are like. They simply don't notice such details.'

'Far be it from me to question your knowledge, Mrs Hibbert, but how do you know this?' the chairman asked.

'Oh, I know,' Mrs Hibbert said. 'I've witnessed patients there. They don't notice anything. They go there as a last resort, depressed people who are desperate.'

'Our benefactor's husband was apparently a manic depressive,' said the chairman.

'Well, there you are,' said Mrs Hibbert.

'I'm not sure – I may be very stupid – that I do know where I am, where we are in this discussion,' he said.

'We are at the point when it ought to be obvious that newly painted walls and fresh curtains make no impression on depressed people – '

'Mrs Hibbert,' the chairman said, interrupting her for the first time, 'I must emphasise that the legacy is bound by the terms surrounding it. Whether we approve or not is irrelevant, whether depressed patients will benefit or not is equally irrelevant.'

'May I just add,' Cecil said, quietly, 'that in my experience not everyone who goes into a hospital chapel is depressed. Some patients go there to find peace and comfort. They may be frightened rather than depressed.'

'Same thing,' Mrs Hibbert snapped.

Cecil took care to keep his tone light. 'I beg your pardon?' he said.

'Same thing,' Mrs Hibbert repeated.

'I beg to differ,' Cecil said. 'Fear and depression are not the same thing.'

'They are linked,' Mrs Hibbert said. 'Depressed people are all frightened of something, or they wouldn't be depressed. It might just be that they are afraid of their own inadequacy, but frightened they are, and their fear is what makes them depressed. Simple. Believe me, I know what I'm talking about.'

Nobody knew how to react. Embarrassment was as thick as smoke in the air. Cecil felt stunned, and then outraged, but before he could comment on how extraordinary he found Mrs Hibbert's self-confident statement, the chairman took charge. Volunteers were called for to buy paint and material, and others to do the painting and sewing. They duly came forward and other business was moved on to. Throughout it, Cecil was acutely aware of Mrs Hibbert, sitting with a fearsomely straight back at his side, rigid with what he interpreted as hostility towards himself. He should not have spoken. The last thing he should have done was get drawn into any discussion about the causes of depression, and he was grateful that the chairman had put a stop to it before he had become properly engaged. But he pondered during the rest of the meeting over Mrs Hibbert's views. What did she know about depression? It seemed most unlikely that she had ever suffered from it herself, but one never knew. At the end of the meeting, he tried to linger behind so as not to exit with his neighbour, but she waited for him at the door. 'I wonder, Vicar,' she said, in a voice loud enough for everyone to hear, 'if I could drive you back?' Politely declining her offer, he pointed out that he had his own car. 'I thought perhaps you were not up to driving yet,' she said, in a tone of such sympathy that an irrational rage almost overcame him and he had to take refuge in a fit of coughing. 'I'm quite well, thank you,' he gasped at last.

Longing to escape her attention he was nevertheless obliged to wait for the lift with her and one other person, a nurse. Everyone else had gone in other directions and it was too late to follow them. He stood in one corner of the lift when it came, and Mrs Hibbert in the other with the nurse in between. The moment the nurse got out, Mrs Hibbert asked if he had yet visited the hospital chapel. He said no, but that he was about to, when he'd attended to another matter (the last thing he wanted was for her to offer to take him there). 'Strange places, hospital chapels,' she said, just before the ground floor was reached, 'but then the older I get, the stranger I find churches themselves. My late husband found churches inspiring, but I can't say I have ever done so. I can do without them, my own faith is independent of them.'

Cecil, watching Mrs Hibbert stalk off, thought he had enough clues now. The woman was one of those people, he deduced, who blamed the Church for some tragedy. They invariably resented that a relative or friend had found refuge in a church and appeared controlled by what they heard there. Either that, or they blamed a vicar for not being able to help their loved one in their hour of need. He'd been involved in a case like that himself. Once, a bereaved woman had hit him, shouting that her son had come to him for help and that he had been turned away, and that this had precipitated his suicide. It was all untrue, he had never turned anyone away, and he had spent hours with that particular young man (though it was true he had not been able to give him the answers he wanted to his impossible questions). But Mrs Hibbert did not seem like that grief-stricken mother. She seemed too sensible. On the other hand, as he reminded himself, the sensible can become foolish under intense strain, and he didn't know enough about Mrs Hibbert to be familiar with what had happened in her past.

The chapel in St Mary's, when he did find his way there, was shabby. Complaints about the state of it were correct. The room itself was small, a mere slot of a room with a low ceiling, making it claustrophobic. Some of the polystyrene tiles were coming away from the ceiling, hanging limply and yet threateningly from the corners. The walls were panelled in fake wood which had been varnished a dull yellow. Only the cross on the little altar table denoted that the room was a chapel – otherwise, it could, with its sad rows of chairs, have been just another waiting-room.

There was a faint antiseptic smell which he suspected came from a concealed air purifier, of the sort used in lavatories. There was no natural light, no windows. He pressed a switch near the door and a harsh fluorescent light dazzled him. Quickly, he put it out. He didn't need such overpowering illumination. Leaving the door slightly ajar so that the light from the corridor gave him some sense of direction, he moved towards the altar and knelt before it. This chapel had, he was sure, witnessed much suffering and agony of mind, and it shamed the trivial nature of his own feelings about Mrs Hibbert. His irritation with her, and his aversion towards her, showed him how far he had yet to come in his constant battle with his own nature. Head bowed, he prayed for tolerance towards others and for the gift of being able to help those who wanted help.

*

Edwina, passing St Mary's at the beginning of the long drive home, saw the vicar driving out of the car park. He had to wait at the lights, where the road she was on passed the main entrance, and she could see him clearly, his clerical collar standing out. He'd brought her luck, or rather her visit to his church had. That very day there had been a postcard from Emma – she'd gone home, upset at her own foolish behaviour, and there it had been, lying on the mat inside the door. It was a cheap, violently coloured card – the sea a garish turquoise, the sand impossibly white – and all it said was 'Cheers! Love, Emma and Luke.' It did exactly what it said, cheered her up. Scrutinising every inch of the card, she saw that it was from somewhere in Greece, though she couldn't make out exactly where. The postmark was blurred and the name of the place written in what she recognised as Greek without being able to understand it.

More cards followed, of the same beach. In fact, they were the same cards with the same message, only the date of the postmark different. Harry was not at all amused. It was, he said, a sign of laziness and of complete indifference to parental anxiety, but Edwina was determined to see it as a joke. She propped the cards up on the kitchen window-sill, and while she washed pans she smiled to see them – they were silly but amusing, surely. They meant Emma was safe and happy, and at least caring enough to establish some minimum contact. But the sight of these cards became less reassuring when, after another two weeks, nothing else had arrived. A month went by and then, just as Edwina was becoming truly worried and had taken the cards down, because suddenly they didn't comfort her, a letter arrived. With it was a photograph of Emma and Luke, obviously taken in some kind of booth, maybe at an airport. It was only a tiny black and white snap, but Emma was smiling (Luke was sticking his tongue out) and looked happy and healthy. The letter was hardly a letter. It was, as Harry pointed out, a paper serviette which had not taken the Biro very well. All it said was that Emma was having a brilliant time, the weather was heavenly, the swimming perfect, and that soon she and Luke would be travelling on but were not quite sure where.

The next card was posted in Tripoli. It said 'Africa! Yeah! On our way south!' Edwina rushed for the atlas. South? South from Tripoli would mean Niger or Chad. The thought horrified her – she was sure Emma would not have had all the necessary inoculations against nasty diseases like cholera and yellow fever and typhoid. Surely, Luke would not think of taking her through those countries. For once, Harry was consoling. South, he said, would just mean *in general* south. They would probably work their way along the north African coast and go south through places like Egypt. Even so, Edwina could not sleep for images of Emma dying of thirst in the desert. Then another card arrived, from Gibraltar. 'Whoops! Change of plan!' it said. That was all. Gibraltar made Edwina happy. It was so near, so healthy. She could tolerate Emma being in Gibraltar easily, even with Luke (who, she tried to remind herself, she might have misjudged).

She wondered, driving home, if she should perhaps ring Mrs Hibbert. It would be kind to let her know that Emma seemed safe, considering how concerned the woman had been when she disappeared. But then Edwina recalled that Mrs Hibbert had been not so much worried as furious that she had been let down. She suspected that Mrs Hibbert might be outraged rather than relieved to be told that Emma was having fun in Gibraltar. Better to do nothing. When Emma returned, she could go and apologise to Mrs Hibbert herself. An apology was what she most wanted.

9

On the Bench

EVERY MORNING, as he descended the stairs, Martin Yates drank a glass of cold water which he'd just taken from the bathroom. Down he went, slowly, not holding on to the banister, sipping the water. He could feel it doing him good. The furred feeling in his mouth cleared, and as the icy liquid trickled down his throat he felt his entire body brace itself for the day ahead. Ida shuddered at the idea of cold water first thing. What she needed was hot, sweet, strong tea, and plenty of it. He made it for her, every morning, always had done. A large pot of tea (loose-leaf, Ida didn't like tea-bags) and with it on the tray a small jug of milk and a bowl of sugar lumps. The tray was a souvenir of the Queen's Silver Jubilee, now much battered, and Her Majesty's image greatly faded, especially her crown. Martin added a plate with two digestive biscuits on it and then he carried it up to their bedroom. He called it 'their' bedroom, but he hadn't himself slept in it for a full night for three years. It was Ida's bedroom now.

Ida slept with the door wedged open with an old slipper so that he could hear her if she cried out. She might not want him in bed with her, but she needed him if she had a bad dream, as she often did. The room was dark, even though the morning was bright. The curtains were thick and lined, and pulled tightly together, though they didn't quite meet, and Martin's first job, once he had deposited the tray on the bedside table, was to part them slightly, though only enough to let a little light in. Then he switched the radio on. Ida groaned. He didn't know which station she had it set on but it always had music coming out of it, music of a sort. She liked to waken to it, she said it made waking easier, something he had never been able to understand. It made his head ache, the jingly-jangly nature of whatever it was. She liked to listen to it if she woke up in the middle of the night, too, she said it took her mind off things. It had maddened him, but he had had to put up with it, bowing to her greater need. Ida, he knew, was as afraid of silence as he was fond of it. All day she had either the radio or the television on, sometimes both, each in a different room, or else she listened to her CDs, mostly the sound-tracks of film musicals. He didn't much care for these either but Ida sang along to them and he loved her to sing, it made her happy. He just wished she would sing on her own, without any background accompaniment.

He opened the curtains a little wider. 'Beautiful morning,' he said, 'beautiful.' He stood for a moment, looking down on the box hedges lining the garden path, draped in cobwebs, swirling delicate webs of white mist laced through the dark green leaves, and at the lawn which paled into silver after the heavy dew. 'Beautiful,' he repeated. 'It'll be a good day. I'll get Mrs Hibbert's hedges cut.' Ida groaned again. He turned to look at her. She had hauled herself up out of the bedclothes and was groping for the teapot, her eyes still shut. A dangerous procedure, but he knew better than to rush over and pour her tea for her. Somehow, she managed to do this without mishap, and took a great gulp. She sighed, and took another, her eyes opening slightly. 'Better?' he asked. She nodded. 'Good,' he said, 'take it easy, no hurry,' and he left the room. She would stay in bed another hour at least. Even as a young woman she had found getting up a daily ordeal. When he'd been working at Cowan's and had had to clock on at 7.30 a.m., it had been hellish getting off on time with Ida comatose and both children bawling for milk or food and needing to be dressed. He'd often left the house without any breakfast, only a bit of dry bread in his hand, worrying all the way to work about Jimmy and Steve and whether they would do themselves some damage before Ida had roused herself. Nothing awful had ever happened, but he'd begun this ritual of taking her tea to wake her up, to try to make sure that it never did, and he'd continued it ever since. She depended on it and he knew it.

Standing in the kitchen, cooking his bacon, Martin gazed out of the window, still mesmerised by the dazzling light of the September morning. He could see shafts of sun already cutting through the mist and turning the dew on the grass into thousands of glittering points. Best time of the day, early morning. He was always telling Ida this, urging her to admire it with him, but she never had done. It was still cold, the sun might dazzle but as yet it had no warmth in it, but he loved the sharpness of the air and longed to be out running in it, breathing in great gulps of air, schooling his lungs to accept it and expand. Once, he'd gone off for five-mile runs at the weekend but he'd had to give them up when he turned fifty, and his right knee, where he'd had a cartilage removed, began to trouble him. He got his exercise gardening, and that had to be enough. Sometimes, even that could prove a struggle – it was heavy work he was called upon (by people like Mrs Hibbert) to do, the cutting of tall hedges, the trimming of trees and suchlike. His strength was his best asset and he had to keep it up.

But he still was strong. At sixty-four, he was still physically powerful, in spite of his knee problem. He never mentioned that to Ida, and if she had noticed his occasional limp she never commented on it, nor would he have wanted her to. It comforted him, when he worried about his knee, to be aware of how muscular he still was, not an ounce of fat on his stocky body, his belly still firm and flat, his chest broad and well developed. Ida had gone to seed. She'd had a gorgeous body when she was young. It had attracted him mightily, just the sight of it before he came to know it intimately. There wasn't a part of it not perfect, in his opinion – she was a stunner, with her lovely full breasts and her long shapely legs. He'd been a lucky man. Not that he'd married Ida for her looks, he hadn't been that carried away, but the prospect of enjoying them had certainly come into his reckoning. She wasn't beautiful so far as her face went – it was rather a bland face, the eyes a little too close together and the nose a little too large – but he'd looked beyond that and seen where her real loveliness lay. She'd felt the same about him, he knew that. He wasn't a good-looking young man but he had a splendid body and, stripped off to the waist, working as a labourer (which was how Ida first caught sight of him) he'd known how impressive his muscles looked to girls. The difference was, he'd always taken care of his body and Ida had not. She'd eaten all the wrong things – cream cakes, crisps, two sugars in her many cups of tea, the list was endless – and never taken any exercise whatsoever. She blamed her excess girth, when finally she noticed it, on having had children (but only two), on operations (various) and on The Change. She couldn't, she said, help being fat.

Mornings like this one, he felt especially sorry for Ida. He was going to be in the open air, working up a healthy sweat, and she was going to be lolling in the house, stuffing herself with rubbish, which would make her feel even more terrible than she already did. She was fond of saying that she got all the exercise she needed from doing the housework and helping to clean the church, but Martin had seen how she tackled both and doubted if she was vigorous enough to burn up a couple of calories never mind scores. He urged her at least to walk more, but she said her legs hurt if she went more than a hundred yards. She had varicose veins, the lovely legs ruined by them, and had resisted the necessary operation to have them stripped out – she said she'd had enough of operations. There was nothing Martin could say to that. The last one had been cruel. They had taken away a good quarter of her left breast and though she was told that this surgery had almost certainly saved her life she had never forgiven them. She hated the scar; Martin hated it too. He'd only seen it once. Once was enough. He was at fault, he knew he was, but the sight of it, soon after Ida came home, had made him feel sick. It wasn't the scar itself, raw and red and jagged though it was, but the idea of what had been taken out behind it, the thought of the flesh, bleeding and blubbery, scraped out, thrown away – he couldn't bear it. And Ida had seen this in his face, though he had said nothing, and he had seen in hers that dreadful mixture of distress and contempt before she pushed him away.

He got his bike out of the shed and checked the tyres. It was only a couple of miles to Mrs Hibbert's, a nice little ride, especially on such a morning. He'd taken his power saw and his strimmer by car to her house the day before, on the way back from another job, leaving him able to cycle today. He looked forward to working in Mrs Hibbert's garden – of all the people who employed him, she had the best garden – but Ida didn't like him to say so. She had never liked Mrs Hibbert, declaring that the woman was a snob, and bossy, and an interfering bitch who thought herself a great deal better than she was with her voluntary work – 'She's too good to be true,' Ida said. The first time they'd gone to the clinic, Mrs Hibbert had been on duty as a Friend, standing right in the middle of the entrance hall, and Ida had insisted on turning round and going out again and finding another way in. It had been excruciatingly embarrassing to realise Mrs Hibbert had seen them and watched them flee in such an undignified manner back out the way they had come. They had then trailed round to the side of the hospital and gone in through the A & E department, which had meant walking along miles of corridors and using two lifts before at last finding their way to the clinic. Ida had been in a rage, saying she wasn't going to set foot in St Mary's again, which was a ridiculous thing to say when she knew perfectly well there was no other hospital for miles around. Martin's own worry had been what Mrs Hibbert would say to him when next he saw her. But she had been tactful, discreet, never mentioning having seen him and Ida. He had reported this to Ida, asking her to give credit where credit was due, but none had been forthcoming.

He thought about Ida's intense dislike of Mrs Hibbert as he cycled along, wondering as ever what on earth had caused it. What, he'd asked his wife, had the woman done to deserve such implacable hostility? Nothing, so far as he knew. In reply, Ida had told him he must have his eyes shut and be deaf if he couldn't see and hear what Mrs Hibbert was like. Hadn't he seen how snooty she was, looking down on folk as though they had a bad smell? Hadn't he heard her being sharp and sarcastic, cutting people down to the size she thought they should be? Martin said no, he hadn't, and asked for examples of such behaviour. Ida gave them to him but Martin had failed to see their significance.

He couldn't agree that Mrs Hibbert was anything but a sensible, intelligent, highly organised woman for whom it was always a pleasure to work. Ida snorted, and said she could tell him a thing or two which might change his mind. Invited by Martin to do so, what she did tell him didn't seem adequately to account for her hatred of Mrs Hibbert. It was a tale about Ida's grandmother having been a charwoman for Mary's mother. Something had been stolen and Ida, who as a child accompanied her Nan when she cleaned, had been accused. Nothing had been proved, but her Nan had been dismissed. Ida had gone up to the Lawson place and made a scene. She was only about 8, but she had screamed abuse at Mrs Lawson, and when Mary had appeared and tried to close the door, Ida had hit her. There'd been a fight between the two children and Mary had been badly scratched. There'd been talk of Ida being taken from her Nan and put into a foster home, but Mr Lawson had sorted things out and everything had quietened down. Ida had hated Mary ever since. There was still some other mystery, Martin sensed that. He sensed that not only did his wife resent Mrs Hibbert but that she was in some way jealous of her. Once, when he first started helping her in her garden, and they had chatted to each other while at work, he had told Ida what an interesting conversation he'd had about global warming, but Ida hadn't wanted to hear. It had been as though he'd implied he never had interesting conversations with her – which was true. It had been true for years. They hardly talked to each other at all, and when they did it certainly was not about global warming. Ida, if she did talk, gossiped about the church, about the vicar and what was happening at the Women's Institute and at Fellowship meetings.

Last week, he and Mrs Hibbert had talked about the so-called war on terrorism and what had happened in Iraq. They'd sat outside her house drinking tea, after he'd toiled for three hours trimming all the beech hedges, including the long back one which needed a stepladder to do it properly. She'd insisted he sit down, in comfort, though he was very conscious of his filthy hands – he hadn't worn gloves to gather up the cuttings – and of the leaves and bits of twig caught in the hairs on his chest. She'd stated her own views first (strong ones, as usual) and then invited him to share his with her. This was what she always did and, though at first he had been bashful and hesitant, she had encouraged him and gradually he had grown more confident, and these days positively eager to express himself on any number of issues. Unlike Mrs Hibbert, he didn't read a daily or Sunday newspaper – he took his news from the television and sometimes the radio – but often she would save pieces she'd read in the *Daily Telegraph* and give them to him so that they could discuss them. He felt flattered that she bothered.

Ida, of course, said that he *was* just being flattered. Perhaps it was true. Mrs Hibbert did make him feel clever, though he knew he was not. He had no qualifications, had never even sat a single exam. He didn't read books, it just never occurred to him to want to. But he wasn't stupid, he'd never thought of himself as stupid. But Ida never listened to him. Instead, she would interrupt – 'Stop spouting, for heaven's sake,' she'd say – and if he tried to discuss something serious she walked away. They had never talked properly about her illness. She told everyone about it outside the house, but she wouldn't discuss it with him. She wouldn't even have it mentioned at home, and this bewildered him. He'd told Mrs Hibbert about Ida's operation and the radiotherapy sessions and she'd been reassuring. She was tactful and also sympathetic, a cheering combination in his opinion. Cancer, she'd told him, was not the automatic death sentence it used to be, and was thought by some still to be. She reeled off statistics to prove that Ida had every chance of surviving many years. But even if Ida had not forbidden him to discuss her with Mrs Hibbert, he would have found it hard to confide to anyone what was really bothering him. It was too delicate, too embarrassing. Ida wouldn't let him touch her. Ever since the operation and then the six weeks' radiotherapy she hadn't wanted to be touched. She wouldn't let him hold her or kiss her, never mind anything else. He could understand this at first, it even seemed natural, but as time went on and she was recovered, well, it became bewildering. His attempts to caress her were met with a sharp 'Don't!', as though he were going to attack her. He stopped at once and said he was sorry. He would have to be patient, and he was. He was a very patient man anyway. He could see how unhappy Ida was, but there seemed nothing he could do to help. Going to their doctor wouldn't help – he could just imagine old Dr Marr's face if he appeared before him saying Ida wouldn't let him touch her. But it had occurred to him that Mrs Hibbert might have had some good advice. There'd been an inkling that she understood such mysteries during the time she'd employed that girl Emma.

She'd liked talking to him about Emma. 'You'll never guess what that silly girl's done now, Martin,' she would begin, and then describe the girl's behaviour in detail, commenting that Emma's relationship with her boyfriend was all about sexual infatuation and nothing more. 'God knows why she's attracted to him,' Mrs Hibbert had said, 'considering he is so ill-kempt, but she is. It's pure lust. She thinks it's love, but it isn't.' Martin had shifted a little uncomfortably on the bench where he was sitting with Mrs Hibbert and had said nothing. He just filled his pipe and puffed on it for a bit, until Mrs Hibbert pressed him – 'Don't you agree, Martin? You've seen the two of them, don't you agree?' Weakly, he'd said he didn't know, and mumbled something about one man's meat being another's poison, and young folk these days being hard to fathom. Mrs Hibbert had been exasperated – 'Oh, come on, Martin, you're not thinking, you're not remembering what it was like at that age – all lust, nothing else.' More shifting on the bench, more puffing on his pipe, and then Martin had been overcome with a flood of memories – Ida looking like an angel in the choir, Ida in a white blouse and summer skirt sitting by the river, Ida at the works' Christmas party in a shimmering red dress. He'd cleared his throat and said, 'You're probably right, but it might mean something all the same, it might go deeper. You can't tell at first, now, can you? It has to start with the attraction, and then time will tell.' Mrs Hibbert had said, very firmly, that because young folk today leapt into bed when they'd known each other a mere five minutes, there was no time to tell anything. They began with sex, they didn't work up to it. 'Not like our generation, Martin,' she ended.

Martin couldn't speak. This was different from discussing capital punishment or the horror of metric measurements. He didn't know which was more excruciating to think about, himself and Ida 'working up to it', or Mrs Hibbert. He couldn't associate sex with her at all, even though she'd been married. Nobody here had known her husband Francis, and there were those (Ida among them) who sometimes doubted he ever existed. Mary Lawson had gone south and come back years later widowed (or, as Ida put it, 'saying' she was widowed). Nobody knew much about Francis Hibbert at all. There were no children, which fuelled the gossip. As far as Martin was considered, Mrs Hibbert was a childless widow and that was that. But there she was, presenting herself as a woman who might apparently have worked up to sex, and expecting him to know what she meant. Well, he did. Two years he'd courted Ida and it had been hell. They'd kissed and cuddled and fondled, and she'd loved it as much as he'd done, but there'd been nothing else till they had married. A white wedding, four bridesmaids, himself in a hired suit. And then the honeymoon, and at last what had been worked up to actually took place. Jim born nine months and one week later, Steve a year exactly after that. A lot had been worked up to. He felt he was letting Mrs Hibbert down by not being open and honest and saying what he thought about young Emma. 'It seems to me, Mrs Hibbert,' he said ponderously, 'that contraception being what it now is, the pill and that, it's changed everything. No sense in working up to things, is there? Might as well get cracking and enjoy it.' 'Martin!' she said. 'You don't really think that, do you? Surely you don't think sex should start things off?' 'Well, Mrs Hibbert,' he said, 'it shouldn't be the carrot for the donkey either.'

He never reported any of this conversation to Ida, of course. She'd have said Mary Hibbert fancied him and that this was disgusting. Ida was always thinking that women fancied him, which was so daft he never replied to her taunts. Ida knew he was faithful and that he always had been. She was his one and only woman, which might have surprised some people. He'd watched Jim and Steve grow into teenagers and been half appalled and half admiring at how many girlfriends they'd had. Over and over again, while his sons were growing up, he'd pondered the same questions: would he have married Ida if he could have had sex with her without marriage? Had he confused lust with love? There had been no other girl he had ever wanted or loved. Only Ida, ever. He'd chased her, pursued her, besieged her. But supposing she had been happy to have sex with him as soon as he'd asked her out, the way his sons' girlfriends did, because they wanted to, not because they were forced, what then? Would he have discovered that he didn't love Ida at all? Because that was what had happened soon enough, this separation of physical passion and emotional feeling. Once Ida had given birth to Steve, she had hardly ever wanted sex. He'd had to plead, and she gave into his pleading only grudgingly, but he never forced himself upon her. His need of her humiliated him – it wasn't as though Ida was attractive any more and yet he still wanted to make love to her. This urge to do so seemed to exist independently of Ida herself, almost as though he was willing her to be the girl he had once been so overpoweringly attracted to. And now, of course, since the operation, that side of their life appeared to be over, and he didn't know what to do about it.

He'd never thought life was meant to be all about pleasure, but nevertheless there had to be some pleasure in it to make it tolerable. Where did he find pleasure in Ida these days? There was none. She didn't gladden his heart. At the best, what he felt for her was pity, that she should be so miserable and afraid all the time, and beyond that only a kind of affectionate loyalty because of their history together. They'd been so young, and their youth had made all the struggling to carve a decent life for themselves easier, both of them good workers, both healthy and strong. It had been a pleasure, then, to come home to Ida after he'd worked such long days. She'd been cheerful and welcoming, thrilled that they had their own two rooms, excited about the coming baby. And when Jim was born this happiness had continued for a while. Ida was always singing, the baby contented, what more could he have wanted? Weekends they went for walks. Ida liked to walk then, she liked pushing the pram. She'd made picnics, just a few sandwiches and a bit of cake and a flask of tea, and they'd walked along the river and found a nice spot and sat there and sometimes he'd fished (illegally).

All gone, long since. But would his life be better, happier, without Ida? He couldn't bring himself to think so. If Ida died and he survived, what would his survival amount to? Lying awake into the early hours, as he often did now, he'd got into the habit of staring at the ceiling, tracing the cracks in the plaster over and over again in the dim light, and longed to be back in his own big double bed with Ida beside him. But they had been 'put asunder' – it came to him suddenly, the words of the marriage service, 'let no man put asunder'. Except it wasn't a man that had parted them but disease, and before that ageing and time and familiarity. Cancer had only finished the process off, or nearly. Death would finish it off. He wanted back what he had once had, and if that meant he still loved his wife then something would have to be done to bring her back to him, but what? Still cycling along, he thought of Mrs Hibbert again, and wondered what she would make of it all.

When she was away, she'd asked him to go into her house now and again to check that everything was in order and to water her plants. She'd given him her key, though he'd been reluctant to take it and had said so, but she'd brushed his anxiety aside – 'Really, Martin, why ever not?' – saying she trusted him implicitly and was offended that he didn't seem aware of that. So he had had to agree to pop in, just a couple of times, but he hadn't been comfortable doing so. He'd taken his shoes off at the back door and almost tiptoed through the house on his stockinged feet. There were plants everywhere, on window-sills and tables. The whole place had been left immaculately tidy, and he worried that he was somehow disturbing the arrangement of things without realising it. Moving from plant to plant (there were five) in the sitting-room with the watering can she'd left ready on the draining-board in the kitchen, he concentrated hard so that he would not spill a drop of water on the beige carpet. The carpet scared him. It was self-coloured, a smooth expanse of pale wool with the chintz sofa and armchairs islands of colour in the middle. He couldn't get over how clean it was – not a mark on it. The window-sill was painted white and was spotless. Between two little flowering plants was a photograph in a silver frame. He guessed it was of Mrs Hibbert's parents, because he recognised her features in the man's face. The mother was slender and pretty, the father imposing, with a square face, big nose, and eyebrows that looked very black. It was a pity, he couldn't help but reflect, that Mrs Hibbert was a female version of her father and not a replica of her mother. There was one other photograph in the room, on top of a mahogany bureau, also in a silver frame. It was of Mrs Hibbert and the man he presumed was her late husband – it had to be, surely, because the two of them were standing in front of what looked like a Town Hall, and she was carrying flowers and smiling. He was smiling too. He looked a nice man, scholarly, wearing rimless spectacles and with a fine head of hair. The hair was very fair, and he looked boyish. Martin stopped peering at this photograph and finished off the plants. It was odd, he supposed, and certainly grist for Ida's mill, but Mrs Hibbert rarely talked about her husband. Maybe it was too upsetting, however long ago it was since he'd died.

What, he wondered, as he checked the bathroom – he'd been asked to see that one of the taps wasn't dripping, even though it had had a new washer fitted – had their lives been like? Mr Hibbert would have lived in a perfectly organised and spotlessly clean and tidy home. His clothes would have been scrupulously laundered, just as Mrs Hibbert's own were – Martin had never seen her less than beautifully turned out. As a wife, Mrs Hibbert must have been a paragon of all the wifely virtues. None of Ida's sloppiness. Just stepping out of Mrs Hibbert's house felt a relief. And yet, as he locked the door behind him, Martin wondered if Mr Hibbert had felt constrained by such perfection? What if he'd found her mania for tidiness and cleanliness constricting? Could any man have felt truly relaxed in such surroundings? But maybe the man had been allowed a room of his own, a study, where he was able to be as messy as he liked. In fact, Martin recalled that Mrs Hibbert had once made a reference to a 'sanctum', that was the word, which her husband wouldn't let her enter except once a year to do a spring clean. 'You have no idea,' Mrs Hibbert had said, 'how appallingly dirty and untidy that room was, books everywhere, all quite undusted.' But she had said all this quite proudly, as though it showed her husband was a true man with a will of his own which he exerted sometimes over hers.

Martin's final reflection on this subject, as he got off his bike, was that he couldn't quite imagine Mrs Hibbert as an amorous wife. (That was how he put it to himself, amorous, though he knew this was a euphemism for what he really meant.) He could see no *giving* of herself. He simply couldn't imagine Mrs Hibbert cuddling up to her husband the way Ida had once cuddled up to him. Martin felt ashamed to have indulged in such speculation, but his conclusion was that however wonderful Mrs Hibbert must have been as a wife he would not have wanted to be married to her. Being well looked after, living in a tidy, clean, extremely comfortable home, was not everything.

He'd been looking forward to seeing Mrs Hibbert again, after her time away, but even before he put his bike in the shed he could see that she was out. The double gates into her drive were wide open, which meant she'd driven off somewhere. Odd, she hadn't mentioned it when he'd dropped his strimmer off the day before, and she'd called out, 'See you tomorrow, Martin.' Well, she'd likely be back soon, and he had plenty to do. He put his overalls on ready to start gardening, wondering if Ida would be up yet. Probably. It was her turn to do the flowers in church and she liked to do it in the morning. He'd offered to bring some chrysanthemums from Mrs Hibbert's garden – huge, bronze heads on them – but Ida had scorned the idea, she didn't want chrysanths, everyone chose chrysanths. It was lucky, he reflected, that Mrs Hibbert never went to church and took no part in any of the organisations to do with it, or Ida would have given them up. She was pig-headed enough. If Mrs Hibbert had joined the Women's Fellowship, or the Bible-reading class, or wanted to help organise bring-and-buy sales, then Ida would have avoided all these activities and the loss to her would've been enormous. She hardly went out if it was not to attend some meeting or function to do with St James's, so what a blessing it was that the woman she disliked had nothing to do with them.

Martin strimmed the edges of the lawn valiantly and thought how strange it was that Mrs Hibbert seemed allergic to the Church. It didn't fit in with what he knew of her. She was a Christian, he knew that, and she'd been brought up a strict Anglican, but she'd told him that she did not approve of what was happening to the modern Church. She disapproved of the new prayer book, of the sayings of various bishops, of women priests, and a whole list of other things. And she had detested the previous vicar of St James whom everyone else had liked so much, saying he had had no dignity and that his pastoral care was quite inadequate, which Martin knew perfectly well was not the case. He had gone out of his way to help Ida. But Mrs. Hibbert had also told him that she read her Bible regularly and said her prayers. She believed in God, and in an afterlife but had no need of any church-going. Martin had found all this interesting. Martin himself went to church only occasionally with Ida. He put his only suit on, spruced himself up, and accompanied her to Sunday morning service. He loved singing the hymns with her. His voice was nothing like as good as hers, but it was a strong, deep tenor and he gave it full rein. People tended to sneak looks at them as they led the singing in the congregation. He even felt that Ida wanted him there, for her pleasure. The only other time she needed him, to take her to the clinic, she resented her need. If she had been able to drive, she would have gone to the clinic on her own.

Martin took as long as he could over the strimming, hoping Mrs Hibbert would come back, but she didn't reappear, and there was no more work for him to do that morning. Rather late, he found a note addressed to him pinned in the back porch where he went to leave the letters he'd taken from the postman. Mrs Hibbert had had to go to a Friends committee meeting at St Mary's and wouldn't be back till later, so she asked Martin just to do the strimming and leave the rest till another day. His disappointment surprised him. Slowly, he tidied up and locked the strimmer in the shed. There were other people waiting for him to come and cut their grass, or trim their hedges, but he felt no inclination to go on to them. Instead, he got on his bike and rode off aimlessly, but in the opposite direction from home. If he went home now, Ida would be back from the church and annoyed to see him. She'd want to know why he was back so soon and why, as she always put it, he had a face like a wet week. Cycling along by the river he frowned and tried to frame in his head what he wanted to say to her, but nothing sounded right.

He was out of the town before he realised it. He'd turned off the river path and gone over the bridge and had taken the second turning at the roundabout without thinking about it. Coming in the roadworks gang to this area from Manchester, as he had done at 18, he'd been amazed at how quiet it was, how few buildings of any description appeared in the landscape once the small town was left behind. Nothing much had changed in all these years. There was more traffic, but it was easily avoided, as he avoided it now, slipping off the main road on to a narrow B-road and then turning off that on to an unfenced road which ran over rough common land where sheep wandered about unconcerned by his presence. He felt like a schoolboy playing truant. There was a pub a few miles on, at a crossroads, and he cycled towards it promising himself a pint of bitter and a packet of crisps. Ida should be with him, enjoying this. But Ida hadn't been on a bike for years and she wouldn't want to be on one, nor would she fancy beer – she'd rather have a pot of tea in a cosy tea-shop.

He reached the pub, had his beer and then sat in the afternoon sunshine for half an hour, watching a glider floating far away over the hills. There was no one to disturb the peace, no other customers at the pub, no one passing on the road, and the publican a grumpy fellow who disappeared the moment he'd pulled the beer. Draining the last of his drink, Martin promised himself that when he got home he would force himself to confront Ida. No good rehearsing what he would say, it would just have to come out, no matter how, just all this pent-up feeling that had been choking him up for so long. But it brought him out in a sweat to think about it and he had to go to the pub toilet and splash cold water on his face. What he should do was be natural, but he couldn't remember what *was* natural, what he used to do. He strained to remember: he used to open the kitchen door and shout, 'I'm back, Ida, how's things?' That was what he used to do, shout 'I'm back', cheerfully, and then walk in and find Ida and give her a kiss. He smiled as he checked this memory and found it to be accurate, but then as he went to find his bike and began the ride home he realised it was an old memory, a very old one. Cycling along again at a steady pace, he thought about how many years it must be since he'd done that. Five? No, many more. Ten? Twenty? Probably. It dated back to when he came home at the same time every day from work, and had that routine, the shouted 'I'm back', the search for her, the kiss. Well, he would try it again. Automatically, he speeded up, fairly whizzing along the road.

He put his bike in the garage and walked briskly to the kitchen door, whistling to calm himself. He felt nervous and excited, eager to carry out this experiment. Clearing his throat as he opened the door, he shouted, 'I'm back, Ida, how's things?' There was no reply, but then there often hadn't been because she might be upstairs or have water running, or the washing machine on, and his voice, loud though it was, would have been masked. 'Been a grand day, hasn't it?' he went on as he walked through the empty kitchen into the living-room. 'I've been playing hookey, went for a bike ride.' The living-room was empty too. He stood still and listened. The television wasn't on, for once. He went to the foot of the stairs and called up 'Ida? I'm back, been for a bike ride.' No reply. He wondered if maybe she'd gone up for an afternoon nap and fallen into a deep sleep, which sometimes happened. He climbed the stairs as quietly as possible, knowing which ones could not bear his full weight without creaking, and gently pushed open the bedroom door. The room was empty, the bed neatly made. He checked the other two bedrooms, though Ida had never ever slept in either of them, and then the bathroom.

She was out, his plan defeated. Slowly, he went back to the kitchen and wondered if he should make himself something to eat. It was just after five o'clock. They usually ate at six. He was hungry, ravenous in fact, what with the cycling and fresh air, and nothing in his belly except beer (the pub hadn't even had any crisps). But Ida always cooked their evening meal, no matter what sort of state she was in, and she'd be offended if he started making something substantial now, so he took a couple of slices of bread from the bin, shoved a thick wedge of cheese between them and ate that. It helped, but not enough. He peered into the fridge and took two cooked potatoes from a bowl. Ida would call it spoiling his appetite but she didn't know how huge his appetite was today. He wandered about the house, feeling restless and impatient, and in the end put the television on. When the news came on, he began to worry. Once it was finished, he worried more. Where was she? The only place he could think of was the church, but not at this time, not today, unless he'd forgotten there was some evening thing on.

By seven o'clock, he was seriously concerned. It was almost dark and suddenly chilly as he stepped out of the house and went to look for Ida. She would not like him coming to find her if she was at some meeting or other but it couldn't be helped; he couldn't sit at home and wait any longer. It occurred to him that if he saw lights on in the church hall then he would know there was, indeed, something happening there and he could just wait patiently outside. There was no one else on the road, but then there never was at this time of the evening. Curiously, he felt less worried than before and turned the corner confident that he'd see the lights of the church hall blazing out. If they were, he thought he might just go back home and wait patiently after all.

He rounded the corner and looked down the slight hill towards both the church and hall with a sudden sense of apprehension. No lights. All six windows in the hall, each set high up in the wall, were quite dark. Slowly, he walked towards it, not knowing what else to do, and when he got there he saw that the heavy double doors were locked. The church, across the road, was also in darkness. Perplexed, he went on standing there, trying to decide where Ida could be if not here. In the vicarage? It was a possibility – yes, she'd had one of her panics and he hadn't been there, and she'd gone running along to the new vicar. Martin let out an exaggerated sigh of relief as he realised this, and went hurrying past the church towards the vicarage, thinking how fortunate it was that he had thought to warn the new chap what might happen. There were lights on in the vicarage all right. Even before he'd gone through the gates and past the huge rhododendron bushes which shielded the house, he saw that there were lights on, three of them, one in the porch, one downstairs to the right of the door and one upstairs, directly over the door. Now, should he wait outside for Ida, or ring the bell?

He couldn't decide. The last thing he wanted was a scene, and if Ida had been compelled to come running to this new vicar then she would likely have been in a state. Irresolute, he stood in front of the door, and then began pacing about, up and down the driveway. Given enough time, Ida would come out. All he had to do was have patience, wait for her calmly. He decided to do this just outside the gate. There was a low wall and he could sit on it quite comfortably. He'd hear Ida's feet on the gravel path before she got to the gate, and he'd be ready. It would be perfectly acceptable for him to say he had just come to look for her.

Martin settled himself on the wall and prepared to wait, but hardly had he done so than a car, coming from the opposite direction to his route home, shone its headlights on him and stopped abruptly. He put up his arm to shield his eyes from the glare, wondering why the devil any motorist was doing this. He imagined it must be someone lost to whom he would have to give directions. But then he heard a voice he recognised saying, 'Martin! What are you doing there? Get in.' He hesitated – how could he possibly explain to Mrs Hibbert why he was here and that he didn't want a lift – but then he heard her say, 'Ida, lean over and open the door for him. I think it's locked on that side.' 'Ida?' Martin said, 'Ida?' and he peered into the car. Ida was staring straight ahead. She was sitting in the back, ignoring him. He tried the back door, which was after all open and not locked, and got in. Mrs Hibbert started the car at once, barely giving him time to close the door. He was quite unable to speak. Several times he cleared his throat but could form no words. It was a very short ride to his house. Pulling up outside it, but not switching off the engine, Mrs Hibbert said, 'There. Safely home. I hope you both have a good night.' Ida got out, he got out. He said thank you, but Ida walked off up the path without a word. Mrs Hibbert drove off immediately.

He felt shaken and bewildered, and followed Ida like an obedient dog. Only a couple of hours ago he had been confident about how he was going to act and now he didn't know what to do or say. Ida went straight into the kitchen, snapped the light on, pulled the window blind down and took some sausages and the cooked potatoes out of the fridge. 'Two, or three?' she asked. 'What?' he said. 'Two, or three?' He saw she meant the sausages. She was dangling a string of them and cutting them off one at a time. 'Not yet,' he said. His voice sounded reassuringly strong, even authoritative.

Swiftly, he strode forward and removed the sausages and turned Ida around. 'Into the living-room first,' he said. 'Food can wait.' There was no resistance. He propelled Ida through to the other room and half pushed her on to the settee, where he sat down beside her and put his arm round her shoulders. 'Now, Ida, love,' he said gently, 'what is all this about, where were you, what's been going on? You must have left the house hours ago, what happened, eh?' She had her eyes closed, but she wasn't weeping nor did she seem angry. Encouraged, he gave her shoulders a squeeze. She didn't react at all. 'Ida,' he said, 'how come you were with Mrs Hibbert? How did that come about?'

Her voice was croaky and thick. 'I went out,' she said. 'I wanted to get away. I walked. I was just resting when she passed and stopped and asked if I wanted a lift. I was tired, so I said yes.' The reply was so simple and direct, and delivered in a tone so unlike his wife's usual one, that at first it seemed both sensible and adequate, but then as they both went on sitting there, Martin decided it begged all sorts of other questions. 'Why did you want to get away, love?' he said, quietly. 'What was wrong with being here, in your own home?' 'It was hot,' said Ida, 'it was hot inside, I thought it would be cool outside. I thought it would be cool, and do me good to walk.' Listening to her, the phrase 'not right in the head' popped into Martin's mind, even though nothing she'd said was mad or nonsensical. He was horrified with himself – Ida was no loony, no nutter. This was just an aberration, an impulse, totally out of character, but there was no need to make anything of it or to be alarmed. A cup of tea would . . . and then he caught himself, seeing that he was doing what he always did, pretending everything was fine, whereas he'd promised himself to be brave instead and conquer his own reluctance to admit things were very far from all right and that cups of tea would solve nothing. Ida wanted something else.

They both sat there a long time. Martin moved his arm from Ida's shoulders and found her hand and held it. Eventually, she started to cry, not noisily, but simply letting the tears slide down her cheeks. He let her cry, not wanting to disturb her by getting up to find something to wipe the tears away. The two of them seemed bound together in a way they hadn't been for years –

he didn't want to spoil the feeling by saying the wrong thing. 'Well, Ida,' he said at last, 'what a pair we are. We both wanted to get away today. I went for a bike ride, don't know why, the bike led itself. I was thinking back to how things used to be.' Ida gave a little groan. 'No good harking back, eh? I know.' He patted her hand. She let him. 'What can I do, Ida, to help?' She got up. 'There's nothing you can do,' she said. 'Nothing anyone can do, it's just me. I have to get on with it, that's all.' She walked back into the kitchen. It seemed pointless now to stop her. He heard the sausages sizzling in the pan. 'Two, or three?' she called. 'Three,' he called back.

10

Pull Yourself Together

DROPPING IDA and Martin off at their home, Mrs Hibbert had felt curiosity rage over her like a rash – she could hardly sit still for wanting to scratch the subject of what was going on between the Yateses. It was maddening not to know, but she resisted the temptation to telephone and inquire after them. She would have to wait until Martin next came to garden and then, if she could get him to sit down and have a cup of tea, the answer to this conundrum might emerge. It might, of course, be that Ida was ill again.

By the time Thursday arrived, Mrs Hibbert, stationed as usual in the entrance hall of St Mary's, was eager to see if she could spot Ida. She didn't. Ida definitely hadn't come to the clinic, not that this proved anything. (Or did it? She wasn't sure.) But she saw Sarah Nicholson and that man of hers, drooling over her. Something was going on there, because Sarah had been to the clinic not that long ago. This time, there seemed no harm in giving way to curiosity. The following week, when she took Dot shopping (she picked her up at the end of the road now, since the disgraceful incident with Adam) she asked how Sarah was. Dot sighed and said she didn't know, there had been some sort of health problem but she didn't know what it was, because Adam wouldn't let her ring up. Sarah's young man (Dot always referred to him as 'young', though he was not) had phoned the week before, which was unheard of, to say Sarah wasn't so well and wouldn't be visiting, but that was all he'd said. 'I'm worried,'

Dot said. 'You're always worried,' Mrs Hibbert said, more sharply than she'd intended, so she hastily added, 'and with cause. It's ridiculous that you can't phone your own daughter whenever you want, absolutely ridiculous. And as for all the performance you go through if Sarah does condescend to visit once in a blue moon – well, really.'

Mrs Hibbert knew all about Adam's banning of his daughter from the house and his instructions to Dot never to visit her. When Sarah did turn up, she knew not to ring the front door bell, but to go round the back of the house and tap on the scullery window at two o'clock in the afternoon on a Monday. This was when Adam apparently could be depended upon to be asleep, because it was the only day he left the house, to be taken in the community bus to have his feet done. He returned exhausted and slept after lunch. Monday after Monday Dot hung about hopefully in her scullery, and Monday after Monday she was invariably disappointed. When Sarah did come, she was let in by the back door and spent an uneasy half-hour in the cramped space, whispering with her mother. It was all so outrageous it drove Mrs Hibbert mad – she declared Shakespeare himself could not have thought up a more complicated plot. In this day and age, to have a father cutting off his daughter merely because she was living with a married man was absurd, and for Dot to allow him to do this, and be reduced to such furtiveness, was almost as bad.

Dropping Dot off that day after shopping, Mrs Hibbert decided it was permissible for her to get in touch with Sarah Nicholson. After all, she reasoned, she only had Dot's welfare in mind, and Sarah might not know how very concerned and confused her mother was. Besides, she knew the girl well enough, surely. In the days when Sarah had been trying to make a living as an artist, painting local views, Mrs Hibbert had bought one of these water-colours for £25. She hadn't particularly liked it, but she'd wanted to support Sarah (mainly to annoy Adam), and there were plenty of places in her house where it could hang unseen. Sarah had been grateful, and ever since they had had a perfectly satisfactory nodding acquaintance. Once she'd seen Sarah go to the clinic, of course, she'd taken a keen interest in her welfare, though she'd quickly come to the unavoidable conclusion that the girl was a hypochondriac. She wouldn't have been able to explain how she knew, but she was sure she could spot them.

So, that same evening, Mrs Hibbert rang Sarah. She took care to make her voice light and friendly, with no hint of reproach in it, when she described how worried Dot was. In fact, she felt afterwards that perhaps she'd rather underplayed Dot's anxiety – 'You know what she's like, Sarah, fretting about nothing most of the time.' Not quite fair, that. 'Maybe you could just pop round on Monday, to reassure your mother,' Mrs Hibbert suggested. There had been rather a long silence before Sarah had grudgingly said that she would try, but Monday afternoon was no longer her afternoon off and she'd had so much leave of absence through being ill that she didn't dare take more, so it might be difficult to manage. 'I see,' Mrs Hibbert said, who didn't like what she saw at all. 'I'm sorry you've been ill. Are you better now?' Sarah said no, she wasn't, really. She said the doctor was concerned about her, and that she was obliged to go backward and forward to the clinic at St Mary's for frequent check-ups. Mrs Hibbert wanted to tell Sarah to pull herself together and stop being melodramatic, but she didn't. 'Do try to visit your mother,' she said instead. When she put the phone down, she felt quite pleased with herself: that call couldn't possibly be classified as interfering.

But in Sarah's opinion, it most certainly was. Nevertheless, she went to visit her mother the following Monday. Slowly, she walked past the six steep stone steps at the front of her parents' house and round the side to the back. She didn't have a key for either of the house doors now. Her mother had wanted her to have them, but she'd refused, saying she would only lose them. She didn't want anything to do with this house, that was the point. She'd finished with it. Big breath, before she rounded the corner of the wall. Her mother wasn't at the scullery window, thank God – it was always too much to bear, the sight of her face, dim through the dirt-smeared window. Gently, she tapped on the window and then without waiting opened the door, taking care not to let it squeak. She looked at her watch: a minute past two. It occurred to her that if she waited five minutes and her mother still had not appeared then she could justifiably leave a note saying she'd been and had been afraid to venture further into the house in case her father heard her and made trouble. But even as she was thinking this, knowing it was not justifiable but that nevertheless she would do it, she heard the closing of a door overhead and the pitter-patter of her mother's feet as she scurried lightly down the corridor. Sarah leaned back against the stone sink and braced herself.

When her mother came in, her expression one of alarm rather than delight, Sarah smiled, but not too much – a tentative smile, a smile meant to indicate that she was frail and must be handled carefully. She watched without moving as her mother put her hand to her mouth and gave a squeak of astonishment and then she bent down as her mother tripped towards her, arms outstretched, and embraced her in the usual awkward fashion. She gave her a light kiss on her cheek, barely touching it, her lips fluttering uneasily over the lined skin. 'Well!' her mother said. 'What a surprise!' She was whispering. 'We don't need to whisper, Mum, do we?' said Sarah, irritated already. 'Not down here?' 'No,' her mother said, but her voice still barely above a whisper, 'and he's got his hearing aid out, he's asleep too, sound asleep, that's why I wasn't here at exactly two o'clock, he wanted his hearing aid out and another cushion for his head, and then he fell asleep straight away.' 'So we needn't stay here?' Sarah said. 'We can go upstairs, somewhere more comfortable?' It was a test, and her mother hardly passed it. A look of agonised indecision came over her face before she managed to nod and say, 'But don't make a sound on the way up.'

Her mother led her along the corridor and then up the short flight of uncarpeted stairs to the next floor, past the kitchen, past the living-room, and into the parlour. It was still called the parlour, always, a room Sarah hated as much as its name, an awful room, hardly used at all and furnished with the heavy mahogany pieces inherited from Adam's mother. The gigantic sideboard was full of her china, and the lace mats along its surface had been crocheted by her. The air was horribly stuffy, with no window having been opened literally for years, but there was no dust anywhere. Every week, Dot polished the sideboard and the china cabinet – a delicate operation, what with trying to keep the polish off the glass – and the huge tallboy in the corner. They gleamed, and stank of the beeswax she used. There were only two chairs in here, both ugly, late Victorian club chairs whose seats had embroidered tapestry stretched across and pinned down with brass pins. Her mother perched on one, but Sarah went to the window, drawing slightly aside the thick, dark maroon velvet curtains to let in a little more light. There was another layer of curtaining behind the velvet, of lace, rather beautiful heavy lace with a pattern of peacocks in the threads.

'Oh, this is nice, this is a treat,' her mother said, 'but if only I could make you a cup of tea and get a bit of cake. I think I could, Sarah, he's sound asleep. I could nip into the kitchen and make some tea in no time.'

'No,' said Sarah. 'No, Mum, I don't want any tea, thanks. How have you been, then?'

'Not so bad,' her mother said, smiling. 'Mustn't complain. But your father, he's . . .'

'I don't want to hear about him. I want to hear about you.'

'Oh, I'm fine, a bit tired, but at my age it's to be expected, getting tired, a bit breathless sometimes. I'm fine. And you, Sarah? You look well, your cheeks are pink, lovely.'

'I've been walking. I walked from the crossroads, it's the fresh air. In fact, I haven't been well, it's quite serious that's why I got Mike to ring you. I had a lump in my breast again.' She saw her mother flinch, and then she gave a little cough, a sign, Sarah knew, of embarrassment. Breast was not a word used in the Nicholson household. She should have said 'chest' – how ludicrous it would have sounded, a lump in my chest, but not to her mother.

'But it was all right, I expect, it was harmless, I expect,' her mother said, her face eager with hope.

'Yes, this time,' Sarah said. 'But they want to keep an eye on me at the hospital, at the clinic there. I have to keep going back.'

Her mother, to her surprise, nodded. 'They're very careful,' she said. 'Mary Hibbert told me, she works there, you know . . .'

'Not *works*, Mum, you make her sound like a doctor or a nurse. She's only a sort of guide there, she helps people find where to go, she doesn't work there.'

Her mother looked humble. 'Sorry,' she said. 'Sorry. I just meant that Mary told me how careful they are and if anyone's worried they have them back even if they don't really need to come.' And then, seeing her daughter's expression, 'Sorry, sorry, Sarah, I didn't mean . . .'

'I know what you meant, Mum, and . . .'

'Oh, don't let's quarrel, sweetheart. I didn't mean anything, let's not talk about it, let's talk about your job. How's it going, how's work been?'

Her agitation was so great, her hands clasping and unclasping so frenetically and her brow creased into such a deep frown, that Sarah let it go. She said the job was enjoyable, she liked the work and the firm was doing well. Mike had the right ideas, she said, it was all down to him, the success they were having. She watched her mother, carefully, to see her reaction to Mike's name: nothing, not a flicker of recognition or interest. 'I wish you'd come and meet Mike, Mum,' she said. 'You'd really like him. You'd see what a good man he is. Why don't you come? Dad need never know. Mrs Hibbert could drop you off on your shopping day, and Mike or I could run you back. It wouldn't take long, Dad wouldn't have any reason to feel suspicious . . .' But her mother was shaking her head, and looked terrified. 'Oh no, sweetheart, I couldn't do that, it would be wrong. I couldn't deceive him.' Sarah stared hard at her. 'You could, if you cared enough about me,' she said.

Without meaning to, she had raised her voice and was almost shouting. Her mother had her hand over her mouth, as though it was she who was doing the shouting. Abruptly, Sarah started prowling round the room, touching things, picking up brass candlesticks and putting them down again with an unnecessary bang. She wanted to do something outrageous like smashing the long line of hideous toby jugs on the marble mantelpiece, or pull the dark green plant from its copper pot, and only with difficulty stayed her hand. All this *stress*, and stress was bad for her, especially this kind, this emotional stress. She felt, turning to look at her mother sitting hunched in the uncomfortable chair, that she was in the wrong. She was behaving in a bullying manner, just like her father, but her mother had provoked her. 'Oh, what a mess,' she said, wearily, 'I'd better go.'

'Thank you for coming, sweetheart,' her mother said, quickly.

'What?' said Sarah.

'Thank you, dear, for coming. When you're so busy, when you haven't been well . . .'

'No, I heard you, it's your thanking me I can't believe. I'm your daughter, Mum, I'm not some guest you have to be polite to. You shouldn't even think of thanking me, you should be wondering why I don't come often, why we don't see each other all the time.'

Her mother looked bewildered. 'But it's your father, he . . .'

'I *know* why, Mum, that's not what I'm asking.'

Then suddenly, there was a noise, a roar, and the crash of something falling over. Her mother was up on her feet instantly and rushing to the door. 'Dot! Dot! Where the hell are you?' they both heard. Her mother turned to her as she went through the now opened door and said, 'Sssh!' and indicated in sign language that she should go out by the front door. She blew a kiss, and hurried down the hall to the living-room. Sarah stood and watched her reach the door and open it, and she heard again her father bellowing her mother's name, and then her mother's soothing tones, her 'there, there' and 'just knocked the stool over' and 'cup of tea', then a series of grunts from her father. She went on standing there, toying with the idea of confronting him. She could just march into that living-room and say she'd had enough of this ridiculous never-darken-my-doorstep stuff, and if he didn't want anything to do with her, her mother did. But it would be useless. Her mother wouldn't back her up. She wouldn't say yes, Sarah is quite right and I won't be forced into keeping her away. She would only cause more trouble, and her mother would suffer.

Instead, she slipped along to the front door and, opening it with only a little click of the lock, left the house. Heaven to be outside. She almost jumped down the steps in one bound, so relieved to be free, but then as she began to walk along the street she was overcome with a vision of her mother trapped in that house with her bad-tempered, miserable father. She'd struggled for years to try to understand how such a union had come about. Once, she'd tried asking her aunt Phoebe, the eldest of her mother's sisters, dead now. Phoebe hadn't looked like Dot. She was much taller and stronger, and she had none of Dot's nervousness – she was tough and sharp-tongued and independent-minded, a business woman running her own little empire, owning three hat shops and very successful with all of them. So Sarah, in early adolescence, when she was at her most bewildered and distressed about why her sweet, patient, gentle mother had married her sour, impossibly bad-tempered father, had begged Aunt Phoebe to tell her how and why it had happened. But Phoebe had been reluctant, for once, to talk. She had been discreet, though not entirely unhelpful. For answer, she had first pulled out an old photograph album and pointed silently at a picture of Adam Nicholson on his wedding day. Handsome, very. There was no doubt about his good looks. Tall, broad-shouldered, square jaw, thick black hair swept back from a noble brow . . . yes, handsome. 'See?' Aunt Phoebe had said, after Sarah had looked. 'And he set his heart on our Dot, wouldn't rest till he had her, she'd no say in the matter.'

This was the bit Aunt Phoebe hadn't been either able or willing to explain, the 'no say in the matter' part. Was it even true? 'She can't have married him just because he said she had to,' the young Sarah had protested. 'Ah, girl, you've a lot to learn,' Aunt Phoebe had sighed. Sarah had said: 'But she must have liked him, it can't just have been his looks.' 'Well,' Phoebe had said, carefully, 'she did fall for him, he could be charming when he wanted. A lot's happened since, Sarah, he's changed, we all change. You can't expect to see him as he was when he went after your mother.' What had changed to account for her father now being so horrible? That had been her next question. Aunt Phoebe had asked if she knew why her mother had had only her, and Sarah had said that, of course, she knew about the first baby dying, how could she not when every anniversary was marked with visits to the cemetery and she was obliged to go too and put a posy of flowers in front of the small white marble headstone. 'It hit your father hard,' Phoebe had said. 'For a man, he took it very hard, you'd be surprised. I'd never seen a big, grown man cry the way he cried when that baby boy died. Your mother cried too, of course she did, and she'd been through all the carrying and having of him, and she wasn't well for months after the birth, but your father took it very hard. He couldn't believe you'd survive when you came along, he was that anxious. But he couldn't forget that boy. Nobody to follow him, I suppose, as he followed his father and grandfather, he knew a girl would never be a butcher.'

All that had made some sort of sense to Sarah then. It was sad, of course it was, but she wouldn't have it that it entirely accounted for the onset of his gloomy personality. She'd pressed Aunt Phoebe further and then heard more about his accident when he was 40, falling on an icy pavement when he was carrying a whole pig carcass into the shop and damaging his right shoulder so badly that he was never pain-free again. 'Terrible thing, for a butcher,' Phoebe had said. 'He had to employ people to do the work he'd always done himself, and he didn't like it, not at all, he wasn't good with staff.' Sarah could imagine that easily enough. And yet still, in spite of feeling some sympathy, none of these attempted explanations for why her father was as he was, were adequate. There must be something else, something Phoebe was holding back, to account for the degree of bullying and nastiness inflicted on her mother by her father.

But if there was, and Phoebe knew of it, she wasn't telling. There were no other useful relatives to bother with her questions. Her father's one brother was unapproachable and Sarah hardly saw him, and both sets of grandparents, who might have been the most useful informants, were dead by the time she was old enough to want to grill them. She remembered her paternal grandparents clearly, though. They were both quiet and somehow shy with her, and she'd always been confused, thinking that they must surely be her mother's parents, not her father's, because they fitted in with her better. She liked them, liked visiting them in their cottage and playing with their two dogs, and collecting eggs from the chickens they kept. It was a mystery to her why her father never seemed to want to take her there – it was her mother who did – and even as a small child she'd noted something odd about the way Grandma Nicholson asked if Adam was all right, was he 'behaving', and the relief on her face when her mother had said he was fine, everything was fine.

All I've ever learned, Sarah reflected as she got on the bus, is that my father is an embittered man who takes his bitterness out on my mother. What I've never been able to learn is why she not only allows this but seems to encourage it. Is it love? Or is it his need of her that she loves? She smiled, and saw her uncertain smile reflected in the bus window. She tried to concentrate on the idea that her mother loved her father, full stop. Loved him more than she loved her only child. Loved him differently, anyway. And I am making a big fuss about it, she thought, I'm jealous. I always have been, and I still am, even though I have someone now who loves me enough to make this not matter. Suddenly, she couldn't wait to get home and prepare a welcome for Mike – champagne, smoked salmon, his favourite olives, a feast. And a smile on her face, the one she'd been unable to put there weeks ago when the good news came.

*

She woke in the early hours of the morning and, though her head ached and she felt slightly sick, she still felt comfortably happy. Just before dawn she fell asleep again and didn't hear the alarm go off or Mike get up and tiptoe out. There was a note from him on the pillow when she woke again, saying that he loved her and that last night had been 'bliss'. She smiled as she read it. Really, it was easy to be happy. She'd been absurd not to realise this. She'd be late for work herself, but she didn't care. Slowly, savouring her lightness of spirits, she got up and showered, unafraid to touch her own body, and went downstairs. The post had come. She saw the St Mary's Hospital stamp on the buff envelope. Well, they'd said they would send her an appointment for next year. She wasn't afraid to open it. There it was, the date, the time, to be at the clinic. It was ages away. She wasn't going to think about it, not for a single minute.

But would she be able to help it, or would the same old anxiety grow?

11

Last Will and Testament

MRS HIBBERT worried about her will. She knew, through having worked so many years for a solicitor, all about the trouble caused when people of substance failed to make a will before they died. She also knew that 'substance' did not have to be very great either for the trouble to be considerable. Anyone who owned a house, anyone who had any investments, anyone who had any money at all in the bank: they should make a will. But her own mother, who had inherited everything when her husband died – he, of course, had made a will – had had a superstitious dread of leaving her affairs in similar good order. 'In due course,' she had said, when the family solicitor had tried to get her to make her will. She had never got round to it, and Mrs Hibbert's sister, the long-suffering widowed Rose, who had returned home and so faithfully nursed her, got no more than the others.

She intended there to be absolute clarity about her own will. There was quite a lot of money to leave, though she carefully concealed how wealthy she was. She had never even told Francis how much she was worth. Sometimes she had felt guilty about this, it did not seem quite right to conceal something so important from her husband, but they had separate bank accounts, in different banks, and she did not know what Francis was worth either. He never asked her for details, and she never asked him. They split bills between them and it all worked smoothly. When he died, she was astonished to find he left her so little because he had so little to leave. He left his sister £1,000 and his niece the same, and she got the rest. The rest was a mere £9,852. Knowing that Francis had had a good salary all his working life, Mrs Hibbert couldn't think what he had done with his money. It rather troubled her: she didn't like to dwell on it.

She often thought how, if it had been the other way round and she had died before Francis, he would have been startled to discover how much he had been left – he probably wouldn't have been able to credit it. In the first year after Francis's death, she changed her will four times as some people, and various charities, went up and down in her estimation. It was a costly and exhausting business, but at the same time it gave her a sense of her own power which she relished. What she had also begun to relish was the secrecy. This had started when she decided to make a few personal bequests, to people she wished to reward. She loved thinking about how astonished and thrilled these lucky individuals would be, and could hardly refrain from giving them a few hints as to what was in store for them. She didn't, though. She was especially careful not to give Dot a clue. Dot was to be left £5,000.

Mrs Hibbert had a copy of the will, of course, and took it out every now and again, usually on a Sunday afternoon, to cast her eye over it. It helped her get through that day, which she disliked intensely. Sunday was the hardest day, especially in the winter – she was never going to forget a certain Sunday in January – when she came dangerously near to feeling depressed, which she absolutely would not allow. She had trained herself to study the local paper on Friday evening and mark any events which could serve as focal points for Sunday expeditions – open days at stately homes, concerts, meetings, flower shows – and she had been very successful at it. Most Sundays, she managed to have plans. But lately, nothing had seemed to appeal. She found herself up and dressed by nine o'clock on wet, dull Sunday mornings when gardening was out of the question, and she dreaded the hours to fill before something acceptable appeared on television. It made her cross with herself but she couldn't help it.

If only she had remained a church-goer, like Dot and Ida, then the problem of how to spend Sunday would have solved itself. All her childhood, Sunday had meant church, morning and evening, and no choice about it. Her family had had a pew right at the front and they always filled it. She'd felt quite proud as they all marched down the aisle to it, passing lesser mortals (like Ida and her grandmother, and Dot and her mother and sisters) who did not have a special pew. When she returned to the town she went only a few times, to show that she was back home as much as anything. It seemed embarrassing to be all alone in that prominent pew and she no longer liked to claim it. In her will, she had instructed that her remains were to be cremated and that there was to be no service. The last burial service she had attended had been her husband's and she had been deeply shocked by the new words used. If she had known that the traditional service was not to be followed she would have objected, but by the time she heard the flat, ordinary phrases of the modern prayer book it was too late. What had been done to the beautiful language of the old prayer book was unforgivable. As she was always telling Dot, the reasons she didn't attend church were not to do with having lost her faith – she was not an atheist, or even an agnostic – but with the mess the Church had got itself into.

It had been hard, having to follow Francis's wishes as laid out in the will he'd written a couple of years before. He'd wanted a full-scale church funeral and had used to tease her about it, saying he certainly didn't want to go anywhere near one of those unspeakably ugly crematoriums. He wanted her to play the part of grieving widow to perfection . . . 'the deepest black imaginable, including a veil,' he'd said, laughing. It was not a joking matter, as she'd told him when he vowed to have this written in his will, but she had done what he had wanted. Indeed, to her surprise, there was some small comfort in doing so. She bought a very expensive black cashmere-and-wool coat, black court shoes, black leather handbag and quite a large black hat with a veil so thick she could hardly see through it and felt like a beekeeper. When she did peer at herself in the mirror before leaving for the church, she thought she looked like the late Queen Mother at the funeral of her husband George VI (which, actually, had been a rather flattering comparison even if she'd had to make it herself). The church had been full of flowers (not lilies, but roses, as decreed by Francis) and lit by dozens of candles, though it was not a Roman Catholic church. She'd wept, but nobody saw, because of the veil, so after all she'd been grateful for it. But the whole business had been a terrible ordeal.

By avoiding a funeral for herself, she was avoiding humiliation after death. This pleased her. The avoidance of humiliation was not the same thing, in Mrs Hibbert's opinion, as having pride. She was often too proud to submit to certain indignities but could, nevertheless, be humiliated by having them imposed upon her, and it was important to resist. Humiliation for the single, elderly woman lurked everywhere. It was at its worst in hospitals. Her feeling for the women she guided to the clinic during her work as a Friend arose out of her own experiences at the hands of doctors, though she never spoke of them. She knew her own body was not a pretty sight (though she also knew that, unlike her face, it once *had* been), but she didn't want the attitude or expression of a doctor to tell her that. Even when she was dead, she wished to retain her privacy, and so in her will she had even described the nightdress she wished her corpse to be clothed, and burned, in. It was an exquisite garment, of finest lawn cotton, with lace at the neck and the cuffs, and lots of tiny tucks across the bodice which fastened with minute pearl buttons. It was the very devil to iron, but she'd enjoyed doing it. She'd only ironed it twice, once before the only time she'd worn it and once after it had been washed, later. It was lying ready, wrapped in tissue paper in the bottom drawer of the chest of drawers in her bedroom. The night she'd worn it had been her wedding night. If she had been anticipating the loss of her virginity then she would never have chosen such a nightdress, but it had seemed to her appropriate to the occasion. Francis had admired it, and she'd been pleased.

Both sides of her family had cared about clothes. No Lawson or Ellis ever looked scruffy – even the working clothes (of those few who had really worked) had been neat and appropriate to the task in hand. The wealthier members, particularly on the Lawson side, had worn tailored garments of good fabric and she had inherited their taste for these. The shoddy workmanship of so many modern garments appalled her – seams coming apart, hems fraying, buttons hanging by a thread. The clothes she herself had were good clothes, properly made, and made to last. She looked after them well, as she had been taught. She'd been brought up always to lay out the clothes she would wear the next day on the night before and to check each item for cleanliness and for its state of repair. Any hole or tear discovered had to be mended before going to bed, or else another garment selected. In the days of silk stockings, she'd learned how to mend ladders and was an expert at darning the heels of woollen ones. She'd also been trained to match colours carefully. Coordination was important, the picking out of a red thread in a patterned red-and-grey-black skirt by the choice of an *exactly* matching red blouse, for example. Mrs Hibbert was very good at this. She never had to take a skirt with her to find a match for it – she could carry the colour in her head. Many elderly women, she had noticed, seemed to decide to forgo colours and stick to navy and black and brown and grey, but she remained faithful to the vibrant pinks and reds and blues she loved so much. The only colour she kept away from was yellow. Her cousin Roberta had pointed out years and years ago: 'Marigold, yellow does to you what navy does to me.' She hadn't known what her cousin meant but she'd understood the message and never worn yellow again. It had seemed hard, in the circumstances, to be named after a yellow flower.

There was a bit in her will about clothes. Clothes made a statement, after all. One of her great terrors was that when she died her clothes would be taken to a charity shop and she absolutely could not bear, dead though she would be, the thought of Adelaide Priest or Lucy Binns or Mrs Jarrett getting their hands on her clothes, pawing them, *pricing* them, and hanging them on those ruinous wire hangers. What she would really have liked to decree was that everything should be burned in her own garden, one great big pyre of clothes blazing away down in the far corner beyond the rhubarb patch. But that would be a waste, positively sinful. There were Harris tweed skirts of the finest quality among her things, and cashmere jumpers, and fine lambswool cardigans, and silk underwear that had cost so much money she'd felt guilty at indulging herself for garments no one would see except herself. She had tossed and turned many nights, trying to solve this dilemma, and had then come across a solution quite by accident. In the local paper, the amateur dramatic society had advertised for clothes of good quality, any clothes, to be given to it for use in future productions. Mrs Hibbert knew it was odd, but she had immediately been attracted by the idea of an actress wearing her clothes. She spent a happy few minutes every now and again imagining the kind of plays for which her wardrobe might be suitable – Terence Rattigan's *Separate Tables*, perhaps, or anything by J. B. Priestley. It made her smile with pleasure to think of her clothes lovingly looked after by a wardrobe mistress.

She still had the blue frock she'd worn for her wedding day thirty years ago. It was a very pale blue with a white broderie anglaise collar and cuffs, and it had a deep blue soft leather belt which had emphasised her slim waist. She'd fretted that it might be too girlish for a woman of 40, but she hadn't been able to resist it. Over the frock, she had worn a dark blue linen coat, and of course she had worn a hat. She would have kept the hat (she had a vast collection of them) which was a pretty navy blue straw trimmed with a white grosgrain ribbon but, unfortunately, Francis had inadvertently sat on it in the train and ruined its shape for ever.

They hadn't had a proper honeymoon, but then they hadn't had what others might call a proper wedding. She and Francis had married in a register office. She couldn't bear the thought of looking foolish in a church, walking down the aisle at her age, and Francis wanted only to do what she wanted. They had a blessing later in church, which Francis had wanted, discreetly arranged on a weekday morning. Only Francis's sister and her husband were present at the register office, as witnesses. She'd worried that it might all feel hole-in-the-corner, furtive, but it hadn't done. They'd had lunch afterwards at an hotel, and then immediately departed for Bath. Francis's choice. He'd called her Mrs Hibbert at every opportunity and she'd loved it.

The complicated train journey (they had to change twice) was something of an ordeal. She'd felt tense the whole time, worrying about the night ahead. She knew quite well that Francis would imagine she was an aged virgin, terrified of sex. But she wasn't. She wasn't a virgin and she wasn't terrified of sex. It troubled her profoundly that she had not told him about her previous experience and nor had she tried to explain her extremely complicated feelings towards him. It was a case of loving him, but . . . and that 'but' somehow too dangerous to expand on.

She had once been a very foolish girl. No one would believe it of her, but she had acted completely out of character in a ridiculously silly way. Whenever she thought of this episode in her past (which occurred soon after she had started working in Manchester), she felt herself blushing. Gradually, she'd trained herself to blot out the memory, so that by the time she had become such friends with Francis she hardly thought of it at all. But deciding to marry him had resulted in such constant flashbacks to what had happened with Stephen Fleming, a man she'd met at the Gardening Club she'd joined, that she had struggled to control the impulse to tell Francis about it. What had stopped her was not knowing *how* to tell him – it was a question of language again. Only ugly words came into her head when she thought of trying to describe how she had felt about Stephen, words like 'besotted'. Nor could she bring herself to use the modern phrase 'fancied him'. She hadn't been that young either, certainly not young enough to excuse the madness which had overtaken her. She'd been 26, young but not a teenager. Stephen was 42, and though she didn't know when she set her cap at him – yes, she'd made the first advance, another thing impossible to admit to Francis in any words whatsoever – a married man with three children.

Stephen had not been to blame, or only a little, in that he didn't confess he was married when first she asked him out. She'd bought tickets for a concert and then lied and said her friend was ill and couldn't accompany her and would he like to? He'd said he'd be charmed, and offered to pay for his ticket but, of course, she hadn't allowed that. It was 1959, women didn't take the lead like that, and doing so, having the nerve, had excited her. Nothing happened after the concert. They had a drink, and he saw her home and bade her a polite good night. But then, a week later, when she had learned how to function in spite of it, he asked her if she'd like to go to the theatre, to see *Much Ado About Nothing*. Nothing happened afterwards. For weeks they went together to plays, concerts, art exhibitions, even lectures. She knew by then that he was married, but she didn't let that put a stop to her hopes, as it ought to have done. Still nothing happening. By the end of the summer, she was longing for him to seduce her (that was the word she used to herself, and shivered) but beyond a friendly kiss and some hand-holding, there was nothing.

This was the worst bit. She'd invited him to have tea one Sunday afternoon. A cold autumn day. They'd been glad to come in from the park out of the bitter east wind which had sent the leaves whirling round them as they'd walked. They'd toasted crumpets in front of the fire. She'd spilled her tea, deliberately, and she'd taken her blouse off in front of him, pretending the tea was scalding her. Her breasts had always been her best feature. His face had changed, and he'd given a sigh and held out his arms and she'd thrown herself into them. Thrown herself. 'I'm married, Mary . . .' he'd reminded her, and she'd said she didn't care, and at that moment she didn't. He'd started to say other things, but she'd stopped his mouth with her kisses. He'd tried to resist, but she wouldn't let him, she'd given him no option. She'd wanted him to make love to her so badly, but 'love' was not exactly what was made. He took her virginity, as she had wanted him to, but the experience was not what she had imagined. She'd been left utterly confused and he'd been so apologetic, saying over and over again how sorry he was, how thoughtless he'd been. She'd told him it didn't matter, without stopping to wonder what it was that didn't matter. All that excitement she'd felt, all that thrilling need, had somehow ended in pain and mess. The tidying up of themselves had been awful, the disarray of their clothes acutely embarrassing. He had been so crestfallen, and in such a hurry to leave, with yet another litany of sorrys. She'd taken a long time to calm herself, and had only managed to hold the tears back by assuring herself that next time would be better.

But there was never a next time. She never heard from Stephen again. She'd been left desolate, inconsolable, and with a feeling that she'd humiliated herself. For the next eight years, till she met Francis, she had trouble making friends with any man, afraid as she was that she would once more come to want physical affection which would lead to another disaster. No man, in fact, ever made any romantic approach, though there were a couple who did become friends and she was glad of their company. Platonic friendships, she concluded, were the best kind. It relieved her not to be in any danger of becoming 'besotted' again and it made her realise how special Stephen had been to arouse such feelings in her. Sometimes, with one man in particular, she had found herself half hoping an approach would be made, just to test her response, but it never happened. It must, she decided, have just been Stephen who could have this effect on her, and that made her pursuit of him seem not so wrong. Sad, but not wrong, to have given herself to the one man capable of bringing her to a state of such passion.

Passion, she discovered in those years, did not exist on its own. She was not plagued by merciless feelings of frustration, though occasionally, usually after watching a film or reading a book, she would experience a slightly disturbing racing of the pulse and an uneasy shifting inside herself which she rather dreaded and tried to quieten with physical exercise. This worked, and she was grateful, fearing what might have happened if she had stayed still and found her body wanting something she didn't care to think about. Was it a waste, to suppress whatever it was she was suppressing? She didn't know, and felt she could now never know, and so she should be sensible and not dwell on it. It hurt though, when people took it for granted that she knew nothing of desire and had her labelled as frigid. Sometimes she was tempted to put them right, but always resisted this temptation, and in any case, as she settled into accepting she was never going to be attracted to anyone that way ever again, it was not so hard to allow herself to be wrongly categorised. By the time Francis came into her life, she had convinced herself that even fantasies of a passionate nature were over.

This, then, had been the problem with Francis. When he touched her, there was none of the immediate response she had experienced with Stephen. He could hold her hand, or kiss her (both these gestures lightly done), and she felt nothing. He was a handsome (though more beautiful than handsome) man, but his looks were immaterial. What she felt in Francis's company was *comfortable*, and this seemed highly significant to her because she was rarely truly comfortable or relaxed in anyone's company. She was always aware, to a lesser or greater extent, of playing a part, or performing. Francis required no such falseness. He made her laugh (not something she did a great deal) and he shared so many of her interests that they matched each other perfectly. He was intelligent of course, and far better educated than herself, but he never flaunted his Oxford degree. They got on famously. In due course, they swopped personal histories, as people do, and she fully expected to hear that, like Stephen, he was married, or at least that he had had lots of girlfriends, because it did not seem likely that such a man could have remained unattached, but he appeared to have had no significant girlfriend. It was puzzling. Eventually, when they had got beyond the need for tact about such queries, she asked him why. He said he expected it was because he hadn't met the right woman.

It took him a long time to convince her that she was the right woman. When he first suggested marriage (suggested it, rather than actually proposed) he had done so in such an offhand way that she had been rather offended. He'd said it would be the 'obvious' thing to do since they spent so much time in each other's company. She'd replied that she could see nothing obvious about it, and that she was perfectly happy with how things were. Then the lease on his flat came up and he said he thought he would buy another in the block where she lived, 'Or I could move in with you. What do you think?' he'd added. She'd said she didn't think that would be a good idea. Her flat was small. It only had one bedroom. He'd laughed, and apologised, and said, of course, what had he been thinking of. But what *had* he been thinking of? She wondered. What exactly was going on? They were friends, companions, colleagues (though she, by then a legal assistant, was not to be ranked beside him, a solicitor) but they were not lovers, nor ever would be. At least, not as far as she was concerned. Yet more and more she'd felt she *did* love Francis, and the thought of spending the rest of her life living with him was attractive. Except for the awkwardness of not being physically attracted to him in the way she remembered being attracted to Stephen. It made her hesitate. It was an awful thing for anyone, man or woman, to have to tell another: I do not think I find you attractive enough to sleep with (though the sleeping part would be no bother – another failure of language).

There was also the age factor. She was five years older than Francis. Not worth mentioning if it had been the other way round, but somehow embarrassing because it was not. There was one woman in the office who, noting the friendship between her and Francis, had made a comment about cradle-snatching. It was clearly meant as a joke, and Mary had to take it as such or else reveal how much this hurt. If she and Francis got married then she would have to endure expressions like that from others and she didn't relish the prospect. It didn't help that she looked older than her years and Francis considerably younger than his – they would always strike people as oddly matched. He might be thought to be her brother rather than her husband. She pointed this out to him and he said he couldn't believe that she cared what people thought. He said that, for his part, he would be happy to share a flat or house with her without being married, but he assumed she wouldn't be comfortable with this arrangement, with her prim fears of what people would think, and so marriage was the solution, 'to make it decent', he teased.

What had persuaded her to marry him after all, in spite of her worries, had been finding the house. Francis had been living, after the lease on his flat ran out, in part of a vicarage where an old friend from Oxford was the curate, but a few months into this arrangement the friend was moved elsewhere and Francis had to leave. He said he was tired of renting and wanted to buy a place, and she'd gone house-hunting with him to help him decide. They looked at awful flats and maisonettes and then, one snowy Saturday, they went to see a small house which was being sold in a hurry (they never knew the reason). The house was indeed small, only two bedrooms and a not very large living-room and kitchen, but the garden was huge. In spite of the snow, they could both see how mature it was, with trees and shrubs they recognised under their icy coverings, and the suspicion of massed roses all along the surrounding walls. It was the garden that did it. Francis sighed and said he couldn't afford the house, though he would love it, and she found herself saying, 'I could contribute.' After that, not to live in the house and enjoy the garden with him seemed ridiculous. She had agreed that marriage was the only way to make this respectable.

Once the decision had been made, she'd been surprised how happy she'd felt about it. It was Francis who had brought up the matter of what would happen after they were married. She'd been acutely aware that he appeared to think that *she* would want reassurance that nothing would change. Didn't she agree, he'd asked, that friendship, companionship, shared interests and genuine affection were enough for any marriage? She'd said that yes, of course she did. He'd seemed so relieved. 'We'll go on just as we are,' he'd said, 'no need to worry that getting married will spoil anything.' She ought to have challenged that. She ought to have asked him to explain himself because she didn't really understand what he was getting at. But what had held her back were the suspicions she had about Francis which she did not want confirmed. She had been cowardly and everything that had followed had been her fault. The fact that her suspicions had been quite wrong made it all the worse.

It was exciting keeping their wedding day secret from everyone they worked with – they'd had bets as to who would notice her wedding ring first. Both of them had been wrong. It wasn't one of the women. It was one of the senior partners, Mr Mason. She took a sheaf of papers in to him and as she placed them on his desk he'd said, 'Why, Miss Lawson, do I see a happy event has taken place?' He congratulated her profusely, luckily in the privacy of his office, and asked to whom was she now married. When she told him, his astonishment was almost comical. He stared at her, his mouth literally open in surprise, and then coughed and spluttered and said, 'Dear me' several times and ended this confusion with 'How very extraordinary'. It was impossible not to feel offended, but when she described Mr Mason's reaction to her news to Francis, watching his expression closely, he laughed. 'Probably thought I wasn't good enough for you,' he said, but she'd felt that wasn't what Mr Mason had thought at all.

Other colleagues were equally amazed but much more tactful. There was a hurried whip-round, and at the end of the week she was presented with some modest gifts – a pair of wooden salad servers, a coffee pot, some linen table napkins and a vase. They were nicely wrapped and had cheerful messages written on the tags attached to them. Mrs Hibbert kept the tags. Nobody sniggered when Mr Gilbert, the other senior partner, made a little speech, and there were no lewd jokes. Everyone was perfectly polite, and called her Mrs Hibbert thereafter in an easy, natural way. She quickly decided that it had been a very good idea to marry. She'd lost nothing by it, and gained a great deal. Francis had his bedroom in the newly purchased house and she had hers and there was none of the awkwardness she had feared. The only tremor of unease she had experienced had been when they'd arrived at the hotel in Bath. They found they had been booked into a room with a double bed. But Francis had acted quickly. He had immediately produced from his wallet a letter from the hotel confirming his booking of a room with two beds, and the matter had been put right at once. He had slept in one bed, she in the other and, though she slept badly, he had slept well, never moving all night. They had each dressed and undressed in the bathroom without any agreement to do so being necessary.

At home, they had separate bedrooms. Separate bedrooms had not turned out to mean an entire absence of physical contact though. They always embraced when they said good night, and when they watched television together they sat thigh-to-thigh, with Francis's arm round her shoulders. They kissed sometimes, though not on the lips, just friendly kisses on each other's cheeks. There was absolutely no comparison with how Stephen had kissed her. She wondered if their marriage was one of what was termed 'convenience', and somehow didn't like the idea. Convenience there might be, but it was not the whole story – there was real feeling, and regard of a high order, in their relationship. Their marriage did not feel a sham even if in one respect she was bound to admit it might qualify as such. Who was to say every marriage should be the same?

She knew, though, that Francis and she seemed odd as a married couple, there was no point in pretending they didn't. Doubtless a certain amount of prurient speculation went on at work, and it certainly did in the mind of her sister-in-law. Sandra had once tried to have a conversation of an unpleasantly intimate nature with her, during the one weekend she and Francis had stayed with her and her husband Brian. She'd chosen the Saturday evening, when the men had walked along to the village pub (not that Francis had wanted to go but he was indulging Brian). Sandra lit the log fire and said, 'Let's be cosy.' Mrs Hibbert had no desire to be any such thing but she was trying that weekend to be amenable and pleasant. She'd hardly met Sandra – only that short time on her wedding day – and wanted to get to know her, for Francis's sake. Sandra was all the family he had and he seemed fond of his sister though not close to her. So the two of them had sat in front of the fire, one on either side, and apart from the glow from a pink silk-covered lamp in the far corner of the room, the only light was from the crackling flames. Sandra was knitting a jumper for her little daughter Chrissie, and Mrs Hibbert had been reading but had given up because she was straining her eyes and yet didn't want to risk spoiling the 'cosiness' by asking for more light. Sandra chatted as she knitted, hardly pausing between anecdotes, illustrating the infant Chrissie's precocious talents, and accounts of how she had been cheated in the butcher's. Asked to agree how difficult it was to match embroidery silks and required to give her opinion on the best way to worm dogs, Mrs Hibbert had struggled to say anything at all. Then the impertinent questions had begun.

'And how are things in the bedroom department?' Sandra had suddenly asked. Mrs Hibbert was so appalled she had said, 'I *beg* your pardon,' with no hint of any interrogative in her intonation, but Sandra had chosen to interpret the exclamation as a question all the same. 'With Francis,' Sandra had said, 'between you and Francis, everything lovey-dovey in that respect?' And then, presumably to encourage confidences, 'I remember when Bri and I were first married, I had the most awful cystitis every time we'd been at it – oh, the agony! But then maybe, being older, you haven't suffered like I did?'

The vulgarity paralysed Mrs Hibbert. She sat quite motionless, silent in her rage, with Sandra's needles clicking and the fire spluttering. 'Well,' Sandra said, at last, finally realising she would get no response, 'I'm glad everything's fine, that's good. It's nice Frank has got married at last. I wish our mother was still alive. She was desperate for him to bring a nice girl home, she could never understand why he didn't when he was so handsome and clever. He just used to laugh and say he hadn't fitted the slipper to his Cinderella yet.' Mrs Hibbert got up. She said she was sorry but she had a dreadful headache and was going to have to retire to bed even though it was so early. Sandra was all sympathy. She jumped up straight away and went off to find some aspirin. Then she insisted on making some cocoa, which Mrs Hibbert did not want, and filling a hot-water bottle which she mysteriously claimed would cure a headache if held to the stomach once she got into bed. The bed was a double one. She and Francis had already been obliged to spend one night in it and very uncomfortable it had been. It was only 4 feet 6 inches. wide and when they turned over in the night they kept banging into each other. Francis had apologised, and said that, as there was only one spare room in the house, he hadn't been able to ask Sandra for separate rooms, and anyway . . . His voice had tailed off and she had known exactly what he meant. There was nothing wrong in his wanting to keep up appearances, and she'd felt sorry for him.

She lay there seething when Francis came tiptoing in two hours later. She feigned sleep. In the morning, he made no comment about the sleeping arrangements, nor did he mention that his sister had said anything. They were both glad to leave. Francis said that next time, they would stay in the pub, which had perfectly comfortable rooms, but there never was a next time. She never told him what Sandra had asked her, not wanting either to admit that she had been upset, or to upset him. All the way home, she had thought of all kinds of rejoinders which she could have made to Sandra's question, and had tormented herself with what her sister-in-law must have made of her silence and hasty withdrawal. She ought simply to have smiled and said, 'Fine, thank you,' and that would have been that.

No one else ever dared to ask her how things were in the bedroom department, not even in a roundabout way. And yet, in resenting Sandra's curiosity, Mrs Hibbert was nevertheless aware that she was not so innocent herself. She would never pose the question Sandra had posed, but she speculated privately all the same and despised herself for doing so. *She* wondered about what went on in the bedrooms of people she knew and did not like the images which forced themselves into her head. Assuring herself that it was natural to wonder what went on didn't quite work. Was it natural? Did everyone speculate in this unseemly fashion? She didn't know, and wouldn't have dreamt of trying to find out. But it did strike her that if it was not natural it might be rather significant. It might mean sex was more alive in her than she allowed. There were some slight indications that this might be true. Sometimes when Francis gave her a cuddle and their bodies were briefly entwined she felt a *frisson* of something which she had told herself she would never again feel. It was horribly confusing, this sensation. Whenever she experienced the strangeness of it, she felt shaken for ages afterwards, but it was uncontrollable. 'What's wrong?' Francis would say, seeing her face (and she wondered just what he did see). 'What's the matter, Mary, are you ill?' And for simplicity's sake, she would say yes, she felt faint, she felt ill, and allow him to go and make her a cup of tea, after which she would recover.

They had all disappeared, these disturbing feelings, when Francis died. She'd been freed of them. Nobody had touched her since. On Sundays, she felt the loss most acutely, the loss of what had been within her, buried deeply but nevertheless there. She felt a deadness, a dryness, a hopeless realisation that everything was over and that indeed it had hardly lived. They had been married such a short time. It had left her bitter towards Francis, which she knew was not fair, but the circumstances of his death increased this bitterness, though she never let anyone know of it. She wished that in her will she could have let those who would read it know that what it contained was not the sum total of what she had been, or of what she had felt. It listed her goods and chattels, it itemised her wealth, but it gave no clue to the riches she had once possessed. Why it should seem important that others should have some inkling of another being who was not the Mrs Hibbert they knew she had no idea. She hated the assumptions made about her and wanted to correct them but could find no way to do it.

She was always so relieved when Mondays came.

12

Happiness is Activity

ON MONDAY, Ida couldn't decide whether to go and see the new vicar or not. If the Rev. Barnes had still been there she would have had no hesitation in seeking what he called pastoral care. She would have gone straight away, without letting a weekend intervene. She'd gone to him on many occasions, often in a complete panic, and he had never failed her. She could just turn up at the vicarage and if he was there he would stop what he was doing and usher her in. She'd sometimes half run to the vicarage, lumbering along with her breath coming in great gasps and her heart pounding alarmingly, and when she got there she was in such a state she hardly had the energy to stagger up the steps and ring the bell. The moment the Rev. Barnes had opened the door, she'd begun to calm down – his arm went round her shoulders at once and he led her into his study, closing the door firmly behind them and ignoring his wife's shout of 'Paul! At least finish your dinner!' He'd made her feel so important, worthy of his time, and that in itself was comforting. They had prayed together, down on their knees, and gradually her fear had always lessened. 'Everyone is afraid of dying, Ida,' he had said, 'but we all have to die. We have to trust in the Lord and He will see us along the path and through to the other side.' Ida had immediately visualised a grassy path, and a fence, and a stile, and herself being helped over it into a beautiful meadow. By the Rev. Barnes.

But the new vicar was different. It hadn't taken her long, in fact, to mark the Rev. Maddox's card and find him wanting in most respects. He was a poor preacher, for a start. His first sermon was highfalutin, his second plainer (had he twigged no one could understand him?) but dreary, and his third hopelessly rambling, with him losing the thread and having to fumble with his notes for an embarrassingly long time. She knew she was not the only one to be disappointed. The church was quite full on the first occasion, with thirty-two parishioners present, most of them women, of course, and there just to look at him. The number was down to a more usual fifteen the second week, and on the third Sunday only the faithful few attended, the hard core of nine who were always there unless ill or on holiday. Nine people, listening to the incomprehensible and smothering yawns. It was a relief to recognise the hymns. But he was over their heads, this new vicar, and his air of aloofness offended them.

He didn't know how to be friendly, either. He turned up, during his second week, at the Women's Fellowship meeting, advised, probably, to show his face by someone on the parish council. Show his face is exactly what he did – he looked round the door of the church hall where they were all gathered and said, 'I'm just saying hello, ladies, don't want to disturb you, carry on.' They all automatically stood up, and Dot Nicholson, of all people, urged the vicar to step inside and be welcomed. He'd been obliged to come into the hall properly and take a seat in their circle, and there he had remained, clutching his knees, while the subject for the monthly competition was decided. A shadow of a smile, hastily controlled, had passed over his face when it was agreed that they would compete to see who could arrange the prettiest wild flowers on a plain white saucer. Ida knew he was sneering, and that he had failed to appreciate that this competition was only a bit of fun, and that they all saw the joke too. His expression had reminded her of Mrs Hibbert's. After five minutes, he'd said he had work to do and must be going. Everyone agreed he was nothing like the Rev. Barnes, who had had no side to him and knew how to jolly everyone along. All that the Rev. Maddox had in his favour was that he was much better looking, and a bachelor. No one said out loud what this might signify. No one had to.

Ida knew that she would never get the warmth from the new vicar that she had received from the old. Rev. Barnes had made her feel brave, too, though she knew she wasn't, telling her how he admired the way she had borne her illness, and it was he who had suggested that she did a shift in the Mental Health Research charity shop when his wife had had to drop out of the rota. 'Happiness is activity, Ida,' he had told her. 'If you stay at home all the time brooding and worrying you'll only feel worse. It isn't enough only to go to church, you need something more. It will help, being in other surroundings once a week, and you'll have the satisfaction of doing a service. Try it.' She had, and he'd been right. She'd trusted him to be right. She didn't trust the Rev. Maddox, but then she hadn't tried him on a one-to-one basis, in private.

She decided to go after all and prepared herself carefully, wanting to appear calm and composed. She walked to the vicarage in the afternoon, taking her time so that she would not be sweaty and red-faced when she got there. Mercifully, she met no one and arrived at the door relieved and remarkably cheerful. There was a long pause after she'd rung the bell and she was just beginning to think that the Rev. Maddox was out when she heard his footsteps and then the creaky old door opened. But not very far. 'Ah,' the vicar said, and 'Yes?' 'Sorry to trouble you,' Ida said, feeling immediately at a disadvantage, 'but could I talk to you? It's personal.' The door did open a little wider, but the vicar took a step back. 'Ah,' he said, again. 'I wonder if you could come back later? In half an hour? I'm rather busy, I'm afraid.' Dumbly, Ida nodded, and backed away from the door, very nearly falling down the first step. Before she had turned round to negotiate the steps properly, the door had been closed again. She felt both humiliated and at the same time outraged – busy? He was busy? With what? One of his awful sermons? The Rev. Barnes had never been busy if she had needed him, even when he was busy he wasn't too busy.

She almost didn't bother going back at all. What could such a man ever do to help the likes of her? She shuddered to think of going to him in the state she'd been that awful day, or on one of those nights when she'd felt the cancer eating its way through her flesh, gorging on her insides and sucking her into its embrace. He'd be worse than useless. And yet, half an hour later, during which time she'd wandered aimlessly across to the churchyard and round it and back again, she found herself ringing the vicarage doorbell once more in a mood of defiance. He thought he'd got rid of her? Well, he hadn't. It was his duty to listen to her. This time the door opened promptly and was flung wide. There was even an attempt at a welcome – unconvincing, but at least it was made, a hand was extended in greeting and he said, 'Do come in.' He didn't take her into the study, where the Rev. Barnes had always taken her, but into the sitting-room. The chill of this room hit them as he led the way in and he made a performance of lighting the fire. It was a coal fire, and she could see at a glance that it would be hard to get going, with so little paper and no kindling showing underneath the coal which had just been chucked on any old how. He fussed with matches, using six, one after the other, and, when some smoke appeared, snatched the leather bellows hanging beside the fireplace and vigorously pumped them. The smoke died down. 'I'm sorry,' he said, 'do take a seat. I'm sorry about this.' Then he saw an electric fire in the corner and rushed to plug it in. It gave off an acrid stench as the elements showed red but he was delighted – 'Warmth at last!' he said, and then, when he'd sat himself down opposite her, 'Now, what was it you wanted?'

It was a simple enough question, one she supposed he was entitled to ask, but she didn't like the way he had phrased it. 'Wanted' made her sound greedy. Why couldn't he have put it differently? Why couldn't he have asked how he could help her? And she didn't like the way he sat, looking so unfriendly, so *official* somehow, so far away across the whole width of the shabby brown carpet – he'd positioned himself as isolated from her as possible, as though she had a bad smell. There *was* a bad smell, too, all round her, coming off the cushions on the battered sofa where the Barnes family's cats had peed. His stare unnerved her and she couldn't think what to say. He was waiting, like a headmaster confronting a pupil, sent to him for chastisement, and it made her remember a teacher she had once had who had terrified her. She licked her lips and gave a little cough, and she saw him surreptitiously looking at the clock on the mantelpiece. It wasn't working. Its hands showed a quarter to six and it couldn't be more than two-thirty. 'I get frightened,' she managed to say, her voice sounding hoarse. He tilted his head on one side, but said nothing. 'Panic,' she said. 'I panic, I feel cancer eating me.' She touched her chest and his eyes became riveted on her breasts. An expression she couldn't quite interpret crossed his face, but she thought it near to disgust, and suddenly she began to cry, not hard, just a few tears escaped. He stared at her, his features rearranged so that he looked simply impassive, and then he sprang up and turned his back on her and began walking about, touching the furniture and talking rapidly. She strained to take in what he was saying. Something about help coming from prayer, and prayer conquering fear, and being on the look-out for help arriving in unexpected ways, and God loving everyone and working in mysterious ways . . . it went on and on, and he was never still and never once looked at her. Struggling to haul herself out of the smelly depths of the old sofa, she said she was sorry to have troubled him and that she'd better go. He didn't move from the window, where he'd finally stopped his pacing. He was watching her as she walked towards the door. She felt dizzy and there was a thudding in her ears – he might have been saying something else, but she couldn't hear it. Putting a hand out to steady herself on the small round table she was passing she touched a lace mat underneath a china bowl full of pot-pourri and brought it crashing down. The table was spindly and couldn't take the weight she put upon it and keeled over on top of the smashed china, taking her with it. She lay in a heap, stunned, the table across her legs and the musty pot-pourri round her head. She closed her eyes to try to stop the spinning in her head, and when it subsided she gave a little sob and tried to get up. She rolled onto her side, cutting her arm on a shard of the broken china bowl, and pulled her knees up from under the little table, but she couldn't lever herself up. Turning, she looked for the vicar, hating him for what he had just witnessed and hating him more for not having rushed to help her. 'I can't get up!' she shouted. 'Can't you see? I can't get up!' She stretched out a hand, but still he didn't move. He had his back to the light, he was in shadow, but she could tell he was transfixed, rigid. Groaning, she rolled away from the table towards the sofa. It seemed so far away and she had to roll over again, her fat unwieldy body refusing to roll easily and needing to be forced painfully, inch by inch. Her dress had ridden up, and her pink slip tore as it caught on the table leg, but she had reached the end of the sofa and grasped the edge of it to help her up. Panting, she got herself half-upright and paused for the last big effort, and at that moment the vicar moved, advancing towards her, his arms outstretched. 'No!' she shouted. 'I'll manage, leave me! I don't need you! I don't want your help! Stop!' He stopped. She was on her feet, but leaned against the sofa to rest a moment. Her head and back hurt, and her arm where she'd cut herself was bleeding, but all she wanted was to be out of the vicarage, away from that man.

'Mrs Yates,' he began, as she stumbled to the door, 'Mrs Yates, please, wait, I . . .' but she wouldn't wait, or speak to him, or look at him. She got through the door and into the hall safely, but the front door defeated her. She tugged and pulled but couldn't open it and he came behind her and she had to move aside to let him open it for her. 'Mrs Yates,' he said again, 'Mrs Yates, this is all most unfortunate, I'm so sorry, I can't think what . . .' but she was out, careering down the steps dangerously, at last away from him. He didn't follow her. She half ran down the drive, only slowing to a walk once she was through the gates. She would never go to the Rev. Maddox again. She'd made a fool of herself, but that was not what concerned her most, it was the fact that she'd gone to see him at all when she should have known better. She'd exposed herself and her fears to a man who couldn't understand them and was repelled by her, a man without compassion who couldn't cope with emotion. Martin couldn't either, but he was of more use, or he tried to be. Now she would have no one to run to when everything became too much, she might as well just wander the roads as she had done that other day and suffer the humiliation of being picked up by Mrs Hibbert.

She didn't tell Martin where she had been and what had happened. Better that he shouldn't know how she'd been let down. But it was Martin who heard something drop through the letter-box just as they were going to their respective beds. He came back holding an envelope with her name written on it in beautiful italic handwriting. She snatched it from him. 'It's from the vicar,' she said. 'Church business.' Martin stood there looking puzzled in that irritating way of his. 'What church business?' he asked, but before she needed to reply he'd lost interest. She put the letter in the pocket of her cardigan and went upstairs, determined not to open it until the morning. She didn't want to be spoken to by that man even on paper. She put his letter on her bedside table, face down, and turned the light off. But as she lay there, sleepless and stiff with indignation, she suddenly realised that the letter might not be from the vicar. She'd assumed it would be, but she'd never seen his handwriting. Who could it be from, then, hand-delivered like that and so late at night? It must be from the vicar. Annoyed, she sat up and put her lamp on and reaching for the letter ripped it open in one violent tearing motion. Yes, it was from the Rev. Maddox.

Only five lines and none containing the word 'sorry'. Instead, she read that the vicar 'regretted' being unable to help her, and that he was 'concerned' that she might have hurt herself in her unfortunate 'tumble'. He looked forward to her calling again, when they might explore the benefits of prayer in more detail. Ida tore the letter into tiny pieces, but that was not enough. She picked up the fragments and dropped them into the glass of water she kept beside the bed, then she stuck her finger into the soggy mess and pushed it further into the water until all the liquid had been absorbed. Flinging herself back down onto her pillow, she tried to compose herself for sleep, but her face was burning and her body hot, and finally she got up and went to the window and opened it. It was a cold night, though the day had been warm. She leaned out, hurting herself on the window-sill. The moon was so bright, and so yellow, it could have been the sun, except for the blackness behind it. Below, on the bricks of the patio Martin had laid out, she saw a tiny animal scoot across. If she fell, she'd fall onto the bricks, but she couldn't fall, she'd have to climb up and throw herself out and she was too fat, the window too small.

Instead, she got back into bed, feeling cooler and less hysterical. She was never going to see that man again, never go into the church so long as he was vicar. But it couldn't be done. It dismayed her to think how little she would have in her life if she took church and church events out of it. Going to another church further away wouldn't work, it wasn't as though the town was big enough to offer her alternatives. St James's was the only Church of England church. And in any case, it was special, special to her, it was *hers*, not this new vicar's, and she couldn't, wouldn't, let him take it away from her. No other church could give her the comfort it gave her. She went into it and immediately felt reassured even if this reassurance disappeared the moment she stepped outside again. She'd been baptised there, confirmed there, married there – the church *knew* her through and through. But the vicarage was a different matter. She could vow never to set foot in it again. And the church hall was not sacred. If the Rev. Maddox turned up at any meeting or event held there, she could leave. With this decided, she drifted off to sleep.

But in the early hours of the morning, she woke up, thinking she didn't want that man to bury her. She would have to make some sort of declaration to that effect, written instructions that the Rev. Maddox was not to conduct, or be present at, her funeral. She would write this request – no, it was an order, a command – down, and then make Martin promise to see to it. He wouldn't let her talk about death or funerals but she would make him listen and make him promise to carry out her wish. One thing, Martin was dependable. Once she got his attention and his agreement he was trustworthy. This thought calmed her again but she couldn't get back to sleep. She kept seeing the Rev. Maddox's face, his distaste, his repugnance when he looked at her, as though she horrified him, and it made her rage all over again. What was wrong with the man? He was a man of God, supposed to be understanding and sympathetic and able to offer comfort and enlightenment. She'd brought him her troubles, her very real troubles, and he'd recoiled from them. She dozed, then woke up, then dozed again, tossing and turning and desperate for real sleep. It came only half an hour before Martin brought her her tea.

She felt awful. Ages after she'd drunk the tea, she still felt awful, and thought about staying in bed for the day, but it was a charity shop day. She had to get up. Her head ached, and the whole length of her spine hurt, but she forced herself to get up and wash and dress, and was ready, just, when Martin shouted it was nine o'clock and was she coming, or not? It was a Tuesday, and on Tuesdays he usually went to Mrs Hibbert's, dropping her off at the shop first. He chattered all the way there about what he was going to do in her garden, as if she wanted to hear. He knew she had no interest in gardens. Gardens did nothing for her. She felt only a momentary pleasure at seeing the flowers bloom, however pretty they were. How Martin could get so excited about the first rose opening out, or his sweet peas climbing up the trellis, she couldn't understand. He took to marvelling at how plants survived cruel winters, as though he wanted to send her a message but, although she understood this more than he perhaps realized, she refused to be comforted by it. 'Life goes on,' Martin said, surveying his garden in spring. The only life she was interested in was her own, and she was not a plant.

She didn't speak all the way to the shop, but there was nothing unusual in that and Martin hardly noticed. Lucy Binns had opened the shop up and was in the back trying to sort out some newly donated sacks of clothes. 'The mess!' she cried, as Ida walked in. Ida stood and looked at all the black bin-liners she was untying. She could tell at a glance that most of the stuff was rubbish, jumble sale standard, jumpers none too clean and with holes in them, blouses with perspiration marks under the arms, trousers with broken zips – people had a cheek dumping such rags in a charity shop, knowing perfectly well they were not good enough to sell. There was only one bag that looked promising. It wasn't a bin-liner. It was a large carrier bag but not one Ida recognised, it didn't belong to one of the chain stores with which she was familiar. She said this to Lucy, pointing the bag out with her foot. Lucy said she'd been told a vicar had dropped it off, so maybe it would have decent items of clothing in it. 'We need good-quality men's clothes,' Lucy said. 'You unpack that one, Ida, and see what you think. Here, I'll lift it onto the table, you don't want to be doing any lifting.' Ida stood aside, pleased, while sturdy little Lucy swung the bag up. She liked Lucy, who was always so considerate and who never forgot Ida had had cancer. Other people in the shop did. Adelaide Priest had forgotten totally. She came out all the time with remarks that showed a complete lack of consideration for the perilous state of Ida's health, and if she was reminded, if Ida, aggrieved, said she couldn't do something because she hadn't the strength due to her operation, Adelaide would say, 'Oh, what nonsense, Ida, you're as fit as a fiddle, you don't want to be treated like an invalid, do you?' This was precisely how Ida wished to be treated, but she could not, of course, admit it. Instead, she glared at Adelaide and said that in fact she was very far from fit and had been told never to over-exert herself. This was not true, but she reckoned that as long as she had to continue to have check-ups at the clinic she was entitled to pretend it was.

The contents of the carrier bag were all neatly folded and obviously hardly worn, but they were puzzling. If Lucy was right, and a vicar had brought them in, then they were very unusual garments for such a man to possess. Ida had anticipated dark-coloured trousers and jackets, with maybe a few white shirts, but the bag contained pale linen slacks and multi-coloured short-sleeved shirts. There was also a panama hat which was so clean round the inside headband that Ida felt it could hardly have been on any man's head for more than a few minutes. She hung the clothes on wire hangers and put them on the rack to await Mrs Jarrett's inspection – it was she who decided whether things should be put through the dry-cleaning machine or sponged down or simply gone over with that vacuum thing. She wondered as she finished doing this whether this vicar had once been a missionary. The missionaries in the pictures in the books they'd been shown at Sunday school when she'd been a child had all worn white suits and panama hats. They'd all been thin and rather frail-looking, like the Rev. Maddox. She flushed as she made the comparison and tried to banish the image of that man in a white suit.

The shop was empty, but then it was still early. There was a chair behind the counter where people came to pay, and Ida was always encouraged to sit on it by Lucy. She needed no urging. If anyone came to the counter, she always stood up to take their money, but otherwise she sat and pretended to read a book, and watched Lucy flit about doing quite unnecessary things to keep herself busy. She was still thinking about missionaries when Dot Nicholson came into the shop. Everyone, except Ida, felt sorry for Dot. She couldn't see why people thought Dot worthy of such sympathy. Nothing bad had ever happened to her, surely. Her husband might be a bully and a miserable person but why that aroused such pity for Dot she failed to appreciate. He'd been a catch, in his day, Adam Nicholson, son of a master butcher with two shops, and certain to inherit the family business. Dot had never known want in her life. Of course, Ida reckoned, this 'poor little Dot' business *was* because she was so very little. Big people didn't get the same sympathy, she knew that. Dot Nicholson was not feeble, but she looked it and her appearance made people want to protect her. If she'd had breast cancer then the sympathy would've been overwhelming. But then, Ida reflected, Dot had no breasts, or none to speak of. She'd never had any. Flat-chested since schooldays. Now that was to be pitied.

Dot had come up to the counter. Ida tried to smile, feeling guilty at the malicious thoughts she'd been having. 'I'm here to find a present for Adam,' Dot whispered. 'He's 75 on Sunday.' Why the woman was whispering, Ida couldn't think – it was hardly an intimate confession. Only Dot would go looking for a present for her husband in a charity shop, of course. Typical. 'What treasure can I offer you?' Ida asked, knowing she sounded sarcastic but that sarcasm would be lost on Dot. Lucy came up to the counter at that point, and Ida took pleasure in repeating, very loudly, that Dot was looking for a very special present for her husband's birthday. 'Well,' said Lucy, brightly, not at all amused or surprised, 'how about a book? We've got some practically brand-new books at the moment, I don't think they've even been opened.' She took an eager Dot over to the shelves and showed her the volumes she meant. Ida knew Dot wouldn't choose any of them, and she didn't. 'A tie?' she heard the helpful Lucy suggest. 'Ties are over here, they've all been dry-cleaned.' They were dreadful ties. Even Dot would see that. Drab brown and navy striped things which had indeed been cleaned but the cleaning hadn't managed entirely to remove the worst of the stains. Besides, Adam Nicholson probably never wore a tie these days, now that he rarely left home. He wouldn't wear a tie on his weekly outing to have his feet done, Ida was sure of that, and Dot had said that was the only time he left the house these days. But Dot had, as expected, spurned the ties. She was scrutinising a table set out with boxes and small ornaments and cufflinks and other clutter. Ida saw her pick up a wooden box and then put it down again. What she finally chose and brought to the counter was a large china mug decorated with a brightly coloured picture of a huntsman and hounds, with the words Tally Ho! printed on it.

'How much is this?' she asked Ida. Ida turned it over. 'A fortune, Dot,' she said. Dot took her absolutely seriously, her anguish comical. 'Twenty *p*,' Ida said, 'can you afford it?' Dot laughed, and produced the money. 'Adam used to hunt,' she said. 'It'll remind him of happier days.' Ida couldn't prevent herself snorting with derision – happy days? Adam Nicholson? – but Dot was oblivious. Lucy had joined them, and was asking if there was going to be a party, or celebration, for Adam's birthday. Dot shook her head. 'We'll just have a quiet day,' she said, as though that in itself was a treat. 'I'll go to church in the morning and then I'll come home and cook a joint of beef, sirloin, with roast potatoes and Yorkshire pudding. Adam's favourite.' Lucy said that sounded delicious. 'Which church do you belong to, Dot?' she asked, clearly just trying to make conversation since there was nothing left for her to straighten or fold, and there were still no other customers. Dot said, 'St James's.' 'Oh,' said Lucy, suddenly genuinely interested, 'that's where the interesting new vicar has just come, isn't it? What's he like?' Dot said he was very nice, quiet, gentle, quite different from the last one, and ever so clever.

Ida waited until Dot had gone, and then waited some more while a young mother pushed a twin buggy round the crowded shop, the twins clutching at clothes and pulling half of them down, which had Lucy chasing round putting them back, and then finally, when there was peace again, she said as casually as possible to Lucy, 'How did you know about the new vicar, then? You don't go to St James's.' Lucy said that her sister, who lived in Manchester, had written saying that their vicar who had had a nervous breakdown had been moved to a quiet parish near where Lucy lived. 'A nervous breakdown?' said Ida, taking care not to sound too interested. 'That's what she said,' Lucy agreed, 'a nervous breakdown. Not something you expect clergymen to have, is it? Not with them believing in God, if you know what I mean.' 'What was it about, the breakdown?' Ida asked. Lucy said she hadn't been told, but her sister had said – and at that moment there was a sudden rush. Three middle-aged women came in together, all carrying large leather shopping bags, and began sorting methodically through all the racks of clothes. Ida could tell at once that they were experts at spotting bargains and were probably going to resell what they found and make a nice profit. They fingered the materials, turning any garment they were interested in inside out, looking for labels and washing instructions, and examining them closely for wear and tear. She and Lucy were silent, both watching the women intently, knowing they were quite capable of stealing even if this was a charity shop. But they would be forced to buy what they'd selected, and they would haggle over the prices. She hoped Lucy would be as firm as she intended to be: absolutely no reductions.

By the time these women had made their purchases (and Lucy was as gratifyingly unyielding as herself) there was a lot to be done. All the colour-co-ordinating Lucy had nobly laboured over was wrecked and she had to start again, with Ida assisting. It was impossible to pick up once more the conversation about the vicar's nervous breakdown and yet she so badly wanted to, feeling she had not yet drained Lucy of every scrap of information imparted to her by her sister. She'd felt such a *frisson* of excitement run through her at the mention of mental instability associated with the Rev. Maddox – she felt desperate to know what had prompted his nervous breakdown and what form it had taken. No wonder he was of no use to her if his own head was in a mess. But instead of this making her forgiving towards the vicar, it only made her angrier. If he knew what it was like to feel you were going mad, why hadn't he been sympathetic towards her tears and panic? He was a fellow sufferer, and as far as she knew he hadn't any excuse, and yet he'd looked at her, and she did have a reason to be distraught, as though she were the lowest of the low.

Later, when there was another lull, and she and Lucy were having a cup of tea at the counter (though they were supposed to have any refreshment separately in the back room) Ida asked Lucy if she saw much of the sister who lived in Manchester. Lucy said yes, she did, quite a lot. They took turns to visit each other for the weekend about once a month, though she was fonder of going to Manchester, where she loved the shops, than her sister was of visiting her. 'She's coming this weekend, though,' said Lucy. 'I wish I'd had a sister,' sighed Ida, deciding to be oblique in her next approach. Lucy agreed it was nice having a sister, and said that she was fortunate to have two, though she wasn't as close to the other one. Ida was hardly listening. 'What will you do with your sister this weekend, then?' she asked. Lucy said that was always a bit of a problem, Janet couldn't sit still, she liked to be out and about, and as Ida knew there wasn't a lot to do here. 'Will you go to church on Sunday?' Ida asked. Lucy said, 'Probably.' 'Well,' said Ida, very, very lightly, and turning away to remove their cups and saucers as she did so, 'why don't you come to St James's and your Janet can see how her old vicar is getting on?'

Lucy seemed quite delighted with this idea. She became more and more enthusiastic, carefully checking the time of morning service with Ida, who was smiling at the success of her plan when Martin picked her up. She wasn't sure exactly what she hoped to achieve by confronting the Rev. Maddox with a former parishioner who knew about his nervous breakdown, and maybe the cause of it (some scandal?), but she was sure she would achieve something. It would mean, of course, having to break her recently made vow never to go into St James's while that man was still there, but then she reminded herself she'd decided only the church hall was out of bounds. Or had she? She couldn't remember, but it didn't matter. Her smile broadened as she got in the car. Martin thought it must mean she had had a good day, and he in turn smiled back. She was bursting to tell someone about the Rev. Maddox's nervous breakdown and Martin was the only person available, so she told him, without any preamble, as soon as they were on the road home. Martin's smile faded. 'Poor chap,' he said. This annoyed her. Nervous breakdowns were not *cancer*. His instant compassion was, in her opinion, overdone. He kept saying it over and over again, poor, poor chap, when what she wanted was for him to speculate as to the causes of this breakdown, to show some real curiosity. He had none. She thought about describing to him how she had been treated at the vicarage the day before, to make him understand why she felt no sympathy for the vicar, but that would only lead to questions she didn't want to answer. Instead, she would ignore Martin and his 'poor chaps'. But just as she was deciding this, he said something else.

'What did you say?' she asked him.

Patiently, Martin repeated it. 'I was saying,' he began, as though she had a hearing problem and not that she hadn't been attending, 'that Mrs Hibbert said she couldn't imagine why the bishop had sent the Rev. Maddox to St James's.'

'Why shouldn't he have?' asked Ida, instantly sensing an insult. 'What's wrong with St James's?'

'Mrs Hibbert says he'll have no intellectual stimulus there.'

'Intellectual stimulus?' shouted Ida. 'What on earth does that mean? He's a vicar.'

'I think she meant nobody like himself to talk to,' Martin said, nervously. 'He'll be a fish out of water.'

'Well, that's his fault,' snapped Ida.

They drove on for a while, and then Martin said, 'Mrs Hibbert's met him.'

'Oh, has she indeed,' said Ida, longing to know how, since Mrs Hibbert never went near the church, but not wanting to show that she did.

'At St Mary's,' Martin obligingly added, 'a committee meeting of the Friends. He's going to be associated with them.'

'Big of him,' said Ida, and 'Associated!' she sneered, but not too sarcastically, because she wanted Martin to carry on. Usually, after three 'Mrs Hibbert saids' she told him to shut up.

'Seems Mrs Hibbert crossed swords with him, but she was impressed, she thinks he is a good man, for all his faults.'

'Good?' Ida felt she was choking. *'Good?'*

'That's what she said. And she knows how to judge character.'

Ida laughed, loudly. 'How do you work that out?' she said.

'She took me on,' Martin said, 'without references.'

'Oh, for heaven's sake!' Ida exploded. 'She took you on because she'd seen you working in Mr Lonsdale's garden opposite her and that was reference enough. And she'd have got rid of you quick enough if you hadn't lived up to her expectations, or if you hadn't turned up when she wanted you to. She's ruthless, that woman, all her family were. They got rid of my Nan soon enough.'

Martin was quiet. He knew that to be quiet was the best way to encourage Ida to continue. But they arrived home and she went into the house without speaking again, her former cheerful mood apparently gone. Something he'd said had upset her, banishing that smile she'd had when he drew up in the car. He should have known better than to mention Mrs Hibbert at all. The rest of the day, he observed Ida carefully. There was something different about her, some atmosphere surrounding her that he couldn't quite grasp. It wasn't that she didn't speak – that was common enough – or that she seemed abstracted, but that she seemed to be concentrating on something. She stared hard out of the window, and he looked himself, following her gaze, but there was nothing to see so remarkable that it held the attention. He did risk asking, 'Penny for them?' but she shook her head. 'Nothing,' she said.

Ida found it hard waiting for Sunday to come. She imagined the scene when the vicar saw his ex-parishioner, Lucy's sister Janet, over and over again. He would be bound to notice her. He'd be shocked, wouldn't he? Knowing she knew about his nervous breakdown and almost certainly its rumoured cause? But maybe not. She reminded herself that Manchester was a big place and that congregations in churches there were possibly much larger. Janet might have been only one of many, indistinguishable from others. Besides, the Rev. Maddox was the sort of man who never really looked at anyone properly. He wouldn't have looked at faces closely enough to remember them. Instead of looking people in the eye, he employed the evasive tactic of looking just above their head, or over their shoulder, as though seeing someone else far more interesting. God, maybe.

When Sunday at last arrived, Ida dressed with exquisite care. She always tried to look her best for church, but this Sunday she wanted to be really smart. She had a bath when she got up and dressed in clean clothes from the skin outwards. The effort exhausted her, but when she saw herself in the long mirror on the wardrobe door, she felt gratified. She had on her navy costume, and navy always made her look slimmer. The waist of the skirt was hellishly tight, even though she'd left the top two buttons undone and fastened it with a large safety pin (nobody would see, the jacket came over it) but she was more than prepared to put up with the discomfort. Nobody these days wore hats or gloves to an ordinary morning service, but she was wearing both, a navy straw hat, nicely trimmed with a darker navy ribbon, and white gloves to match her white blouse. Only her shoes let her down but there was no alternative. She couldn't get into the navy court shoes that had once gone with this outfit because her feet were so swollen, so she had to wear her flat, black Ecco shoes. Still, she looked good enough to be going to a wedding (which was precisely how the navy costume had come to be bought).

Martin was digging in the garden as she left. He stopped digging to tell her how nice she looked. He liked her to look 'nice' and she knew why – he interpreted it to mean she was feeling better. If she'd bothered to dress up, then she couldn't be in a panic. He didn't realise the reason could be the precise opposite. She often used the need to get dressed smartly for church to force her into controlling herself, and the struggle was always tremendous. The battle to select clothes and put them on in the right order would make her head pound, and she would break out into such a sweat she wanted to tear them all off again, and throw herself on the bed and stay there. It was often touch and go whether she would or she wouldn't. But this Sunday she'd felt wonderfully calm. Although it tired her, getting ready had in other ways been almost a pleasure. Her short walk to the church was as a consequence quite stately. She passed someone she knew and she could see them noting how well turned out she was. It struck her, as she entered the church itself, that if asked she would have to say that she felt *well*.

She sat where she always sat, in the sixth pew from the front, on the right-hand side. Only Mrs Gibbon and Mrs Hardy sat in front of her. Across the aisle, she could see Dot, on her knees, praying. Behind her, she heard the Teasdales – mother, father, daughter – file in, the father coughing, as usual. The Proudfoots would rush in at the last minute and sit right at the back. Nine of them, so scattered about that the church looked even emptier than it was. The Rev. Barnes, whose congregation was always twice, sometimes three times, this number, used to urge everyone to come together, and for a while everyone did, filling the front pews on both sides, but then, over the following weeks, they would drift apart again and he would once more have to remonstrate with them. But Ida had the feeling that the Rev. Maddox actually preferred his congregation to be as spread-out as possible. It made them less threatening, easier to ignore. The church might be small, but when he was in the pulpit there was no sense of intimacy as he preached. His manner and delivery were more suited to a cathedral – he pitched his voice to carry a great and unnecessary distance. Maybe his Manchester church had been huge and he had not yet adapted to St James's dimensions, but that was the kindest explanation and one Ida did not believe.

She wondered where Lucy and her sister Janet had chosen to sit, but was determined not to turn round to see. Patiently, she sat through the service, singing the hymns lustily as she always did (and aware that no one else did). The sermon was about harvests but, though it began with the harvesting of corn, it moved on to souls and she was lost. Her mind wandered hopelessly as she stared at the Rev. Maddox, trying to see him in a mental institution in a strait-jacket though, of course, she knew perfectly well he would probably have been at home taking sedatives. She dressed him in the linen slacks she'd found in the carrier bag unpacked at the Save the Children shop and put him in one of the lilac shirts. They suited him, but the hat, the panama hat, didn't, so she took it off. He'd combed his hair very carefully this morning, as carefully as she'd combed hers. It was dark and thick and the parting on the left side very neat. He'd looked in a mirror to get that parting, which suggested he was vain. He wasn't as young as they'd all thought he'd be. It was just that he had the sort of skin which aged well, but now she was scrutinising him she could see lines where she hadn't noticed them before. He was 50, at least, she was sure. He was very clean-shaven, his chin and upper lip without the faintest hint of any growth, and he had dainty lips, prettily shaped . . .

She didn't fall asleep but staring so intently at the vicar she felt she'd hypnotised herself and had to shake her head to clear it. The service over, the Rev. Maddox strode to the door, looking neither to right nor left, and positioned himself there dutifully. The first week, he hadn't done this. He'd stayed at the altar till everyone had left. But he'd been tactfully told that the custom at St James's, and surely at most churches, was for the vicar to bid farewell at the door to each and every one of the congregation, saying a few appropriate words every time he shook a hand. The trouble was that though he had thereafter followed this custom, he had difficulty finding any words at all. His awkwardness made his congregation feel awkward and they were coming to dread the mumbling which ensued, and had started rushing out with unseemly haste so that the handshakes had already become perfunctory. Ida didn't hurry. She wanted to be last out so that she could study the effect that seeing Lucy's sister had on the Rev. Maddox. But she saw, as she stepped into the aisle, that Lucy had not attended the service. She knew all eight of the people ahead of her and none of them were Lucy and Janet. Her disappointment made her gasp 'Oh!', and Dot, in front of her, said, 'Ida?', and she had to pretend to cough. But as she made her way behind Dot to the door, she clung on to the fact that even if Lucy and Janet had not shown up she still knew about the vicar's nervous breakdown and she meant to let him know that she knew. She held herself back a little, giving Dot, who followed on after the Teasdales (only the father shook hands) plenty of time. She could hear Dot twittering on about Adam's birthday and the special roast cooking at home, and then she had scuttled off. Ida moved slowly forward, consciously trying to look dignified.

He flushed dark red. There was no mistaking it – red from the neck up. He could hardly get out the words, 'Nice to see you, Mrs Yates, how are you this fine morning?' Ida had intended to be magnificently cool and remote, but she couldn't manage it. 'Never mind me, Vicar,' she said, with what she hoped was unmistakable emphasis, 'how are *you*? Well, I hope?' She was going to add 'Quite recovered, I trust', but didn't. He had his hand sticking out but she hadn't yet taken it. She took it now, and squeezed it. Her hand was strong, her grip firm. She held his hand until he had to free it, with difficulty. For once, he was meeting her stare, but his eyes didn't have in them the expression she had expected and looked for. They were sad eyes. 'Quite well, thank you,' he said, very quietly. 'Good,' Ida said. Something was slipping away from her, all that lovely power she'd felt, and she wanted it back. 'Good,' she repeated, 'because I heard you haven't been well.' He raised his eyebrows, and Ida knew this meant that he wasn't surprised, that he was well aware the whole parish had known he hadn't been well, which was why he had taken up his position so late. He seemed to be pondering how to respond, and she was not going to help him. 'A friend,' Ida said, 'in Manchester . . .' and then it was her turn to blush. 'Ah,' he said, 'I see,' and he nodded. There was nothing she could do but nod back, and say good morning, and walk away, but she couldn't walk as quickly as she wanted to because her legs were stiff. She felt suddenly dreadfully ashamed, and then resentful that she had to acknowledge this – it wasn't fair, it wasn't how things should have turned out. All she'd been looking for was for *him* to have been made ashamed of how he had treated her.

Martin was still digging. 'Good service?' he said, cheerily. She didn't answer. She felt ill.

13

Awaiting Events

THE WEEKEND over, Rachel was, as ever, perfectly happy to be going to work, even though she loved the Sunday gliding lessons. She liked her office. It was small but not cramped, and it faced south so that it got any sun going, and she'd made it a pleasant place, with David Hockney reproduction prints on the walls and always a jug of flowers on her desk, natural-looking flowers, not stiff stems, lilac in May, scented stock later on. Mr MacAllister had let her choose the carpet five years ago when all the offices were being refurbished and she'd chosen a self-coloured jade green which looked pretty. The one easy chair, for clients to sit on, was covered in a green and white material, tiny white daisies on a green background. Her office, she considered, was a soothing place, a surprise to visitors, and it contrasted markedly with the austere atmosphere of the rest of the building. Walking up the dark staircase with its panelled walls and dark grey carpet, Rachel looked forward to the burst of light as she entered her own room.

Miriam, the young work-experience girl, niece of one of the partners, came in. 'Good weekend?' she said. Rachel said, yes, very enjoyable. 'What were you up to, then?' Miriam asked, in that old-fashioned chatty way, which was somehow disconcerting in one so young. Rachel smiled. Miriam amused her. She was the only one in the building who had any curiosity about other people. It had been so easy, three years ago, to take a month off work to cover her operation and treatment, and pretend she was going on holiday. If Miriam had been there, she would never have got away with it – there would have been questions about where she'd gone, questions about what the weather had been like. Without Miriam, there had been no questions. A couple of colleagues had said, 'Good holiday?' and not stayed for an answer. No one had noticed that she was pale and didn't look as though she'd had a holiday at all, and she had felt relieved. There had been no need to invent any holiday history.

She told Miriam she was learning to fly a glider, a piece of information received with intense interest which then had to be curbed – Miriam would talk for hours, if encouraged. She was such a bouncy sort of girl, her very walk was jumpy, and Mr MacAllister himself was reported to have complained that the floors of the old building could not stand much more of Miriam's elephantine movements. Once she'd bounced out, Rachel worked steadily all morning, and then at lunchtime she walked into the town centre to buy a sandwich and take it to eat at her desk. On the way back, she met the only other woman solicitor in the practice, Judith Holmes. 'Keeping well?' Judith asked, and 'Lovely day, isn't it?' and then 'I must rush, bye.' She rushed. Rachel followed slowly behind, thinking about how people so often asked if others were well without seeming to appreciate what a difficult and complicated question it was. Sitting in her office again, eating her sandwich and looking out of the window over the tops of the chestnut trees, she wondered if she was really, as she'd replied to Judith, keeping well.

How could she know? She'd always been well until she was told she was not well. She'd been superbly fit and healthy until she was pronounced disease-ridden. And she had had to accept and believe the verdict without, to her, any proof. Doctors had the proof. They'd explained, they'd drawn diagrams, they'd produced pathology results, they'd given her leaflets to read, but none of it had made sense. She'd felt absolutely fine until they started giving her treatment and then she'd felt ill. So, how did she know, when the Judiths so lightly inquired, if she was keeping well? She might be, she might not be. It was important, she'd been told, to be optimistic and have a positive outlook.

Why? They didn't seem to know, beyond having some theory that cancer might be either caused or encouraged by a fatalistic attitude. Such rubbish. She only had to think of many optimistic, strong women who had succumbed to the disease, to know there could be no truth in it. This hint that a patient could influence the progress of her cancer by her mental and emotional approach to it made her angry.

All she felt she could do was eat well, take exercise, stay calm. And it was as she was reminding herself of this that she felt a stab of pain, just a little stab, gone in a second. Cautiously, she put the wrapping from her sandwich into the waste-paper basket. Probably indigestion, probably she'd eaten too fast (but she knew she hadn't). Sitting down again, this time back on the swivel chair behind her desk, she composed herself and took deep breaths. Fine, she was fine. But she remained quite still for a good few minutes before reaching for the folder in front of her. No pain at all. Starting to read the papers in the folder, she had to force her mind to concentrate. She succeeded. Fifteen minutes later, clear of anxiety, she bent to the right to open a drawer. This time, several quick, sharp, fleeting pains all along her breast-bone. No mistaking them. Her whole body tightened, her right arm quite rigid, with her hand gripping the drawer handle. It took an effort to straighten up and sit back in her chair. Her heart was racing and she felt not so much dizzy as vague, as though she were not really present. She slipped her hand into her shirt and felt along the bone, pressing lightly with her fingers. Nothing. No lumps or bumps, no pain.

The thing to do was be sensible. Await events, see what happened next, keep track, note down what was taking place. Drawing a pad of paper towards her, she carefully wrote down the date in the left-hand corner and then the times. '1.47 p.m.', she wrote, 'small stab of pain, while eating a prawn sandwich in office.' Was the prawn information necessary? Or the place where she'd eaten it? How absurd it looked, written down. '2.05 p.m.', she wrote underneath, 'three or four stabs of pain while opening drawer.' She'd been stretching. Could the pain be muscular? But she hadn't been stretching the time before. No, rule out muscular. Miriam charged in, carrying mail. 'Hi again,

Rachel,' she said, dumping the mail on the desk, and then 'Ooh, you've gone all white, are you all right, Rachel, are you all right, shall I . . .' 'I'm fine,' Rachel said, 'just the sandwich I had was a bit odd-tasting,' and she gestured towards the bin, desperate to provide evidence. 'Maybe you'll sick it up?' Miriam suggested, hopefully. 'Maybe, but I don't think so. I'm fine, really, just a bit queasy, it will pass. Thank you, Miriam.'

It had passed. No more pains all afternoon. At home, she took the sheet of paper she'd made her solemn little notes on and put it in the folder which held all her hospital details and her clinic card. She was remembering now what Mr Wallis had said when she'd pressed him to tell her what to look out for, what signs there might be that the cancer was active. One of the things he'd told her was that the pain with cancer was constant once it started. Her stabs of pain had not been constant. They'd come, they'd gone. Surely that was a good sign? But then perhaps she hadn't understood properly what Mr Wallis had said. She would have to ask him again, and then he would think her neurotic. Well, she was. Cancer had made her neurotic about her own body. How could she possibly have gone travelling with George, as he'd wanted her to, three years ago, so far away from medical help if she'd needed it? Illness, George had said, was a luxury a traveller such as himself could not afford. Pompous, she'd called him. Maybe, by not going with George, she'd saved her own life. Maybe, by being alert, she was saving it now.

But the business of monitoring the workings of her body was exhausting. Every day, there was some trivial ache or pain or some difference somewhere which might mean something sinister. Her throat would be sore in a way it had never been sore before, or she'd develop an ulcer on her gums she had never had before, or she'd suddenly find swallowing difficult, or she'd start coughing and hear a strange wheeze – the list was varied and endless. Always, she controlled her terror and awaited events. These things cleared up, settled down, but only for other things to take their place. Her body had become a tyrant, demanding and receiving full-time attention. Years of hardly knowing how it worked had been replaced by a horrible awareness of its most minute tickings – she could easily have presented herself at her GP's or the hospital clinic every single day. But she hadn't.

She wasn't going to go to either of them now. The piece of paper was put away, another victory gained. She saw, as she slipped it into the folder, the letter which had come from the counselling service at St Mary's. They'd asked if she would like to attend a group meeting of women who had breast cancer, to share experiences with each other which they all might find mutually helpful. She hadn't been able to imagine anything worse, and nor did she want a one-to-one session, also on offer. She was on her own with this thing, and had to deal with it alone. Talking about it wouldn't help her, not even, if it had been possible, talking to George, though she had often, in the past three years, wished he was with her. Every time she looked at the first date on her clinic card, stuck at the front of the folder, she was struck by the neatness: 2 p.m., Thursday, 9 April 2000, the day George left. She'd said goodbye in the morning, not even telling him about the lump or the appointment, and then she'd gone to St Mary's. Those who liked to think stress caused cancer would be triumphant, but she rejected this thinking. She had to, or otherwise it would happen again. She was a survivor, and intended to go on being a survivor, and to that end she had to keep her mind clear of all conspiracy theories. Control, of herself, was essential.

Only once had she lost it. She could hardly bear to remember the consequences, what she had put herself through. It had been a pain then. In her hip, her right hip. It had never crossed her mind that this might be suspicious. A pain in her hip seemed almost a pleasure to go to see her GP about. She'd been quite relaxed, and eloquent describing it. 'It's when I walk,' she'd said, 'I get this sharp pain, it shoots from my right hip down the front of my thigh, and it's so searing, I have to stop and rest. Do you think I've pulled a muscle or torn a nerve or something?' No, her GP didn't. He thought it might be sciatica, though he explained that in that case the pain would run down the back, not the front of the leg. But then he said, 'In view of your history,' he thought she should have an X-ray. She hadn't understood at first. 'My history?' she'd echoed. He'd emphasised that it was unlikely that this hip pain had anything to do with her recent medical history, but it was best to be sure. She went for the X-ray in a state of such agitation she could hardly keep still for it to be done. How she had continued to work she could not imagine. And then, even worse, the bone scan following the X-ray result. Going into that tomb-like room, surely all black, black everywhere, and yet she knew it could not be, of course it couldn't, wasn't, the walls were white, the low ceiling white, only the machine was black, a huge, round iron-black thing which travelled slowly along her body as she lay there, weak and already dying. It came very low over her head, throbbing as it went, and she'd begun to sweat, the claustrophobia intense, the desire to jump up and scream almost unbearable. But she did bear it. She kept still, as instructed. There seemed to be no one there but herself, no sound louder than the sinister hum of the machine. When it finished its eerie progress down her body, a technician appeared. 'You can get down now,' she said. But she hadn't been able to for a minute. 'It's over,' the technician said, impatiently, and still she hadn't moved, the effort of levering herself off the bed so enormous she had to force herself to swing her legs down first and test their strength before the rest of her body could follow.

It had been a farce. First, a shadow had been seen that looked like 'something'; then the bone scan showed 'hot spots' in her hip bone that could be 'something'; then the somethings were declared nothings, or, to be accurate, arthritis. So they said. Arthritis. She was young, but arthritis, she was told, was no respecter of age. Did arthritis run in her family? Yes, it did. Well then. She had an arthritic hip. It responded to a course of anti-inflammatories. The pain faded, only to reappear if she walked up very steep hills which she hardly ever did. But the agony she had gone through did not. She felt that if she had awaited events, the pain would have settled down anyway. She'd tried, ever since, to control her fears that every pain was cancer. But it was wearing, this constantly watching herself, being on guard, permanently worrying that she would be caught out and that on the one occasion she didn't report a pain, that would be the fatal one.

Control. That was what was important. Lean on no one, be sensible, await events. Oh, but it was a harsh instruction to have to give oneself. No wonder, she thought, that she'd wanted to learn to fly.

14

The Clinic

MRS HIBBERT, driving to St Mary's, almost stalled her car on the steep hill going out of town. There, flying down on the other side, was that girl Emma – she was sure it was her – and behind her, on another bike, that boy 'Sluke, both of them shrieking and laughing, not a care in the world. What annoyed her, and momentarily distracted her from concentrating on her driving, was the unworthiness of her thoughts. She knew she ought to be glad to see Emma back safe and sound, and obviously in excellent spirits and health, but instead she felt resentful, as though she had been made a fool of. Had the girl come to say she was sorry for her abrupt departure? No, she had not, and very probably was never going to. Emma didn't care about her. Better to put Emma out of her mind.

She arrived at St Mary's, feeling that she had a great deal to do. There was, first of all, her appointment with the Rev. Maddox. It had been agreed, at the last committee meeting of the Friends, that it would be an act of kindness to take him on a tour of the hospital to give him some idea of what their work was about. She felt quite comfortable with the idea of being in charge of the Rev. Maddox but rather suspected, from the encounter they had already had, that he might not be so comfortable with her. She'd asked him which college he'd been a member of at Oxford and when he'd told her St John's, she had said her late husband had gone there too. This had not seemed to create between them the bond she had anticipated. He was a shy, nervous man, the Rev. Maddox, she could see that, without any small talk. This was rather admirable – she had no time for small talk herself and heaven knows she had suffered enough from it in the company of Dot and others – but on the other hand it made all conversation, or at least the starting of it, a strain. She was going to have to choose her topics carefully and let him know that she was not an idle chatterer.

Then she had to find out what had happened to Chrissie. She'd heard the alarming news weeks ago that Dr Harrison had left and was rumoured to have given up being a doctor. Rita, to whom she'd again given a lift, had told her. It was the talk of the clinic – everyone was shocked. Mrs Hibbert had at once telephoned Chrissie, and when there was never any reply, after repeated attempts, she'd written her a letter, which in turn had received no answer. But Chrissie was back in St Mary's, according to Rita (giving her a lift had become a regular event), and Mrs Hibbert was determined to find her and discover what had been going on. She also wanted to express her relief that Chrissie had come back and had not shirked her duty.

The Rev. Maddox was waiting. He stood near the door of the Friends' room looking embarrassed, his hands clasped in front of him, rather high on his chest, and a frown on his face. This frown only lifted marginally when she strode up to him and said his name, and he was slow to hold out his hand to be shaken. She suggested that first they have a cup of tea in the Friends' room, which was fortunately empty, and he agreed that that would be appreciated. Together they went into the room, and after she had put the kettle on, Mrs Hibbert closed the door firmly. 'Do sit down,' she urged. The Rev. Maddox perched on the edge of a chair, hands on knees, and cleared his throat. Mrs Hibbert looked inquiringly towards him, thinking the throat-clearing heralded some utterance, but none was forthcoming. 'So,' she said, giving him his tea, 'I believe your last parish was in Manchester?' 'Indeed,' he said. 'And did you like Manchester?' 'I found it difficult,' the Rev. Maddox said, not looking at her, 'but it was not because of the place or the people. It was for personal reasons. I liked Manchester very much, but I was unwell while there. Shall we begin our tour?'

All the time she took him round the hospital, explaining what the Friends did, she was thinking about that word 'unwell'. He'd been 'unwell', not ill. She thought she knew what that meant. Francis had used it when he'd been struggling to tell her what he'd felt for years, 'unwell in the head', he'd called it. He'd been to church that day, to evensong, but she'd had a cold and had not accompanied him. It always surprised her how devout Francis was, and how much he enjoyed going to church, whereas her faith wavered and actually going to church never seemed important to her. The church Francis belonged to seemed to her very high-church and she had preferred the simplicity of St James's, the church she had gone to as a child. He'd come home in a strange mood, talking about the sermon he'd heard. He'd tried to précis it for her but she wasn't really interested and her attention wandered. And then suddenly she'd heard him say, 'I must be honest with you, Mary. I haven't been honest, and I should have been, the vicar made me see I should be.' For a moment, she had felt a tremor of real alarm at the thought of some awful thing he might be going to tell her, but once he began talking this had been replaced by bewilderment. Whatever was he saying? What did this peculiar 'unwell in the head' business mean? Francis, normally so fluent and articulate, had stumbled over words and faltered.

It appeared to be, so far as she could make out, something to do with feeling he was not in the right body. He'd wondered if this feeling meant that he wished he was a woman, but he'd come to the conclusion that this was not the problem at all. Nor did he think he was a homosexual, afraid to admit it – it wasn't that, he wouldn't have been afraid. All his life he'd felt his mind and body were not properly fused. His body didn't seem to obey the commands of his mind. Nobody suspected how peculiar he was. He had never, he told her, had any fully realised sexual experience, and it was her acceptance of his condition (though she hadn't known what it was) that had made him love her. She'd made no demands for him to have to satisfy.

She'd wept, how she'd wept. How could a wife not cry her heart out, hearing this? But what she'd wept for was her own failure to realise there had been something wrong all the time with Francis. How could they have been such friends, so very close to each other, so happy in each other's company, and yet she had not known that most important thing about him? It had been stupid of her, and insensitive, not to have deduced that her husband must be in some way abnormal to have no desire whatsoever for sexual relations. She supposed that somewhere in her mind she had had suspicions that he might secretly prefer men to women, but that she had accepted this and simply did not mind – it was part of the unspoken bargain between them. To find that she had been quite wrong, and that Francis had been tormented by his 'unwellness', this lack of desire, seemed a reflection on her own lack of understanding. He hadn't been able to speak to her, that was the very worst aspect of his suffering.

After his confession, things were never quite the same – an awkwardness lay between Francis and herself which worried them both. Silently, she cursed the vicar's sermon, with its exhortation to be completely honest. Honesty, in this case, had decidedly *not* been the best policy. She wondered whether she ought to encourage Francis to seek treatment of some sort, but when she tentatively made a reference to this possibility he shuddered and said he had tried psychotherapy years ago and it had not helped. She went on feeling she should do something about Francis and his 'unwellness', but embarrassment prevented her from consulting anyone. Meanwhile, he grew quieter and quieter. He said he simply felt tired, but since tiredness was such an easy thing to talk about she managed to persuade him to go to his GP (who was not her own doctor). He went, and came back a little more like his usual cheerful self, which made her wonder if his doctor had got more out of him. At any rate, some medication had been prescribed. She didn't find out till later that the tablets he took were anti-depressants.

When she found Francis still heavily asleep at lunchtime that Sunday she hadn't felt any particular sense of alarm. He sometimes did sleep late if he'd been working on papers into the early hours, as he had been doing. It had annoyed her, that this was necessary on a Saturday evening, especially since she'd cooked an especially delicious dinner and they'd shared a bottle of Chianti – it seemed an insult to the meal for Francis to go off into his room claiming important work that had to be done for Monday. She'd shouted, in the morning, that coffee was ready, but he hadn't appeared. But by noon she was seriously irritated at his behaviour and uncertain whether to prepare lunch or not. So she'd gone into his room, saying, 'Francis, it *is* nearly lunchtime,' and it was not his lack of reply which had alerted her to there being something very wrong but his breathing.

She'd noticed at once the empty container beside his bed. When the paramedics arrived, she handed the Nardil packet to them. They said there should be a warning card somewhere, because Nardil had a high overdose rating, but she had never seen one. From the beginning, travelling in the ambulance, she had been adamant: Francis would *never* have taken an overdose. He had been tired, he'd been working very late, he must simply have misjudged the dosage. She remembered, when questioned at the hospital, that he had complained the evening before that his vision was blurred, which was why it was taking him the weekend to read through the documents he had. They asked what he had eaten and drunk the day before, and she listed (with some pride) the fillet steak, the potatoes, the broad beans, the salad, the Stilton and the wine. It was not until the inquest that she heard how Nardil reacted with all these things, and the inference was that Francis must have known they would. But nevertheless, the verdict had been one of accidental death, to her enormous relief. It was a verdict she believed to be absolutely correct – she would not allow that Francis had been either intending to kill himself or making a cry for help. Nonsense. She had been there to help, he had not been without it. Only a small, inner voice asked if it had been the kind of help he had wanted, and she silenced it.

*

The Rev. Maddox made little comment during their perambulation of the hospital, and she gave up trying to interest him in anything. By the time they parted, she had decided his 'unwellness' had not been the same as her husband's. She didn't know what had been wrong with him (maybe was still wrong), though she suspected that, in his case, the problem was his homosexuality, his inability to 'come out', but she was quite certain he would not be a good chaplain. He would never know what patients wanted, never know how to talk to them, let alone comfort them. He was quite clearly one of those unfortunate individuals unable properly to communicate with anyone. She was sure he would have few, if any, friends, and his illness was probably due to this inability to establish human contact. 'No man is an island' Mrs Hibbert said to herself, but the Rev. Maddox was trying to be one. She could have told him it wouldn't work. If he was really so repelled by his fellow human beings then he should go into a monastery or else have treatment. There. She would wipe him from her mind.

But her mind was still full of him as she hurried down the corridors to find Chrissie. She didn't like it when she had to admit she had failed with someone, had failed entirely to break through their reserve or, in some cases, their distrust of her. She wanted to be seen as decent and fair and eager to help, a safe pair of hands. It hurt when she sensed people were suspicious of her and that clergyman had been very suspicious indeed *without cause*. When she got to the clinic, she was still troubled, and struggled to concentrate on what she wanted to say to Chrissie when she found her. Finding her proved difficult. The clinic was in semi-darkness, not a light on and no one about. She looked at her watch: 1.25 p.m. Of course, it was much too early, Rita had told her she never arrived before 1.45 even if the occasional patient did. Mrs Hibbert was not going to sit on one of those uncomfortable seats and wait. Instead, she retraced her steps along the thin yellow line, walking very slowly, as though she were patrolling. She turned a corner and hesitated. She had no means of knowing from which direction Chrissie would come. Sporting her Friend of St Mary's armband, as she did, she could wander into most departments of the hospital at will, but she did not know where Chrissie would be. It was not sensible to leave the clinic, and so she was obliged to return and stand like a sentinel at the door. When, after a few uneasy minutes, she saw Rita approaching, she felt embarrassed.

'Why, Mrs Hibbert,' Rita said, 'what brings . . .'

But Mrs Hibbert interrupted her. 'I'm looking for Dr Harrison,' she said. 'Will she be along soon?'

'She won't be along at all,' Rita said, putting lights on and opening up her cubicle. 'She's transferring.'

'Hospitals?' asked Mrs Hibbert, reluctant to follow Rita into the clinic. 'Hospitals?' she repeated, shouting slightly. She could see Rita shake her head. 'Jobs,' she said. 'Doing training, some research thing.'

'Are you sure?' Mrs Hibbert said.

'Sure as sure. Came in this morning apparently, looking good they say, after her break, and told everyone. She wants to do research, I don't know what sort or where.'

'Well,' Mrs Hibbert said, 'well, that's a pity, it's a shame.'

'Is it?' said Rita.

Was it? She left Rita organising herself and made her way back to the entrance hall and her duties. Was it a pity, a shame, a waste, that Chrissie had given up her work in the clinic? She wished that she understood what this 'research' was, whether it justified Chrissie's decision. There was a dull, sad feeling in her mind. She felt let down. Chrissie hadn't listened to her when she'd tried to help her. She'd ignored her afterwards. And then she'd gone ahead and done what she wanted, taken the easy way out.

*

Here she was, in the entrance hall, back again in front of the glass doors. Consciously, she straightened her back and held her head high, bracing herself against the onslaught – how they surged in, these people. They all wanted attention, they all wanted kindness, they all wanted to be made better – they were full of want. But so was she, though it was her job to conceal this. She stood impassive, rock-solid, as she always did, searching the faces, identifying the weak and fearful. Poor Francis. She found herself saying this over and over in her head, every time she was on duty. He had never set foot in St Mary's Hospital, or in this town, but nevertheless she could not help thinking of him and how she had failed him. Poor Francis. What had he really wanted? What could she have given him?

There was a woman standing quite still just inside the doors. She was in the way. People had to walk round her, and she was being jostled as the crowds pressed in. A middle-aged woman, slightly overweight, neatly dressed in a spotted skirt and a dark jacket. She looked appalled, as though in front of her was a scene of horror instead of the ordinary jumble of an hospital entrance hall. Mrs Hibbert could see she was holding an appointment card in her hand. A first appointment here, undoubtedly. She couldn't even get as far as the inquiries desk. Mrs Hibbert found herself sighing, but it was a sigh of something approaching satisfaction: she knew what this woman wanted, she knew what she needed. A calmness came over her, a feeling of peace. Slowly, taking care not to move in any way abruptly, or make any sudden movement of her hands, she walked towards the woman. 'Can I help you?' she said, as gently as possible.

Help, that was what was wanted, that was what she had to give, whether it was accepted or not. Knowing this was what gave her strength, and at that moment, approaching the terrified woman, she was full of it. What fools people were to think they could manage on their own.